ALL SECRETS DIE

ANDREW WATTS

DALE M. NELSON

SEVERN RIVER PUBLISHING

Severn River Publishing
www.SevernRiverBooks.com

This is a work of fiction. Names, characters, businesses, places, events and incidents are either the products of the author's imagination or used in a fictitious manner. Any resemblance to actual persons, living or dead, or actual events is purely coincidental.

ISBN: 978-1-64875-579-8 (Paperback)

ALSO BY THE AUTHORS

The Firewall Spies

Firewall

Agent of Influence

A Future Spy

Tournament of Shadows

All Secrets Die

BY ANDREW WATTS

The War Planners Series

The War Planners

The War Stage

Pawns of the Pacific

The Elephant Game

Overwhelming Force

Global Strike

Max Fend Series

Glidepath

The Oshkosh Connection

Air Race

To join the reader list and find out more, visit

severnriverbooks.com

"Man is not what he thinks he is, he is what he hides."
— André Malraux

1
_____

Havana, Cuba

Colt McShane was gray.

The problem was, gray was not the goal. Moving through the sweltering and broken streets of Havana, Colt needed to be *black*, he needed to be invisible. But in a place like this, one never knew. It was one of the many things that made Havana dangerous. Colt was here to meet an asset. To do that, he would spend six hours wending his way through the city's crowded, tropical miasma to ensure he wasn't followed. Colt was two hours into that surveillance detection route (SDR) now, and already he'd sweated through his shirt.

He'd left his room at the Hotel Saratoga and taken a cab to the Ministerio de Ciencia, Tecnología y Medio Ambiente de la República de Cuba, the country's science and technology ministry. This was his third day in Havana. Colt had spent much of the previous two days at the ministry meeting with various bureaucrats. Or, more accurately, sitting in stuffy, smoke-filled waiting rooms under slogging ceiling fans for hours until a functionary decided it was his time. Colt had posed as a foreign development firm executive looking to improve Cuba's struggling cell phone infrastructure. He'd taken these meetings and spent those interminable hours to backstop his cover so that today, when he took the chugging cab from the Saratoga to the ministry's secondary offices in Cuba's capitol building, any minders wouldn't waste their time loitering outside, assuming it would be another long day of meetings.

Colt spent thirty minutes inside the capitol's wide, marble lobby, a brief respite from the unrelenting sun. The building shared the same eighteenth-century architectural style as America's own capitol. He'd identified himself to one of the first of many gatekeepers and said he had an appointment. Upon being told he had no such appointment (Colt knew by now one could be had for the right price), he thanked the functionary and asked that his name be placed on a waiting list. Both of them knew the name would never be called. Colt said he was stepping out to call his contact within the ministry so that they could clear up what was obviously an oversight. He left El Capitolio, after being harassed only once by a solider with an AK-47 lazily slung on his shoulder. Once outside, Colt worked a zig-zag pattern, up one block and over two, gradually working his way west on foot. He doubled back twice, pretending to look at his phone for directions and checking to see if anyone had followed him out of the capitol. If anyone had, the blazing noontime sun won out and they had long since given up.

Colt picked up a city bus on Avenida Simón Bolivar, waiting for longer than he wanted for it to arrive, lamenting that apparently only the fascists could make things run on time. He rode the bus for a long string of blocks, hopping off to walk to the Terminal de Omnibus Nacionales, Havana's national bus terminal. Colt pushed his way through the crowd and into a restroom. Inside a stifling stall, Colt folded his tan tropical-weight blazer and dress shirt into his computer bag and replaced them with a white camp shirt. He traded his dress shoes for a pair of canvas sneakers. Finally, he pulled on a navy ball cap and pair of Randolph aviators.

Colt slung his computer bag across his back and left the crowded bus terminal on foot. He took care to avoid the National Revolutionary Police Force officers stationed at various points throughout the building. Cuba's cops were generally lazy, ineffective thugs. That didn't make them any less dangerous, but usually one could escape their attention with a good cover story and a fast bribe. Besides, It wasn't the Cuban cops he worried about; it was the DGI. The Dirección General de Inteligencia had been one of the

CIA's most challenging opponents of the Cold War, second only to the KGB that trained them. The DGI were formidable, pervasive, and relentless.

And they hadn't lost a step since their Soviet patrons collapsed.

The odds were good the DGI would have a plain-clothes operative in the terminal watching for anything suspicious. Still, the crowded station was the best place to lose a tail, so Colt considered it to be an acceptable risk.

He found a cab outside the bus terminal and gave the driver an address further west, on the far side of the Rio Almendares, the river that sliced off Havana's westernmost neighborhoods.

Cab drivers were another necessary risk. They were unrepentant underground capitalists and many maintained links to the black market. Most were also informants. You could pay a cabbie to get you anything, take you anywhere, but there was always the chance the second you left the cab their next call was to the revolutionary police.

Colt paid the cabbie in Cuban pesos and got out. It was easier now that they'd done away with the dual money system. The Cuban government previously maintained a separate currency for use by foreign travelers. It was as unnecessarily expensive and complicated as one might expect a communist-designed monetary system to be and they'd finally eliminated it in 2022, likely to make it easier for foreigners to do business here. American dollars were illegal to use outside the airport and thus were highly prized on the black market.

Especially by cops.

Speaking of cops, Colt clocked a pair of them at the other end of the block, cooling their heels in a Russian-made Lada squad car. Every officer in the Agency could spot one of the those a mile away. Legacy of the bad old days and Moscow Rules. The cab dropped him in a residential neighborhood, down the street from the Italian Embassy. Colt walked north a block, now not far from the water, and found a cafe where he bought a small sandwich and some water. Give some time for the cops to move on.

Colt checked his watch. Four hours until his meet with Hazlett.

Hazlett insisted on Havana.

Colt didn't like it, but he understood Hazlett's rationale. And his paranoia.

Paranoia could keep you alive in Havana.

Assume everyone is watching, assume everyone will sell you out for the price of a coffee.

It wasn't far from the truth.

The Cubans had a kind of neighborhood watch program they'd run since the Cold War. It wasn't unlike domestic security initiatives in America —if you see something, say something. Only the Cubans amended the first part to, "if you see anything, tell your local political officer and get paid." The first and only commandment: Suspect thy neighbor.

Every idling cab with a hack driver huddled behind an old newspaper. Every shopkeeper with a broom whose gaze lingered just a little too long. Anyone could be an informant.

But what the Cubans *didn't* have was the pervasive digital surveillance of more modern countries. And it was those electric eyes that Hazlett feared. Because Howard knew that "they" were watching, and the only way to avoid that was to meet in a place without eyes.

Colt understood that better than most. He'd been burned in Hong Kong, his identity compromised. Now, with the Chinese intelligence service collaborating with so many of America's antagonists worldwide, the Agency feared the Chinese were sharing the identities of known intelligence officers. The Cubans hadn't modernized. Information that moved at the speed of data ran into the cinder block wall of communist bureaucracy and stalled. Even if the Chinese shared Colt's identity with their DGI counterparts, the time it would take to manually correlate that with the national police's passport control, to make the connection and act on it would hopefully be far longer than he was on the ground.

The CIA had learned recently that the Chinese and the Cubans had formed a partnership. At a minimum, the Chinese were opening an electronic and signals intelligence outpost here, though the Agency assumed it would go much deeper than that. Colt wasn't worried about his cover or the national police's ability to unravel it. What he did worry about was being grabbed by the DGI. They liked to harass Americans—because they could, because it was tradition, and because they knew CIA still had a bug up their ass about Cuba. If the DGI did pull him in, the chances that they could figure out he was CIA, especially given this new cooperation with the Chinese foreign intelligence service, increased exponentially.

Colt would be looking at long years in a dark prison.

But it was worth the risk.

Hazlett was a relatively new asset, recruited in the last six months. He was a Brit who officially worked for a global development company. The kind of firm that rolled into struggling nations bringing deep pockets and bold promises. Maybe he actually did those things. Colt didn't know or care.

The only thing Colt cared about was that Howard Hazlett worked for Archon.

Hazlett's recruitment earlier that year had been a major blow against Archon, and was the first time they'd actually turned someone on the inside.

Colt killed the last of his water and checked the street before heading out of the café.

He stepped out into the blazing sun.

"Excuse me, señor?" Colt knew before he turned that voice belonged to a cop.

Colt had learned about Hazlett the winter before, courtesy of LONGBOW.

LONGBOW was the product of an intelligence operation years in the making. It started with a mission Colt ran years before, where he'd secured the source code for the chip that drove the current generation of smartphones. That gave the Agency's technical division complete access to any device using that series of chip. Subsequent operations helped the CIA get LONGBOW on multiple models from a variety of manufacturers. LONGBOW enabled an agent to use the infrared sensor on the camera on one device to connect to the camera on another phone. Once inside, the device installed an application that gave the Agency complete control of the phone. They could remotely control the device or see anything a user had installed, read any form of communication—regardless of if it was encrypted—and even spoof that user.

Nadia Blackmon had gone undercover inside Guy Hawkinson's company, HawkTech. Over the course of a year, she worked her way into his inner circle. She covertly loaded LONGBOW on his phone and, for several weeks, the National Technical Counterintelligence Unit (NTCU) was inside Hawkinson's comms loop. The NTCU identified all of Archon's inner circle and council of deputies, which led them to one Howard Hazlett.

Once they had Hazlett's identity, NTCU hackers got onto his corporate email and secured his travel itinerary.

Colt had made his first pass in Berlin.

Hazlett worked for an international development bank and was in Germany for a meeting with a client looking to finance a new mining operation in Africa. Colt was waiting for him when he checked into the Waldorf Astoria and completed a LONGBOW shot from across the lobby. Following along the texts, the NTCU learned Hazlett was going to meet a colleague at the Waldorf's bar that night. NTCU hackers sent a text from Hazlett's phone canceling the meeting, then immediately deleted it before Hazlett could see. Unaware, Howard Hazlett showed up at the agreed-upon time for his drink.

Colt found a seat at the beautifully rendered art deco bar, which was done in rich browns, blues. and brass. He ordered a Warsteiner and made a few passes at casual conversation. Hazlett ignored him. When the bartender was out of earshot, Colt said, "You're going to want to put your phone down, Howard."

"How do you know my name?"

"I know a lot about you," Colt said. "I also know a lot about Archon."

"I don't know what you're talking about."

"We both know you do. When you're ready to chat, call me. Just don't wait too long. Last man standing when the music stops and all that."

Colt left Hazlett at the bar with a card that had a phone number with a UK prefix.

There's an old CIA joke about Cuba.

The Cubans assume everyone with an American passport is a spook.

And every Canadian is an American spook using a Canadian passport.

"You have identification, yes, señor?" The man's English was good. It was the language of commerce, after all. Colt had memorized the revolutionary police ranks as part of his pre-mission prep. This man looked like a captain. That wasn't saying much—Cuba's rank structure was as inflated as their currency. A second police officer took up a position to the captain's right, blocking any escape route Colt might have taken.

"*Sí*," Colt replied and carefully withdrew his passport wallet. He opened it, "accidentally" flashing the American dollars in the wallet's adjacent fold. He removed the passport and handed it to the police officer.

"Carrying around American money is dangerous," the cop said, taking the passport. "It is not legal to use it here."

"The gentleman at the bank told me I could have it, I just couldn't use it."

"Unfortunately, these men, they do not keep apprised of the law."

"I'm sorry, officer. I certainly don't mean to cause trouble." Cuba, like many repressive governments, had a thriving black market. People were going to find the things their authorities denied them and would take considerable risk to do it. Of course, the supposed "authorities" were among the black market's most vigorous consumers. The cop might be assuming Colt was here to buy things on the underground economy, though other than cigars, there was little one could get here that you couldn't find in Miami at far less risk. Most of Cuba's black market was full of creature comforts.

The police officer flipped the passport open and used a thick index finger to roughly swipe the pages. He scanned each one before moving on.

"What is your business in my country, Señor Hodges?"

"Business. I work for a telecommunications development company. We're proposing a project to build out a 5G cell phone infrastructure." The so-called "Cuban thaw" moved at a glacial pace. Even after the Castros finally relinquished control, Havana maintained a strong communist legacy. As a result, the Cuban Treasury Department heavily regulated which U.S. businesses could operate here. Colt had chosen telecom because it was one of the types of investment the Treasury would allow. It was also something the Cubans desperately needed.

"You don't think our cell phone network is very good, eh? You cannot get your Facebook here?"

The police captain was tall and well muscled. Colt put him at forty-five. He was deeply tanned and clean shaven. A blue ball cap sporting the NRPF logo cast a dark shadow over his face, which did nothing to hide the contemptuous gaze shining from his black eyes.

"No, it's not that at all. We're just here to evaluate interest in investing in modernizing the telecom infrastructure." Colt knew he had to tread carefully here. The government maintained control by denying its people access to information. If the captain was a hardliner—and judging by his relative youth, he likely had this job through political appointment—the implications of Colt's imaginary project might anger him.

"What are you doing *here*?" he said, pointing at the street with the hand holding Colt's passport.

"Having lunch. I was at the Ministry of Science earlier, but there was a problem with my appointment. They told me I couldn't get in to see anyone today."

"How long have you been here?"

"Three days," Colt said. That information was stamped on the passport. "I've been meeting with people from the Ministry of Science and several of the committees."

The captain turned to his subordinate and barked an order in Spanish. The man nodded quickly and ambled over to their car.

"So, I have an American businessman who is far from anyone he could do business with. What am I to make of this?"

"It's something of a site survey," Colt said. "I'm testing coverage in the area for my report."

"Is that so?"

<hr />

Hazlett didn't immediately call the number on the card, so they took his recruitment up a notch.

Colt flew to London and followed him to and from work. The NTCU knew from watching his phone that Hazlett hadn't reported the initial communication to his superiors at Archon. Unless he'd done so in person, and that seemed unlikely.

Colt tracked him using the GPS on his phone, walked up behind him, and grabbed his arm. "Let's have a quick chat," he said, and guided Hazlett into a waiting car driven by Tony Ikeda, a CIA covert action officer Colt worked with frequently.

"I can protect you from Archon, but I can't help you if you don't help me."

"What makes you think I need protection? And this is bloody kidnapping."

"The two chaps from MI5 in the car behind us think this is a friendly chat. Turn and smile for them."

Hazlett did not turn, nor did he smile.

"Archon has been exposed. They got careless and too aggressive. That got Samantha Klein killed. Guy Hawkinson disappeared and a host of governments dismantled his company for espionage. We know who runs Archon. Do you really think that Quentin Wales, Rhett Bolton, or Mariano Emmanuelle are going to come help you? Are they going to pay for your legal counsel? Spoiler alert, they will not."

"Who are you?"

Colt chuckled. It was a dry, brittle sound. "Oh, we are not at the 'you get to ask questions' stage of our relationship, pal."

"What do you want?"

That was more like it.

"My subordinate is checking to see whether you really met with anyone at the Ministerio," the captain said. "However, this could take some time to verify. What hotel are you staying at?"

"The Saratoga. I'm returning to the U.S. tomorrow."

The cop raised an eyebrow at that. It looked like a caterpillar doing yoga.

The cop then looked back over at his subordinate in the car, still on the radio.

Colt saw his opportunity.

"Is there anything that we might be able to do to resolve this misunderstanding, Captain?"

The man chortled and Colt smelled old tobacco on his breath. "I am glad to see your country wishing to invest here in Cuba. This is good, yes? But, you should not carry so much cash around. While I am sure this is a mistake," he placed a hand on his chest, as if to physically show his magnanimousness, "another police officer may not be as understanding."

"Thank you," Colt said. In a swift, controlled motion, he swept the dollars out of the wallet and folded them into his left hand. He traded the money and the wallet with a move that would've made any three-card monte hawker envious and offered to shake the cop's hand. "I am gracious for your understanding."

The captain pocketed the money with practiced disinterest. "Enjoy your stay in Cuba." He handed the passport back.

Colt thanked him and departed quickly.

He walked three blocks to the beach, where he found a cab loitering in front of a hotel.

They drove east, crossing back over the river to the other side of town. The hack driver, sensing bait, asked Colt if he needed anything. Colt thanked him and said he was fine. The cab let him out near Havana's sprawling cemetery. It was something of a tourist attraction, and his being there wouldn't draw attention. Colt disappeared inside.

Over the next two hours, he worked his way east through a combination of walking, double backs, and cabs.

By the time he'd made it to the long street along the port, Colt was certain he hadn't been followed.

The situation with the police captain unnerved him. It wasn't the first bribe he'd paid. In fact, he'd been greasing his way throughout the town. That was just how things worked here. Still, there was a shrewdness, a cunning in that cop's eyes that Colt hadn't liked.

He alternated street time with cooling his heels in a couple cafes along the route to El Malecón. This got him out of the sun, and gave him a chance to hydrate and to calibrate his surroundings. Several blocks from where he was scheduled to meet Hazlett, he'd spotted a pair of national police slouching against their Lada. He ducked into a café on the opposite corner and nursed a glass bottle of Coke for fifteen minutes. Still, there was no sign of them leaving. His earlier encounter with the police captain had him spooked, and Colt wondered if maybe the cop called him in. If these two detained him or radioed his name back to headquarters, there was a chance they'd hit. Even if they didn't figure out who he was, he'd certainly miss his meeting with Hazlett.

Colt checked his watch. It was past time. He was three minutes late for the route he'd planned.

Beads of condensation crawled down the side of the empty Coke bottle as if they, too, were scared to move.

The old man at the counter asked Colt if he wanted anything else. Colt told him no and pushed back from the old wooden surface. He stepped out of the cafe and turned right along the crumbling sidewalk, heading north toward the water. Colt knew better than to immediately look behind him to see if the police were following. That would be too easy a giveaway. One technique he often used, especially when posing as a tourist, was to vamp taking a selfie and look for tails on the phone's display. But the Cuban police were touchy about phones and were just as likely as not to confiscate it. Instead, he tried another trick. He pulled up the map function on his phone and stopped, as if trying to orient himself. Playing the clueless tourist, he looked around in a few directions, then back down at the phone. Finally, he turned around, checked behind him quickly, and then back down at the map. He looked up one last time and saw the police officers hadn't moved from the corner.

Colt turned and hurried to the beach.

Because of the time burned waiting for those police to leave, Colt had to move much faster than he'd planned.

Part of the reason he'd chosen this location was the simple grid pattern of the surrounding streets. He turned left and checked behind him, cleared it, walked up a block, and turned left again. Colt repeated the process several times until he'd reached the waterfront. El Malecón was Havana's famed strip that faced the Florida Strait, looking northward from the city. Ever since the 1920s, people flocked here at sundown to watch the blazing reds and oranges become violet as the sun disappeared, lighting the evening sky with fading swaths of tropical color. Malecón was a wide strip of often broken concrete sidewalk, ending in a seawall with a stubby, rocky shore on the other side.

Colt crossed the boulevard and walked back the direction he'd come, seeing the ever-growing groups of people massing in small clusters. He saw lovers stealing away, fisherman and laborers huddled around bottles of beer and families, showing the children the natural beauty of sea and sky. Colt heard as much muted English as he did vibrant Spanish, with accents ranging from American to Canadian to British.

Their meeting spot was opposite the Parque de la Juventud, a concrete skate and BMX trick park. *Way to stick it to the imperialists*, Colt mused. There was a large crowd gathered here to watch the sunset, but Colt saw Hazlett immediately, wearing a lime green linen camp shirt and white pants. Hazlett had a folded-up newspaper and a pen in his lap. Colt walked past him and said, "Take a walk," without breaking stride. He heard a brief shuffling as Hazlett turned and stood, quickly trying to match Colt's pace.

"What've you got for me," Colt said when Hazlett appeared at his side. Colt kept his vision focused forward, scanning the crowd, the street, and the opposite sidewalk.

"No one knows where Hawkinson is," Hazlett replied.

"Do better."

"I don't know what you want from me," he said, a pleading tone in his voice.

"You know exactly what I want from you, which is why we're having this conversation instead of you having it with MI5. And you know what the alternative is. You people almost started a war between my country and the Russians. I don't have a lot of sympathy for how hard you've got it."

"I'm only a functionary."

So was Himmler, Colt thought. And he knew Hazlett was much higher in the orbit than he made out. He said, instead, "Why don't you know where he is?" Guy Hawkinson had disappeared about six months earlier. The NTCU linked Russian cyberattacks to a server farm in Argentina covertly run by Hawkinson. Hazlett claimed the broader Archon leadership council, which they referred to as the "board of directors," didn't sanction the attacks and didn't approve of them. Colt didn't believe him, but admitted there were grains of truth in it. It wouldn't surprise him at all to see Hawkinson acting on his own.

Hazlett continued. "No one knows where he is. He's masking his location, even from the board. We believe he slipped out through southern Europe, but after that?" Hazlett held up his hands.

"Why do you think he's keeping his location secret?"

"I don't really know, other than to say he doesn't trust anyone. The board won't grant him a seat, but they can't kick him out of the organization."

"Because they fear reprisal?"

Hazlett nodded. "Yes. Hawkinson runs most of the operations. They don't want those capabilities turned against them. And they still need his uncle's support."

Guy's uncle, Preston Hawkinson, was a United States senator and a presidential candidate. Though the formal nomination wouldn't take place until the party convention at the end of the summer, it was effectively his.

"But the board is still in contact with him?"

"They are, though he said he tossed all of his phones and computers in a burn bin."

Colt had assumed that, but the confirmation was useful. Since they hadn't been able to connect to Guy's phone since his disappearance, the NTCU feared he'd ditched it.

"And he's still directing ops?"

"That's right, though the board asked him to dial it back. Frankly, they're all concerned over how quickly Hawkinson's operation was rolled up."

Colt recognized this for what it was. Hazlett wasn't a spy of conscience. He was a traitor only because he'd gotten caught, and he'd go back to exactly what he'd been doing before if Colt let him off the hook. Hazlett wasn't a true believer. He simply saw Archon as the quickest path to power.

"What's going on with Hawkinson's businesses?" Colt asked, redirecting the questions to his information requirements.

"He moved HawkTech and the other companies he owned to a holding company last year so that there wasn't any direct link to him. He's selling them now. I'm facilitating the transactions."

"To whom?"

"Other Archon-owned businesses."

One great shell game.

"I'll want the names," Colt said.

Hazlett removed the newspaper that he'd tucked into the crook of his elbow and handed it to Colt. Colt noticed the pen was still clipped to the paper.

"And the other thing?"

"It's there," Hazlett said. "I acquired that at great personal risk, so please use it judiciously."

"I'll be in touch," Colt said. He stepped over to the road. A '57 Chevy Bel Air convertible rolled past, painted in an electric lime green that matched Hazlett's shirt. Colt enjoyed seeing the classic cars here, even if the only original parts were the bodies. He checked the street, ostensibly for traffic, but more for tails, and crossed.

Back in his hotel room, Colt opened his laptop and navigated to a browser for international news. He clicked on a particular word in the header, entered a pass phrase (there was no prompt or any other sign that he'd navigated over a new window), and a secondary login screen appeared. He connected a USB drive to the laptop, which contained an encrypted authorization key.

Colt typed the list of companies that Hazlett had given him, tore up the paper, and then burned it in the ashtray.

Next, he removed the pen clip by unsnapping it. He pulled out a carbon sliver and inserted that into a small slot in a different thumb drive, which he then connected to the laptop. The "sliver drive" was a micro-scale hard drive Hazlett had used to smuggle one of the biggest coups in the Intelligence Community's war against Archon.

It held the encryption cipher used to encode all of the board's message traffic, the private communications reserved only for Archon.

The NTCU could now watch the Archon decision loop in real time.

2

Beijing, China

Beijing was burning, and the world didn't know.

The Chinese started turning on anyone with Western press credentials. Reporters were hounded with claims of counterintelligence by the state police, or worse, the Ministry of State Security. Officials ejected foreign journalists from the country if they were lucky, jailed them if they were not. Those who remained were told what they could cover and what they could not. The government forbade any reporting that wasn't a cultural enrichment puff piece, a softball treatment of China's thriving tech economy, or a laudation of the country's emerging role as a global peacemaker. They charged journalists caught violating that policy with sedition and jailed them.

It was like reporting from the center of a black hole.

All so the world wouldn't see that Beijing was burning.

Rioters took to the streets at night, first with signs and then with bricks. Emboldened by the fourth night and in response to fierce beatings by police, they hurled Molotovs at police cars. Students screamed and raged. It was Tiananmen and yet, it was not.

This was unlike other protests in the country's history

It was brazen, a courageous refutation of authority.

This was an uprising.

This was a *movement*.

And Lacy James couldn't touch it. It wasn't what she was here for.

At least, not entirely.

She'd entered the country on a tourist visa a week earlier with a burner phone and a laptop she'd bought on a layover in Tokyo. Anything that connected her to her paper, including legal protection, was back home in San Francisco.

Three different uniformed police officers stopped her, two municipal and one state, on her way to the park. Each demanded to know what she was doing in Beijing. They became more aggressive when they learned she was a "tourist." They demanded to know if she was a journalist. Lacy told them no.

Lacy had the cybersecurity beat for the *New York Times* and over the last few years, her job had taken her to some unexpected places. She'd covered tech luminary Jeff Kim's rise and staggering fall. The quiet mutterings of possible espionage and Kim's rebirth as a presidential advisor on AI. She'd reported on the emergence of a techno-terrorist group called "Archon," an organization that wanted to upend the world order and replace it with, what, super-intelligent machines so that people didn't have to do the hard work of governance? And she'd covered the Russian government's hacking and subsequent opening of a dam on the American River outside Sacramento. The resulting flood took hundreds of lives, caused billions of dollars in damage, and flooded California's capital city for weeks. And it brought America and Russia the closest to armed conflict since the end of the Cold War.

Lacy's most recent story, tipped by a hacktivist she knew only as "Bashe," was about a security breach at the world's three largest social media platforms. Someone accessed accounts at scale and dumped the passwords on the internet before blasting notifications on Discord, 4Chan, and Reddit. They even spun up a YouTube channel that had usernames and passwords in a constant scroll. The shockwaves that the story caused were still being felt in the tech community. The leak also included China's leading social media platform, WeChat, but she'd left that out of the initial story. She knew the Chinese would deny the leak and if she published the WeChat leaks, the Chinese government never let her in the country. It had been an enormous story in a huge news year for information security, or InfoSec to those in the loop.

But Lacy felt all of that paled compared to the lead she was chasing now. The implications of this story, once she'd considered them, left her shaking.

She was here to meet with a source, someone who had information on the unrest that was so explosive, she didn't feel safe sending it to Lacy digitally. Not even with the many precautions Lacy took to anonymize the transmission. Of course, against such pervasive digital surveillance and two of the world's most egregious cyber espionage outfits—the Ministry of State Security and the People's Liberation Army Intelligence Directorate— such caution was warranted.

Lacy walked through an elevated plaza in Beijing's Zhongguan district at sunset, following path as it curved through the manicured landscape. Zhongguan, China's version of Silicon Valley, was home to the country's startup ecosystem, top technical universities, and both domestic and international tech firms. According to Lacy's contact, tonight's protest would take place here. This evening's riot would be the biggest yet. The rioters chose Zhongguan for the symbolism, because so much of the tech developed here in Zhongguan was used to spy on Chinese citizens. Some seventy-five percent of Chinese citizens used the WeChat app for social media, communication, and commerce. They used it for real estate and travel. And the company that owned it answered to the CCP, the Chinese Communist Party. They turned all data over to the state, and the state monitored every transaction, every chat, every message that crossed its electronic wires.

The protestors avoided any social media developed in China.

That was new. These demonstrations showed a level of organization China had never seen. Lacy knew from colleagues and peers who covered the Chinese government that the party was nervous. For the first time, it seemed, they feared they couldn't keep a lid on the boiling pot. The *"why"* was the story. Part of it, anyway. No one knew who was coordinating these protests, now into their second week. Most nights, they occurred in a different location than the night before, but it was always random. Except that it couldn't possibly be. The mysterious organizers expertly planned and tightly coordinated each nightly event in a way that was something more than organic student protests. It was clear that Chinese youth were becoming more and more opposed to their autocratic rulers.

Lacy's interest here wasn't in the riots themselves, but in the fascinating juxtaposition. Each night activists stormed the streets and threw fire at police, damaging the edifices of authority. Yet somehow, the Chinese government hid all evidence of it from the world. It shouldn't have been possible. That in a country where the state controlled or monitored all digital communication, these rioters could still organize and outwit them was truly incredible. One of a journalist's most vital skills was pattern matching, the ability to find discrete points of data in the steam of informational noise and piece them together to reveal the story. Lacy believed these events were linked, somehow, to the social media hacks she'd reported on two weeks before.

And no one could figure out how they'd done it.

To Lacy, this all felt connected.

Lacy strode down the concrete path, ground lights illuminating her way. The sky was a burning orange and it would be dark soon. Already, Beijing's electric night erupted around her. She saw a woman emerge from a nearby building and walk toward a bench on one of the perfectly groomed boxes of grass, a bag slung over one shoulder. Lacy made eye contact across the distance and the woman offered the hint of a nod in recognition.

Tian Meiling was perhaps the most courageous woman Lacy had ever met.

Being an objective journalist in China was akin to being a revolutionary in any other country. Meiling's husband, an activist, was in his seventh year of a one-year sentence for the brand of political dissent the CCP called "sedition." Last Meiling heard, he was at a work camp somewhere far to the west. She kept up a brave face, but Lacy didn't think the woman had any realistic expectations of seeing her husband alive again. Meiling worked for a Taiwanese newspaper that had been repeatedly attacked by the information warfare arm of the People's Liberation Army (PLA).

Lacy sat next to her on the bench.

"How are you tonight, Meiling?"

"Tonight will be something," she said cryptically. Meiling didn't share her contact within the movement, and Lacy agreed not to publish anything until she returned to the States. Not that she would have. An InfoSec expert she interviewed had coached her on how to communicate securely, *really* securely, and how to protect herself and hide her identity online. But even with the things he'd taught her, Lacy didn't feel comfortable filing her story from here.

Meiling handed her a local newspaper, folded in half. Lacy accepted it and tilted it up, sliding the contents into her palm. It was a computer's peripheral cable.

"The thumb drive is concealed in the USB port," Meiling said.

This was raw footage of the riots.

Footage that would show the world what was happening.

This was what Lacy had risked her life to get.

Once they realized the riots were more than isolated incidents, the CCP had restricted internet access in the country. They'd hoped to degrade the dissident's ability to coordinate. Though it might still have been possible for Meiling to send this footage to Lacy over a secretly created VPN, they agreed it was an unacceptable risk. Instead, Lacy had taken the substantial risk of traveling here to get the footage herself. And that wasn't all. There were also stories, saved as anonymous text files, detailing the government crackdown and what the protesters were doing. Anything to show the world what was unquestionably happening.

But having this in her hand made Lacy complicit in the "insurrection."

"You need to leave," Meiling said.

"What are you hearing?" Lacy reached for her notebook, but Meiling was already moving to her feet. They'd been sitting less than a minute.

Lacy guessed their interaction showed up on at least twenty cameras.

Meiling didn't look at Lacy as she spoke. Her voice was clipped, almost harsh. "A friend working for Bellingcat was arrested a few hours ago. It's too dangerous for you here." Meiling was already walking away. When she was about ten feet away, Lacy caught her say, "Make the world see."

Lacy knew the protest wouldn't start right here. There was no way Meiling would let Lacy anywhere near it. The protestors started their activities at different times to keep the security forces guessing. It was a week-night, and Lacy had a hunch things would kick off soon. Start during the evening rush to tie up the response forces in the traffic. Lacy wanted to experience it in person. She knew that would add much to the story, but there was something in Meiling's tone that said this time would be different.

Lacy descended to the street level and started walking east. Her hotel was in the financial district. The *Times* travel mavens, screaming about how much it exceeded her per diem, hadn't wanted to spring for the Ritz-Carlton, but staying at Western hotels was safer. It didn't eliminate the risk by any means, but did buy it down a little. Lacy just said she'd cover the difference. She walked about half a mile until she found a subway, but saw a couple policemen loitering outside the station, watching the crowd. Lacy had no way of knowing whether the authorities were tipped to tonight's demonstration or simply expected it. Regardless, she'd find a different way back.

Lacy waited on the corner for the walk sign and joined a surging mass of commuters as they crossed a street. She looked up and saw the image of someone being publicly shamed for their social reliability score in between ads for a market and a new WeChat game. Lacy half expected to see her own face pop up with "AMERICAN JOURNALIST" underneath in angry, glowing red.

She made it to the other side of the street and kept going.

Lacy hailed a cab and had him drop her at the hotel. She paid in cash, wanting to leave as light of a digital footprint as possible. She made fast steps to her room.

Once inside, she set her pack with her laptop down on a chair and thought about what to do next. Then she noticed something out of place. A retired spook she'd once interviewed and since befriended had taught her a few things about traveling in hostile countries. He'd advised her to place things in her hotel room deliberately and memorize the locations. Then, leave the "do not disturb" tag on the door so the cleaning staff wouldn't mess with it.

Lacy had left the TV remote at a forty-five degree angle on the night-stand so that it pointed to the corner. It was now off by several degrees. Her glasses case was also a few inches over from where she'd set it. Lacy felt a crawling sensation down her spine and had to fight back a shiver. She opened the drawers and saw indentions on the neatly folded articles, which were no longer in the precise stacks she'd left them in. In the closet, her suitcase had been opened, the packing cubes inside reorganized from the way she'd left them. The jacket she'd left in the closet was off just enough on its hanger for Lacy to know that someone had taken it down and rifled through it. Lacy didn't know if they'd intentionally left things out of place to send the message that they'd been here, or, perhaps more likely, whoever had been in her room enjoyed the complacency of an untouchable government and simply didn't care that she knew.

The knowledge that someone has been In your private space without your permission is a deeply unsettling one. Not long after college, on her first job as a cub reporter, Lacy's apartment had been broken into. She'd never gotten over the feeling that someone had walked through her home, touched her things, had breathed in her air and exhaled their own. That place was never the same, and she'd moved out within a few weeks.

Lacy packed her things and called down to the concierge desk for a cab. Whoever had been in here had taken nothing. Her passport and other identification never left her person. Same with the laptop and burner phone. It was just the knowledge that someone had been in her room and left it just out-of-order enough that she'd know someone had. They'd known she was a journalist the second she'd entered the country. That was verifiable. She'd expected a little harassment given the state of things. Still, she hadn't expected this.

At the checkout counter, the smug manager with a British accent asked her why she was leaving early.

"Was the room not to your liking?"

The room was fine, just not who was in it, she wanted to tell him. "I've decided to catch an earlier flight home. I have to get back to work."

"Ah, I see. What line of work are you in?"

She remembered the tips her ex–intel officer source had given her. Almost everyone here is a collector. Hell, they were teaching counterintelligence in kindergartens now. "I'm a travel writer." She forced a smile. "Don't worry, this was just vacation, though I'd have rated your hotel favorably."

"Very good."

She settled the bill and met her cab. Lacy didn't know if she'd be able to get a flight out that night, but she'd rather spend the night at the airport than stay in the hotel. Spending a few weeks in an American jail to protect a source is a far cry from being banished to a black hole on the edge of civilization because you got caught doing your job in a dictatorship. That did not meet Lacy James's bar for a noble sacrifice.

And if they caught her with the micro-drive hidden in the USB cable, Lacy would face serious prison time. The state security service had persuasive means of extracting information. It would only be a matter of time before they got Meiling's identity from her.

After some cajoling with her carrier, Lacy could get a red-eye to Minneapolis but had to spring for international business class. She charged it to the company card. Let the travel office fight her on that. Even though she was based in San Jose, Lacy would go directly to New York from Minneapolis. She needed to sit down with the senior editor face-to-face and talk about what had happened.

Lacy moved through the throng of security and the multiple looks at her passport. Even on the way out, they wanted to know what she was doing in their country.

She didn't get scared until they pulled her bag.

They took her out of the line and over to a table where they dumped the contents of her luggage and rifled through her things. They didn't care about the clothes, even though they spread them out over the table, anyway. The public security officer focused on her electronics and her phone. They opened the laptop and took apart the phone. They dumped the pouch she used for the peripherals. A second immigration officer appeared and, after a quick exchange, began examining her computer equipment again.

"Can you tell me what's going on, please?" Lacy put a calculated amount of irritation in her voice. She couldn't push them, she knew, but thought it was equally dangerous to just roll over. If they sensed guilt, she might not make it out of here. The customs officer snapped something in Mandarin, which she didn't understand.

Lacy hadn't had time to inspect the file Meiling gave her. She didn't even know how well the thumb drive was hidden inside the cable. When Lacy packed it in her cable pouch back at the hotel, it looked like any other piece of computer hardware. But she hadn't exactly given it a thorough examination.

The customs officer held up the cord and Lacy saw that the USB connector was slightly bent. He jiggled it with his thumb.

Lacy thought she was going to puke.

The customs officer stared at her for a moment. In halting English, he said, "You need a new cable."

And with that, they let her through.

Lacy stuffed her things back in her bag and walked out of there as quickly as she could without making it look like she was fleeing. She checked into the Delta lounge and resisted the urge for a stiff drink. There would be time for that on the plane. She logged onto the airport Wi-Fi, which she assumed the government monitored, and emailed her editor to let him know she was coming home early. And would meet him at the *Times* office tomorrow night.

Lacy opened up a secure browser and checked the dummy email account she used to communicate with one of her Chinese sources. She knew him only as "Bashe," which was a mythological python who ate an elephant. Bashe was a hacktivist and had provided some of her best leads over the last year, including tipping her to these protests even before they started. Despite Bashe's accurate and damaging information, Lacy remained cautious, as she didn't know who they were.

Bashe's email had an attachment.

Lacy logged out and shut down her computer. That would have to wait until she was on U.S. soil.

Lacy opened Bashe's email again when she was in Minneapolis waiting on her flight to New York. Her normally lithe fingers trudged over the keys, jet lagged and hungover from the multiple scotches she needed to calm down.

It's not every day you get to watch a bomb go off in real time.

Bashe's attachment was a trove of documents, classified cables between senior PLA staff officers and CCP party officials. The government wanted to label the protestors as Taiwanese agents provocateurs. They wanted to paint the riots as a massive intelligence effort intended to cause instability on the mainland. In one communiqué, a party official demanded to know how ready the PLA was to invade if the government demanded a "punitive exercise."

"Holy shit," Lacy said.

Lacy's story went live later that week.

Her footage was undeniable (though *deny* was precisely what the Chinese government did). The Defense Department and CIA press liaisons blasted the *Times* for not revealing the source of the leaked cables. The paper defended their actions and stood by her. News services across the world lit up with the possibility that the Chinese would use the protests as justification to invade Taiwan. That wasn't the actual story, however, and Lacy feared the world would miss it.

The real story was that someone outside of an intelligence agency had hacked into the top-secret cables between the CCP and the PLA leadership. Encased within a fortress of quantum key distributions, homomorphic encryptions, and layers of cryptographic algorithms, the data in these organizations was guarded by a virtually impenetrable wall of encryption that dwarfed the computational power of most supercomputers. This, on top of the recent breaches at the world's largest social media platforms.

Hacking these digital fortresses was not supposed to be possible.

3

Istanbul, Turkey

"We have a longstanding relationship with the Turkish National Intelligence Organization. Every U.S. administration going back twenty years has clashed with Erdoğan in some fashion or another, but we remain tight with the NIO, which is what makes this so tough." Meredith Banks leaned back in her chair, cradling a cup of coffee with both hands. She was the CIA station chief of Ankara.

"Did you soft pitch this to NIO?" Hoyt Bennett asked. Bennett was deputy Chief of Station, Athens, and Erica Cano's boss. He'd come with Erica on the trip over from Greece. Ankara Station had reached out to Athens for a capable case officer for help with a short-term assignment. They couldn't use any of their own people because Turkish intelligence knew them. Cano had volunteered and flown up with Bennett to prep.

Istanbul was hosting the Shanghai Cooperation Council's annual summit. Turkey wasn't a member, but the SCC was courting them hard to join. The Chinese had created the SCC to act as an operational and ideological counterpoint to NATO, so scoring Turkey as a member state would be a huge coup, not to mention a major embarrassment for the Americans. Washington worried about Ankara's growing economic and political ties to

China and Russia. As a NATO member, the Turks proved a sketchy ally in the new millennium. A few in military circles counted on them to be there if called upon. Many quietly viewed Turkey's continued NATO member-ship as one of those instances on the friends-close-enemies-closer continuum that only made sense in realpolitik. In a strategic move, the SCO changed the summit's location from New Delhi to Istanbul to court Turkey's government—and to slight NATO.

Banks continued. "Overall, this is low threat. However, assume that Chinese and Russian intelligence will be at the summit."

"What about the Turkish?" Cano asked. Cano was in her eighth year in CIA and had loved every minute of it. This kind of thing, what they were asking her to do, was exactly what she'd signed up for.

Banks nodded as she spoke. "Yeah, so we assume NIO is there, which is why we aren't. They're going to be trolling for possible recruits, just like we would. NIO has the lead for counterintelligence, but the law prevents them from conducting operations, so any arrests would be handed off to the Turkish National Police Force."

"If I can ask, ma'am, why are we keeping this from the Turkish?"

"Fair question. We don't know exactly where they fall right now. We kicked them out of the F-35 partnership after they bought Russian surface-to-air missiles. The Chinese have infrastructure projects here as part of their 'Belt and Road Initiative,'" Banks said, laying on some annoyed air quotes and snide undertones on the latter. "And it's been tense in NATO lately. They tried to block Sweden from joining and are generally dragging their feet on supporting Ukraine. They're a lot closer to the Russians than we like and are, for all intents and purposes, a fully functional dictatorship. Given Ankara's increasingly close orbit to Moscow and Beijing, we couldn't risk telling NIO."

"Understood," Bennett said. "So, what does Erica need to do?"

Banks smiled. "She's going to bug a meeting between the Russian and Chinese presidents."

Cano spent two days working with the Ankara team rehearsing the hand-off before traveling to Istanbul, under cover as a journalist for the World Press Syndicate news service. Cano checked into a hotel near the International Congress Center, which Ankara Station had secured for her. She used the first two days of the summit to orient herself to the sprawling convention center and mingle with her fellow journalists to backstop her cover. She even attended a press reception hosted by the Chinese Ministry of Foreign Affairs. It was stomach-churning propaganda.

For much of the third morning, she listened to a Russian functionary drone on about economic investment and the importance of international collaboration in these "times of strife and uncertainty." The Russians had no appreciation for irony, she mused. The audience laughed at a bad joke and Cano knew the Russian was wrapping up his speech.

He'd graciously allowed ten minutes for questions and that was Cano's queue to leave. She stood and quietly slid out the door and into the hallway, a small artery off the main hall. Cano found a coffee shop, ordered a coffee, and steered herself toward another portion of the hall. Banners throughout the International Congress Center extolled the virtues of the SCC and the summit's grand objectives. Cano's eyes made a quick pass over the main hall and clocked a pair of Chinese men loitering next to an elevator bank. She put the odds that they were state security at fifty percent.

Time for the plant.

The Agency had substantive intel suggesting what the two presidents would discuss today, and they wanted that on tape. The Chinese told the world they wouldn't provide lethal aid to the Russian war effort in Ukraine. Technically, they would not. In a move with echoes of Iran-Contra, the Chinese covertly transferred arms to an intermediary, who secretly imported those weapons into Russia in exchange for oil and certain rare earth elements.

The two leaders would take part in several sessions together, aping for the cameras in a show of diplomatic might and solidarity. And there would certainly be breakout sessions between them and their various functionaries, not to mention state dinners and grand events. The CIA didn't care about these. What they were interested in, what they'd spent a year planning, was the quiet word these two dictators would share in an alcove secured by their respective security services.

Which would take place in about three hours.

Erica left her position in the convention center's main hall and walked down the lushly carpeted hallway. Both the Chinese and Russian intelligence services had been through the room on the floor above already and cordoned it off. No one, certainly not an American journalist, was getting within fifty yards of that spot.

At exactly 11:52 a.m., Erica stood next to a large floral arrangement in the main hall. She raised her coffee cup and gave it a quick shake, as though seeing how much liquid remained inside.

That was the signal.

"Are you through with that, miss? I can take it for you." A man with the convention center staff uniform appeared and asked Erica in accented English, gesturing to her styrofoam coffee cup.

"That'd be great, thank you," she said and handed the man her cup.

He took it, locked eyes for a moment, and disappeared back into the crowd.

The handoff completed, it was time for Erica to make herself scarce.

She'd taped the bug to the bottom of the coffee cup. It looked like a watch battery. Özgür would remove the bug and discard the cup. He'd affix the bug to a decorative vase in the alcove where the two dictators would have their quiet word. Özgür was a support asset, one of the small army of trusted locals the Agency used to conduct operations in a country. He had no connection to the Turkish National Intelligence Organization or the General Directorate of Security. Özgür was simply a good man who was looking to earn a little money for his family. He wasn't overly political and Erica had the sense that he enjoyed the cloak and dagger. They hadn't met before now, and Erica knew him only by his first name.

Because of the heightened security around the conference and the fact they didn't know who Turkish intelligence might be surveilling, the CIA couldn't give Özgür the bug before this moment. They didn't want to risk it falling into the wrong hands or his not showing.

Erica looked to her left and saw a Turkish man in a dark suit and no tie leaning against the wall, watching her.

She faded into the crowd.

Erica pushed her way through a throng of people, looked back over her shoulder, and saw that the man was gone.

The crowd was thick and progress slow going. Erica reached her right hand across and tapped the crown on her smart watch, sending a signal to the local cell network. Even the smartest electronic intelligence sensor (of which they assumed there were many deployed here) would see this as a single data ping on the network that would immediately be lost in the digital noise.

One ping only, Erica said to herself, smirking.

If only the Russians could appreciate irony.

Erica maneuvered through the crowd in the direction of the main doors.

She felt a prickle at the back of her neck, like a spider with pins for feet was crawling across her skin. The sensation was hard to describe, harder to quantify. But it was what they taught you at the Farm: Trust your instincts. If you think you're being watched, you probably are.

She spotted the Turk in the dark suit midway through the hall, looking around.

Looking for her.

Erica quickly ran through her options. The ladies' room only worked if you had backup coming. Law enforcement wouldn't care about social conventions, and it was almost always a bottleneck, unless it had a second exit. Instead, she reversed direction and cut across to the main exhibition hall where they were setting up for the next event. It was a cavernous expanse that could host a regulation football game and provide stadium seating for an audience. Erica slipped past a convention center employee who tried to keep her out and found herself on one of the middle tiers. To her left were descending rows of seats leading to a wide floor and a stage. To her right, rows extended to the upper levels. The seatbacks, walls, and carpet were all a garish red.

Erica made fast steps across the tier to the exit on the far side. It felt like she was running through a cave.

As she walked, Erica pulled out her phone, looking down at the screen and then up at her surroundings. Phones were great tools to amplify a cover. They were ubiquitous, and people were so attached to their screens that someone saw a person looking at a phone, or using it to orient them- selves to anything, it tended to fade into the background. Erica stole a glance behind her and didn't see the man.

She pushed through the doors and found a set of stairs. Two flights down, Erica found a service door, which she took, and it dumped her in a large hallway. To her right, she saw a long row of double doors, all open, that connected with a loading dock. She headed for that, passing confer- ence center employees pushing large containers on dollies. Erica entered the loading dock, her ears filling with the sounds of moving vehicles and cargo and someone barking orders in Turkish. An attendant with a clip- board spotted her and shouted something in Turkish that she didn't under- stand, but she guessed by the tone was probably something along the lines of, "You can't be in here."

Erica held up her phone and said, "Can't get a signal."

She took a short staircase to the dock floor, and that really pissed off clipboard guy.

Erica lengthened her stride, leaving him in her wake. She needed to get to a main street so she could start cutting an evasion pattern. Ankara Station had another support asset who'd gotten his hands on a cab. That was supposed to be her ride out of here. He'd be waiting two blocks east of the convention center right now. Erica slipped between a parked semi and the wall, emerging into the bright sunlight that fell on a large driveway.

A Turkish police car blasted up the drive.

Erica heard shouts behind her, now rough voices in English mixed with the angry Turkish tones.

Uniformed officers and men in suits converged on her from the right, a wide concrete plaza overlooking the conference center grounds.

This was not good.

Erica gripped her phone. She pressed the lock button twice and the down volume button three times, hoping the distress signal made it out. Turkish police officers swarmed her like compass points converging around a needle. A man in a dark suit, though not the one from the convention hall swaggered up and sneered. He reached for her badge. "Ms. Alicia Evans?" He followed it up with a condescending hum.

"My name is Chief Inspector Mehmet Bal and I need you to come with me, immediately."

"This is outrageous. I'm a journalist," she said, holding up her press badge to ward him off. "I want to speak with my embassy staff."

"Oh, there will be plenty of time for that, I'm sure," he said in syrupy tones. "But first, you and I are going to have a chat. When you get to speak with your consulate depends entirely on how truthfully you answer my questions."

"I don't know what you're talking about, and this is preposterous. I'm a journalist. You have no right to detain me."

"Conducting an unauthorized intelligence operation on Turkish soil is a very serious crime, Miss . . . Evans, was it?"

Rough-looking policemen closed around her. For the first time in her CIA career, Erica Cano felt truly alone.

4

Washington, DC

In Will Thorpe's more than twenty years in the Federal Bureau of Investigation, he'd never known an evening summons to the White House to be a harbinger of good news.

If the phone call had come from literally anyone else short of the FBI or CIA directors, he'd have turned it down for lack of time. There was too damned much to do. As head of the National Technical Counterintelligence Unit, Will's job was to stay on top of a continually evolving landscape of technological threats against the United States. In the last few weeks, that picture had changed dramatically, dangerously, and possibly irrevocably.

His unit was investigating a series of security breaches targeting the country's largest social media and dating platforms. Some unknown actor had sliced through their security systems like they were nothing, ripped user data—names, passwords, private messages, everything—and dumped it on a dark web server. Then, they posted messages on various chat servers to draw attention to it. The tech industry scrambled to implement fixes while users, public and private alike, raced into damage control mode. Several prominent business executives, two congressmen, and a national news anchor all had extramarital affairs exposed. And that was just in the first two days. People were still poring through the trove of data. Then, on heels of that, the NTCU learned the same thing had happened with enterprise email systems.

Billions of private messages showed up on the dark web servers.

A hacker, equal parts enterprising and horrible, had created a generative AI plug-in to sift through those messages using keywords. People quickly zeroed in on politicians, celebrities, executives, exes, and rivals. The most private communications of some very public figures flashed around the internet, leaving humiliation, scandal, and worse in their wake. Police were overwhelmed with assault calls as citizens responded to their exposers, and the FBI's cybercrime division was catastrophically overwhelmed. The NTCU deployed its personnel and tech resources to trace the source, but so far it had proved impossible. No one could figure out how the attackers got in so effortlessly.

And it was just beginning.

Thorpe had still been at the NTCU office at the CIA headquarters, so it was a fast trip into the District. Well, fast for DC anyway. There'd been no information provided on why *he* needed to be in the national security advisor's office as fast as he could. Jamie Richter's chief of staff said only that it was an emergency and he couldn't get into it on the phone.

Thorpe had more interaction with Jamie Richter, the national security advisor, than he wanted. On balance, Will liked Richter a lot. He was smart, capable, and good at his role. Will just wasn't comfortable with the kinds of conversations that took place in the West Wing on random weeknights.

Will parked and cleared security, a uniformed Secret Service officer checking his credentials against the list of authorized visitors. They waved him through to one of Richter's staff, who was on hand to guide him to the advisor's office. Once there, Thorpe found another surprise. With the national security advisor was the head of CIA's National Clandestine Service, Dwight Hoskins. The Agency's rank-and-file operations officers believed Hoskins was a politician and a ladder climber, they didn't trust him. However, he had backed Thorpe and the NTCU up on some key operations when he could have cut ties for political expediency. Also in the room was Hoskins' predecessor, Jason Wilcox. Wilcox was an old-school clandestine warrior, beloved by the operators he once led. Wilcox had been the youngest head of the clandestine service since Allen Dulles. After the rampaging senator Preston Hawkinson had forced him out of the role, Wilcox joined the secretive organization known as Trinity. Though few outside this room knew that.

"Thanks for joining us, Will. I hope I didn't disrupt your evening too much."

"Nothing dinner and a show won't cover. My wife is used to it by now."

"Great," Richter said, already moving on. He was a tall, narrow man with a slight build and an angular face. "Can I get you something to drink? We've got water, coffee, and bourbon. I don't have good news, so you may want something to take the edge off."

Will could see all three offers in equal amounts on the desk and tables. Wilcox had a tumbler in his hand.

"I guess I'll have one of those," he said, pointing at the whiskey. Richter poured him some from a decanter. Will accepted it and sat down.

"Okay, gents, let's get Will up to speed first."

Hoskins, standing, set his glass on a table nearby. "Two days ago, Turkish intelligence rolled up an Agency operation to bug a meeting between the Russian and Chinese presidents at a summit in Istanbul. We didn't coordinate it with them because we knew we couldn't trust them with it. They arrested one of our ops officers and have her in custody."

Richter took over. "The Turks haven't told the Russians or the Chinese what we tried to do, and they're asking a pretty steep price to keep their mouths shut. For openers, they want back in on the F-35." Turkey had originally been part of the coalition of international investors in the Joint Strike Fighter. The intent had been to export that fifth-generation jet to allied nations in a way of improving tactical coordination in coalition combat. Officially, the U.S. kicked Turkey out over the planned acquisition of the Russian-made S-400 surface-to-air missile system. And there were broader concerns about whom the Turks might leak the fighter technology to if they found it politically expedient. Richter continued, "They also want the president to formally retract America's recognition of the Armenian Genocide."

Will drank. These would be major foreign policy embarrassments for the administration at a time when they certainly didn't need them. Preston Hawkinson's campaign would rake them in the ad cycle and in the debates.

Hoskins picked the thread back up. "We don't believe there's a double agent or that one of our own sold us out. The support asset had been polygraphed and worked for us for years. There's a counterintelligence (CI) team deployed to Ankara right now and they've said everyone there is solid. We think that only leaves a communication breach."

"Deputy Hoskins is aware of this already," Will said. "We're investigating an alarming number of security breaches, outside of what you're seeing on the news. I think you're all aware of what's happening with the social media platforms. An automaker just reported their entire EV lineup for the next decade leaked online, including not yet disclosed plans to change suppliers. The French haven't publicly acknowledged this, but all of their diplomatic cables between Paris and their African embassies just turned up on a dark web server. This isn't all, but it paints a picture of some very serious hacking chops."

"You think this is AI?" Hoskins asked.

Will shrugged. "We don't know. Our analysts can't find a common denominator. The scale of the attacks suggest it might be. Otherwise, it's a small army of hackers."

"You read Lacy James's piece in the *Times* last month?"

"About the hacked CCP and PLA emails? Yeah. We've got the article tacked on the corkboard in the unit." He didn't say that someone wrote underneath it ". . . and find out."

"Well, Beijing is blaming us for it," Richter said. "They're claiming we broke into their classified network and leaked the cables to the press . . ." Richter's voice trailed off in the manner that was a roundabout way of asking a question. Hoskins looked at Will.

"It wasn't us," Will said.

"Cracking diplomatic traffic is no small feat. How do you think someone could pull it off?" Wilcox asked.

Will shook his head. "Honestly, Jason, I don't know. There's no common denominator. It's a combination of public and private targets, citizens, government officials, celebrities. We've even got CERBERUS on it, but there's nothing in the link analysis to point us anywhere. But, whoever did it . . . they've pulled off some of the most sophisticated cyberattacks in history. We're talking about closed loop, encrypted, diplomatic cables. Now, the Chinese had two successful cyber espionage operations against us in 2009 that targeted diplomatic cable traffic, but we've made substantive improvements since then."

CERBERUS was the NTCU's AI system that rapidly pattern matched number of enormous datasets, able to complete queries in hours that would've taken human analysts months. For instance, CERBERUS could identify the source of each hard-to-find component of a quantum computer, eliminate the ones obtained for other purposes, and then correlate those findings with scores of other data points to provide a picture for intelligence analysts. CERBERUS connected to every classified and unclassified computer system the federal government owned, except for the ones that were air-gapped.

"So have they," Hoskins said dryly.

"Cables transit the public internet, though, right?" Richter asked.

"Typically, yes. But they're encrypted in a few ways and often require special hardware with ciphers to download and decrypt them. Without that, you just get gibberish, noise. For example, to decrypt our top-secret traffic, you'd need a supercomputer with nearly unlimited processing power and time. I have to assume the Chinese are using similar encryption standards."

"What about Archon?" Richter asked from behind a tumbler of bourbon.

"I don't know if even *they* have that capability," Wilcox said. "Hacking into a corporate email server or our outdated air traffic control network is one thing. Diplomatic cables and top secret military comms are something else. Archon has done the chaos-for-the-sake-of-chaos thing before, and I think they've moved beyond it. All that said, I don't have any specific indicators about them.

"We hit them hard and Archon has been quiet ever since. I have high confidence they aren't behind this." Will wasn't about to say, in this forum, that the NTCU had an agent inside Archon. Not in the West Wing. "My guess is, we're looking at a new player," he finished.

"Beijing is mobilizing forces. They're calling it a 'naval exercise,' but this could be a prelude to something bigger. They're itching for an excuse to invade Taiwan, and this might be it," Richter said.

"You don't think they'll actually start shooting over this, do you?" Wilcox asked.

"They're blaming us now. What happens if there's another leak? Which brings us to why we're really here." Richter paused and took a drink. "Will, do you still have your asset in their intelligence service?"

Liu Che. A Chinese spymaster who ran one of the most disastrous espionage rings in U.S. history. He'd actually maneuvered to get his asset, a Navy admiral, a seat in this very building. Colt captured Liu, Will arrested him personally, and they'd eventually turned Liu into an asset. Albeit a reluctant one.

"We do," he said.

"Okay, good. We need a back channel to the Chinese. We need them to know this isn't us. How quickly can you work?"

"His handler is out of the country right now, but I can recall him within a few hours."

"Do it," Hoskins said.

Richter walked over to his desk and leaned against the edge. "Now, the other reason I've called us all together is that we need to talk about what we're going to do about this. Will, before you arrived, Jason, Dwight, and I were discussing options. We have the whole of the Intelligence Community engaged on this. The NTCU is the community's expert on Archon. Your team did exemplary work taking the fight to them and, you're right, you struck a major blow. But Guy Hawkinson escaped, and that organization still exists. I need you to run this one down, Will."

Be careful what you wish for, Thorpe said to himself.

Richter turned to Wilcox. "Jason, you're in a position to see things that we can't. What do you know about this that we don't?"

"I agree with Will that Archon has been quiet. And you're correct about Hawkinson. He's vanished. I can't even find him. That doesn't mean they aren't involved in this. I just don't see it," Wilcox said.

"Gentlemen, I need options to give the president."

"We'll get our source working on the back channel," Hoskins said. "Will is going to start fleshing out the Archon angle."

Though the NTCU was a joint unit, comprised of personnel across the Intelligence Community, the majority came from the CIA and the FBI. The NTCU now reported up to the CIA's newly created Technology Mission Center, further bringing the unit into the Agency fold in ways that made Thorpe uncomfortable. It wasn't that he distrusted the Agency brass. Besides, their teams worked well together. It was just that as the balance shifted closer to one organization, it became difficult to ensure competing priorities and, to Thorpe's mind, legal authorizations aligned. As a career FBI agent, he still felt uncomfortable taking direct tasking from the number-two man at the CIA.

The meeting broke and Hoskins stayed to discuss something with Richter.

Thorpe left the White House. Once he was outside, he stopped in the Washington summer night, the air heavy and charged, and dialed the NTCU ops center from his unit-issued mobile phone. The ops analyst who answered asked him a challenge question to verify his identity. Once Thorpe responded with the daily code phrase, the analyst said, "How can I help you, sir?"

"I need you to recall McShane immediately."

The analyst whistled into the phone. "He's not going to like that."

"Tell him I'll owe him a beer. He needs to be back in DC by tomorrow."

"Roger that, sir."

Thorpe hung up and spent a few moments in silent contemplation. The air felt electric, like the hours before a storm. Quiet, but tense, loaded. Thorpe would miss the work, certainly. Running the NTCU would be the highlight of his FBI career. His team did God's work, but they also never caught a breath. The nature of technical counterintelligence in the modern world was that there were always threats. Almost every modern nation had some cyber espionage capability, and most of them trained it on the United States. Even America's allies occasionally tried to breach her digital walls. Terrorist groups and even corporations hunted for trade secrets or ways to circumvent the rules.

Some of those companies were just attacking each other, but it fell on the NTCU and the FBI to identify those threats and counteract them. And then of course, there was Archon.

The threats were as persistent as they were pervasive. The NTCU responded to hundreds of attempts every day by foreign governments and terrorists to attack some system, public or private. The number only increased. Artificial intelligence amplified the threat level by orders of magnitude they hadn't yet been able to quantify. Whereas just a year ago, a human being conducted all the network attacks NTCU operators countered, now many of those were launched by ever more sophisticated AI. Hell, Archon had developed an AI that continually trolled the dark web for security vulnerabilities and aggregated them. From there, they would sell those vulnerabilities to other hackers or exploit them themselves. The NTCU determined it was the most efficient distribution of security vulnerabilities ever, causing hundreds of millions of dollars in damage. The breach even caused a prominent investment bank to collapse. A hacker gained access to the client base and sent targeted messages to the bank's commercial customers, pretending to be an SEC regulator. He recommended they withdraw their funds because of pending "bank irregularities."

It never ended, and Will Thorpe was tired. Worse, he was spent. One can only stay on the wall for so long.

He'd miss it, but part of him longed for the simpler life of running a small squad chasing money launderers.

"It's a lot to take in," Wilcox said. Thorpe hadn't even heard him approach. "How are you holding up?"

"I'm tired," Thorpe said. "Tell me, Jason, what are you *really* seeing?"

Wilcox declined his head. Thorpe knew his former boss was cagey. They liked and trusted Jamie Richter, but he was still the president's national security advisor, and therefore he was a politician. Information was currency in his world. The trust an operator extended to a policymaker differed from the trust they gave a peer.

Wilcox said, "It's worse than they think. SwissBank was hit. NATO headquarters, Europol. Someone got into Arkady Gorev's personal phone, which is funny because about ten people on earth have that number. They dumped a bunch of texts and voicemails from his phone to the web. Apparently, that started a panic among the Russian general staff that a Night of the Long Knives was coming."

Gorev was a Russian oligarch and one of the world's most notorious arms traffickers.

"We're going to need help, Jason," Thorpe said. "I'm at half strength now, after General Burgess threw his little tantrum and pulled all the National Security Agency personnel. We lost most of our offensive cyber capability."

"I won't ask you to get into specifics on the White House lawn," Wilcox replied dryly. "But I think there are things we can do."

Though, the thought dawned on Thorpe that perhaps *this* conversation was the real reason he and Wilcox were here tonight. Damn, Jamie Richter was a hell of a chess player.

"I suspect that my deputy and your deputy are discussing that very topic as we speak," Wilcox said.

"I doubt that very much," Thorpe said, allowing himself a thin smile.

5

Colt left Havana at his first opportunity and flew to Miami International.

He had an hour to kill before his flight to Barbados.

Colt purchased a local newspaper from a kiosk and then went to go find some breakfast. After wolfing down an egg sandwich, Colt grabbed his coffee in one hand, folded the paper under his arm, and headed for Gate E15. Once he was there, he took out the pen he'd gotten from Hazlett and started working on the day's crossword puzzle.

"Is this seat taken?" a woman asked.

"It's all yours," Colt said.

She was in her early thirties, brown hair cut short, large dark eyes, attractive. She wore jeans and white shirt with the sleeves rolled up to her elbows. She was also a CIA analyst assigned to the NTCU named Alison D'Angelo.

Colt folded the newspaper, clipped the pen in the upper fold and set it between them. He looked at his watch.

"Well, I guess I better be heading to my gate."

"I hope it's nice wherever you're going," D'Angelo said, amiably. "Oh, you left your paper," she said.

"Keep it, I'm through with it," Colt said.

With practiced ease, D'Angelo palmed the pen—with Hazlett's thumb drive safely in the clip—and deposited it in her bag. Then, she unfolded the paper and pretended to read. She'd be on a flight back to DC about the same time Colt left for Barbados. D'Angelo was good, and he was proud of her. Getting analysts into the field gave them an opportunity to experience a little of what case officers did every day, and he was a firm believer that it made them better at their jobs.

Colt wouldn't have chosen to take personal time in the middle of a crisis. Though, it seemed like ever since he'd joined the NTCU, the times in between crises were few and far between. But Thorpe had ordered him to take time off. Under any normal circumstances, there would be a mission debrief before he did anything else. When someone could define "normal circumstances," Colt hoped they'd let him know. There was also the matter of where he was going and who he was seeing. Thorpe would never vocalize it, but Colt's relationship with Ava was their best source of information on Trinity and their operations. If Colt could get anything useful from their time together, Thorpe believed it was time well spent.

Colt thought through what he'd learned from Hazlett's file, mentally preparing his debrief so he could focus on enjoying his time with Ava.

Archon had indeed gone to ground after Hawkinson's escape and subsequent disappearance, but that didn't mean they'd dried up and withered away. Rather, they were gearing up for something big. The NTCU didn't know if Guy's uncle, U.S. Senator Preston Hawkinson, was aware of Archon's existence and his nephew's role in it. Was he content to receive support from some anonymous benefactor? Was he fully complicit, or did he just accept that someone wanted him in the White House, treating it the same way he might money from a political action committee? They didn't know. What Hazlett's information confirmed, however, was that Archon was proceeding with their effort to hand Preston Hawkinson the presidential election.

In the file, Hazlett had detailed their electioneering campaign.

He also gave insight into what Hawkinson intended to do—or, more to the point, what Archon intended for him to do once there. A President Hawkinson would gradually unravel constitutional protections, disguising them as necessary reforms to an antiquated system. Once the ideological head of the so-called "anti-technologist movement," Hawkinson would implement sweeping changes to the federal bureaucracy, replacing "outdated and inefficient" offices with AI. He'd reduce the size of government by orders of magnitude, streamline processes, and make it outwardly appear more accountable.

Small government federalists on the right would laud him and the technocrats on the left clamoring for modernization would do the same. They just wouldn't know who was pulling the digital strings.

With the money he'd save from cutting tens of thousands of jobs from the federal payroll and the attendant support contracts, Hawkinson would invest in a national IT infrastructure. Modernize the grid. Ubiquitous cell coverage, internet for all, smart grids in most cities.

And that was where it became truly terrifying.

Similar to the Chinese Belt and Road Initiative, this infrastructure investment would mean every packet of data in the country passed through a government-built network. Lurking in this network would be Archon's AIs, intercepting and reading every message, every phone call, every internet search.

It'd be enough to make Orwell say, "You've gone too far."

It would be a practically uncontested race. Archon's systems would digitally manufacture damning evidence against Hawkinson's political opponents, even deepfake conversations. They'd move rivals out and replace them with sycophants regardless of political ideology.

By the end of Hawkinson's first term, America would be unrecognizable.

Guy Hawkinson's HawkTech had built "secure voting technology," which they'd deployed throughout the world on UN projects. They'd even tested them in several voting districts in the U.S. at his Uncle Preston's urging. Now that Guy was a global fugitive, Archon manufactured the sale of that business to another Archon-controlled enterprise. Even now, they were in talks with municipalities across the country to run proofs of concept. It was too soon to affect the outcome of this year's election, but by the time the next one rolled around, there would be enough that Archon could assure the results. Whether Preston Hawkinson was at the top of the ticket or not.

Following what they'd believed to be the decisive blow against Archon last year, the NTCU's new masters at the Technology Mission Center wanted the unit to pivot to other threats.

Colt hoped that with this new intel, he could convince them the fight against Archon was far from over.

Colt tossed his empty coffee cup in a recycling bin and found his gate. Next stop, the farthest he could get from Langley in the time they'd given him.

The Coral Reef Club was an exclusive resort on Barbados's western shore. Colt padded across the cabana's tile floor to the bar, where he scooped ice into two tumblers and poured a few fingers each of Mount Gay XO rum. He picked up both glasses and joined Ava on the porch, where she was enjoying a radiant Caribbean sunset of glowing pastels. The blue sky faded from light blue to pink, then blazing orange at the horizon. Colt handed her a glass and sat in the white wicker rocker.

He drank in silence for a time.

Ava took a drink and rocked slowly in the heavy tropical air. "I could get used to this," she said.

"Yeah, all we'd have to do is cut the undersea telecom cables and this place would be actual paradise."

"Don't tempt me," she said. Then she added dryly, "Plus, there'd still be satellites."

Ava had arrived from London the day before. Colt had flown in that morning, once he'd wrapped up his operation in Havana and sent a cable to Langley with his mission report.

Their reunion had been . . . less than he'd hoped for.

Colt didn't know precisely what he expected, just that it wasn't what he'd gotten. Ava had already checked in and wasn't in the room when he'd arrived. On the choppy flight over from Miami, Colt nursed a fantasy in which she'd be waiting for him in a bed they wouldn't leave for hours. After some searching of the grounds, he'd found her in the pool, casually swimming laps. She got out when she saw him, but the passionate embrace he'd been thinking of for the last few months was denied because she needed to towel off. It just got more awkward after that.

It was as if they didn't know how to act around each other now that the restrictions were gone. Well, given Ava's position in Trinity, their relationship likely broke a whole new and exciting group of Agency ethics regulations. Thorpe, to his credit, agreed to turn a blind eye to it. Of course, that had more to do with Ava's value as a source within that organization than it did any slack he'd cut Colt.

Ava suggested Colt change and join her by the pool. So much for a lazy afternoon in the cabana, he noted sourly. Colt changed, fixed a rum and coke, and resigned himself to figure out the invisible wall of tension between them.

It didn't take him long to see that Ava was stalling.

Finally, he asked her. "What's wrong?"

"What do you mean?"

"Ava, you've all but kept me at arm's length since I got here. I don't know what to make of it, other than I don't like it."

She took a drink and in her profile, he could see the corners of her mouth turn down.

"It's not that, Colt. Well, actually it *is* that. I don't know how we do this."

"How we do what?"

"This, us, everything." Ava shook her head. "Every time we see each other, it's because the world is about to end."

Colt was about to laugh when he realized she wasn't joking.

"Those bad things are going to happen whether or not we see each other," he said.

"I know that, but that doesn't make it any easier to turn off. It's not that I can't compartmentalize it, I just . . ." Her voice trailed off.

"You and I have seen things no one else should have. I think that's what makes this work. We're probably the only two people on earth who understand each other."

"I don't know," she said dismissively. "There was this guy when I was at Mossad. He was very understanding, and very pretty."

Colt felt like someone was pulling his heart through his chest. He couldn't believe what he was hearing. This is where she broke it off. God, couldn't she have just dropped him over the phone so he didn't fly all the way—

Was she laughing?

"You should see your face, darling," Ava said, chuckling.

"What?"

Ava turned in her chair and grabbed his hand. Colt was still dumbstruck and thoroughly confused.

"I was teasing you. There wasn't an understanding, handsome commando at Mossad. Well, there were several, but I didn't sleep with any of them."

"If this is still teasing, you should stop," he said flatly.

"Listen to me. I love you. This is just very hard, and I thought it was complicated before."

"I understand." Colt's pulse returned to normal, but he was still thoroughly confused. "But, if we just . . ."

"Colt," Ava said. "Stop talking." She grabbed his hand and led him inside.

Well, that clarified things, Colt reasoned amid the twisted sheets. He half-sat in the bed with a fresh drink on the nightstand and Ava resting her head on his chest. The cabana was quiet, cool, and a muted indigo color as the last vestiges of the pastel sunset drained away.

Ava spoke first. "I almost didn't come here. Not because I didn't want to see you. I needed to see you, but there's just so much to do."

"I get that. Thorpe basically ordered me to take the time off. Everyone is panicking, though I can't say that I blame them." Ava shifted next to him and then pulled herself up to sit. "The tech indexes are in a free fall because of these leaks."

"I saw. It's making my day job hell." Officially, Ava ran a technology portfolio for a London-based venture capital firm. It was a cover for her role in Trinity and gave her the ability to find promising advances in AI that

Trinity wanted to cultivate. "I know you won't tell me, but I'm going to ask anyway. Did you pull off that Chinese dip cable hack?"

Colt shook his head. "Oh, I can tell you. That wasn't us. We don't know who did it, which is a large part of the problem. Washington is lighting itself on fire over this because they're afraid *our* dip traffic isn't safe. Who knows, it probably isn't. There have been a lot of security breaches in a short amount of time. That's the part that troubles me, that whoever is doing this is doing it at scale."

"Do you think it could be dozens of different actors?"

"It seems too pervasive to be random and uncoordinated," Colt said.

"I agree, but here's what I've had my team thinking about: We know that when your government raided Hawkinson's offices in Switzerland, they didn't find much. I think Archon anticipated this and started selling his businesses off, to Archon-owned front companies, we assume. We've been following the money for eight months. My team has been going after their front companies. It's like a Russian nesting doll of shell corporations. Just one after another. That bioweapon they developed? That tech is still out there in the wild. But what we think is going on is they might be creating franchises. What if they gave some of their tools to terrorist groups, the North Koreans, the Iranians? Hell, even unscrupulous corporations looking for an edge? We know Guy's people developed an AI that trolled the dark web for security vulnerabilities at scale, which let them get into God-only-knows how many systems."

The implications of Ava's statement were terrifying.

With Archon, they had a firm target. It was still a nebulous, poorly understood organization, but because it spun out of Trinity, they knew who the leadership was and could monitor them. If Ava was right and Archon was distributing tech to any number of different actors, security services and corporations alike could spend *years* playing whack-a-mole against them just to keep the threats at bay.

And all the while Archon would retool, reconstitute, and recalibrate for their broader objective.

Colt wondered if all of that would stopped if Archon put Hawkinson in office. It wasn't a bad strategy—Hawkinson shows the world the solution to the crisis and gains immediate credibility. He'd never be able to convince any of those antagonists to stop, but it seemed highly likely Archon could develop technology that made their attacks irrelevant.

"We're hitting them hard, but it still doesn't feel like it's enough. Do you remember in the nineties? After the Cold War ended, one of your generals said that we killed the dragon, but not the snakes?"

"It was James Woolsey. He was the CIA director then," Colt said. Everyone at the Agency knew this quote by heart and the situation that inspired it. "He was talking about the Clinton Administration gutting the Agency's budget. Woolsey said, 'We killed a dragon but the snakes remain.' He was talking about all the other threats we'd ignored, like terrorism, because we'd been singularly focused on defeating the Soviets."

Ava exhaled softly, but completely. Colt felt her breath on his chest. "That's what this feels like," she said, her voice distant.

Colt desperately wanted to tell her about Hazlett. He wanted Ava to know that he was doing his part. He also wanted her to know that she wasn't alone in this fight. But he couldn't say a word. Agent names and locations were the most sacredly guarded secrets the Agency had. Colt would not violate that, not even for Ava.

She would just have to trust he was doing all he could.

Instead, Colt said, "We know they've exported some of their AI cyber weapons to a host of non-state actors. Hell, the FBI arrested some kid in Glendale that had a clone of Archon's open source crawler last week. It feels exactly like what Director Woolsey said. If what you say is true, we could be tied up for years chasing all of those." Colt slid out of bed, walked over to the bar, and refreshed their drinks. This was a conversation that felt like it needed a little fortification. He handed Ava her drink and slid his legs back under the sheet. "The thing I can't figure is how they're just destroying some of the most advanced encryption out there. A Gmail account is one thing, but a top secret diplomatic cable between the People's Liberation Army general staff? *We* would have a hard time with that." Colt smirked and added, "Probably."

"I worry there's an iceberg in the water. If this keeps up, the whole notion of privacy is just . . . *gone*." Ava sipped her drink. "This is something none of us have ever seen. I'll admit to you, I'm scared. Trinity only works because of secrecy. We've had to do some . . . necessary things that our governments might not agree with. What happens to us if that gets out? What happens if a friendly government that used to shield us seizes one of our labs? Now they've got the most advanced AI research in the world and we're at the whim of a popular vote."

Trinity held the belief that the breakout potential for Artificial General Intelligence was so great that a government shouldn't be entrusted with it. The political tides shifted too quickly and, worse, could be manipulated.

Colt didn't share Trinity's belief and frankly, the idea scared him. He did, however, agree with the dangers Ava talked about.

Colt now knew several of Trinity's members. His former boss and mentor, Jason Wilcox, headed the group. Ava, of course. He understood why those scientists founded it during the Cold War and he even agreed with some of their goals. Except that they'd already split once. What happened if there was another ideological break? Artificial General Intelligence—a machine that can think and reason like a human and do so across any number of domains. Its ability to learn wouldn't be constrained by the need to sleep or eat. Hypothetically, AGI could learn everything humanity knows about say, physics, in a single session. What could Trinity do with that kind of power if they stopped being the good guys? They weren't accountable to anyone.

"You could come work with me, you know," she said.

There it was. Colt had feared this would happen. When Ava first told him she was leaving Mossad for Trinity, she'd asked him to come with and he'd told her no.

"Jason wants you on board. He didn't say so, and would never ask me to ask you, but I know where his head's at."

"Yeah?" he said, noncommittally.

"He knows everyone is fighting an uphill battle. This is perfect for you, and your time as a venture capitalist couldn't be a better cover. I want you to think about it, Colt."

For eight years, Colt worked directly for Jason Wilcox on what the Agency termed a "nonofficial cover." They installed him in a commercial company—in this case, a tech-focused VC firm—and in every respect, Colt lived a double life. He was undercover every minute of the day. He didn't set foot inside of Langley for almost all of that time. Colt collected economic and technological intelligence on governments and corporations alike. Occasionally, Wilcox would have a covert assignment more in the traditional Agency model, such as when Colt injected the Agency's Sci-Tech Division–designed remote jailbreak of smartphone firmware into a Taipei chip factory.

Colt didn't want to leave the Agency, but the work was definitely changing. He'd never truly been an insider at CIA. He'd gone directly from working undercover for Wilcox to the NTCU. Though their office was in the bowels of Headquarters Station, the NTCU had a dotted line to the director of national intelligence. After the National Security Agency backed out of the mission and pulled their assets back to Ft. Meade, the CIA moved the NTCU under their newly created "Technology Mission Center." Nothing was official, but Colt knew that when Thorpe returned to the Bureau, which he planned to do next year, the TMC would replace him with an Agency person. That would likely cause the Bureau to pull the rest of their special agents, leaving the NTCU with CIA personnel and a handful of analysts from across the IC. Losing the FBI would mean losing their ability to operate inside the U.S.

The problem with that was that technology didn't recognize national borders.

Maybe Ava was right this time.

The battle against Archon had been a costly one for Colt. He had few friendships outside the Agency anymore. There just wasn't time, and even if there had been, how could he relate to someone on a meaningful level after the things he'd seen every day? Some officers were far better at compartmentalizing their lives than he was. Archon, through Senator Hawkinson, had forced Wilcox's premature departure from the CIA. Many thought Wilcox was a lock to be one of the few CIA officers to be appointed director of central intelligence. For Colt, it was as professionally damaging as it was personally. Because Colt spent his entire Agency career before NTCU undercover and reporting to Wilcox, no one at HQS knew him. He had a very small professional network and no political top cover. There were no senior officers guiding his career or helping him avoid the political landmines that lurked unseen in Langley's halls.

Fred Ford, Colt's friend, boss, and partner in the NTCU, had finally retired after the unit's re-org. The Chinese intelligence officer, Liu Che, shot Fred and almost killed him during their first attempt to grab him in a Washington park.

Fred, reasonably, decided that was the last bullet he was going to have to dodge.

The Agency's war against Archon was littered with the casualties of hasty decisions and half measures. It was the mark of fighting an enemy they didn't understand on a battlefield they couldn't comprehend.

Ava held her drink on her lap above the covers, hands cradled around it. She looked at him, an unreadable expression heavy in her dark eyes.

Perhaps it was time.

And yet he said, "I can't leave now." Colt drank, held his glass, surprised at himself. Was that just a knee jerk reaction? He could still take it back. It was just the two of them. But he pressed on. "I've got some things underway. I don't want to say any more than that. It's just . . . I can't leave now," he repeated.

"I understand," Ava said, distantly. Did she? Ava had always been the lighting in a bottle. The primal force one could only hope to slow down, never to contain. When she decided she needed to act, she did. Ava never equivocated. It frustrated her when others were not as decisive. She often bristled at Colt's insistence on following the rules.

Ava didn't argue with him and didn't press him. She left her statement stand. He wondered what that meant.

Colt was about to suggest they order dinner when his phone rang.

He replace his drink with his phone and looked at the number. "Undisclosed Caller."

He sighed, knowing what was coming.

Colt answered. He listened to the brief message, said he understood, and then hung up.

"Shit."

6

Washington, DC

"Good morning, Mr. Kim," an aide said as Jeff cleared White House security. "Follow me, please."

Jeff wore a tan linen suit and a blue shirt without a tie. He hated wearing suits, but even he recognized that the laid-back attire of the tech community could only go so far. This was the White House, after all. He matched the aide's stride as they headed inside.

Technically, Jeff held a position in the administration. The year before, the president had appointed him "Special Advisor for Advanced Technology" in the wake of a Russian cyberattack that opened up California's Folsom Dam and devastated Sacramento. Kim had helped stop the attack, and prevented it from being so much worse. His was largely an advisory role and didn't merit an office in the West Wing.

Not that he'd have maintained one anyway.

The aide asked him if he needed anything to drink. Jeff declined, and the aide guided him to Jamie Richter's office.

The national security advisor had started his career in the State Department before moving to academia. He'd maintained tenure at Georgetown University, teaching graduate courses in international relations and foreign policy, but also spent much of his post-State career at some prominent DC think tanks. Richter's office bore the marks of station one would expect: photos with world leaders, engraved awards, and a framed copy of *Foreign Affairs* which bore the title of his seminal essay, "A New American World Order?".

Jamie Richter looked tired.

It wasn't even ten a.m. and his jacket was already off, sleeves rolled to the elbows. Richter's desk looked like a trailer park after a tornado. Papers and other official debris were everywhere. A Yeti coffee tumbler with the Georgetown logo teetered precariously on a stack of legal pads. A whiteboard crammed between a table and the window was covered in a scrawled list of U.S. government departments and agencies, corporations, minimal governments, and nongovernmental agencies. It also displayed the names of several foreign governments, UN committees, and NATO activities.

Jeff had been so focused on Richter, he'd failed to notice Dr. Candace Khatari, the president's "Cybersecurity Czar," seated at the table. Jeff knew Dr. Khatari well, not that they got along. She had been an early member of Google and rose through the company quickly, exiting with more money than she could likely spend in two lifetimes, and went on to co-found a moderately successful firm specializing in intrusion detection and post-attack remediation. After selling that company to Palo Alto Networks, Khatari went on the lecture circuit. She and Jeff had both sat on a SXSW panel a few years ago, where they'd vigorously debated whether artificial intelligence was a security liability or a force multiplier. She was a noted critic of placing trust in AI, and Jeff suspected she was behind some of the torpedoing that undermined Janus.

Janus was the system Jeff designed and deployed at the president's request to prevent an attack like Folsom from ever happening again.

Based on Jeff's landmark AI, "Saturn," he'd created Janus and trained it to run cyber defense systems. In the Roman pantheon, Janus was Saturn's partner, the god of gates and pathways. Janus continually searched for vulnerabilities on the systems it monitored, including trawling the dark corners of the web where hackers stashed exploits. The system immediately deployed patches and was programmed to notified law enforcement when applicable. It monitored all email traffic, searching for phishing and social engineering attempts, insider threats, unauthorized disclosures, and policy violations. The system enforced a zero trust architecture, which assumed that an attacker was always present in the network. Janus interrogated every outside connection attempt to a protected network—whether or not it was from a trusted source—and shut down any unverified or unauthorized connection immediately. Janus kept a threat and vulnerability database, which it shared continually with the cybersecurity divisions within government and industry, expanding on an initiative the White House had attempted in the mid-2010s. It was the most comprehensive cybersecurity initiative ever attempted.

And it was doomed from the start.

Jeff knew the failures of bureaucracy, which is why he did his best to steer clear of them. This initiative would stay in play as long as it was politically expedient. Even under the best of circumstances, Janus would face incredible pressure just to stay alive. There were billions of dollars in government consulting at risk, and multiple firms had already filed lawsuits against the administration because the president enacted this through an executive order. It didn't matter that Janus was a direct response to a Russian-led cyberattack that killed hundreds and nearly destroyed an entire city. The industries surrounding the Beltway wouldn't allow those lucrative contracts to just slip away. Beyond that, there was bureaucratic intransigence. Jeff's technology put contracted and civil servant security and IT specialists out of a job. This spurred additional lawsuits from industry and protests from the civil service unions.

"Thanks for coming, Jeff. Be with you in a sec," Jamie said. He stood in front of his desk and issued directions to the three aides clustered around him, then asked for the room. The aides cleared out, the colonel closing the door behind him.

"Sorry for asking you to fly out here. I know it's a pain in the ass, but this isn't something I can talk to you about over the phone. Not even a secure one."

"I understand. How can I help?"

"Have a seat," Richter said, motioning to a nearby chair. Jeff took it. "In the last week, we've seen the largest number of security breaches since . . . well, ever. Everything I'm about to tell you is top secret. You're not to discuss this outside of this room." Jeff nodded his understanding and Richter continued. "It started with the Chinese. The *New York Times* broke a story—"

"I'm familiar," Jeff cut in.

"Right, well, it's since spread like wildfire. Pardon the expression."

Jeff had a storied history with wildfires. It was not, as one might conclude, a good one. Though pitching his fire prediction software had been what secured him a meeting with California's governor on that fated day the year before.

"Anyway, we're now seeing breaches on nearly all social media platforms, in industry, and across the whole of government. This includes classified information and diplomatic cables, stuff that's supposed to be inaccessible."

"Jamie, if we hadn't paused the Janus rollout—"

Richter held up both hands. "I know, and I don't want to re-litigate that, Jeff. That's not why you're here. Frankly, some breaks happened in Janus-protected systems."

That got Jeff's attention.

"We had an Air Force Special Reconnaissance Team operating in Crimea, keeping tabs on Russian troop movements. Someone hacked their state-of-the-art encrypted tactical radios. They recorded the transmission and dumped it onto a Google drive and shared it on Twitter. That's not supposed to be possible. Thankfully, we evac'd them before the Russians found out about it. I owe the president answers and I don't have any to give."

"What does National Security Agency say? Or CISA?" Jeff knew the answer or he wouldn't be here. If the alphabet soup of three- and four-letter agencies knew what was going on, Richter wouldn't have called him. Still, it'd be useful to know what ground had already been covered.

"The NSA assumes it's an AI," Richter said.

"They think it's one of yours," Khatari said dryly.

"Candace, please."

"What do you mean, one of mine?" Jeff asked.

"The National Security Agency's assessment is that only a bleeding-edge AI could do this much damage this quickly. They believe someone stole yours and trained it to do all this."

"That's preposterous. The practices I use in my company are stricter than what I'm deploying through Janus." He flicked a sidelong glance at Khatari. "At least, they were until you pulled Janus's teeth out."

"Well, I think we see where placing too much trust in AI has gotten us," Khatari snapped.

"That's enough. Dr. Khatari, I'll remind you that the president requested Jeff's help with this. We don't have any answers. But Jeff, there is something to whether or not this might be one of your systems. We know Guy Hawkinson stole quite a lot of your IP and sold that to the Russians. Do you think it's possible that they've corrupted your tech and made it offensive?"

Jeff shook his head. "I didn't design Janus, or the system it was based on, to have offensive capability."

"But it could learn," Khatari broke in.

"No, it couldn't," Jeff said archly. "I've designed safeguards into my systems to prevent them from harming people. They can't be 'taught' to override that. The only way—"

Khatari broke in. "Oh of course they could. You don't—"

"The only way they could be overridden is if someone hacked deep enough into Janus to convince the system that nefarious actions would actually be in accordance with its goals. However, I've anticipated this and designed guardrails against that. I assure you, if there is a scenario that Dr. Khatari has envisioned, I've thought of it."

"Could an AI hack one of your systems?" Richter asked quickly before Dr. Khatari could return fire.

"We're getting into a highly hypothetical area here. It may technically be possible. It would have to be a more advanced system, faster, smarter and capable of outmaneuvering mine. However, you're conflating two independent problems. Hacking into an email system or a social media platform is a matter of finding a vulnerability and exploiting it. Diplomatic cables and tactical military radios are entirely different. Breaking encryption differs from exploiting a security vulnerability, which Dr. Khatari well knows."

Khatari narrowed her dark eyes at him, but said nothing.

"Go on," Richter said.

"What do you know about quantum computing?"

A mix of irritation and impatience flashed across Richter's face. Speaking with people who weren't on his technical level frustrated Jeff tremendously. He felt it necessary to explain concepts before getting into the substance of the matter so that the other parties could communicate. Unfortunately, that was an investment in time.

A wave of righteous indignation crashed over Khatari's face and as her mouth opened to assault Jeff with protest, Richter broke in. "Just get to the point."

"This is important," Jeff said, his turn to show irritation. "The simplest definition is that quantum computers work differently than traditional machines, even supercomputers. A classical computer, like the one you're using now, uses bits to store and process information. A bit can be either a 0 or a 1, just like a light switch can be either on or off. But quantum computers use qubits instead of bits. A qubit is a lot like a regular bit, it can still represent 0 or 1. But unlike a bit, which can only be in one state at a time, a qubit can exist in both states at once. It's like having a light switch that can be both on and off simultaneously. This phenomenon is called 'superposition,' and it's a fundamental property of quantum mechanics. Because of superposition, qubits have the potential to perform multiple calculations all at once, giving quantum computers some truly mind-boggling computational powers. Think of it like this. A classical computer might process data step by step, doing one calculation after another. But a quantum computer, with its qubits in superposition, can explore many different possibilities simultaneously, making certain tasks much faster and more efficient." Jeff paused and waited for questions.

Seeing there were none, he continued. "The technology is nascent, but at least fifty nations—including the Russians and the Chinese—have some level of investment in it. I bring this up because leading computer scientists and quantum physicists believe this technology will render all current forms of security irrelevant. Today, a classical computer would take three hundred trillion years to break a 2048-bit encryption key. A quantum computer of sufficient power could do this in ten seconds."

"That's impossible," Khatari said. "At least now. And anyway, quantum computers can't even talk to traditional computers."

"Apparently you haven't studied rudimentary physics, Dr. Khatari. Quantum mechanics holds that there is one state where they can and one where they cannot." This wasn't entirely accurate, but Jeff needed to back her down so he could get his point across. Several scientists, Jeff included, had conducted successful integrations of quantum and classical computers. It was more complicated than designing an automated programming interface, or API, but conceptually it was the same problem. "As I was saying, our fear is that quantum computing can defeat all extant cybersecurity and encryption protocols. NIST is currently working on this problem, but they aren't much past the position paper stage. Now, I will reluctantly agree with the good doctor on one point," he allowed, nodding toward Candace. "It should be currently impossible. No current quantum computing array in existence can create enough stable quantum bits to generate the computational power necessary to do this. Research efforts underway by the Chinese and American governments are close, but they aren't there yet. A private organization called the Cyber Futures Foundation also shows promising results. None of them have reached Q-Day yet. They will reach this milestone within a year or two, but are not there now."

"What I'm hearing is that it's hypothetically possible, but no one has done it yet. Is that what you're telling me?" Richter gripped his steel coffee mug.

"He's talking out of both sides of his mouth," Khatari said. Richter sent her a withering look.

"Jeff, go back. What's Q-Day?"

"It's the point at which we believe there is sufficient quantum computing power—the stable qubits I mentioned earlier—to defeat all encryption." Jeff closed his eyes and weighed his next words. This would change everything. The nature of his relationship with the government, possibly even his deal. Having Khatari in the room now certainly didn't help. He liked Richter and could work with him, but Jeff threatened Khatari's position and stature in the administration. She ran committees, wrote papers, and chaired interagency meetings. Jeff delivered a solution, and she hated him for it. Such was the nature of this town and the reason he avoided it. Jeff exhaled heavily. "I achieved Q-Day. About four months ago."

"And you didn't think to mention that?" Khatari snapped.

"I'm expected to disclose all of my trade secrets now?"

"When they constitute a national security threat, yes."

Her argument was as ridiculous as it was hyperbolic, political theater for Richter's benefit.

"Another point where I will reluctantly agree with Dr. Khatari is that this could result from technology stolen from Pax AI. Working with some top physicists, I designed a quantum array about five years ago. We've been continually honing the design. I am farther along than everyone else, but only by two to three years. This is all the technology that Guy Hawkinson stole from me. It's possible that he would've sold that to the Russians, but I doubt it."

"Why?" asked Richter.

"He'd want to keep it for himself."

"I'll bite this time. Why?" Khatari said.

"Guy Hawkinson would never sell something an adversary could use against him. As I understand that situation, his relationship with the Russians turned sour quickly. We've seen Hawkinson weaponize my technology in the past. There's no reason to think that he hasn't done so again."

"Fine time for a revelation, Jeff."

"I'm sorry, Candace, but I disclosed everything he took to the FBI and the NTCU in my voluminous debriefings on the matter. They must not have decided you needed to know."

"That's about enough of that, Jeff," Richer said firmly. "Guys, I can do without the urinary olympics. I get enough of that here already. I don't care if you two don't care for each other. Like it or not, Candace is the president's cybersecurity advisor. Jeff, you're here to provide solutions. So, let's fast forward to that part and skip the part where you two bicker for another hour."

"Right, sorry," Jeff said. "The other part that's relevant is the number of instances. You mentioned about ten."

"That's right."

"Now, all severe on their own, and high profile. But not, I think, systemic. If an AI were directing this, I believe you would see relentless assaults on all systems. That doesn't appear to be the case."

Khatari said, "Is it a hardware limitation? I'm not an expert, but I know quantum computers are incredibly expensive."

"That's correct, prohibitively so for most organizations. Gold electrodes, lasers, and most designs require special cooling. This leads me to conclude whoever is behind this has not implemented a solution at scale."

"Sure seems that way," Dr. Khatari quipped.

"I mean at scale for a machine. There are also few scientists with the requisite expertise. I'm sure that the number willing to work for Guy Hawkinson is probably a much smaller one."

"Jeff, I know you disagree," Richter started, cautiously. "But there have been a lot of attacks. Would it be possible for an AI using this quantum computing to break down our encryption?"

"Hypothetically, yes."

"Which brings us back to the point about *your* systems," Khatari said.

"So, what are the options?" Richter said, again cutting off the rebuttal.

"Well, for starters, we need post-quantum encryption factors," Khatari said, leveling a hard gaze at Jeff. "And, yes, I have read the NIST papers."

"You're right," Jeff allowed. "But that will take years to implement. And that's being generous."

"What team are you playing on, Jeff?"

Jeff sighed. He was tired of having to continually explain things to lesser minds. "First, we have to agree on a standard, and then it has to be implemented across the whole of government. Janus could expedite this, but you've worked behind the scenes to undermine it. I assume that's because you feel that I'm encroaching on your turf. I don't care about politics, Candace. The president asked me to solve a problem, so I did. You and some others didn't like the answer because it wasn't business-as-usual."

"Easy, Jeff," Richter said in a warning tone.

"No, Jamie, she needs to hear this. Frankly, so do you. Rolling out a post-quantum security protocol will take a long time, so we should start now. Focus on essential systems like diplomatic, military, and IC communications and critical infrastructure. The government already has a prioritization schema for protecting assets. Start with that. But, considering the fact that the whole reason the Russians hacked Folsom in the first place, or Hawkinson's people hacked the air traffic control network, was because those systems haven't been upgraded or even patched in years doesn't leave me with a lot of confidence in your ability to rapidly deploy a solution." Jeff folded his arms and his eyes narrowed. "You can debate ideas, but you cannot debate objective fact. And here's another thing. I will not be blamed for this. If this is indeed Guy Hawkinson and his lunatic fringe of true believers, I'll remind you he used privileged access as my security contractor to steal that technology. He murdered my employees and caused a wildfire that burned tens of thousands of acres. When I asked the government for help, you did nothing. And when his senator uncle buried it, you still did nothing. It wasn't until you needed my help that you agreed to act. I want this perfectly understood." Jeff turned to face Candace Khatari, so that there was no possibility of missing the message. "If I hear so much as the whiff of a rumor, or, God help you all, some kind of leak in the media, I pull Janus. I go away forever and you can figure this out on your own. I will not help you. And when you come calling me to understand how he's wormed his way into your networks, I'll just smile and say 'thoughts and prayers.'"

The room was silent for a long, cold time.

It was probably just a few breaths, but the resonance of Jeff's anger hung in the air like a specter.

"Candace, would you give us the room?" Richter said, not taking his eyes off Jeff. "We'll catch up later."

"Jamie, I really think—"

"We'll discuss it later, Candace."

Khatari's stare could have lit Jeff on fire. She had more dignity than to slam the door, but she closed it hard.

"You're really going to have to learn to play well with others if you're going to get along in this town, Jeff."

"I don't want to get along in this town. I want to be back home working. You asked me to come out for something important, but all I seem to be getting is a lecture from someone who isn't capable of doing her job. Or maybe she can do *that* job, and that's the problem."

Richter pinched the bridge of his nose. "I will control Dr. Khatari, and you have my word that no one will not blame you for this. Now, what do we do about it?"

Jeff knew there was only one way to solve this problem, but he doubted they had the resolve to do it.

"You need a post-quantum encryption standard, and you need to start now. But I wasn't being hyperbolic. That will take years to roll out, even if you use Janus to deploy it. Which . . ." Jeff's voice trailed off, leaving the rest unsaid.

"I understand, and I'm dealing with that. For what it's worth, POTUS is pissed off that people are slow boating this and he's going to deal with it."

"Jamie, if you want to solve this quickly, and stop it from getting worse, you need to act decisively."

Jeff didn't know with absolutely certainty that Hawkinson and that Archon group of his was behind this. But it was a reasonable conclusion given the factors at play. It was possible that another entity had developed a quantum system on par with his own design, but Jeff didn't think it plausible.

"Jeff, for once, I need a straight answer from someone. What do you mean by *decisive*?"

"Guy Hawkinson is the only one, in my estimation, with the capability to launch these attacks. You have weeks, not years, before the damage is irreparable. That is the reality you're facing right now. Social media hacks are a big deal, because they affect nearly all your constituents. But what about the private keys for cryptocurrencies? We've already seen the two biggest, ForgeCoin and CryptoBase, go bankrupt in a matter of weeks. People have lost millions of dollars. That will not go unnoticed."

"This administration does not support independent currencies and strongly recommends Americans not invest their money in them. The president and the Treasury secretary have been clear on this point."

"Then you're out of step with your base, at least the ones that you want to court. These are the kinds of people who are going to flock to your opponents if they don't think you're going to protect them. These are tech-savvy investors, and most of them are the ones who understand the nature of this threat. And that's not it. Hell, I've read NATO's 'red line' strategy for Ukraine, and I've seen the private cables where you've said exactly what

weapons you'll provide and what you won't. I saw them on a Discord channel, so you'd better believe the Russians have, too. That's national security
stuff, clearly your wheelhouse. What's going to happen to the pharmaceutical industry when drug formulas and clinical trial results start showing
up? You're looking at bankrupting whole industries. What about DOJ criminal investigations? Good luck keeping up criminal surveillance when
people know they're being looked at. This problem is so much bigger than
you're giving it credit for, Jamie. You need to deal with Hawkinson, and you
need to do it now. For two years, this administration has dealt in half-
measures."

"That's hardly fair. This is a big ship, Jeff. You don't know how much
work it takes to turn it."

"I don't care, Jamie. It's the hard truth and you need to hear it. What's
the current buzzword, radical candor? This is simple math, my friend.
Unless you solve for Guy Hawkinson, all your secrets are at risk. And not
just yours, everyone's. How do you operate in a world where no secret is
safe?"

7

Taiwan, Republic of China

Tony Ikeda stepped into the electric daylight of Taipei's famed Shilin Night Market. The tantalizing smells of a dozen different food vendors immediately hit his nose, reminding him how long it had been since his last meal. Night markets were a staple of Taiwanese culture, and Shilin had been in continuous operation since 1899. Here, one could sample a panoply of local street food, browse a multitude of curious shops, and burn hours at arcades and karaoke kiosks. Densely packed stalls offered anything imaginable under the brightly colored neon or more modern LED signs advertising their wares.

Tony found a small gap within a large group of people standing at the market's main entrance and pushed his way through. He maneuvered through the crowd, which looked like a mix of university students, tourists, and locals. It was still early, about nine, but this was peak for the most varied collection of patrons. Soon, the families and regular shoppers would drop off and the market would take on a more carnival-like atmosphere.

Tony twisted his body so that he could slice through the crowd, using his left shoulder as a prow. Once he reached an intersection, Tony turned left and then right, moving deeper into the labyrinthine confines. He repeated this once more, finally arriving at the alley he was looking for. Halfway down the row after his last turn, Tony found a collection of shops hawking postcards, curiosities, clothes, and candy. Tucked away behind a stall of knockoff Americana, Tony found what he was looking for, a narrow bookshop. Tony pretended to browse for a few moments until the owner, an older man of about sixty with silvery hair and a mustache, peeked around a rack and asked Tony if he needed help finding anything.

"Do you have anything by Chang Ta-chun?" Tony asked.

The old man eyed him appraisingly and held up his index finger. "I think so. Let me check in the back," he said, and disappeared behind a wall of books. Tony stepped deeper into the shop. The heavy, multitudinous sounds of the market faded away a little, muted by the walls of old books.

The old man returned with a well-worn copy of *The Guide to Apartments*. He handed Tony the book.

"This has some of Chang's best short stories," he said.

Tony opened the paperback's back flap and removed a slip of paper which he immediately slid into his pocket.

Tony flipped through the book, as if perusing its contents, and then handed it back to the old man. "Thank you for showing it to me," he said.

"Happy reading," the old man said and accepted the book back.

Tony stepped out into the alley and navigated back to the market's main thoroughfare. He found the first drinks vendor that he could, ordered a bubble tea, and paid in cash. Drink in hand, he removed the paper from his pocket and read it. On it was the name of a vendor, his stall number, and a time. Tony checked his watch. It was about twenty minutes from now. He memorized the note, took a final sip of the bubble tea and transferred it to the hand holding the paper. The condensation on the plastic cup acted like glue and the paper stuck fast. Tony dropped both in a nearby trash can.

They knew the Chinese were coming.

Once the CIA hacked into the Chinese intelligence network, they were able to find the proposed invasion plans for Taiwan. The PLA was inscrutable, and their planning activity nowhere near as coordinated as their counterparts in the American military. Eventually, the military analysts deciphered the invasion strategy and the Agency went to work to thwart it.

For decades, the United States had maintained a policy of so-called "strategic ambiguity" regarding Taiwan's defense. Though nebulously codified in law, it was written in such a way that a president wasn't specifically constrained to physically defend the island if the People's Republic of China decided to push across the Taiwan Strait. Recently, that ambiguity had crystallized as the Chinese government blamed America for the leaked *New York Times* story in which the PLA's general staff questioned whether victory was even possible.

Beijing blamed the U.S., claiming it was an "act of cowardice and deception" intended to weaken the "supreme resolve" of the People's Liberation Army. Langley feared that action was a prelude to war, that Beijing would *have* to act to prove they could do it. Today, the president maintained an iron grip on the Chinese Communist Party, the intelligence services, and the military, but that grip weakened each year as economic supremacy eroded and the domestic outlook became increasingly worse. Langley believed Beijing would direct the invasion. They needed the economic revenue from Taiwan's position as the global manufacturer in computer chips and they needed to take the island while the U.S. was still formalizing the alliances designed to prevent it.

Tony, a covert action officer with CIA's Special Activities Center, was deployed here immediately as fears of a Chinese invasion grew. And he hadn't come alone. The Agency also covertly deployed U.S. Army Special Forces teams attached to SAC's Ground Branch. The Green Berets would do what they did best, foreign internal defense. They integrated with the Taiwanese forces and were, at this moment, deployed at the PLA's proposed invasion sites, hiding and waiting.

Thanks to Tony's friend Colt, the Agency had a digital spy in the Chinese intelligence network. That system not only created untraceable virtual private networks to covertly report intel back to headquarters, it also wormed its way through the electronic corridors to implant itself in other systems. They were now inside the PLA's Second Department network. They learned Beijing had indeed ordered advanced echelons of the PLA special forces and covert operatives from their foreign intelligence service to lay the groundwork for an invasion.

Thanks to their electronic mole, the CIA knew exactly where the covert insertions would take place, what China's targets were, and how they planned to achieve them. The Agency even had copies of the execute orders.

The operation would begin tonight, with covert insertions of sappers from the PLA Navy's new Type 22 corvette. Designated "Houbei" by NATO, the Type 22 were stealthy, high speed catamarans that could quickly close the distance on the Taiwan Strait. They would penetrate Taiwanese-claimed waters, insert special forces teams, and disappear. In areas with heavier maritime traffic, the PLA planned to use commercial fishing vessels. Once ashore, their special forces would take out key coastal defenses and radars. Cyberattacks would blacken the island. After a night of chaos, civilian ferries would take army troops across the Taiwan Strait to capture the western ports. At that point, they could bring soldiers and vehicles across at their leisure. Contrary to many of the war-game scenarios, the Chinese didn't want to obliterate the island. They needed the industrial base, so that precluded the wanton destruction feared by so many.

At the same time, covert operatives for the PLA's intelligence arm intended to carry out targeted assassinations of key Taiwanese military and political figures. The intent was to cause the government to rapidly implode so that they would have no choice but to accept China's terms of surrender. The assassinations would be a combination of close-quarter kills and violent explosions, both intending to send the message that Beijing could strike down their Taiwanese rivals at will.

Because the Chinese justification for invading Taiwan was their fabricated claim that the U.S. had leaked their cables, Washington took Taiwan's defense seriously and spared no resource in assisting them.

Taiwan was a counterintelligence nightmare.

The country shared indelible ethnic, cultural, and familial ties with the nation that wanted to annex them and destroy their government. Finding Chinese spies and their handlers was a daunting challenge. Over the last twenty years, as the PLA's Department Two and the Ministry of State Security's operational acumen improved considerably, China had carried out successful penetrations of the Taiwanese military and security service. They'd even turned a former intelligence officer and police colonel on the presidential protection detail. When the CIA shared knowledge of the invasion plot, Taiwan's intelligence agency, the National Security Bureau, asked Langley for help.

The Taiwanese president was, at this moment, aboard an unregistered Agency aircraft bound for Tokyo, where she would spend the next three days at a "summit." Given the tensions, the Agency wasn't sure whether the Chinese would actually scramble fighters if they saw an official aircraft depart, and no one wanted to risk the potential for civilian casualties by putting her on a commercial jet. The meeting was a convenient pretext to get her off the island until the crisis was resolved.

Tony's job was to prevent the assassination of Taiwan's minister of defense.

Tony pushed through the busy night market.

The assassin was a former special forces soldier recruited into PLA's Department Two. The plan called for planting an explosive device within the defense minister's office, hidden inside a telephone. CIA knew that a sleeper agent had created a set of identification credentials for the assassin and acquired a uniform that would get him into the Ministry of Defense headquarters. What they didn't know, until now, was the agent's identity.

The bomb ended up being the key to it.

The old man in the bookstore that gave Tony the slip of paper was a Taiwanese national police officer and a highly valuable longtime source for the Agency's Taipei Station team. Using his network of informants, the old man learned that an arms smuggling ring in Taipei arranged to provide concentrated plastic explosives and a detonator to an unknown buyer. Separately, using their previous electronic infiltration of the Chinese intelligence network, the CIA identified the name of a PLA special forces officer that was purportedly being positioned in Taipei. The Agency's assessment was that he was the "buyer" and would carry out the assassination. Delivery would take place tonight at the Shilin Night Market. The old man hadn't learned the exact location and time until earlier that day. The bookstall belonged to his cousin.

Tony found the location the old man gave him, one of the few sit-down places in the market. There was a single, narrow line of round stools that ran the length of the counter, disappearing into the building, with barely enough room to move past. Tony watched for a few minutes as the chef prepared beef, vegetables, and noodles in a wok and then handed those across the counter to the customers waiting on the stools. At exactly 9:30, a man that Tony put to be in his mid-thirties wearing blue pants, a t-shirt, and ball cap pushed his way through to the fourth of the ten stools at the counter. There was an awkward shuffle and a sidestep as the man who'd been sitting there stood.

Tony watched them as the two men made eye contact for an instant. He slid to one side to get a better view and saw the man leaving had left a backpack on the ground beneath the counter and the stool.

The second man, the one in the ball cap, sat and ordered. He paid for and accepted his food, then stuffed a few perfunctory bites into his mouth with the accompanying chopsticks. He set the paper bowl on the counter, reached down and grabbed the backpack, and stood.

Tony activated an app on his smart watch. Made to look like any number of fitness trackers, this would send Tony's location over an encrypted network to Taipei Station. They'd coordinate pickup with the National Security Bureau.

The target left the food stall and melded with the crowd. Tony followed.

According to their intelligence, the man's name was Wu Chen. He'd held the rank of "Shang wei," equivalent to a captain in the U.S. military, serving in the elite "Oriental Sword" SOF unit, assigned to the Beijing Military Region. The PLA's intelligence department recruited him five years ago for training in covert action. He was not that dissimilar to Tony Ikeda.

Wu found a side exit and left the main market building. Tony followed him to the street outside, which looked as though the market had burst at the seams and spilled vendors out into the adjacent alley. Tony pretended to check out a kiosk when Wu checked his rear for potential surveillance.

He turned and continued on his way. Tony waited a few seconds, turned, and followed.

Wu snaked through dark alleys, connecting with side streets that still held a myriad of vendors. Power lines and colored lights hung between buildings on the narrow street. There were slightly larger eateries here, though still tiny by American standards, and produce vendors and tea shops. All still going strong into the night hours.

Tony quickened his pace, closing the distance with Wu, just as he was about to approach another alley.

When he just a few feet behind him, Tony said in Mandarin, "Captain Wu?"

It was an old counterintel trick. Instinct and habit overrode training and Wu cocked his head to the side, hearing his name and rank. Tony grabbed Wu from behind and forced him into the alley. Immediately, the ex-soldier responded, whipping around with a wild punch.

That was unwise.

Covert action officers have intense hand-to-hand combat training in a variety of disciplines. Tony had earned black belts in jiu jitsu and judo by the time he'd graduated high school. He'd paid for his undergrad at UCLA by teaching martial arts, and continued to train, earning a black belt in Uechi-Ryū karate by the time he left college.

And that was all before the CIA taught him everything they knew about fighting.

Tony deflected Wu's punch with his right wrist, twisted it, and clamped down on Wu's. Tony yanked him forward, off balance and landed a swift kick to the outside of the captain's knee. Wu countered, corking his body over and hitting Tony with his opposite hand. It wasn't hard, but it landed, and Tony lost his grip on Wu's wrist. The soldier stepped back to give him distance and drew a pistol from a holster concealed under his shirt. He assumed that would be the end of it.

Before Wu had a chance to set himself, Tony propelled off his back foot, closing the distance. His left arm shot out in tight arc, overpowering Wu and deflecting the gun's line of sight. He grabbed Wu's wrist and yanked the man forward while delivering three lightning-fast strikes with his right fist, middle knuckle pushed forward to a point. His punches all landed on the side of Wu's head. Tony immediately followed up with flat-hand strike to Wu's throat.

His opponent staggered backward, choking for air. Tony grabbed the pistol from him.

"Make one move and I kill you," Tony said in Mandarin.

It was over, just that fast.

"Put the bag on the ground," Tony said. "Very slowly."

Wu did.

"Turn around. Lace your hands behind your head." Once Wu did that, Tony added, "Get on the ground."

Wu turned and side-kicked, but Tony was just out of his reach. His foot hit the pistol, knocking it out of Tony's hand. The kick was a calculated risk. It disarmed Tony, but Wu landed with his back to his opponent. By the time he spun around to face Ikeda, Tony was ready. He lunged, grabbed Wu's arm, and pulled him off balance using his forward planted right leg as a fulcrum. Tony dropped to the ground, half pinning Wu and pummeling him with several strikes to the face. Wu was losing steam quickly, but still fought back in an increasingly desperate attempt to escape. Tony adjusted his positioning, wrapping an arm around Wu's shoulder to get him into a pin. He quickly switched that up to a headlock, which he held until Wu passed out.

Tony was just getting to his feet when a vehicle appeared at the end of the alley.

"Hard part's over," Tony said, dusting himself off as his peers from the National Security Bureau and a Taipei Station officer filled the alley.

There was an unwritten rule among the world's intelligence officers that was nearly universally observed. When a security service finds a foreign officer operating in their country, they might expose, harass, or detain them, but they were never to be harmed. Even in the darkest days of the Cold War, the KGB honored this. The rule's basis was not unlike immunity for the overt diplomatic staff. If the Russians discovered a CIA officer in Moscow and killed him, the Agency would launch a worldwide campaign actively targeting any and all suspected SVR and GRU operations. They would have their officers and diplomatic staff ejected not just from the United States but from dozens of America's allies. The Russians could quickly find themselves blinded, exposed, and unable to act in a large part of the world.

The rules on stopping assassinations were a little murkier, but Tony also recognized Wu's intelligence value. Tony acted in self-defense and spared the man's life. Captain Wu would be looking at a very long prison sentence which the Taiwanese, given the state of affairs with the bully across the strait, were unlikely to be motivated to negotiate his release.

Two hours later, Tony had a bottle of Gatorade and a coffee at the CIA station inside the American Institute in Taipei. Having an official embassy in Taiwan would go against the "one China" policy, so the AIT compound served as the de facto American embassy and consulate in Taiwan. They'd quickly debriefed, but the rest of the operation was still unfolding. The National Security Bureau officers arrested Wu and took him to an undisclosed location. That group was a small, trusted cadre that (unknown to them) the Bureau's head had asked the CIA to thoroughly vet before assigning them to the special detail, to make sure none of them were double agents. At midnight, they were joined by the institute's defense attaché, Marine Colonel Thomas Hoult. Hoult acted as the liaison between the Taiwanese forces and U.S. military components involved in the operation. The Defense Intelligence Agency (DIA) managed the attaché program and occasionally supported CIA activities. Colonel Hoult was an infantry officer who'd spent his entire career in Marine special forces, including in command of a raider battalion.

Like himself, Tony suspected the colonel would much rather be in the field right now alongside the snake eaters than in the de facto embassy.

Colonel Hoult had a tactical radio and was in communication with the special forces team leads. They were positioned along the island's northwest coast at the expected invasion sites, embedded with ROC Marines. Hoult also coordinated with the operation's maritime component, which was conducted from a U.S. Navy destroyer in the South China Sea.

Two years before, at the start of the current tension, the U.S. Navy had deployed unmanned underwater autonomous vehicles (UUAVs) to patrol the Taiwan Strait. Six months ago, they'd quietly deployed the new Sand-shark-class UUAVs. Currently, the Sandsharks were silently and invisibly following the Chinese Type 22 corvettes as they crossed the strait. Apparently, there was some debate within the military on whether to actually fire on any Chinese landing craft, but both the president and the secretary of defense were clear that the rules of engagement forbade it.

Not that the People's Liberation Army Navy had to know that.

"Site Delta has spotted landing craft on night vision. Small insertion craft," Hoult announced shortly after midnight. "They count three craft. Six in each."

One of the local CIA officers pulled up the UUAV feed for Site Delta. They had a drone hovering right offshore that would give the station personnel a real-time feed in night vision or infrared. The Chinese SOF team landing at Site Delta, according to the operations plan, would separate into two groups, fanning out along the coast for a protracted mission. An elite team of saboteurs, their first targets were the Thunderbolt-2000 Multiple Launch Rocket Systems (MLRS) the Taiwanese Army deployed along the coast to fire on amphibious landing craft.

The Americans had to convince the Taiwanese not to fire at the advancing ships, fearing that would trigger a full-scale conflict that would lay the island to waste.

Once these were quietly dispatched, one team would move to the petroleum storage yard at Houcuo Village and set remote charges on the tanks. This was purely a distraction intended to cause chaos and tie up first responders. Even now, the PLA Second Department (Intelligence) cyber warfare teams lurked inside the Taiwanese critical systems, ready to shut off power for most of the island and flood their emergency services with conflicting calls.

The two teams would reconvene and make their way to Taoyuan International Airport near the oil field. Taoyuan was Taiwan's largest commercial airport. The saboteurs would hit its fuel supply, radar and control tower. The objective was not to destroy the runway, as the battle plan called for the PLA to turn Taiwan into an "unsinkable aircraft carrier," a forward deployment base with which to project power into the greater Pacific.

Only instead of MLRS positions, they'd find a company of very pissed off Republic of China (ROC) Marines and American Green Berets.

The Taiwanese had operational control of this phase, with the U.S. troops there just in a support capacity. They waited until the Chinese soldiers were just emerging from the water when snipers took out their inflatable boats, cutting off any escape route.

Then they hit the lights.

The ROC Marines had vehicles positioned along the beachhead and augmented their own lights with additional spots. They lit all of them as the Chinese troops were running for the shore, illuminating their advance in bright light.

A few minutes later, Hoult leaned back in his chair and announced. "We have eighteen CHICOMM troopers in custody. No shots fired."

He looked like he was ready for a cigarette.

Exhales around the table.

It was a dangerous gamble, and could easily have broken into firefight. Luckily, the Chinese realized how far outmatched they were.

Now, the Taiwanese actually wanted one PLA SOF team to reach their shore, because they wanted to catch them in the act. The prisoners would prove a valuable chip to play against Beijing and there could be no denying what they were there for. But they didn't want them all.

Next, on a signal from the destroyer, USS *Raphael Peralta* on station off Taiwan's east coast, the Sandsharks sent sonar pings to the Chinese corvettes they followed. The corvette skippers wouldn't know if they were Taiwanese, American or what, just that something underwater painted them as a target. As they did, Taiwanese destroyers and frigates positioned along the west coast and intended to show as berthed immediately departed for intercept courses.

Each of the Chinese corvettes reversed course and returned to the mainland.

Taiwanese frigates intercepted "fishing vessels" aiming for Taipei's main port on the west side of the island. They stopped them under the auspices of a routine inspection. One turned tail and ran, a second stayed to be boarded. Taipei Station would later learn from their Taiwanese counterparts that there was a bit of a mutiny on board with the SOF commander trying to force the boat captain (a Chinese naval officer in civilian clothes) to outrun the frigate. He refused.

By first light, it was all over.

China's attempted covert takeover had failed.

The situation would only get worse from there.

8

Singapore

Jet lag was a bitch.

The trip was two days or three, Colt couldn't remember which, because international dateline math always messed with his head. Traversing the globe was easier in the Navy because ships moved at a pace that let you keep up with the time change.

Thorpe recalled him to HQS with orders to report immediately. Colt might have been able to find a flight that night if he'd tried really hard. But what was supposed to be a weekend in paradise with Ava had been cut off after just a few hours. So much for his first vacation—hell, his first day off —in nearly a year. Colt felt the CIA owed him a solid. He didn't push it too hard. He left early the next day and was back at the NTCU by early afternoon, where Thorpe caught him up on the end of life as it was currently understood.

To be sure, there had been ten, perhaps fifteen, incidents worldwide that the IC was aware of. They knew it would get worse and would only grow. Analysts red teaming potential outcomes postulated that medical records, court records, corporate and personal banking data, and all communications traffic were now at risk. It wasn't an understatement to say that the foundation of modern global society was based on the secure transmission of data, and that was now jeopardized.

Stock markets across the world reacted accordingly. The government downplayed the situation, but since the *Times'* story was already out, with multiple follow-ups by several media outlets, they couldn't keep pace. Because leaked cables and radio traffic and electronic correspondence were showing up on Google drives and Discord servers, on the dark web and, with some embarrassing news about the French president, being anonymously emailed to journalists, there was no more keeping it a secret. Tech indexes plummeted. Social media companies debated whether to pull the plug until they could secure their systems (if that was even possible), or if they should stay up in order to push new information. Ultimately, only a handful of platforms paused operations. The rest assumed the risk and stayed active. Their official positions were to serve as critical communications paths for their users. Colt guessed it was more accurate to say none of them wanted to be offline if news of a solution broke or if a competitor shut down.

So, they'd recalled Colt into a shitstorm and given him one of the strangest assignments of his career.

Make sure the Chinese government knew it wasn't us.

He messaged Liu Che over their covert communications tool, a CIA-designed app on a phone they'd issued Liu. It leveraged the same firmware jailbreak Colt secured working for Wilcox. It was as secure as anything else these days, but he'd still been cagey about the reason.

Singapore was hardly middle ground, but Liu was a senior intelligence officer in the Chinese Ministry of State Security and he couldn't just dip out to Hawaii or LA on a whim. Especially since he had been burned in the States.

They had an interesting relationship.

Colt had saved Liu's life, and they'd formed the sort of bond that could only exist in the surreal world of international espionage. Were they adversaries? Absolutely. However, Liu was still an agent and still reported on his government's activities now that he was back home. They trusted each other in the strange way that only intelligence officers could understand.

Their two countries were also on the brink of war.

It was tense now as any point since the 1958 Taiwan Strait Crisis.

Colt nursed a local energy drink with a label he couldn't hope to decipher. It was too damned hot for coffee and it was six o'clock at night. He walked slowly through Singapore's futuristic Gardens by the Bay park. Designed to maximize green space, it was a sprawling park filled with trees and local flora, but its distinctive feature was the twelve "Supertrees." Rising one hundred and fifty feet off the ground, these structures were vertical gardens, with plants running their entire length. "Branches" reached out from the top, creating an artificial canopy with LEDs that glowed bright purple at night.

The now familiar form of Liu's precise posture and measured gait moved into view. Colt wore a linen camp shirt and lightweight pants and he was still sweating. Liu, on the other hand, looked perfectly comfortable in a tropical weight tan suit, white shirt, and dark tie. Colt realized he'd never seen Liu wear anything other than a suit.

Colt rose from his bench, forced down the last of the energy drink, and dropped the can in a nearby recycling bin. He closed the distance to Liu, smiling as though he were meeting an old friend.

"I'll admit to being quite curious to know what got you on a plane to fly all the way out here," Liu said ruefully, then added, "Particularly now."

Colt held his smile, but there was no humor behind it. The question, and taking initiative in the conversation, was Liu's subtle reminder that he wasn't a typical asset and didn't adhere to the assumed officer–agent power dynamic.

"You have the cyber strategy we talked about?" Colt asked, trying to regain the initiative. One of Liu's standing information requirements was to uncover details on his country's expected cyberattack strategy in the event they invaded Taiwan. The CIA knew that if that ever happened, the People's Liberation Army intelligence department and their proxies would bombard targets not only in Taiwan, but also in the U.S., the latter to make America's entry into that conflict more costly.

"I'm working on it," Liu said. "It is challenging, as I'm sure you can appreciate. And there are preoccupations." The rivalry between Liu's own service and the PLA's intelligence department was long and bitter, each vying to be the country's premier intelligence service, regardless of what

doctrine or organizational design might say on the matter. The ever-nebu-
lous nature of information operations only blurred the lines and intensified
the rivalry. "However, I can tell you that a primary target will be municipal
power infrastructure on the West Coast, particularly around your naval
installations. The primary goal is to cause as many fires as possible, especially in Southern California."

"Make the families panic and distract everyone deployed on the
mission."

"Precisely."

That was truly diabolical. It was also what Fred Ford would call "a
tomorrow problem."

"I suspect that is not why you are here, however," Liu said.

"No. I need you to convey a message to your superiors," Colt said.

"Is this a joke? Or are you just trying to get me arrested?"

"Che, the United States did not break into your diplomatic and military
cables. And we certainly didn't leak the contents of those messages to the
New York Times. Nor did we fabricate the entire thing as part of some deception op. Your government thinks otherwise. Secure communication around
the world is getting pulled apart. We, collectively, need to deal with that. We
don't need your government escalating the situation any further in Taiwan.
This breaks bad all kinds of awful ways unless you and I can come up with
a plan."

That's the understatement of the year, Colt said to himself. He'd learned
about the sub just before leaving Langley. That was a dangerous move. The
Chinese boat was in Taiwan's territorial waters, but sinking it was an act of
war. The U.S. Navy had used a top secret robot submarine and could make
a defense claim, based on the fact that the sub's sonar suite detected an
attempted insertion of frogmen.

The move was bold—no, reckless—but so far, the Chinese were
backing off. They could disavow the special forces soldiers that came
ashore and the sleeper agents who were all now in Taiwanese custody. The
submarine was a trickier subject. Officially, the Chinese government
admitted only that they'd lost contact with a submarine conducting a
routine training exercise. They were not saying how. The move put the U.S.
in a thorny diplomatic position, because whether those waters were China's

or Taiwan's depended on who was asked. The United Nations had not formally recognized Taiwan as a sovereign state, so they technically could not claim the twelve mile limit assumed to be territorial waters of full nations.

It appeared, for now, that the U.S. and the Chinese were both quietly backing away from the aborted invasion. The Chinese were eager to avoid the embarrassment of it being so quickly wrapped up, and the Americans were all too happy not to face repercussions for having covertly slashed a Chinese sub.

No one knew how long that tenuous quiet would hold, which is why Colt was here.

"I would have assumed a call from your president to ours would have sufficed," Liu said.

"Apparently, that didn't go over well." Colt knew, but would not say, that the CIA director had attempted to contact his counterpart at the Chinese Ministry of State Security, but they rebuffed him. The Chinese assumed he was lying, that this was another layer in an elaborate espionage scheme.

"My friend, there is the minor problem of the fact that I cannot simply tell my superiors your country did not do it." Liu said. "If, indeed, you did not."

"We didn't," Colt said, irritated. "As for the first part, I have an idea."

"Oh, I'm quite interested to hear this."

"We'll need to make up a source."

Liu laughed. It was a solid, barking guffaw, though Colt couldn't tell if it was honest or playacting.

"We'll create an asset that you would have plausibly recruited when you were running Admiral Denney."

"I would have reported this. It will raise flags."

Colt noted ruefully he didn't say "red flags." Probably because they all were.

"You'll think of something. You made a rather hasty exit from my country, as I recall. Certainly you didn't contact all of your assets," Colt said. He studied the man for a reaction and got none. He assumed Liu still ran agents in the U.S. despite telling him he'd closed those networks down. "I'll periodically give you intelligence through this channel, which you can report on. This has the added benefit of preserving your cover and hiding our work."

Liu thought it over.

"I will grudgingly admit the latter is of use to me."

"Good. My people are already working on the cutout. We'll have it up and running by the time I get back home."

"In your service?"

Colt couldn't help but detect the slightest sense of expectation in his voice.

"Dear God, no," Colt said, now with his own chance to laugh. "You're getting a disgruntled contractor at the Defense Intelligence Agency."

"Wonderful," Liu said dryly.

"This is serious."

"So, if it isn't you, who is it?"

"I don't know yet. That's the truth. But I don't think it's a long list, especially not if we take our respective services out of the mix."

"How easy is it for you to come to Singapore? Could you do this periodically?" Colt asked.

"Easy enough. Certainly within a few days' notice. I have . . . interests here," Liu said with a wry grin.

"It's safer if we don't communicate inside China."

"I agree," Liu said.

"I'll send the intel through Singapore Station. They'll use a support asset to relay it to you via a dead drop. You'll receive your first batch tomorrow."

"I thought you said it would take a few days to prepare."

"They're completing the cutout, but this messaging can't wait. You'll have a rough persona and a name in the packet you receive. Everything else will be in subsequent dispatches. I'll signal you through our COVCOM that a pickup is ready. The local team will handle everything else personally. It's the only way we can ensure the transmission isn't compromised."

Liu said, "Then I guess we'll be in touch."

Liu watched Colt disappear into the burgeoning darkness, then turned and walked in the opposite direction. He returned to his hotel, taking care not to be followed. Once he was in his room, Liu produced a device his service had created to resemble a tube-shaped portable speaker. He swept this over the room, sweeping for the electromagnetic signals that would reveal a hidden surveillance device. He'd cleared the room once already, but had been out several hours and needed to reconfirm before he made his phone call. Satisfied the space was clear, Liu closed the heavy curtains.

He retrieved his service-issued phone from the room's safe and dialed an American number.

Singapore time was exactly twelve hours ahead of Washington, DC. Mia would just be getting ready to leave for work at the Pentagon.

Mia Denney was the prize in his stable of agents. Born in Hong Kong to an American hotelier and a Chinese national, Mia lived through the transition from a British protectorate to the city's repatriation. She'd attended university, where a keen observer noted her intelligence, natural charisma, and facility for languages. That professor, who served his nation faithfully as a talent spotter, shared this information with the service. A senior officer approached Mia and offered her an opportunity to perform a vital role for the people. She accepted and enrolled in "State School No. 228," where they'd trained her as a spy.

Under Liu's expert direction, Mia cultivated a young U.S. Naval officer named Glen Denney, who fell for her immediately and completely. They married. She placed the aviator in a compromising position on their honeymoon, leveraging a faked gambling habit. Her "uncle" Liu Che was more than happy to help get the newlyweds out of trouble with the Macao government, for a small favor, a reasonable exchange of information among friends.

Liu manipulated Denney's career, and placing him in opportunities to advance and to provide intelligence critical to the People's Republic. Denney acknowledged this relationship for what it was (always believing this was solely to help his wife) and rose eventually to the rank of three-star admiral with a position on the White House's national security staff.

In an ironic twist, which Liu in no way found amusing, it was his own now-handler, Colt McShane, who uncovered Glen Denney's espionage.

Glen died tragically and Liu mourned him. A handler and a source often develop a strange yet close bond, after all. Liu still had Mia, however. Despite her years of deception, she genuinely loved her husband, and his death cut her deeply. But Mia remained a loyal subject of the People's Republic. Her ability to compartmentalize was like nothing Liu had ever seen. Even at Glen's memorial service, she devised a way to place an exploit on the phones of half the flag and general officers in attendance. After a suitable period of mourning, Mia approached one admiral for a job. Her language skills, two and a half decades as a navy wife, and career in hotels made her a reasonable enough candidate for a new role looking at lodging and force support in the Pacific. The Navy refused to admit such a senior officer as her late husband could have been capable of espionage, especially since the Navy's own counterintelligence function completely missed him. They chalked it up to the CIA looking for someone to pin it on. The brass gave Mia what everyone assumed was a token position in the Joint Staff J4. Mia quickly proved her value to the organization and was promoted, eventually moving over to J3 Future Ops to lend expertise to basing and bed down planning with a focus on the Pacific theater. Frequent trips to the U.S. Indo-Pacific Command (USINDOPACOM) headquarters in Honolulu gave her opportunities to meet with members of Liu's staff.

"Good morning, uncle," she said. The honorific was a running joke between them.

"Good morning, my dear. How are you today?"

"Well. Looking at colleges. Oh, I will be TDY to Pearl again in about two weeks."

"Excellent," Liu paused a moment to frame his thoughts and consider, again, his meeting with Colt. The overly elaborate plan to create a source and feed his government information, his government's apparent refusal to cooperate. This felt to Liu like a double-blind. He need to make sure he wasn't walking into a trap. "Mia, I need you to look into something for me."

9

Langley, Virginia

Colt, thankfully, wasn't in Singapore long enough to adjust to local time, so his transition back to the East Coast was easier than his way out. His body was reasonably certain where on planet Earth it was. Thorpe wanted to see him first thing. There was no time to rest.

Before meeting with the boss, Colt checked in with Alison D'Angelo, the officer who'd met him at Miami International for the handoff. She'd had the lead for sifting through the intel they'd gotten from Hazlett and was the targeting officer specializing in Hawkinson and Archon.

D'Angelo reached the same conclusion Colt had: Archon was putting all of their resources behind getting Preston Hawkinson in office.

Colt entered Thorpe's office for their meeting and closed the door behind him. The boss was on the secure phone and held up a hand. "Welcome back," Thorpe said, once he had completed the call. "You hear from Liu?"

Colt shook his head in the negative. "Not yet. He said he needs a week to sell it. Some bullshit about how he has to prepare his superiors for this new source he hadn't told them about before now."

"You need to stay on him. Since all of our other avenues appear to be closed off, this is the one chance we've got to convince the CHICOMMs we didn't hack them." A grim smile broke Thorpe's face. "I mean, in this specific instance."

"That's what I wanted to talk to you about. Everyone else is engaged in this security thing," Colt said. "We're the only ones who have any insight into Archon. Based on what we learned from Hazlett, I feel like also trying to run down whether they're doing these hacks has us chasing down two totally different things."

"I'm not going to give you the 'walk and chew gum' speech, Colt," Thorpe said tentatively.

"Hear me out, boss. What if it's both?"

"What do you mean?"

"So, one of the main goals of any AI is to do the things a person could do, just millions of times faster and at scale. Hypothetically, they could have AIs running all of these hacks while they're focused on propping up Preston Hawkinson. The only thing I can't square is *how* they're doing it. Hawkinson built the system that would enable them to do this, but even that relies on vulnerabilities they can take advantage of. Some of what's going on right now is codebreaking. That's a totally different technology problem and something that I think a lot of people are conflating here. One is finding a crack and exploiting it before it can be patched. The other is impossibly hard math done very fast."

"It's a sound theory, I'll grant you. Need something more than a guess, though. Do you have anything from the cipher we got from Hazlett?" Thorpe asked.

"We've deployed the cipher he gave us and we're inside the board's communication loop—it's like their version of Signal. That's only been active for two days and they don't keep messages, so we can't look at previous traffic. It's worth noting, they're not talking about the current situation. At least not in this format."

"Good tradecraft, unfortunately."

"Yeah, it's almost like they're good at this."

"Okay, so why else do you think it's Archon?"

"I don't think anyone else is as advanced. I honestly don't think the Russians would risk anything else after the strike on the GRU's cyber facility last year. Iran, North Korea? No. Who else could it be? The Chinese wouldn't leak their own communications just to frame us."

"You should know that very opinion is getting a lot of traction, especially in the Pentagon. DIA's analysts are convinced. INDOPACOM and Joint Staff J2 both concur. Even after what happened, a lot of senior Pentagon people think the Chinese are so hot for invading Taiwan, they'd hatch a global deception campaign to do it. You can't read a DoD slide deck now without tripping on a Sun Tzu quote. They argue that the rest is just sideshow, to throw everyone off the scent."

"The Chinese aren't that good. I'll spot them the social media hacks and even some lower level DoD stuff. But the diplomatic cables or our COVCOM in Turkey? No way. I think that given the amount of Jeff Kim's R&D that Guy Hawkinson made off with, they've got the capability to do this. There's another possibility, which is that it's not one bad actor but several."

"I don't follow."

"Something Ava told me, which corroborates what I learned from Hazlett. When they knew Hawkinson was too far out in front that he was going to get arrested, they started parceling off his businesses in secret. They were sold off mostly to shell corporations that Archon already owned. It's one of the reasons why when the FBI raided his offices, they didn't find much. What if Archon gave this tech to a whole host of bad actors? Remember how Al Qaeda fragmented after we invaded Afghanistan? You had dozens of little franchises of dirtbags we're *still* chasing down."

Thorpe tented his fingers, deep in thought. Finally, he said, "When we were chasing Hawkinson down last year, you said something that not a lot of people picked up on. It was in our briefing with the Euro Division team, and we were trying to convince them why we needed to get someone inside HawkTech. This was in the context of painting Hawkinson and Archon as a strategic threat. You were trying to get people to sit up and pay attention, because nobody wanted to listen. You said one of the things Hawkinson stole from Jeff Kim was quantum computing. At the time, it was all theoretical, but you said that in time, scientists thought quantum computers would have so much computational power, they could crack any form of encryption we had in seconds. So, a minute ago, when you said one of these problems was impossibly hard math done very fast, I remembered that conversation."

"Hawkinson built one," Colt said. "Nadia saw it. It was at his Geneva office. There was another one in Buenos Aires."

"Which we melted down," Thorpe said. "I understand from our conversation those things aren't cheap."

"They are not. You need specialized experience to build them, plus some rare materials, and there isn't a single agreed-upon design yet. Nadia worked on one in her grad school program. It's not like a regular computer where there's one basic way to build it and the advantages come from who's got the better components."

"Where is Nadia? Can we get her in on this?"

"She's at the State Department language school learning Mandarin. Goes to Taipei Station when she graduates, but it's an eighteen-month program. I can go talk to her."

Thorpe nodded. "Do that. Now, how sure are you? Not gut level. I mean in terms of actual intelligence?"

"I've got the CERBERUS team looking at all the rare materials used to construct a quantum computer now. We should know where in the world everyone is by the end of the day."

Thorpe said, "How solid are you on this theory?"

Colt gave a solemn nod, then realized Thorpe was looking for actual words. "I'm convinced."

"Good. I was just on the phone with the national security advisor. He wants us to brief him today."

That was . . . not normal.

What in the hell was going on, Colt wanted to know, that the national security advisor wanted to meet with a pair of operational-level people in a tiny unit no one had ever heard of. Yes, Colt had briefed the advisor once before and yes, there was a global security crisis unfolding right now. None of that justified two people of their level going to the White House.

"Pack up everything Hazlett gave you."

"Right now?"

"Yes. We're leaving as soon as security gets your cover ID over to the Secret Service. You're driving."

"Why do we always do it this way?"

This was the second time in Colt's CIA career he'd been at the White House. The first one had resulted in an argument with Director of the National Security Agency and Commanding General of U.S. Cyber Command, Lieutenant General James Burgess. *That* had ended in the general losing face in front of the president, which spurred Burgess's retaliation to pull all of NSA's personnel from the NTCU.

So, it wasn't much of a surprise when, after the two of them had cleared security, Thorpe said, "Watch your mouth this time." Colt held a locked courier bag in his hand.

Jamie Richter greeted them and guided them into his office. "Don't worry, Colt, POTUS is in Brussels for a NATO summit. You can speak your mind today."

Colt, red-faced, said nothing.

"What have you got for me, Will? The last time we spoke, I said I needed options to give the president regarding this security situation. What about that back channel with the Chinese?"

Thorpe said, "Colt?"

"Yes, sir. I've met with my source, personally. We've created what we call a cutout, a made-up source that we can use to pass information. That helps our agent maintain his cover."

"Will it work?"

"We'll know pretty fast if it doesn't," Colt said.

"Good enough. Now, Will, you told me the NTCU has new intel on the security situation?"

"Yes, sir," Thorpe said.

Colt felt a wave of anxiety wash over him. Thorpe had likely oversold Colt's theory to get them in the room. They had multiple independent pieces of intelligence, but nothing linking it all together yet. Colt prayed it didn't backfire on him. He unlocked the courier bag and opened it, withdrawing a highly modified iPad, similar to what the Presidential Briefing Team had started using in the last decade. Colt powered up the device and pulled up the reports his team had compiled from Hazlett. A source's identity was the Agency's most sacredly guarded secret, so Hazlett was referred only by his cryptonym, EMBER MOON.

Colt handed the tablet to Richter.

Thorpe continued. "We think Archon is most likely responsible for the security crisis, though we aren't ruling out the possibility that they've sold the technology to others as a way of increasing the level of opposition for us and our allies. Archon took most of the technology Hawkinson developed and redistributed it to other Archon-owned activities through a large number of shell corporations. It's a game of three-card monte on a global scale."

"I'm with you so far," Richter said, swiping through reports on the tablet. "What's the end game?"

Thorpe said, "Colt?"

Colt cleared his throat. "Sir, I have credible, firsthand human intelligence that Archon's primary objective remains getting Senator Preston Hawkinson elected president."

"That's EMBER MOON, I take it? You come up with this? It sounds like a cartoon my kids watch."

"They're randomly assigned, sir," Colt said. *I wanted to call him PRANCING POODLE,* he thought, *but it'd be too easy to figure out.*

"Tell me about this source. What you can, I mean."

"He works for one of Archon's leaders. As you may remember, they're organized like a corporation with a board of directors. Each board member has a particular specialty and they've got complete control over their department. Operations, finance, intelligence, strategic planning. EMBER gave us a code that lets us access the communication system they use. He's shared message fragments with me, where they're discussing it."

Colt then discussed what he believed Archon's plan was, using Hawkinson to eliminate opposition within the government and conduct electronic surveillance on nearly everyone.

"I agree with you, Mr. McShane, regarding their plan to put Hawkinson in office. I'm not sure if you've seen, but his only viable challenger for the nomination just dropped out. Apparently, there were some emails leaked from his personal account to a young woman that is not his wife." Richter exhaled heavily. "The part I'm not clear on is how all of these security breaches help further Archon's objective."

"In that collection of reporting, you'll see similar efforts to undermine the electoral processes in pivotal democracies. The UK, France, Germany, Japan, Canada, Israel. Key positions within the UN and EU. They can prop up dictators with money, that's already happening. About a year from now, there will be a swift coup in Russia."

"I might actually support that," Richter deadpanned.

"It'll be someone worse," Colt countered. "But the world won't see it that way. Everything they've done over the last two years has been to undermine democracy. It's not about one political ideology or another, it's removing debate from the calculus. Putting Archon in power. Once they are, they'll have the ability to manipulate the systems in such a way that we can't get them out. All of this will be a facade to show that the current system doesn't work. That governments can't keep pace with technological threats. They'll put Preston Hawkinson down the hall, sir, and he will tell the American people we need a shield of intelligent systems to defend against attackers like this. He'll deploy them, and the war is over."

"Colt has a hypothesis, which I agree with, that Archon may be using quantum computing technology to break through the firewalls and unravel encryption," Thorpe said.

Richter set the pad down. "Jeff Kim was in here three days ago and said the same thing. He's convinced that only a quantum computer could slice through these other systems so easily. He believes, with his customary modesty, only his design is far enough along to pull it off."

Colt and Thorpe traded a knowing look.

"So, where do we go from here?" Thorpe asked.

Richter walked over to his window and looked out at the White House lawn. Colt saw what he interpreted as a troubled expression. "I'm going to be incredibly candid, gentlemen. A rarity here, I know. It should go without saying," he turned to face them, "but what I'm going to tell you does not leave this room. POTUS's reelection chances aren't looking good. We've had one national security crisis after another, which the opposition is seizing on. Once we make these concessions to the Turkish government to keep them from blowing up our bugging attempt, Preston Hawkinson is going to run roughshod over it. Normally, I wouldn't share those concerns with a cop and a spook, and I'll spare you the tired line of politics and bedfellows. If a group trying to overthrow the current world order did not also back the leading candidate . . ." Richter's voice faded. "Jesus, it sounds ridiculous even saying it out loud."

Richter returned to his desk, as though sitting behind it gave him a kind of agency. "Colt, you've risked your life against these guys more than once. You opened my eyes and the president's to a whole new awful world of threats."

"Sorry about that," Colt said. Richter responded with a wan smile.

"I'm not mincing words when I say that the possibility that Archon could have a Manchurian candidate in the Oval Office is the most terrifying scenario I can imagine. Our way of life just . . . goes away. Now, our biggest problem is that aside from the three of us, the president, and Dwight Hoskins, no one in government knows who Archon is or believes they exist. Even after last year's events, people are reluctant to believe a non-state actor has that kind of power. And, Senator Hawkinson used his position on the Senate Armed Services and Intel Committees to go after anyone who breathed a word of it. Called it a witch hunt. 'Ghost chasing' was the term I think he used."

"What are you getting at?" Thorpe asked. Colt was wondering the same thing.

"I've tasked every agency in the Intelligence Community to find out who is hacking our networks and breaking into our communications. Ours and the world's. Military intelligence is doing the same. I've had a long conversation with the secretary of defense about it. The point is this: No one else knows or believes Archon exists, except for the NTCU. I've got every other agency running down rabbit holes so that when Preston Hawkinson and whatever spies he might have wonders what America is doing about this crisis, they'll know we're looking everywhere but at them."

"It's Operation Bodyguard," Colt said, mostly to himself.

"Exactly right," Richter agreed. Bodyguard was an Allied deception campaign designed to mask the D-Day invasion site by tricking the Nazis into thinking they'd come across at Calais. They even gave Patton a fake army of inflatable tanks. "I've spoken with Hoskins and he's on board. He's going to give you the top cover you need at Langley. It should keep the Technology Mission Center off your back." Richter paused, considering his next words. "A year ago, the president issued a finding that authorized a covert action against Archon. Colt, in proving Archon's culpability in those cyberattacks last year, you and your team probably stopped us from going to war with the Russians. That finding is still in place," Richter said, letting the words linger between them.

A "presidential finding" was the legal justification for the CIA to conduct a covert action. It let the congressional oversight committees know that he'd authorized an operation, but still gave the administration plausible deniability if the operation failed. Their previous finding was vaguely worded so that it wouldn't draw attention to the fact they were targeting a senator's nephew for fear that it would appear that the administration was trying to punish a political rival.

"Gentlemen, you have until the election to take Archon off the board. Find out how they're getting into all of our most protected secrets and end it. If you can't do that before November, it won't matter. I suspect we'll all be in prison."

***

Colt dropped Thorpe at Langley and headed east.

When political headwaters forced him out of Langley, Jason Wilcox honored a longstanding promise to his wife and got the hell out of Washington. They retired to a quiet home on Maryland's eastern shore on a wooded tributary of the Chesapeake Bay. Knowing he'd need at least two hours to get there, Colt didn't return to work. Thorpe understood, and they both agreed this was a better use of Colt's time.

He hadn't been to see the Wilcoxes in weeks. When Jason first retired, Colt was here at least once or twice a month for crab boils and mentoring sessions, twelve ounces at a time. He'd had to stop their visits when his ops tempo went vertical.

Colt phoned before he left DC to say that he was on his way and to make sure Jason was home, knowing the odds were about even that he'd be here or in London. Wilcox greeted him at the door. "Sorry, I didn't bring beer this time," Colt said as his former boss led him into the spacious home.

"I assumed it wasn't a social call since it was in the middle of the work-day. We'll stay inside."

Wilcox led him into the living room and explained that his wife was out for the afternoon. He sat opposite Colt in his favorite chair. "So, what's going on?"

Jason Wilcox's living room wasn't exactly a SCIF, but it was as secure as a private home could be. There's an unwritten rule that you never truly retire from the senior intelligence service, as evidenced by Wilcox's frequent trips to the White House and Langley in recent months. Agency security personnel had proofed his house against surveillance when they'd moved in, and still conducted periodic update checks. There were small devices beneath each of the many windows that created tiny vibrations on the glass, therefore making it impossible for a laser to decode and translate the conversations happening within. When people spoke, their voices created invisible vibrations in the air that cause windows to vibrate, lasers can detect this and allow an eavesdropper to listen. Wilcox had other tech, of Trinity's design, that proactively interrogated his home network for any intrusion and eliminated it in real time.

Colt wasted no time in sharing his theory about Archon and quantum code breaking.

"What are you seeing?" Colt asked, once he had explained everything.

"I think your conclusion is sound. I also think it's the only reasonable one you can make. The DoD theory is shit. Every government stands too much to lose getting caught, and no terrorist group has this capability."

"Do you know where Hawkinson is?"

"Guy? No. His sister Sheryl moved her kids to a private school in Switzerland. She's still running her VC firm in Silicon Valley. The FBI doesn't want to move on her because there's no direct link to her brother's activities. There's also the political risk to consider. If they move on her for anything less than murder in the middle of Times Square, it'll look like they're just going after a political rival's family. It doesn't matter if she's guilty, that's how the Hawkinson campaign will spin it. Guy disappeared. We think through a pipeline in Eastern Europe, but we don't have any secondary confirmation. He hasn't popped up on anyone's screens since. I'll tell you, Colt, I've been at this a long time. I've *never* seen anyone disappear so completely." Wilcox leaned forward in his chair and his eyes narrowed. "If I were you, I'd concentrate on Quentin Wales. He's the board member for operations. If they're behind this, it'll start with him."

Jesus, Colt mused. *Word travels fast.* He'd just come from the meeting with Richter. Unless Wilcox had just assumed Colt was going after these guys.

"Colt, I took your advice to heart. We're not sitting this one out."

"That's good to hear," Colt said tentatively. They'd had tense conversation in Athens the year before, where he'd gotten in Wilcox's face about Trinity's lack of involvement. Colt had pointedly told him the world could no longer afford to have Trinity focusing solely on research while Archon actively worked to undermine Western civilization. Wilcox tried to explain that it wasn't that simple, and Colt said some things he regretted.

"Look, Jason, this thing is serious. Already, we've got the CHICOMMs claiming this is an elaborate fake-out to cover an operational that got leaked to the press. That's all bullshit, but it's where they are. If we—collectively—don't stop this now, it goes south fast. For everybody."

"You don't have to sell me, Colt," Wilcox said, somewhat gruffly. "Our entire society is built on secrecy and protection. Confidentiality is the foundation for everything we do. Without it, there are no bank accounts. Hell, there are no banks. We lose commerce and diplomacy and journalism. We lose the law. My—our—assumption is that Archon wants to expose every secret everywhere."

"My best guess at their endgame is to destabilize everything until after the election," Colt said. "Once Preston Hawkinson is in office, he normalizes their actions. He probably launches a sweeping technology initiative designed to reduce the size of government, streamline decision making, end the bureaucracy. Hawkinson's administration will save billions eliminating overhead, redundancy, and labor. He'll look like a hero."

"While an Archon AI gradually takes over running the government," Wilcox said gravely.

"Then, it's just a matter of time before that permeates the corporate sector," Colt continued. "With that much raw data, the systems will improve at geometric rates. They've already deployed their so-called secure voting technology across the country. Once Hawkinson is in office, rigging an election will be child's play. Their family of AIs will eliminate waste and make the government run faster. They'll pump the money they save back into tax cuts first, and then programs to benefit the electorate, keep people happy. Gradually, we move toward this supposed 'techno-utopia,' but at the expense of civil liberties and freedom of speech."

Wilcox agreed. "It won't be overnight. But five years from now, ten on the outside, this country will be unrecognizable."

"What are you going to do?" Colt asked.

"Not wait on others to act," Wilcox replied.

10

Langley, Virginia

"Abso-goddamn-lutely not," Nadia thundered.

Colt hadn't seen her in months. When she'd returned from her assignment in Geneva, after a long stretch of well-earned leave, Colt got her reinserted into the Clandestine Service School to complete her training. Nadia was a hell of a natural case officer, but she needed polish if she was going into the field again. Hilariously, she'd spent more time actually undercover doing the job than she'd had training for it, so when she got back to the Farm she had more practical experience than most recruits would get on their first operational tour. And other than the rare paramilitary officer or analyst who made the jump to operations, Nadia was probably the only officer to graduate the Farm with an intelligence commendation.

Now, she was at the State Department's language school in Arlington, Virginia, learning Mandarin for her first "real" operational tour at Taipei Station. It was a dream posting for an action-oriented, hard-charging young officer like Nadia, in the thick of a simmering conflict with the highest stakes. People were already saying Taipei was the new Vienna. You could operate in the clear, but the opposition was everywhere, and it was dangerous.

She'd reacted to Colt's pitch about as he'd expected she would.

"No. Way."

"It's a temporary assignment, a couple of weeks and you're right back here."

"No," Nadia said, folding her arms. They'd found a tree on the grounds to chat beneath, but it did little for the relentless Virginia summer heat. "I earned this."

"You sure did. You're also one of a handful of people in our service who understand how real this threat really is, what they're capable of. Nadia, I wouldn't ask if it wasn't important."

"Language school isn't a yoga class. I can't just pop in and pop out when I feel like it."

"You're three weeks into an eighty-eight-week program," Colt said. "You can make it up." Nadia was about to protest again, but Colt closed the distance between them. He shouldn't be discussing this outside of a cleared space, and certainly not outside of Langley proper, but it was what he had to work with. Colt dropped his voice just above a whisper. "We have authorization to take Archon out. Once and for all. That will mean going after Guy. I've got an FBI agent on the squad already."

Nadia had spent a year undercover in Guy Hawkinson's company, and when he discovered her true identity thanks to one of Archon's AIs, he tried to have her killed. He'd come damn close. Colt knew what he was asking of Nadia being here. He knew why she pushed back, but he also knew that if anyone deserved to be on the team that finally took Guy down, it was her.

"He's still got an uncle in the Senate. Even if you get him, he'll just duck it like he always does."

"Not this time. We're going to get his uncle, too. Guy won't get away. Everyone agrees that we need to take him down. Everyone."

Nadia stared Colt down for a long, silent moment and thought.

"No bullshit this time? No half measures. You're really going to do it?"

"We are."

"I don't want to live looking over my shoulder."

"Nadia, we're going to get him."

"Then, I'm in."

"Good afternoon, everyone," Colt said. He stood at the head of the table in the NTCU conference room. Thorpe sat at the other end. "Most of you have been in the NTCU a while, but I'm not sure everyone has worked together. Of course, I'm never here, so you might all know each other already," Colt smiled. "I'm also going to introduce two new faces, and then we'll get to it. Nadia Blackmon was on this team for about a year and a half, running an undercover operation in Guy Hawkinson's company. Everything we know about his operations is because of her. If you don't recognize her, you've certainly seen her intelligence. We owe her a debt." He paused to allow for grateful nods around the table.

"Next up is Tony Ikeda. Tony comes to us from the Special Activities Center. He assisted us in a snatch-and-grab op last year, and on the takedown of Hawkinson's activities in Argentina." Tony had also just returned to Langley after an extended op abroad, which he hadn't been able to tell Colt about.

Colt turned to face one of the other members. "Alison D'Angelo is a targeter, focusing on Archon's board." Targeters were specialized intelligence officers who focused on a single subject, like a dictator or terrorist leader, to learn everything about them, helping to predict their moves and inform operations. "Special Agent Keith Ricci will handle the arrests. Finally, Solomon French from cyber operations rounds out the team." By now, the NTCU team members were all well aware of the ongoing cybersecurity threat, but Colt spent a few minutes recapping the most recent events for Nadia and Tony. Then, he moved on to Jeff Kim's theory that Archon was using quantum computing technology to do it.

"Team, we're calling this one QUIET TITAN. Before you say anything, it's a randomly generated name. I did not pick it. While we still believe Guy Hawkinson is driving this, no one—and I mean no one—has seen him in six months." Colt looked at Nadia, who nodded, understanding the secondary meaning. "Instead, we're going after Archon's board of directors. Our primary objective is to take them down, but we hope that also flushes Hawkinson out. Thanks to a source we have inside the organization, EMBER MOON, we now have all of their identities. Alison is constructing profiles. Our plan is to capture each board member individually and bring them to a secure location for questioning."

"I don't want to sound harsh, but why not kill them?" Ikeda said.

"It's a fair question, considering," Colt agreed. "Alison?"

D'Angelo nodded. "Each board member has a different focus—ops, finance, political affairs, strategic planning, R&D. Each of them has some type of operational discipline, which means if their head of operations was taken out, they could still function. The way they are designed, no individual board member knows what the others are doing or how. They have no insight into their activities. It's a security measure. We also know from EMBER MOON that if a board member dies, they have a successor that the other board members don't know about, who carries out their instructions. At that point, they basically spin off an Archon franchise, if you want to call it that."

"It's like cutting off the head of a hydra and not getting to see the other heads that grow back," Colt said.

"Okay, so assassination is off the table," Tony said dryly.

"Tony raises a good point, though," Nadia said. "If the board members have these backup plans, don't those just kick in if they get arrested?"

"As we understand the contingency protocols from EMBER, they automatically activate if a member dies. They don't necessarily activate if a member is arrested, because the board members assume they'll be able to get themselves out quickly," D'Angelo said. "Here's the most important part. The secondary echelon is used to being dark for long stretches. It's not uncommon for them to go weeks, even months, without hearing from their principle. So, in theory, we could capture a board member and hold them for some time for interrogation without the second echelon ever knowing."

"That takes care of the rank-and-file. But what's stopping the rest of the leadership from getting clued in once we bag one? Won't they notice the absence?" Nadia asked.

"Good question. The board rarely, if ever, meets in person now. They know what we can do with link analysis. However, we're inside their comm system. They've got their own secure messaging system, which we've penetrated thanks to EMBER. As we take one off of the board, we'll just spoof them on the net, just like we did with Guy and LONGBOW. And, thanks to

Alison's profiling, we'll be able to impersonate them pretty well. That said, we've got to move quickly. Impersonating them will become more difficult the longer this drags out."

Tony raised a hand. "What do we know about the board?"

"Four Americans, three Brits, one Spaniard, and one Swiss. Only two of them joined after the schism with Trinity. Most of these guys are patriots who believed in Trinity's original mission that developing Artificial General Intelligence was a means to an end, a pathway to a safer world. Over time, that belief got corrupted into thinking AGI would allow them to run society better than our existing forms of government. Then there are two, including our first target, who were never true believers. They always saw Trinity and later Archon as a path to power, a way to guide global events as they saw fit. Alison, why don't you bring everyone up to speed on our first target?"

"Sure thing." D'Angelo tapped the keyboard in front of her, and a face appeared on the conference room screen. "Target number one is Quentin Wales, formerly a major general in the British Army. He commanded the Special Reconnaissance Regiment and later the 6th Division and NATO Regional Command South in Afghanistan. He left active service in 2010. Wales joined Trinity in the nineties, so he was part of what we now call the 'revolutionary cadre,' the group who pushed to form Archon. Once he retired, Wales founded the private security company Praetorian, which he still runs."

"He sounds a lot like Guy Hawkinson," Nadia said.

"That's right," D'Angelo agreed. "He was Trinity's original hawk. Wales was the one who pushed them to be more aggressive. Following 9/11, he wanted to use their technology to find and kill Bin Laden. He saw Guy as a protégé, and we believe he handled Guy's recruitment. Worth noting, he also recruited Samantha Klein."

"What kind of security, and what is our operating environment?" Ikeda asked.

"Wales is a hard target," Colt said. "He's never without a security detail and runs a company staffed with former special operators. There are a lot of parallels to the Hawk Security Group here. Wales lives in Monaco, which is going to complicate things. We've got the Monaco police to consider. Monaco has more high-wealth citizens than just about anywhere else in the world—Russian oligarchs, movie stars, Formula One drivers, tycoons, and royalty all call that place home. The Monaco police respond quickly. They're very good and they don't ask a lot of questions. They've recently implemented a new surveillance platform, not unlike what the Chinese use. Heavy on facial recognition, pattern matching, and link analysis. Anyone want to guess who sold them the platform?"

"Praetorian?" French, the cyber operator, said.

"Nope. A UK-based InfoSec firm called Counterthreat, whose majority investor is a private equity fund that Archon controls through a series of front companies. Now, beyond the Monaco police, the principality is located entirely within France and close to Italy. They have agreements with federal law enforcement in both countries. Beyond the security issues I just described, this city's street map looks like abstract art. It's built up around the side of a mountain. We do not want to get into a situation where we're in a chase."

"You mentioned an Archon-owned company designed the Monaco police's new security surveillance system. Any reason to suspect your face, or mine, is already in the database?" Nadia asked.

Colt stopped to consider that question. "I think it's possible, yes. We've got tools to spoof video surveillance, and Solomon is already working on a backdoor into that system."

Nadia gave a thumbs-up and looked back at the screen.

"Are we involving MI5 or MI6?" Ricci asked. "Or, hell, DGSE?"

"Not initially," Thorpe said. "The fact is, we don't know whether Archon has compromised their information systems. Until we do, TITAN stays confined to this room. The director and the deputy director, the national security advisor, and POTUS know. That's it."

"I don't like it," Ricci said, shaking his head. "We're talking about apprehending a citizen of our closest ally without informing them. If this gets out, we're looking at a full-blown diplomatic crisis, which I don't think anyone needs." The FBI agent, emotions clearly rising, gestured at Wales's image and bio on the screen. "This guy is a highly decorated senior military officer and we're just going to disappear him? How would we feel if someone had scooped up Colin Powell over WMD charges? This . . . Look, I'm sorry, but we can't do this."

"Keith, I understand your concerns," Thorpe said. "But this is the difference between law enforcement and covert action."

The FBI agent flashed red. "That's not good enough. We don't even know that he's done anything. There's no probable cause! What, are we just going to ditch him in Guantanamo when we're done with him?"

Colt broke in. "Keith, we have first-person knowledge that he's an Archon board member. We also have secondary confirmation through SIGINT. That alone should be enough. We've also got a presidential finding authorizing the operation." Colt didn't like using the finding as justification. He'd hoped the stakes and the mission would be enough. He didn't know Keith Ricci well, but Thorpe thought highly of him and had personally recruited him into the NTCU. Ricci had been part of the FBI team that raided Liu's house in Washington that fateful night and arrested his wife. Without that move, Colt wouldn't have had the leverage he needed to turn Liu into an asset. Every operation needed a conscience, a voice of reason, someone to challenge the norms. Different from being a "devil's advocate," which was dissent for the sake of argument, people like Ricci were an invaluable inoculation against the groupthink that so often plagued large organizations. Even Langley . . . *or especially Langley*, Colt thought. But Colt believed the FBI agent was also missing the point, which Thorpe had clearly spelled out. Colt understood the optics of failure. The sheer gravity of consequence should give them all pause.

It didn't mean, however, that they should reconsider.

There weren't other options.

Ricci pressed his point. "Yeah, and if you're wrong—or even if you're right and Archon figures it out—this gets plastered all over every newspaper in the world and we take the fall for it. Then, Senator Hawkinson gets a hold of it and makes the Church Committee look like a Sunday afternoon in the park."

"I don't like it either," Colt said. "But it's us. We're the only team in the field on this. Most of the Intelligence Community refuses to acknowledge that Archon exists. Those that do are too afraid to stick their necks out in case Hawkinson wins the election. I'm not talking about violating the

Constitution or breaking any laws, but I'll stretch them as far as they go. This goes for everyone. Before we get started, I need to know that you can do this. If you can't, I understand."

The operation was questionable, Colt knew that. What choice did they have? But they could not afford for someone to decide they couldn't go along with it and blow a whistle. That would signal to all their enemies that they were coming.

Colt looked around the table. The faces staring back at him were grim but determined.

"Good. Our first objective is to capture Quentin Wales."

11

The Principality of Monaco

After a week of surveilling Quentin Wales, they'd concluded he was a man of parade ground discipline and excellent tradecraft. He woke every morning at five-thirty, exercised vigorously for an hour, alternating days with thirty minutes on a treadmill or in his lap pool followed by another half hour of weight training. Land was in such short supply in the microstate's surreal geography that for Wales to have a fifteen-thousand-square-foot villa with a pool overlooking the famed Monte Carlo neighborhood, he must have paid a legitimate fortune. Of course, when you belong to an organization that can manipulate investment markets in your favor, large expenditures are no longer so risky.

The house itself was a difficult target. It was built along a steep slope, not unlike the archetypal cantilevered houses synonymous with the Hollywood Hills, and accessed via a narrow private road. The neighborhood had twenty-four-hour surveillance and a dedicated private security force to swiftly protect their elite clientele; Wales's neighbor to the right was a Qatari arms dealer, and to the left lived a former supermodel. Much like Jason Wilcox's place, the windows had sonic scramblers that prevented electronic and optical surveillance. Even Tony agreed the house would be nearly impossible to hit.

Wales departed for his office each day at eight-thirty in an armored Range Rover with a driver and two members of Praetorian's executive protection detail. They took a different route to and from the office each day. There was also a chase car that followed, presumably to check for tails. The car rotated each day and, as far as they could determine, was randomly assigned from the vehicle fleet. It was typically an Audi S6 or BMW M5, though they'd seen sport SUV versions as well. They counted seven different chase cars.

"You sure we want to start with him?" Ikeda quipped as Wales's Range Rover disappeared into the Odeon Tower. The tower was a forty-nine-story shark fin of concrete and blue glass, the first new high-rise constructed in the principality since the 1980s. The Odeon Tower lorded over the hillside above the Mediterranean on Monaco's northern end, on one of the city's snake-twist roads. Another few feet and they'd be in France.

Tony, driving, rolled past the Odeon in their rented Peugeot.

"I mean, it's not the least accessible place," Colt said. He unbuckled and got out of the car. "See you at the marina."

"Roger that," Ikeda replied.

Odeon Tower was a mixed use facility, with offices and shopping on the lower floors opening to high-end residences above.

"I've got line of sight on the office," Nadia said into their earpieces. She was posted with her laptop on a rooftop two turns down the twisting coil of road. Nadia controlled two mini-drones with her computer, which gave the team multiple angles into Praetorian's offices. They wouldn't have audio, but could at least maintain visual confirmation of Wales's activities and location. "Looks like he's going right into a staff meeting," Nadia said. The drones were small, both about the size of a hummingbird, and would be nearly impossible for someone to see through the tinted glass. The downside was their short battery life, so Nadia staggered their loiter time and brought one back to replace the battery while the other was on station.

Only Nadia, Tony, and Colt had deployed forward to Monaco. The rest of the team worked from a safe house in Vienna. They were expecting to be gone for some time.

The only advantage they had was that they knew exactly where Wales would be today.

If their target were anyone else, their plan would've been to hack into his business systems and create an offsite meeting at a location favorable to capture. This was how they'd bagged Liu Che in Geneva the year before. However, Praetorian's information systems, controlled by a sophisticated AI presumably designed by Archon, were set to immediately alert to network intrusion and shut the connection down. They had no security vulnerabilities to exploit and patched immediately if the system discovered one. So, getting Wales while he was at his office was out.

Taking Wales at home was not an option either. Between simple geography and the quality of his private security, they'd never get out in time. There were too many chokepoints. Plus, Monaco was one of the least navigable cities in the world. A car chase here would only end in disaster. They'd ruled all these options out during the weeks of planning leading up to the mission, and being on the ground in Monaco only reinforced that decision.

The only actual option they had left was to separate Wales from his security detail and get him into an escape vehicle quickly.

Knowing they couldn't hack into Praetorian's network in the weeks before the operation, even with the NTCU's best resources, they'd decided on the next best thing. Colt had Hazlett provide a short list of names, potential clients for Praetorian's services. They'd settled on a minor Saudi noble, one of the myriad cousins in the constellation of princes that loosely orbited the royal family. This one ran an international development company, which was how Hazlett knew about him. Solomon, the team's cyber operator, easily hacked into the Saudi's systems and requested a meeting with Quentin Wales about hiring Praetorian. Colt, acting as the prince's assistant, provided the voice. They used an AI deepfaking algorithm to affect a British-tinged Saudi accent. Solomon intercepted any phone and email communication from Praetorian to the Saudi.

They'd scheduled the meeting at Port Hercule, just below Monte Carlo, on the Saudi's boat. Colt originally proposed getting Wales onto a yacht, using CIA paramilitary officers to act as the Saudi's private security. Once they'd gotten Wales out into international waters, they'd interrogate him.

Despite the presidential finding, however, Thorpe shot that proposal down immediately because it had too large of a footprint. Colt reasonably asked, "Do they actually wanted me to capture this guy, or do they just want me to make a show of it, blow something up and come home?"

"You're the super spy, figure it out," Thorpe countered. "Get it out of your system and come back with a refined plan that keeps eyes off of this. You know damned well we can't have the Brits asking why we bagged one of theirs without talking to them first."

Instead, they'd settled on grabbing him at the marina. The pretext was that Wales would meet the Saudi on his yacht for the meeting. Posing as the prince's "business manager," they'd explained his highness did not wish private security aboard his ship. The terms were non-negotiable. Wales agreed. His people would remain at the outskirts of the marina in their vehicles.

Colt, posing as one of the prince's men, waited for Wales on the frontage road that ran along the dock to usher him into the blacked-out Audi Q8. He would make a show of driving Wales around a corner to the yacht in a grand display of the prince's hospitality. This would separate Wales from his security detail. He'd hit Wales with a tranquilizer and pick up Ikeda, who would follow the convoy from Odeon Tower as it headed to their safe house in a French village about thirty kilometers from Monaco. Nadia would meet them there. They would interrogate Wales and, eventually, extradite him on a CIA aircraft.

They needed at least four more officers to make this work.

Instead, they had just the three of them.

There was an arm's length of problems with this location, but it was also the only way they could think of to separate Wales from his security team with the time and resources they had.

"Target is moving," Nadia said.

Colt and Ikeda both rogered.

"I've got the target vehicle," Ikeda said. "Chaser is a black Mercedes G-class."

Colt wished he had Tony in the car with him. Having a backup to manage Wales's security team would've been helpful, especially if they decided they wouldn't play nice and follow along with their prospective client's demands. However, Nadia didn't have experience tailing someone in a car, and Colt didn't have confidence that she could do it in heavy traffic and on such complicated streets, so that left her on digital overwatch online and with the drones. If the security team presented a problem or didn't act as expected, Colt would say the duress command over the net and Tony would ditch his car, emerging from a hidden location in the marina. He'd pose as an additional member of the prince's detail.

Colt, wearing a tan suit, robin's egg blue shirt, and navy tie, sat in the idling Q8 listening to Ikeda relay Wales's position every half mile as it made the trip from the tower to the marina. Facing the city through the tinted windshield of the SUV, Colt wondered at how they stacked buildings upon the tiered ribbons of land that climbed up the mountains. Bright sunlight streamed down through broken clouds, so brilliant Colt could practically see the individual rays. He had a forty-caliber Glock G27 in a concealed holster under his jacket and a microinjector designed to look like a fountain pen. This would deliver the tranquilizer that would knock Wales out until they got to the safe house.

"Approaching Boulevard Louis II," Ikeda said. "Entering the tunnel." They were less than a mile out now. The last part would take Wales through a long tunnel that would exit just north of the marina, to Colt's right. Colt couldn't fathom how they pulled off car races on these streets.

Colt idled in a parking spot, facing the mainland on a small manmade isthmus that extended out into the Mediterranean with a marina on both sides. Yachts lined up to his right. Colt believed the spot belonged to the owner of one of these berths, and he was surprised that no one from the yacht club's management had demanded he move yet.

He saw the caravan before Ikeda called it in as they cleared the pill-shaped, five-story waterfront shopping center on Quai Louis II. The boulevard descended at an angle with a sheer face of waterfront apartments on one side and the marina on the other. The two Praetorian SUVs slowed and pulled into a hairpin that would take them into the marina proper, with Ikeda following in a Peugeot hatchback several cars back.

Colt eased the Q8 forward to the end of the row and parked it at a diagonal. He opened the door and stepped out into the afternoon heat as the Range Rover pulled into the hairpin to reverse direction into the marina.

The Range Rover was about a hundred feet from Colt when he saw several high-speed streaks flash across his field of vision.

It was a brief, bright flash. If Colt hadn't been exactly where he was, he wouldn't have seen it.

The streaking blurs crashed into the vehicle's rear passenger window. The SUV, still traveling at least twenty-five miles an hour, jerked hard to the left, crashing into the wall. Sparks flew into the air with the impact, but it kept moving at the same speed. Colt assumed the driver was out, too. The Range Rover crashed into the side of the marina's main building.

Colt broke into a run for the wreckage.

"What happened?" Nadia radioed.

Tony's voice crackled in. "Was that—"

Colt's shoes hammered on the pavement as he closed the distance with Wales's vehicle. He was just skidding to a stop when the Mercedes G-Wagon chase car roared through the traffic circle and onto the frontage road.

Colt heard the high-pitched sound of an outboard motor split the air. He turned to see a speedboat racing out of the marina.

Wales's security detail boiled out of the G-Wagon, every one of them a close cropped ex-special operator, wraparound sunglasses and earpieces, pistols out. They flanked their principle's car, but not before Colt got close enough to look through the hole in the window that—whatever that was— had flown through. If that was a bullet, it had been packed with explosives. There was no question Wales and everyone else inside was dead.

The ex-general's head slumped against the far window, which was covered in gore and viscera. Colt felt hard hands grab him and yank him back from the vehicle, demanding in harsh, British tones to know who in the hell he was and what in the hell he was doing.

"I work for the prince, you fool. I was here to meet General Wales," he said, trying to sound nervous and scared.

"Wait the fuck over there," the ex-soldier half-shouted, pointing to a spot on the curb.

"What's going on here?"

"I said wait over there. Not telling you again," the security man said.

"I don't like this," he said nervously. Colt backed up to the Audi and climbed in. The vehicle was still running, so he threw it into drive and raced down the quay to the frontage road. Security men dove out of the way and Colt sped up.

"Target is dead," Colt said into the radio.

There was hurried movement and at least two men piled into the G-Wagon to chase Colt. He bolted out of the marina, pulled a tight hairpin to reverse direction on the upward slope of Boulevard Louis II, and then made a hard right into a parking garage. Because he'd reversed direction, he was behind the Praetorian Mercedes when it hit the roundabout, so they likely didn't see him pull into the garage. Colt parked the vehicle, wiped it down, and exited.

He moved between vehicles, trying not to look too suspicious, knowing that he was certainly on camera. Colt found a set of stairs and took them two at a time to the shopping plaza on the level above.

———

They parked illegally in a residential space outside a waterfront condominium building on the French side of Avenue de Princess Grace. The condo building was a thin wedge a little larger than a road median, but it was four floors with only a two-lane road separating its residents from the ocean. They were about two miles from the marina, but in Monaco's M. C. Escher geography, it felt much further.

They'd at least had their things with them, so didn't need to chance going back to the rented flat they used as a staging area. The plan was always to leave Monaco once they had Wales. They'd rented the Audi with a credit card that linked back to an anonymous bank account and a name that didn't exist, so that was clear. Now they just had to figure out who had killed Quentin Wales.

"There's no way this is a coincidence," Colt said. "Those odds just don't exist." He was coming down from the adrenaline high and though his hands shook, his mind worked. It did not surprise Colt that someone would murder Quentin Wales. But to do that right in front of him? His mind hovered between two possibilities, both likely wrong, but the only options that made sense right now.

Either someone wanted to send him a message, or they wanted him to get blamed.

In retrospect, perhaps the high-speed exit hadn't been that smart.

"You think we got hacked?" Nadia asked.

Colt shrugged. "I don't know." No form of covert communication was truly secure. Ultimately, it was about reducing risk to an acceptable level that allowed the mission to go forward. Technology gave you an advantage to stay several steps ahead of the opposition. It was never a guarantee. Given what they'd seen over the last few weeks, Colt didn't fully trust anything, let alone the comms they'd used in the field. But, in order to hack them, an adversary had to know where to look. They had to know that Colt and his team were here. Unless the breach was at Langley.

If Archon was behind the quantum hacks, it didn't follow they'd assassinate their own head of operations.

A dark thought passed through his mind.

Trinity knew they'd be here.

Or, at least they could puzzle it out. Wilcox gave him Wales as a target. And earlier than that, Ava told him Trinity would take more active measures. Assassination was not her style, though he had to admit that Ava was dangerously short on grace after learning that Archon had murdered her parents.

Still, the part that didn't fit was waiting until just before Colt and his team captured Wales to pull the trigger.

Unless Trinity wanted to send a message. How many times had Colt admonished Wilcox or Ava for them to get in the game, to clean up Trinity's own mess? Could they have done this to remove any doubt?

That didn't seem right, somehow, but he couldn't find a more cogent explanation at the moment.

There was also the question of Wales's contingency plan. If Hazlett was to be believed, Wales's second echelon was now spinning up its own, independent enterprise that no one knew anything about.

"I'm in," Ikeda said. Tony's entry to the CIA's covert action division was through black information operations, the kind of hacking that goes unacknowledged, save for the most senior levels of Agency leadership. His mentor helped write Stuxnet. Once recruited into the Special Activities

Center as a black hat hacker, Tony had been trained by the Agency into a full covert action officer. He plied both trades regularly. Currently, he'd hacked into the Monaco Police Department's (MPD) computer network. Though they'd contracted with Praetorian for their new digital surveillance system, MPD still used a mundane Microsoft Windows–based operating system, which Tony could access in his sleep.

"You know, something else occurs to me," Colt said, still facing the city. Tony and Nadia were both seated in the Peugeot behind him. "It could've been the Saudi we used. He was pretty dirty. The king used his company to funnel money into black ops in the Yemen war. If the Iranians were watching him, they might have struck at Wales to send a message to the Saudis. Tony, can you see if the Monaco police have any intel that Wales's life might have been in danger?"

"No, but ours might be."

"What?"

"Look," Ikeda said and turned his laptop so Colt could see the screen. Colt saw pictures of him walking back to the Audi just after Wales's Range Rover crashed. There were also photos of Tony staking out Odeon Tower in the Peugeot. Nadia pushed herself up in the back seat to peer over Ikeda's shoulder. She read the scroll in French on the screen.

"That's an APB, boys," she said.

"Jesus, they've got the car registration and shots of Colt and me from multiple angles. They've got a pic of Nadia, too, though it's not very clear."

"Any names?" Colt asked.

"Hold on." Ikeda taped a few more keys, pulling up an Agency-designed translator API that layered over the browser and converted the text to English. "Doesn't look like it." He turned to face Nadia. "Can you translate something for me?"

"Just give me your computer. It'll be faster," Nadia said, and they went through the awkward juggling of computers in the tight space. "What am I saying?" Nadia asked once she had Tony's laptop.

"I'm in the MPF's dispatch system there on the top left," Tony said, pointing. "Put in an update on the suspects heading west toward Nice in a black Audi Q8."

"Got it," she said. "Done." Nadia handed Tony his laptop back, and they got ready to move.

"Oh shit," Nadia said. "We're all over the French Gendarmerie network. Monaco police shared everything with them. They're on their way right now."

"I think we're being set up," Tony said.

Colt got behind the wheel, with Tony and Nadia staying on their computers, connected via a secure sat link. Ikeda traded off navigating and following Monaco police traffic. Nadia stayed dialed into the Gendarmerie's network to keep track of their movements.

"If we stay on this, heading uphill, we'll eventually connect with the A8. I think our best bet is to drive to Menton on the border with Italy," Tony said.

"Even if we get a fresh car to cross the border with, they've still got our pictures. They'll certainly share that with the Italian border guards," Colt said. "I agree with heading to Menton, but not along the A8. I'm afraid they'll have that patrolled. It's also the fastest way for the responding officers to get here."

"Okay, Princess Grace goes along the coastline, but I think it'll be slower. And there are no ditch points. God, the traffic patterns in this place are insane. No wonder everyone has a boat." Tony typed a few commands in. "Best bet is going to be Boulevard du Larvotto, going northeast through the city. There's no way on or off once we get going, but it'll be faster. Take that to Avenue Varvilla and stay on it until we hit Menton."

"Got it," Colt said and put the car in gear.

Colt waited for a break in the afternoon traffic and pulled out onto the road, heading left along the coast.

Then he spotted a pair of black SUVs in his rear-view mirror.

"This is gonna get sporty," Colt said. He pressed the gas down and leapfrogged two cars in front of him, swerving back into his lane and narrowly avoiding a silver Ferrari rumbling in the oncoming lane.

Nadia looked behind them. "How'd they find us?"

"My guess is they're tied into that new surveillance system," Colt said. "They probably saw us crossing the border."

"Turn up ahead," Tony called out.

Colt sped up again, leaping around another car. He followed the road up the slight incline, away from the ocean, flanked by trees on either side. The road curved into a tight U-shaped corner, again reversing direction. Colt pressed the gas out of the turn and blasted down the road, closing with the car in front of him.

Even though their instructors admonished them to use these skills as an absolute last resort, every graduate of the combat driving course fantasized about putting their training to use in a high-speed chase. Colt was no different. He just wished he was piloting something other than a Peugeot 308 hatchback. The car was small and nimble, if lacking pickup, and was good for weaving through traffic. But there was no way Colt could outrun those big-engine Range Rovers for long.

"You'll want to go straight here," Tony said, "up onto that bridge."

Colt raced forward, ignoring the directions and instead pulling a hard right.

"I've got an idea," Colt said.

"I hate it when you say that," Nadia muttered from the back seat. He jerked right again as if to enter the Monte Carlo Country Club's parking lot, then reversed again, taking the car back left. Instead of going under the bridge Tony had told him to drive over, Colt reversed a third time, pulling onto the corkscrew on-ramp. He hoped the cluster of trees in the median would hide them from their pursuers, at least for a moment.

From the back seat, Nadia watched the first of the Range Rovers completely miss the turn and blast into the Monte Carlo Country Club, going the wrong direction. The two behind it slammed on their brakes to navigate the tight turn.

In an urban plan that could only make sense here, they found themselves back on Avenue Princess Grace, climbing steeply. Colt slowed to take the lefthand corner and continued uphill, engine whining. He saw another of the corkscrew roundabouts up ahead, this one somehow connecting three or four entries and exits on at least two different levels of traffic. Colt checked the rearview and didn't see the SUVs. Traffic was swelling now, and he suspected their rapid exit was over. Colt turned left, which took him down a steep ramp and into the hairpin traffic circle, reversing their direction yet again. They'd just entered the cover of a wedge-shaped apartment when he saw the SUVs coming up the hill. Colt followed the road up the steep incline.

"How long are we on this?"

"It's a straight line for several miles. No ditch points."

"I don't love it," Colt said quietly.

"Wait—up here, on the left." Ikeda pointed to a road that just appeared on the left behind a wall. Colt checked the rearview. The SUVs hadn't made the turn yet. He turned hard off Avenue Varavilla and then immediately into the small walled-off parking lot of an apartment building. He parallel parked in front of a car along the tan brick wall, completely shielded from traffic on Avenue Varavilla below them.

Colt turned in his seat. "Nadia, do you have battery left in the drones?"

"Sure do," she said.

"Can you launch one out the window?"

She ripped open her backpack, powered on the micro drone, and launched it out her open window. The mosquito-like whine quickly faded away as the drone climbed into the afternoon sky to over the road. She positioned the drone right over the turn off Avenue Varavilla to give them the best approximation of distance.

"I've got them," she said. "There are two . . . and the third is about a tenth of a mile behind them. Must have taken some time to get outta Club Med." She tapped a command on her laptop, targeting the first vehicle. "Six hundred feet, speed is forty miles per hour." Nadia continued counting off closure in fifty-meter increments. Once she reached fifty, she told them the vehicle was slowing.

Tony lifted the hem of his shirt, revealing the concealed holster attached to his hip.

They were boxed in. There was no exit from this parking lot, except on foot. Those Range Rovers had armor plating in the doors and bullet resistant glass. Colt knew a gunfight would not go their way.

"Okay, the first one is continuing on Avenue Varavilla," Nadia said. Then, nervousness edging her voice, "the second is turning."

No one spoke. No one breathed. Colt put one hand on the door and the other inside his jacket. He could use the car behind them as cover and hopefully get a lucky shot when they opened their doors. He didn't exactly want to get into a shootout without knowing who he was firing at. Monaco had a small intelligence service and a criminal investigative division. Either of those would make sense, and he'd assume they could continue the pursuit of a suspect into France. It didn't follow that any of the French Gendarmerie's specialized units could respond to this quickly, certainly not the France's foreign intelligence service, the DGSE.

As far as they knew, only their faces appeared in the all-points. It did not include their cover identities, true names, or association with the CIA.

"Second vehicle is continuing on Chemin Des Grottes," Nadia said. She'd studied both French and German while posted to Geneva, mostly as something to do in her off hours. Though Swiss was a Germanic language, its proximity to and shared history with France meant invariably high linguistic cross-pollination.

"What's the third one doing?" Colt asked.

"He's slowing down," Nadia said.

"Waiting to see if we doubled back," Tony said.

A chorus of car horns they could hear even from their hiding spot said the SUV would not loiter for long. Nadia reported they continued on Avenue Varavilla. They agreed to stay here another ten minutes, with Nadia keeping overwatch with the micro drone. It didn't have a long range, but she could send it a half-mile up the road, making sure that the Range Rover didn't turn around or pull off to ambush them.

While Nadia was watching the road, Colt and Tony planned an alternative route, one that would take them off the main roads and through the mountains. Nadia spotted two Gendarmerie vehicles, lights and sirens, on Avenue Du Président Kennedy—the road "above" them, racing back toward Monaco. There was no other police presence that she could see. Colt asked her to recall the drone and once she did, they turned about in the small lot and headed back to Avenue Varavilla.

Colt drove them uphill to where Varavilla merged with Avenue Du Président Kennedy, around a curve following the mountain's contour. He turned off onto Avenue Du Serret, heading further up the mountain and into more distant residential areas.

Their route took them through the riviera's impossible geography, wondering at how the industrious and likely half-mad builders attached houses to even the slightest horizontal scrap of land. Though they could've taken a straight line into Menton, operations security now dictated a more circuitous path, with an improvised surveillance detection route. With Tony plotting their course in real time, Colt drove a series of loops, switchbacks, and meandering routes through the idyllic seaside community. Eventually, they settled on ditching the Peugeot at the port. If their pursuers had a way of tracking the vehicle, Colt hoped this would throw their scent off for good. Rail was the logical exit from France if they had a burned vehicle, and the one they intended to take, but there was still a valid case to make a run by sea. They could charter a boat anonymously to take them into Menton's Italian sister city, Grimaldi, just a few minutes' travel and out of the jurisdiction of the Gendarmerie. Though France and Italy enjoyed an open border, it could be closed. That was unlikely, but Colt still wanted to avoid traveling by car.

Colt pulled onto the coast road and headed east. It was early evening now, and the sun hung golden and low over the water. Tourists packed the beaches and traffic sluiced like spilled paint. Tall palms flanked the road on the seaward side and green and brown dappled mountains rose in the distance, now crowned with gray-white clouds that suggested rain. Tony spotted a carnival to their right, set up in a large parking lot next to the marina, and the three agreed that would be the perfect spot to ditch the car.

"We sure we don't want to just make a run for Italy? I mean, the border is right there," Nadia said, pointing to the mountains to the east, rising up out of the water, where they swallowed up the road. Tony looked to Colt as if it say, *It's your call.*

"It's a fair question," Colt said. "It comes down to acceptable risk. France and Italy have an open border, but they each have a police station on either side. We don't know if they'd stop us or not, and the original APB for was for two men and a woman in a red Peugeot."

Nadia picked up the thread from there, realizing his logic. "But if we take the train, we can stagger our departures, or leave at the same time but on different cars."

Colt nodded.

"And three train tickets are a lot more palatable to HQS than us stealing three different cars."

Nadia snorted and Colt saw her smile from the rearview.

Colt pulled into the lot and orbited for a few minutes until a spot opened up. He parked, got out, and wiped the car down. Humid, heavy sea air hit them as soon as they stepped onto the pavement, and it immediately triggered memories of Colt's years in the Navy. Most of his career had been aboard destroyers traversing these very waters and he recalled a dozen port calls "between Nice and Greece," as an old master chief he served with used to say.

Colt, Tony, and Nadia took the train to Milan, where they split up to take different paths to Vienna. The rest of the team had the safe house set up on the outskirts of the city. Colt had just returned from a trip to Vienna Station at the U.S. embassy to send Thorpe his mission report . Dwight Hoskins told the Vienna Chief of Station that Colt and his team would occasionally use Vienna Station to send cables back to HQS, but they were otherwise ghosts. The station chief was an old hat who had joined the Agency during the Cold War and spent most of his time fighting the KGB and its vile successors in Europe ever since. He knew well the flavor of unacknowledged work the Agency had to do here and told Colt if there was anything he needed, just to ask.

For now, they believed the Agency's intelligence cable network—a closed loop system—was still safe.

Thorpe shared Colt's concerns about the improbable timing of Wales's murder. Colt did not share with his boss that he thought the operation was a complete failure, hastily planned and under resourced, and was beating himself up over it. They should have taken months to plan an operation like this. Rehearsed it until they could execute it in their sleep. Colt was exhausted. They moved on the timetable the White House had given them and, but if they ran the rest of QUIET TITAN like this, things would go south fast.

"Got something for you," Nadia said the second Colt walked in the door from his run to Vienna Station.

"What am I looking at?" Colt said.

"This is the system that Archon-owned InfoSec firm, Counterthreat, created for the Monaco police. They call it 'advanced security analytics,' but it does large-scale pattern matching and link analysis. What does that remind you of?"

"CERBERUS," Colt said grimly. The NTCU had created the tool to trace technical threats at machine scale and speed. It was now being rolled out to the CIA more broadly and expanding its datasets to include mission areas ranging from nuclear proliferation, human trafficking, and counterintelligence. CERBERUS remained a black program, off any accounting ledger. They'd worked with a private software development firm to build it. The CIA just didn't have the expertise to build a program of that scale and sophistication, though their own software engineers had changed it heavily after delivery. "We need to make sure that the firm we partnered with to build this didn't get hit, too."

"I wonder how long this has been going on," Nadia mused.

"If we believe Kim's theory, only six months. But I'm coming to believe that anything is possible. Anything else?"

"Just one thing. Monaco police also had a contract with Praetorian for what they're calling 'high value asset protection,' and—you're going to love this—'problem-solving.' Digging around some of their reports, I found out they've used Praetorian's security details to protect some people they'd rather not assign official support to. That Russian arms dealer who used to own the soccer team, they've got a group on him. Sounds like the deal is, they don't want these guys rolling in with their own heavies."

"Makes sense," Colt said, but still didn't see how this related to their mission.

"The problem-solving part is what's bugging me. They don't keep any files on this. They do, however, have a hotline. And then, I found this. Do you know the name Marcel Bénichou?"

"No," Colt said.

"French Algerian terrorist. He was meeting in Monaco two months ago, allegedly to plan a series of bombings in Paris to coincide with the French Open. Intelligence Division notifies Praetorian. Bénichou's body turns up about a week later, badly tortured before being shot in the head."

Private security and intelligence firms were common, especially in

Europe, where governments didn't have the massive budgets America did. That these firms had their own field operatives was a reality that existed in the gray space between a poorly kept secret and an unfortunate truth better left unsaid. But that one of them answered to Archon was extraordinarily dangerous.

It meant their adversary could put an army in the field.

12

Weeks ground on with few fresh leads.

Colt was so far beyond tired, his vocabulary didn't even have the words to describe it. When he closed his eyes, Colt just saw the endless steps that he would walk disappearing into the horizon.

The team was running on fumes, the last light of a guttering candle. Duty and anger kept them moving. They worked relentlessly from the Vienna safe house. Colt didn't even bother setting shifts; the team just worked. They'd taken a deployable version of CERBERUS with them, and though it couldn't hook into the usual government or IC networks in the field, they could still use it for open source analysis. That alone saved tremendous time.

Not that it seemed to do them much good.

It felt like a losing battle.

Three of Archon's board members were dead.

Quentin Wales, head of operations.

Rhett Bolton, head of finance, had died two weeks before when his air taxi collided with a flock of birds and crashed in the Hudson River. The

National Transportation Safety Board was still trying to puzzle out how all eight of the air taxi's rotors had been shredded in midair. The pattern was close to a bird strike, but not close enough for them to call it. Then, just two days ago, someone had shot the Swiss-born scientist Mariano Emmanuelle, Archon's head of research and development, at his home in Basel. Authorities hadn't released the details, but the NTCU learned through intelligence channels that the Swiss federal police had found a remotely operated, fifty-caliber sniper rifle hidden on the grounds of Emmanuelle's home. Colt's first thought was it seemed eerily similar to the weapon Archon shot Ava with in Greece the year before.

One thing was clear—someone had declared war on Archon.

Someone else, Colt mused dourly.

Short months ago, only the president, the national security advisor, and select members of the Intelligence Community knew of Archon's existence. Not long after the Russian hacking crisis, word broke in the media not long of a shadowy "techno terrorist" group calling themselves "Archon." The *Times* cybersecurity reporter, Lacy James, had the exclusive. The NTCU wanted the FBI to raid the *New York Times* and get their source, assuming it could only be an internal leak. The White House denied the request. The official claim was that they had their hands full and couldn't stand another crisis, but Colt knew what they really meant. They couldn't stand having every journalist in the country against them in an election year.

Even after all that, many in the intel community still refused to believe Archon existed.

Colt didn't believe some dark arm of the U.S. government was taking out Archon's board members.

Thanks to their connections with Trinity, the British code-breaking agency, General Communications Headquarters (GCHQ) and the Secret Intelligence Service (MI6) knew about Archon, though whether that extended to the British prime minister, Colt didn't know. For now, he wasn't ruling out MI6. This felt like one of theirs.

And then there was Israel. Mossad knew about Archon at an operational level, and they did have a damning history of quietly eliminating enemies of the state. Archon's DNA-targeted bioweapon and its Holocaust echoes had shaken Ava to the core when they'd learned about it. Colt had to assume Mossad's involvement was at least possible, if unlikely.

Of course, Guy Hawkinson had a long list of enemies. Perhaps one of them was taking more aggressive action. He'd double-crossed Russia's intelligence service, the SVR, which resulted in the Russians using a space-based kinetic weapon to launch giant tungsten spears at a Caribbean island where Hawkinson had created one of Archon's first physical operations. If anyone had a grudge against Archon, it was the Russians. Still, given the number of assets the CIA had inside Russia's security apparatus now, it would be a minor miracle if the Russians were going after Archon and the Agency didn't know about it.

The last possibility was Trinity.

And of all the potential actors, only Trinity knew the board members' identities.

Colt denied the possibility for weeks, actively subverting his own intuition. He couldn't bring himself to believe that Ava would do it, or that Wilcox would permit it and then hide it from him. He couldn't believe they'd shoot Quentin Wales. Certainly not with Colt right there and damned near framed for the job.

He couldn't believe Wilcox would countenance a murder.

Watching her parents' murder had changed Ava. She'd taken an understandably hard edge that day and cloaked herself in a cynicism that she had never fully shed. Colt wouldn't deny her that, nor its righteous justification. But Wilcox had taught him everything he knew about the ethics of their profession. He'd shown Colt how to navigate the surreal and complex moral waters of intelligence work. It was impossible to conceive that the same man was ordering extrajudicial assassinations.

Unless, of course, Wilcox had determined the threat severe enough to justify this. Or had his firing to assuage the righteous indignation of a U.S. senator been the final straw that ended his belief in the system?

As with Ava, Colt couldn't fully deny the justification. He also didn't want to believe it was true.

Regardless of who was behind the murders, Colt and his team needed to capture the rest of Archon's leaders before it was too late.

They already had the risk of three independent clandestine spin-offs starting up. The only thing in their favor right now was the fact that Hazlett worked for Bolton, so Colt's team had insight into those plans.

He'd just returned from Vienna Station and the six-hour SDR. They had multi-spectrum cameras covertly installed on every side of the house, which allowed them to scan in the visible and nonviable light. They secured it against electronic eavesdropping. It was as safe as any field location could be, nestled in a village outside Vienna at the end of a long street, surrounded by trees.

Colt gathered the team in the dining room, where they'd taken to conducting briefings. He poured a fresh coffee as he waited for everyone to gather. Once they'd all taken their seats, he started. Colt's voice was thick and plodding, like gears that had been ground down.

"Cable from HQS this morning. There's been another leak and it's . . . it's bad This one is against the Brits. It exposed a joint MI6-GCHQ operation within the European Union. Apparently, the Brits were worried about relations with their neighbors post-Brexit and were tying some soft influence ops to turn sentiment back in their favor. They also had agents in several European governments. The leak has already hit the major news outlets in Europe and at home. So, brace for impact within the UN, the EU and, especially, NATO. Agency's early analysis is that this significantly widens the divide between the UK and the Continent and is a major erosion of trust."

"With good reason," Alison D'Angelo said.

"The GCHQ snooping is going to be the bigger problem, because it blatantly violates the EU's data privacy laws."

"Does this affect our timetable at all?" Tony asked.

"I think it has to. We have unknown opposition, and they are moving quickly. Faster than us."

That last part frustrated Colt immensely. This group moved with lightning speed compared to many of the operations he'd been on in his career, and yet some unknown adversary was lapping them.

"Maybe we just let them," Nadia said. "I mean, that's the goal, right? Take these assholes off the board?"

"The goal is to capture one of them so we can find out how they're beating everyone's encryption," Solomon French said.

"What's the difference? They've clearly made some enemies. Why not just let them take the board members out?" Nadia retorted.

"Because then we lose the ability to see how deep the threat goes," Colt said. "That has ripple effects beyond just our team."

"Colt, cut the Seventh Floor bullshit," Nadia snapped. "I don't know when you started talking like management, but not here, not with us. You of all people know what Archon is capable of. We've got top cover. I say we nail them to the wall with it. Someone wants to take out Archon's board members for us? Cool. Maybe we can beat them to the punch and grab a couple first."

No one spoke. No one even breathed. It was like seeing something deeply unsettling in public, like a violent argument among strangers. Observers knew was it wrong, but social pressure prevented them from speaking up. Nadia was way out of line, and the expressions on the faces around the table showed it.

Colt let Nadia's comment slide for now. Though comparing him to Langley's Seventh Floor stung. He was certainly the only operations officer in recent memory to run his mouth off in front of the president of the United States and the heads of two intelligence agencies, so he could cut Nadia a little slack. He also knew where her anger was coming from. They'd tried to kill her, and came damned close.

"We're not in the assassination business," Colt said.

"And I wouldn't count on that top cover," Tony added.

"We have a presidential finding," Nadia insisted.

"Yeah, and that's the first thing that gets burned in a White House ashtray if this goes sideways. Remember, they had a finding in Nicaragua, too. My group has a lot of scars over deniable ops that got denied because it didn't go right and somebody found out about it," Tony said. "And it doesn't change the fact that Colt's source is saying that their contingency plans go into effect if their board member is dead."

"I don't like the idea of us being scooped," D'Angelo said. As the targeting officer, Alison had a steep personal investment in understanding and analyzing every aspect of the board members' lives, their histories.

She'd consumed and distilled every bit of intelligence the free world had on these people. "Someone having better intel than us on Archon is deeply concerning. And it pisses me off." Colt watched the heads around the table nod in agreement. That sentiment seemed to unify everyone.

Colt tried to get them back on track. He almost wished Keith Ricci were here so he could remind everyone of the law, but they'd pointedly left him at home until their targets shifted to American citizens. Colt knew they might need to take some actions that would be better off unwitnessed by a cop. "The rest of our list is a little complicated, which is why we started with Wales. Cameron Braithwaite is a member of Parliament. We assume he's off the table. Alison, can you give us the rest of the list?"

"Yeah. Okay, I'll start with the non–U.S. citizens. After Braithwaite is Jin Yoon. He's one of the world's top AI minds. He's got a nationally funded lab in Seoul and a TV show. He's a minor celebrity in South Korea."

"Yeah, let's definitely start with him," French said.

D'Angelo continued. "Next up is Carlos Marin. Spanish entrepreneur and futurist. Considered the father of Spain's tech community. Marin founded the Artificial Intelligence Research Institute at the University of Barcelona with an anonymous grant of fifty million dollars. I'll give you two guesses where that money came from, but you're only going to need one. He currently lives in Ibiza. After that, we have the Americans. Dr. Heather Fleet is a resident researcher at Caltech. She rarely leaves California, so we'd need cause to arrest her. And then we have Reece Craddock."

"Holy shit, he's Archon?" Nadia said, laughing.

At one time considered the godfather of computer security, Reece Craddock had enjoyed a fast and abrupt descent into infamy. Originally wanted by the U.S. government for tax evasion, he fled the country and hid out in Belize and Costa Rica before disappearing entirely. Craddock brought his funds with him, keeping them in a plethora of tax shelters, furthering the IRS's ire. Many dismissed him as a tinfoil hat conspiracy theorist. Craddock contended that the government hunted him relentlessly for decades with black helicopters and special operators. He was reportedly addicted to cocaine and never without a sidearm.

"It's entirely for show," D'Angelo said. "The tax evasion thing was real, but the rest of it was an act. He was certainly an odd choice to join Trinity, but had been a kind of fringe member since about 1987. He was active in the organization until 1995, when he fled the country. Trinity leaders asked him to keep his distance. He stayed away until the 2003 schism. After that, what eventually became Archon's board offered him a seat at the table. Craddock is largely, if quietly, credited for turning Costa Rica into the computer science hub that it is today. The only problem is that he's totally off the grid. We don't have any idea where he is. No one does."

"Which brings us to number nine. Your favorite and mine, Guy Hawkinson."

"I thought Guy wasn't on the board," Tony said.

"That's right, he's not," Colt replied. "But I want him to be part of the discussion. He's the one who stole Jeff Kim's tech, which means he's the most likely to be behind the breaches. Second, there is the possibility that Guy is actually going after the board members."

"Oh, this is all we need. Archon civil war," Nadia grumbled.

"We know from EMBER that Hawkinson has a grudge against the board," D'Angelo mused. "They didn't elevate him to the table, even after everything he's done for them, not to mention the incredible losses he sustained, both financial and public. Guy is now a global fugitive and will never set foot on his home soil again, unless his uncle wins the presidency. Colt painted an effective, if dystopian, picture of Hawkinson being the surviving member of Archon with the technology to undo any form of encryption. Not to mention having his own soldiers." Hawk Security Group was defunct, but they'd known he kept his most loyal troops with him.

The world was full of horrible actors who'd pay legitimate fortunes for the technology Hawkinson possessed.

"Does this mean Guy is back on the table?" Nadia asked.

"Guy was never off the table," Colt replied. "We just don't know where he is. If we can't find him, we can't bring him in. I'm raising it only because I want to keep the objective front and center of everyone's mind. We assume Guy is leading the quantum code breaking, but we can't find him, so we grab a board member. The hope is that the board member, even if they don't know where Guy is, can explain how they're getting into all of our encryption."

"And if they don't know?" Tony asked.

"That's worth something, too. It means that Hawkinson works alone or, God forbid, that there's a new player."

"Are we looking in the wrong place? Or, maybe better to say, are we looking for the wrong thing?" Nadia asked.

"What do you mean?"

"Well, this stuff is scarce, right? You couldn't build a quantum computing array in your garage, at least not one powerful enough for all this. When we kicked this off, you had CERBERUS look for the raw materials."

"We got hits, but nothing decisive," Colt said.

"This is just a theory . . . and, I'm caveating this with the statement that I had *one* class on quantum computing in grad school." Nadia grabbed a piece of paper and sketched a hasty diagram. "But there's an idea that quantum computers can create linkages with each other to form networks."

"That's like, basic computing," Solomon said.

"No, it's, *like*, not," Nadia retorted. "Because the data is expressed as these quantum bits—qubits—and transmitted at the subatomic level, it's not only untraceable, but hypothetically unbreakable. That could be why we can't find Guy Hawkinson. If Archon has one of these quantum networks, it's possible they're communicating that way. That's where they could launch their attacks from. These things aren't cheap and"—Nadia gave a knowing glance and a slight smile to Tony—"they've already lost one. Maybe they didn't build a new one, they just co-opted some existing labs. So, rather than concentrating on looking for building blocks, maybe we should see if we can find connections between these board members and known quantum computing facilities."

"If that's true, that could mean Guy is still on their side," Colt said.

"And someone else is assassinating their leaders," Nadia concluded.

"Can you run that down?" Colt asked.

"Sure can. You know, it'd be really useful if I could talk to Jeff Kim. Is there any way to make that happen?"

"Why?"

"The part that I'm not clear on is that I don't understand how the linking works." She shot a hard side eye to French, who didn't catch it. "It's not like a classic network, and there's no such thing as a subatomic internet.

At least, not yet. I legit don't know how two quantum computers talk to each other. When I was in school, which was not that long ago, our professors didn't even know if it was possible, let alone how to do it. I want to run this theory by Kim and see what he thinks. We know a quantum computer and a classic computer can talk to each other over a regular network connection. You just need a quantum networking protocol. People are still trying to figure that part out, to be able to do it reliably at scale."

"I don't think there's many people who could've come up with that. I'll run it by Thorpe when I check in tomorrow."

By now, Vienna's Chief of Station had put together that Colt (whom he knew to be the number-two man in the NTCU) was here working on the encryption problem. Of course, he didn't know just how aggressively Colt's orders were to prosecute it, but he led off that morning by asking the younger officer if there was anything at all that he needed. Colt settled on a secure phone call and a private office.

Thorpe led off. "I didn't want to put this in a cable on the off chance that someone at Vienna Station would see it," he said. "Their chief probably knows, but I don't know what he's told his staff, and I don't want to cause a panic."

"Panic over what?"

"The entire Intelligence Community is frozen, Colt. After this MI6 debacle, ODNI issued guidance—delivered via courier—which was to assume no communication is safe. They're literally talking about putting all message traffic in diplomatic bags."

"Jesus. That's unhelpful," Colt said. While the dangerous reality of the current crisis was clear, many were forgetting the fact that no adversary could target every communication path simultaneously. Even if augmented by a massively parallelized AI, whoever was behind this still couldn't monitor every secure system in the U.S. government, let alone the world. The probability that the phone call he was currently on was being listened in on was so small it wasn't worth worrying about. The senior intelligence officials should know that. Though Colt also understood the optics of crisis management. If they assumed business as usual and there was another leak, heads would roll that the Agency hadn't taken sufficient protective measures.

"This doesn't change your mission, but I wanted you to be aware of what's happening at home. Okay, your turn. What've you got for me today?" Thorpe asked. Colt summarized the previous day's analysis of Archon's remaining leadership.

"I think it's worth noting," Colt said, concluding his review, "that not one of these attacks happened the same way. There was what we assume to be a high caliber sniper, an aircraft crash of indeterminate cause, and another long-range gunshot through a second-story window. Still deadly, though of a much lower caliber than what killed Wales."

"What does your gut tell you?" Thorpe asked.

"I think we can rule the Russians out. Their specialty is old school tradecraft and traditional hacking, but this is way outside of their capability. Plus, we've got so many ears inside the FSB and SVR right now. If they were doing this, I think we'd know."

"Well, pulling on that thread, we're getting reports that there was a power grid overload at Russia's National Quantum Laboratory yesterday. This is coming from the Chinese intelligence network. The Russians have not made it public. The Chinese are placing their labs under enhanced security. I think we can cross them off the list as well."

Colt exhaled. "Will, I see only two plausible explanations right now. One, Hawkinson created the quantum decryption algorithm using Jeff Kim's designs. He's acting alone and is taking out board members to get control of the organization."

"But, according to EMBER, he couldn't access the next level down."

"That's true. It might be that he doesn't care. If we're tied up chasing them down, we're not going after him. It's a variation on the theory that Archon is using the security breaches to create a big smokescreen before the election."

"With you so far. What's number two?"

"It's Trinity. Other than the NTCU and whoever has read our intelligence, Trinity and Hawkinson are the only ones who can identity Archon's leadership."

"Do you really believe it could be Trinity?"

"I don't want to, I really don't, but . . ." Colt's voice trailed off as he considered his next words. "Frankly, the thing that keeps me up at night is the possibility of Archon and Trinity going to war with each other. Do you have any idea how fast and how destructive a war between AI superpowers would be? Neither of them are accountable to a government or recognize national borders as a factor. Will, this is all the bad things at once."

"What'd Wilcox say to you the last time you spoke to him?"

"He'd never admit that Trinity would launch an assassination campaign. He just said he was taking my advice, and that they were taking active measures."

Colt couldn't count the number of times he'd replayed that conversation in Athens back in his mind. His pressing Wilcox was out of frustration that, because Trinity wouldn't act, they were trying to push the CIA to do something. Colt, meanwhile, was stuck between what he knew to be right and what his government would allow. He pushed Trinity into this and now, maybe, pushed them too hard.

"I haven't spoken with him since that meeting at the White House," Thorpe said.

"I'm going to see Ava in a couple of days. I'll ask her directly if they're doing this."

"And if she says they're not?"

"If she says no and I think she's lying, go to Wilcox. You have a different relationship with him. He might tell you things he won't tell me."

"Why do you think that?" Thorpe asked.

"He's not trying to protect you," Colt said matter-of-factly.

"I'm fine if you go see Klein. I can't stop you, and if you think there's a chance she'll acknowledge their involvement, it's worth a shot. But have you thought through what you will do if she says yes?"

That was a damn good question, and one Colt had not fully considered. He did not know.

"Colt, if Trinity is doing this and Ava knows about it, she will be responsible for the murder of an American citizen. The FBI will arrest her. We'll be obligated to go after the rest of Trinity, and that includes Jason Wilcox."

"I know," Colt said.

"Do you, Colt?" Thorpe asked, growing increasingly serious. "Have you truly thought this all the way through? Have you considered what happens if we have to arrest a former deputy director of the Central Intelligence Agency and a former Mossad officer, and God knows who else, for murder? Do you know what will happen if they don't go quietly? Their organization is home to some of the world's most advanced technology. What if they decide to fight back? We know what Archon can do. Trinity will be so much worse, not just because of how advanced they are, but because of all that we've trusted them with."

"Well, given all that, should we treat them as any other potential intelligence target?"

Thorpe was quiet for a time as he considered the question. After nearly a minute, he said, "No, I think it's still valuable to put the question to Klein personally. They could probably pick out any electronic surveillance we'd use anyway. I know she's ex-Mossad, but given your relationship, there might be a visual tell you can pick up on."

There was little else to say. It stung that Thorpe would even question Colt's loyalty.

"One last thing," Colt said, ignoring the sting. "I'd like to reach out to Jeff Kim, to see what he might offer. If this really started with Hawkinson stealing his tech, he might give us something to look for. Nadia's got a theory about—"

"It's fine," Thorpe said, cutting him off. "I won't understand the ask anyway, so I'm just going to tell you that you can do it."

Colt told Thorpe he'd be report back after he met Ava and then hung up.

"So, I'm supposed to spy on my ex-Mossad agent girlfriend because my boss thinks she might be an enemy of the state. Jesus Christ, I have a weird life." Colt stared up at the ceiling. "And now I'm talking to myself."

Colt thanked the Chief of Station for letting him use his secure phone line and made his way out of the massive embassy complex. He crossed the busy street in front of the embassy to the sprawling Stadtpark, where he pretended to enjoy a few minutes in the shade before exiting the other side and walking several blocks to a Strassenbahn station. He took the train north to the edge of Vienna. There, Colt walked another three blocks to where he had parked. He drove a circuitous route through the city, taking the better part of the afternoon and cutting back and forth across the Danube. Colt even drove through Vienna's airport as an additional measure before finally turning to make his way to the farmhouse in one of the outlying cities to Vienna's southwest.

13

Amsterdam, The Netherlands

Colt didn't tell Ava that he was operating in Europe, just that they needed to meet.

Amsterdam was easy for them both to reach and was a popular international tourist destination. Additionally, since Schiphol was one of the world's busiest international airports, it was common for travelers to spend a layover wandering the city. Colt landed at eleven a.m. with his backpack and joined the tightly packed train into Amsterdam. He wasn't staying overnight. Colt exited at the Niuemarkt Station and zigzagged across the canals, working his way to the west to Scheepvaarthuisbuurt.

Colt found the dockside cafe where he was to meet Ava, grabbed a table, and ordered an Amstel and a basket of fries. The Europeans were suffering through the worst heatwave in the modern era, and since most buildings on the continent weren't designed with central air, they flocked outdoors looking for anything to escape the heat. It made for excellent cover.

Ava arrived twenty minutes after he did.

Colt stood and greeted her with a handshake. They'd agreed that until they knew no one was watching, better to keep their interactions distant. For today, they were just two travelers sharing a beer.

"I'm surprised you're here," Ava said, casually popping a fry into her mouth.

"Why?"

She reached for her beer. "They haven't identified you yet, but the French shared your photo with Europol and they pushed it out across the continent. You're lucky the Dutch National Police didn't grab you at the airport."

"They only have my picture," Colt said.

"Still. You need to be careful, Colt. What the hell were you doing in Monaco anyway?"

"How'd you know about that?"

Ava glowered at him and didn't say anything for a few beats, instead taking another sip from her stein. "We have hooks into most of the law enforcement databases. One of the visual recognition apps picked it up."

"Nice to know you're keeping tabs on me."

"It's a security measure. Ever since Archon tried to brand us all as terrorists, we've had to be careful about who might be watching our members. Jason extended that to you, Thorpe, and some other members of your team, at least the ones that Trinity members have ever been seen with in public. Seriously, what were you doing there? Wales has an army around him at all times."

"It doesn't matter what I was doing," Colt insisted. "What matters is what happened when I was there. Someone murdered Wales right in front of me. Then, amazingly, my photo shows up in half a dozen police databases. The pictures came from local surveillance cameras linked into the Monaco police force's new intel system. It'd take a pretty sophisticated link analysis and facial rec to connect all that."

"What are you getting at?"

"I think whoever did it is trying to hang Wales's murder on me," Colt said.

"Why?"

"Can you think of a better way to get my team out of the picture? I don't think they knew we'd be there, but I can imagine my image alerting on a system and taking it as a target of opportunity."

"What are you implying?"

Colt turned away from her to look at the water. There was a line of bushy trees between the street and the concrete piers, half of which had boats moored to them. People bunched at the bases of the trees, seeking refuge from the heat.

Colt knew he had to choose his next words carefully. Ava had just admitted to using facial recognition tech to keep tabs on him. It wasn't a great logical leap to guess the same tech could've been used in Monaco. Dark thoughts swirled in his mind. Would Trinity, would *Ava*, frame Colt and his team to provide a smokescreen for their assassination campaign? Put suspicion on the CIA so they could eliminate Archon?

There was a world where that logic made sense, but Colt didn't want to believe it.

"I'm not implying anything, Ava," Colt said, his eyes still on the harbor. "Someone is taking out Archon's leadership element before they can be brought in for questioning."

"That seems like a strange thing to equivocate on," she said.

"If they're dead, we can't figure out how they're defeating everyone's encryption and bringing global communications and commerce to a standstill."

"If they're dead, they can't do it either."

"Except for the contingency protocol that activates in the event of a board member's death." If Ava knew about that, she wasn't giving it away. Her face was blank. One of the hardest things a spook can do is try to interrogate one of their own. "Every board member controls some aspect of the operation. They have their own organization, which the others don't know about. Their subordinates don't all know they're part of Archon. Most don't. Their leaders designed it that way so that if one of the board members was arrested, they'd only have so much they could give up." Colt assumed Ava knew that part, given Trinity and Archon's shared history. He didn't think she knew about the deadman switch. "If one of them is killed, a backup plan goes into effect and the lower tiers carry out some instruction. They spin off and create other 'Archon-like' activities, but no one knows who they are, what their objectives are, or where they're based. Nothing. Except the board."

Again, if Ava knew any of this, her expression betrayed nothing.

"I'm worried that someone is taking matters into their own hands without full context."

Ava snorted. It was an abrupt and caustic sound. "Didn't you get into Jason's face and tell him we needed to do something about this?"

"I did. You'll remember that was after Trinity gave me infected code to inject in Hawkinson's network. That almost got Nadia killed. I said it, and still agree that Trinity cannot stand around while my service and others try to stop them. Especially when most governments refuse to acknowledge they exist. I assumed you'd use your tech to expose their businesses, go after their money and political influence. Expose their leadership."

"You can't have it both ways."

"And you also can't rely on people like me to fight your battles for you."

"Maybe we're not," Ava said. "I know you well enough to know when you're talking around something. What aren't you saying, Colt?"

"Did you kill Quentin Wales?"

"Ah, so you want someone else to solve the Archon problem, but you also want to decide how it's done?"

"Ava, he was murdered on a city street in Monaco. Whomever did it could have killed other people in that crash. Other people were—his security detail just had the misfortune of working for an asshole."

"You wouldn't say that if you'd known them."

"Okay, then how about Rhett Bolton's air taxi crashing in the Hudson River?"

"Maybe he should've taken a cab and not a quadcopter," she quipped.

"Tell that to the pilot's family. He was just the guy who was on the flight schedule that day. This is serious, Ava. God knows the Brits have their hands full right now, but Bolton was an American citizen. It's not public yet, but the FBI is investigating his death as a murder. This is going to have repercussions."

"What did you hope was going to happen? They'd arrest him? I can just imagine that trial. Mr. Bolton, do you run a secret techno-terrorist group? No, Your Honor. Case dismissed."

"You're deflecting. There are only two groups with direct knowledge of Archon's leadership element. My unit is one, and it wasn't us. The other is yours."

"You're leaving one out," she said, her voice clipped. "Archon itself. Maybe one of them decided they're no longer going to play nicely with others. I mean, if their entire plan is to replace bureaucracy with artificial intelligence, why not lead by example?"

"Did you do it?" When Ava didn't respond, Colt said, "A car bomb is hardly a scalable solution." He immediately regretted it. Hastily, he added, "We've been sending Hellfires at Al Qaeda's leaders for over twenty years. Someone always just moves up to take their place."

"Maybe you haven't been killing them fast enough," Ava said. Her voice was definitely darker now. "But illiterate terrorists in a cave are hardly the same caliber opponent as the head of a multinational technology firm or a world expert on artificial intelligence. Those aren't exactly renewable resources."

"Ava, I—"

"No. Anyone can build a car bomb and anyone can fire a gun, but we have nations putting the full weight of their economies behind artificial intelligence. Anyone can be a power in this fight and anyone can be a serious threat. Archon is an existential threat. This fight isn't only about killing the bad guys, it's about preventing them from unleashing a technology they can't, or choose not to, control. Even if we agree that AGI won't be achievable for decades, we can't allow developing an artificial intelligence that extends beyond our ability to safeguard it. Archon brought down your air traffic control system and the oil distribution network using an intelligent system to find the vulnerabilities in those systems. There was a human-on-the-loop then. Next time there might not be."

"So that's your answer to the control problem? You just murder everyone that you think is evil? Who do you answer to? No one. What laws or safeguards ensure innocent people don't get hurt?"

The "control problem" was one of the fundamental questions in AI development. Though rooted in philosophy, there was also the hard technical question of how to ensure AI systems would only benefit and aid humans and not harm them, even inadvertently. An algorithm sees that people who bought wooden chairs also often bought rope, so the helpful shopping app says, "People like you also bought this item." Now, the app serves up the shopper a chair and rope. For the program, it's simply fulfilling its purpose in recommending products that other shoppers also bought, but a critically thinking mind could see the potentially grim and unintended extension.

The center of Colt's conflict was the fact that Ava wasn't wrong. Well, at least in her characterization of AI's potential for weaponization. Though, like fire, even when used for benign purposes, AI could be uncontrollably dangerous. When trying to characterize the problem for the Agency's nontechnical leadership, Colt referenced a recent hypothetical he'd read in an article. A scientist suggested an AI tasked with solving a complex problem determined it needed more computing power to achieve the goal its creator assigned. It then determined that humans were the top consumers of computing power, so it removed them from the equation. In the example referenced, it was just cutting humans off from computers, but there were logical extensions of this argument that could encompass far worse outcomes. Unlike any other technology developed, AI was not only self-learning and self-improving, but it did so far faster than humans could react and respond. The potential that it could get out of control too fast for humans to do anything about it was real, and Colt, among many others, felt that the scientific community was racing so quickly to push the technological envelope that they weren't considering all dangers.

He'd hoped Trinity would play the role of society's technological conscience. Unfortunately, they'd spent so much of their time working in secret that when their existence was finally revealed, it was by their adversaries who tried to paint them as a techno-cult.

"You mean, like when a CIA drone strikes an innocent person because the intelligence was wrong?"

"Exactly like that, actually. We held the people who got it wrong accountable. This is not a problem we can just murder our way out of, Ava. At some point, one of these people has to be captured and questioned. If we don't do that, how are we ever going to clue the public in on the threat?"

"Most of the public uses their kids' birthday as a password. You can't have it both ways, Colt. You can't demand someone else take action because you can't, and then question the actions they take."

"You still haven't answered me."

"And I'm not going to." Ava's eyes shone with an angry light, an inner fire he'd only seen once before, and he knew he'd pushed the subject too far. She waited several inexorable moments before she spoke. When she did, her voice was dangerously flat and calm. It was a tone of warning. "Colt, I love you, but I will not allow you to use our relationship as a source. If you want to know what Trinity is doing, you need to join us and find out. Also, your country has a fifty percent chance of putting an Archon agent in the White House, so please don't lecture me on the merits of the system." Ava pulled her phone out, pointedly ending the conversation. She scanned a message and swiped it away, then returned her phone to her pocket. She stood and left.

Colt paid the check and returned to the airport.

14

Ibiza, Spain

Carlos Marin had moved to Ibiza full time about ten years earlier, when he'd transferred operational control of his companies to a collection of trusted lieutenants, opting instead (he noted with more than a little irony) to take positions on the company boards. He still maintained a direct role in the three AI-focused research institutes he'd founded, which allowed him to discreetly motivate the areas of exploration. He made two trips a month to Barcelona to meet with the researchers in person, though they remained in daily virtual contact.

His home, a stately Spanish country villa of white stucco, turquoise glass, and exposed wood, was in the island's far northeast corner, just outside a resort community called Cale de San Vincente. Marin had never married, but surrounded himself with a nearly constant string of models, actresses, and one notable tennis star. At one point, Quentin Wales had admonished him to keep a lower profile, arguing that his prolific and sensational love life attracted too much attention. Marin explained once, and once only, that a Briton could not possibly understand Marin's responsibility to maintain such an image, and that it would be more conspicuous if he did not. And, Marin reasoned to himself, it wasn't as though women were throwing themselves at the pockmarked, sour-faced former general. Someone had to pick up the slack.

He'd never cared for Wales, who represented a side of the organization Marin thought would be better left unexplored. Wales insisted that the group act as global puppet masters, manipulating world events in their favor. Carlos thought that sounded exhausting. Was not the point of this entire endeavor to create a world where AI could perform the arduous work of managing a global society? No, Carlos Marin—himself to be granted the title of First Marquess later in the year for his scientific and business contributions to Spain—was not sorry to see Quentin Wales go. He was, however, sorry that Quentin Wales *went*. It was a subtle distinction most wouldn't appreciate. Of them, Wales was the most likely to have made the flavor of enemies who would seek revenge by assassination. Certainly, Wales's life before joining the organization netted him no small number of enemies, and his current business dealings outside of it attracted the wrong kind of attention.

This thing with the Saudis . . .

Marin, of course, had cautioned against that. Not that Wales listened to him. Or anyone.

If it had *just* been Wales, Marin would've thought put it down to an old enemy, a rival or, perhaps, a name off the long list of people Wales had offended with his security business. Many people moved to Monaco to hide in plain sight and didn't appreciate Praetorian selling the national police a sophisticated law enforcement network.

But then Bolton and Emmanuelle died, and now there was something to be concerned about.

Those deaths, in such proximity, could only mean that someone was hunting them. The question was—who?

To Marin, the Americans were the obvious first choice. They had uncovered Samantha Klein's alliance with Hawkinson which was how, he surmised, the CIA learned of Archon's existence. MI6 was possible, but less likely. Braithwaite had that service well monitored, and if there had been an active move against the group, he would know.

Hawkinson had certainly made an enemy of the Russians, but they were cold shadows of their former selves. Also, with the rest of the world tearing itself apart over the complete loss of security, it seemed doubtful they'd also be able to muster the wherewithal for an assassination campaign.

Only Trinity could identify their board of directors and even then, half of them had joined after the schism. Archon gone to great lengths to obfuscate the identities of the newer members and their respective organizations.

Hawkinson, Marin mused, and made a mental note to get in touch with him. Hawkinson had been Wales's acolyte, but perhaps it was time to reevaluate that relationship now that the general was dead. They could never admit him to the board, Guy was too well known, but there were other options. Marin understood his lingering anger over not being elevated, but surely Hawkinson had to understand they couldn't admit a lightning rod such as he. And had that not been the whole point? Give the Western security services a few shiny objects to chase? Guy Hawkinson on the one side, and a cult of computer-obsessed Trinity cultists on the other.

Guy was crafty and knew how to think like the opposition. He would likely have useful insight into this situation. The other board members wanted to keep him at arm's length after the debacle in Argentina, but Marin was never one to throw a useful tool away just because the sheen had dulled a little.

Marin slid out of his shirt and dropped it on a lounge chair atop a folded white and blue striped towel. No set schedule today, no prescribed number of laps, just a need to work out some stress. After that, a drink. After the drink, Carolina. He smiled.

Standing at the edge of the pool, Marin glanced to his left to see one of his guards walking the perimeter fence that looked over the blue-green Balearic Sea. Having guards around all the time took some getting used to. Marin was a deeply private man and had never traveled with security before. Much of the reason why he'd moved here was to avoid exactly that. But after the three suspicious deaths of other Archon board members, even he agreed a personal security detail was a necessary evil, at least for the time being.

He looked up into the perfectly blue sky, watching a bird turn lazy circles in the coastal thermals above his home. The bird pitched slightly, starting to dive.

Must have found a fish, Marin said to himself.

He dove into the pool.

He was underwater when it exploded.

The shockwave killed him instantly, but the force of the blast was strong enough that it launched a massive geyser of water (and Carlos) arcing high into the air. The detonation took out one of his guards and blinded another.

All that was left of the pool, the deck, or any of the surrounding furniture was a blackened, smoking crater.

15

Vienna, Austria

"Connecting me with Jeff was a great idea," Nadia said. Hearing the old infectious enthusiasm back in her voice made Colt smile. She sounded like the feisty former Air Force cyber ops officer he had recruited out of Cornell grad school. He'd been worried about her for the last year, and even after she'd gone back through to finish the Clandestine Service School, he didn't know if she would never truly be "back." Watching her tear apart this highly complex technical problem with such joy made his heart leap.

"So, here's what we've got," she continued. She'd flown out to Langley to meet with Jeff in person about this. "I was right, Jeff created a networking solution. He—actually, his AI, Saturn—proposed the design. It relies on a device called a quantum repeater. This is an overly simplistic explanation, but it's kind of like a Wi-Fi extender. It's a device that allows you to extend the transmission. See, the problem is that when you transmit qubits over long distances, they go through a process called 'decoherence,' in which they gradually lose connection to their quantum state because of interaction with electromagnetic radiation, photons and electrons. A repeater kind of re-energizes the quantum state. Jeff's design used a lab-created diamond as a kind of hard drive, with the—"

"Nadia, I'm loving that you're so excited, but I need you to explain it to me like you were briefing the DCI."

"Right, sorry. TL;DR, the quantum and classic computers talk all the time. You can do it over an ethernet connection. You just need to create a process for the two systems to talk to each other. It's a little more complicated than an API, but not much. If fact, quantum systems rely on classic systems for processes they aren't good at, or mundane tasks you wouldn't waste the processing power on."

Colt smirked. "TL;DR" was coder slang for "too long; didn't read," what the military would call BLUF, or Bottom Line Up Front.

"So, there's no issue with them connecting on the internet?" Colt asked.

"No. Again, you need the protocol to enable them to communicate, but it's not hard. And a quantum computer can transmit over the internet, though all the problems I described earlier still apply."

"This decoherence?"

"Right," Nadia said. "Jeff said that hypothetically, you could create these quantum repeaters and deploy them along the transmission path, and they'd . . . re-cohere? I'm actually not sure what the right term is."

"You're telling me Jeff hasn't done this yet?"

"Not at scale or outside of his lab yet, no."

Back to the beginning, with no idea how Archon—or whoever—was doing this. It occurred to Colt that Trinity might know the answer to this problem. Or, at least have a system that could figure it out. Unfortunately, that door had closed. Colt had other ways into that group outside of Ava, but he didn't think they'd talk to him now. Going to Wilcox would just put his old boss in between himself and Ava. Besides, Colt already knew what Wilcox would tell him.

Colt had tried to patch things up with Ava in the week following their fight, but when he'd called, she'd simply repeated the refrain she'd given him that night. No more free rides. Colt loved her and wanted to have a future with her. Though, most days if he was being honest with himself, he struggled to understand what that future might be. He tried to balance their ephemeral concerns about their relationship with the very real concerns of the current crisis. Colt had hoped Ava would share what she knew about Archon for the greater good; instead, she'd taken it the opposite way and accused him of trading on their relationship for intelligence.

"He offered another theory," Nadia said, excitement palpable in her voice. "If you could create a transmission protocol, you could use existing fiber-optic cables. Jeff said no one has successfully done it yet, to his knowledge. However—"

"However, Hawkinson has had this tech for over two years, and we know he built a quantum computer at least as late as eighteen months ago."

"That's a year and a half. He could've had a system working on this problem. Since the concept of time operates differently at the subatomic level, it's entirely possible Hawkinson has already solved this problem."

"Does Jeff think that's likely?"

"He said he thinks it's likely they could've created a solution for a single network. The virtue of a quantum computer network is it gives you exponentially more processing power, which is how he surmised they've been able to break through so many forms of encryption. He thinks that if we concentrate our search not on the computer itself, but on the routing protocol, it might be possible to triangulate the network that way. Once it detects an intrusion, it'll backtrace it to the source. It just needs to know what to look for."

Colt had never felt so far out of his depth before. He was being pushed into a space in which he had only a cursory understanding of an incredibly complex technology, and yet he needed to devise the operation that would counter it. His next words were a familiar refrain, almost a homily to pushing unknowable problems through the bureaucracy. "Let me see if I've got this. He thinks it might take too long to find the computers themselves, but we could do it by creating a program that searches for a quantum routing protocol. Like a packet sniffer for quantum IPs?"

"That's totally wrong, but I know where you're going, so yes."

"And we know how to do this?"

"We will in . . . about twenty four hours. I'm flying to Palo Alto tonight to work on this in person. Assuming you approve my TDY, that is."

"Thorpe can do that," Colt said.

"I know, and I asked him. He said that if he can't explain it to the travel office, he can't authorize the trip." Nadia snickered. "I'm mostly kidding, but he wanted me to run it by you first."

Colt laughed. "Okay. No problem, of course. But, say you two write this software. Where do we deploy it? The internet's a big place."

"I recommend we deploy it through CERBERUS. That gets us access to almost every government system, in addition to a mess of civilian and corporate networks that allowed us to use it. The snooper won't be a big app, and will only call back to the NTCU ops floor when it detects an intrusion, highlighting the backtrace to the point of origin."

This would be covertly deploying an app no one had authorized them to build across most government owned-IT systems. There was no question CERBERUS could handle the extra workload, but there was no time to seek authorization for this. Not to mention that if they tried, the plan would die in bureaucracy. Each agency would demand that their own IT or information security department oversee the effort, and invariably someone would disagree with the approach or the intent or just because it encroached on their territory.

"Ok. Do it. I'll clear it with Thorpe and Hoskins. I'll just assume this is part of that presidential authorization. Can you make it so that none of their antivirus programs pick it up?"

Nadia laughed again. "Child's play, boss. The administration's already tapped Jeff to create an AI-based InfoSec platform."

"Yeah, Janus. I heard about it."

"Well, we'll just have Janus recognize it as an authorized program. But I can easily write some code to obfuscate it on the systems Janus doesn't monitor. It won't be hard to do, since I already know the operating systems are their vulnerabilities. What I don't know, our cyber ops team will."

Nadia had no shortage of initiative. The challenge with her was dialing it back and focusing her energy in a positive direction. What unnerved Colt was how quickly she'd devised this plan. That could only mean Jeff Kim had helped, and Jeff always played his own game. Given Kim's previously divided loyalties, Colt was uncomfortable bringing him in on this. He'd only wanted Nadia to consult with him on a technical level. The last time they'd brought Jeff in on an operation, it was only because they had damning leverage over him—proof of espionage—and knew they could control him. Yes, the president's pardon had cleared him of all that (which the NTCU knew about courtesy of Jamie Richter), but it didn't mean Colt trusted him now.

Colt wondered what Kim's price tag would be for this.

Colt admonished Nadia to be careful and not trust Kim with too much. He reminded her he was once a Chinese asset, and that only by the grace of the president and political necessity was he not rotting in a federal prison.

Nadia said she would, but her tone sounded like a teenager saying "Yeah, Dad." That was how she usually spoke, so it was hard to tell, but it didn't leave Colt with a lot of assurance.

Colt thanked the Chief of Station for the use of his secure phone and made his way out of the labyrinthine embassy complex.

By now, he knew Vienna well.

During the month they'd been working here, Colt had spent his scarce free time wandering the city, getting lost and figuring out his way back. He created a mental map of the city, committing the major streets and landmarks to memory. Having been to the city before helped, but he put himself through a crash course in Viennese geography. Colt took cabs and busses and rode the Strassenbahn, Vienna's light rail system. He donned his running gear and jogged through the Stadtpark and along the canal. All to commit the layout to memory so he could plan SDRs and improvise on the fly.

Like he needed to now.

He'd spotted the tail on the train, but he didn't know how long they'd been there. Colt's mind had been on Ava and the mess he'd made of things, not on his environment. That kind of mistake can get you killed. Instead of continuing on, he hopped off the U-Bahn, Vienna's subway, at the Michelbeuern station. There was a hospital, a medical school, and a Strassenbahn station that would have plenty of taxis right outside, so it would be easy to blend into the crowd. This was where the countless hours he'd dedicated to learning the city paid off.

The summer evening was warm and still bright. It didn't get dark until around nine, which had thrown him off his first few nights.

Unfortunately, his assumption about the ubiquity of taxis in relation to subways and hospitals was incorrect, and as Colt stepped into the small plaza in between the looming U-Bahn station, the hospital, and the medical school, he had the distinct feeling of being in a box canyon. He realized that he'd only ever seen this plaza on a map, and hadn't actually been here himself. He didn't have a clear way out.

Colt clocked the tail coming out of the long, descending covered walkway from the U-Bahn station. He jumped on a Strassenbahn headed back in the direction he'd come. Colt put his two pursuers in their early-to-mid thirties, white and athletic, both wearing loose clothing and sunglasses. They quickened strides to make the train, but they didn't run and didn't seem to lose their bearing when they missed it. That told Colt one of two things. Either they had a large surveillance team and could hand it off to another group, or they had another way of tracking him.

Once he was moving, Colt pulled out his phone and called Tony Ikeda. "Hey, man. Did you catch the race this afternoon?" It was a coded message. The phrase "catch" meant Colt was being followed, and "race" indicated it was ongoing. The reference to "afternoon" was a throwaway phrase to make it sound conversational.

"No, I missed it," Ikeda said. The response meaning their team wasn't currently monitoring Colt's position.

"You should try to pick it up on replay if you can. I think it'll be on channel four soon."

"Got it," Tony said and hung up. He'd be running for the car.

"Pick it up" was the code for requesting immediate backup, and "four" referenced one of their five predesignated spots in the city for Ikeda to meet him. Colt hopped off the S-Bahn at the Nussdorfer Strasse station, which was a large gray building with a teal roof, in stark contrast to the usual marble stations with orange tile roofs.

Colt walked east on the sidewalk. To his left was a Jewish cemetery walled off by a tall wire fence and a row of trees. He made the corner of a busy intersection, two to four lanes of traffic coming from three different directions, and passed beneath an elevated S-Bahn track. A red and silver city bus chugged by. The sidewalk swelled with commuters. Colt took the crosswalk heading under the train bridge, then crossed onto Heiligenstäder Strasse. Typical of Western European construction, Viennese buildings were all connected, so that they took up an entire city block with no gaps between them. Often, these structures formed a ring with a courtyard in the center of the block. The architecture, which gave the impression of walking through a labyrinth, was clearly not made for espionage. When trying to lose a tail, there was rarely an alley to slide into when someone needed it. The only option, usually, was to enter a building or a parking garage, both of which could be problematic if the escapee didn't know whether there was a rear exit. Colt briskly walked to the end of the block.

What he needed was a cab. Unfortunately, in the age of ride-sharing and travel apps, taxis in most Western cities were fewer and farther between.

The block's end was welcome chaos. It was a wide intersection with roads curving in from several directions, bars and restaurants hung on every corner, and a large Strassenbahn terminal. Colt crossed to the trian-gular-shaped median in the center of the three-way intersection, pulled his phone out and mimed looking at the map, turning to orient himself to the output on the screen. His eyes lifted to scan his surroundings. He couldn't immediately tell if anyone was following him. The intersection swelled with commuters, tourists, and traffic.

Colt crossed to the Strassenbahn and rode it north several stops to Spit-telau before jumping trains and heading back in the opposite direction along a different line. The light rail took him along the Donaukanal, a trib-utary of the Danube that broke off from the main river and wended through the city.

Colt crossed the Donaukanal on a pedestrian bridge.

When a fresh pair picked him up leaving the Strassenbahn station at Landstrasse, Colt knew they'd coordinated their movements over the radio. This new duo followed him four blocks to the bridge. He caught them when he cut a stair-step to the north. It was a technique for identifying street surveillance by going up a block, cutting over one or two and then going up again. Sometimes they stayed with him, other times they guessed his direction and raced the length of the block, hoping to grab him. Likely, they had help, perhaps from a vehicle or maybe even drones.

Colt stepped off the pedestrian bridge and walked down the block to the meet site, an expansive park in Vienna's northeast quadrant called Krieau, named for the city's famed 18th-eighteenth-century horse racing track. Colt pulled his phone out as he walked, pretending to take a picture of the park's entrance, but he flipped the camera angle to selfie mode. He angled the screen up just slightly so he could see over his shoulder and spotted the two new agents behind him. Colt crossed the street and entered the park.

Tony stood just off the footpath in athletic gear, pretending to stretch. He wore scrambled and encrypted earbuds that linked to his phone. It wasn't as secure as a military tactical radio or some of the specialized gear the covert action teams used, and no electronic signal was unbreakable, so the team still needed to coordinate in code. Tony spotted Colt. A civilian looking at him would see a man in a slight hurry, but Tony could tell Colt was edgy.

He picked up the two guys behind Colt. They were about thirty feet back and closing fast. Ikeda guessed they were looking to make a grab. "Heading out for a few laps," Tony said through the team's closed-loop comms channel.

Tony started jogging.

To his right, he spotted Solomon French filming the park with his smartphone. If he could get Colt's pursuers on camera, they could feed the video into the image rec software in CERBERUS.

Tony closed the distance between himself and Colt's tail. He watched his partner turn north, heading deeper into the crowded park. It was full of unsuspecting people enjoying the warm summer night.

Colt lengthened his stride, and the two men behind him did the same. Tony angled for one of them.

He barreled into one man in the lead and they both crashed to the ground. Tony was on his feet instantly, hands up in apology. "*Entschuldigung! Est tut mir leidt.*" I'm sorry, it's all my fault. The guy was on his feet, face twisted in anger that he fought to control.

Tony wanted to hear him respond so he could gauge the man's nationality.

Instead, his hand dropped to his hip.

Tony was ready for that, too.

He wasn't worried about this pair. Any weapons they had would not be a factor.

The second one grabbed the first, pulling him back. They slowly backed away, not taking their eyes off Tony.

Whoever they were, they were spoiling for a fight.

Just not today.

It took them three hours to get back to the safe house, driving far out of their way and doubling back innumerable times to ensure no one followed them.

It took them less than thirty minutes to pack it up.

Colt rode back with D'Angelo.

French picked up Tony.

Both cars made sure they weren't followed. Colt had a tough choice to make. Assume they were burned, in which case they had to vacate the safe house immediately, or assume the pursuit was an effort to flush them out into the open, in which case they should hunker down in the safe house.

Colt opted for the former.

For tonight, they were spread between three small hotels in Vienna's outlying communities, Jägerwaldsiedlung and Kordonsiedlung. They'd have to figure out a new safe house in the morning, which would require logistical support from Vienna Station.

The group had a back corner table in a local restaurant. The place was empty for a weeknight. Most European restaurants assumed that a table belonged to whoever sat there for the night or until they left. There was no rush to turn the table over for the next patron. Once their food was served, someone came by every thirty minutes or so to see if anyone needed another beer but otherwise left them alone.

There was no one else in the restaurant and the bar was on the other side of the large room.

"Any idea who they are?" D'Angelo asked.

Colt wouldn't normally have authorized a debrief in a gasthaus, but it was their best option for the night.

"No," Colt said.

"The one I bumped didn't say anything," Tony said.

"Vienna still has a Casablanca kind of vibe to it," Colt said. "In some ways, they never shook off the Cold War. The Russians have always been very active here. Iran too, given the IAEA. Though these guys were Caucasian. It wouldn't surprise me to learn they were SVR."

"You don't think the Russians are bugging us, do you?" D'Angelo asked.

"No. Not at all. Sometimes they just pick people up coming out of the embassy to screw with them. Rattle their cage and see what happens. It's a good way of training people for field work. Plus, they're assholes. That said, we can't rule out Archon. They have access to two dedicated private security forces, and those are just the ones we know of."

"You don't think it's Trinity, do you?" Tony asked. "Tell me if I'm skirting a line here, but given how that conversation went . . ." Colt had confided in Tony, because Ikeda knew about his relationship with Ava. The others did not, but didn't interrupt to ask. "You don't think that Trinity tried to move on us, do you? Like, maybe they think we're going to stop them or something?"

Colt took a deep drink of his beer. "God, I hope not. No matter how bad it gets with Ava, I cannot imagine Jason Wilcox ordering them to disrupt us. He created this unit."

"Wait, who are we talking about?" D'Angelo asked.

"Not now," Colt said. "Not relevant."

"Seems like maybe it is?" French interjected.

"Guys. Not. Now."

Ikeda's voice was solemn. "Colt, you and I both know that bad things get justified in the name of the greater good. That happens literally every time our service gets themselves in trouble."

"I think the key question is, are we burned?" French asked. It was his first time in the field and Colt recognized the anxiety.

"Nadia, Tony, and I all had our pictures taken in Monaco, but they didn't connect them to our legends or true names. Other than what just happened, we have no reason to suspect the operation is compromised. I think it's possible this was just the Russians, or someone like them, picking a target at random and seeing what they could do. We can't rule out private intelligence companies either. Solomon, see what you can turn up with CERBERUS. Look for any traffic on a possible botched grab. We've got a tunnel into an SVR system. Use that. We haven't been able to get into Praetorian yet, but maybe try again." Colt didn't think they'd be successful this time, any more than they'd been at the last several attempts to crack through Praetorian's firewall. He just needed to give French something to do to keep him occupied.

"Alison, I'd like you to monitor the Archon messaging system. See if they're talking about this."

"On it."

"Tony, I need you to thoroughly red team our operation. How vulnerable are we here?"

Colt went to Vienna Station the next day and explained the situation to the Chief of Station, or as much of it as he could.

The chief coyly told him they had "a number" of properties in the greater Vienna area that were used for a variety of purposes, and that he'd make one available for Colt's team.

Colt sent a COVCOM message to Thorpe, telling him in code phrases that he wouldn't be sending cables for a time and that the unit was going dark. Because of the risks around Archon breaking their encryption, Colt only relied on his Agency-assigned covert communications tool for emergencies. If their unknown opposition had hacked their comms, they may have puzzled out the COVCOM as well. Let them try to unpack what the string of innocuous gibberish meant.

Solomon interrogated each of their smartphones and laptops, all Agency-issued and heavily modified. He could find no trace that another agency had penetrated any of their devices.

They each took turns flying the micro drones in sweep patterns outside the house, pushing the tiny devices out to their maximum range, hunting for any signs of surveillance.

Colt concluded they'd gotten away clean. Tony assessed their risk of exposure as moderate to high, but he didn't recommend they pull up and set up a base camp somewhere else. At least, not until they had a more definitive confirmation of exposure. Still, he changed the plates on their cars and recommended they establish new surveillance detection routes.

Colt issued new instruction to the team.

Assume we're being watched at all times and act accordingly.

D'Angelo stayed on the Archon messaging network, which contained a hail of furious communication. The day before Colt's tail, Carlos Marin had died in an explosion at his home in Ibiza. Archon's leadership element had dwindled down to just four—Braithwaite, Craddock, Fleet, and Yoon. Plus, whatever odd status they'd conferred on Guy Hawkinson. Archon's people were scared. Half their number was dead, and they had no clue who was behind it. The remaining Brit, Braithwaite, assumed it was an MI6 operation. Craddock thought it was Hawkinson, while Heather Fleet, the Caltech professor, argued it was the work of some unknown third party. Yoon was radio silent, not even responding to his board fellows' missives.

With Solomon's help, D'Angelo hacked into the Spanish National Police's computer network and got access to their case file on Marin's murder. Security camera footage at the home captured a drone hovering in the distance beyond the property line and then something impacting the pool at high velocity, followed by the explosion. They believed it was a suicide drone.

"Colt," D'Angelo called from the upstairs office where she'd set up shop in the new location. "I've got something." Colt climbed the stairs to the second-floor bedroom *cum* Archon manhunt central. Angela had an incredible memory, which meant she wasn't generating reams of documentation and plastering the walls of her room with it. Everything was in her head. If they needed to bug out of there in a hurry, all she'd need to do was grab her computer.

"What's up?" Colt asked.

"Reece Craddock is turning himself in."

16

Vienna, Austria

"Reece Craddock," D'Angelo said. Craddock's face appeared on the television screen, hooked through her laptop. "Considered by many to be the godfather of cybersecurity. His 'C-Dock Virus Protection Suite' was one of the first and most successful commercial antivirus programs available. After graduating Caltech in 1979, he worked at Xerox PARC and then for the Rand Corporation, where he first learned about computer viruses. He left Rand to form Craddock and Associates in 1986. In 1987, he releases the C-Dock antivirus program. By 1992, he IPOs the company, and he's personally worth about five hundred million. Around this time, Heather Fleet, his classmate from Caltech, recruits him into Trinity. Craddock stays on the fringes of organization, not really getting involved, mostly jumping in on information security topics and voicing concerns about digital surveillance." D'Angelo advanced to the next slide, showing Craddock's rap sheet.

"Fast forward to 2004. Craddock is now wanted for tax evasion and defrauding the U.S. government. Now, what's _really_ interesting about this is that at exactly the same time, news is breaking about the existence of ECHELON." ECHELON, the NSA's sweeping, global electronic surveillance program created in the 1970s to snoop on the Soviets. By the early twenty-first century, the NSA, in collaboration with multiple foreign governments, was using ECHELON to eavesdrop on electronic communications across the globe in the name of counterterrorism. Though full disclosure wouldn't come for another decade, by 2004 investigative journalists had uncovered the program's existence in an exposé that received widespread attention. A former CIA director had confirmed but downplayed ECHELON's existence back in 2000. "Reece Craddock went on the offensive, arguing on television, in the press, and online that his tax problems were because of whistle-blowing related to ECHELON."

"It's really strange to me that someone that so . . . unglued . . . could make their way onto Archon's board," Ikeda said.

Solomon French added, "Yeah, I always thought Craddock was the mayor of crazytown."

"I think that was mostly an act, a ploy for the government to dismiss him and underestimate him. However, we do have clear evidence that sustained time on the run takes a heavy psychological toll, so some of the post-2004 behavior may be legitimate. And he did a lot of coke."

"I don't want us to get too far off track," Colt said. "But Craddock actually disclosed ECHELON's name and gave the first actual evidence of that, right? Do we think that was at all connected to the Trinity–Archon split?"

D'Angelo smiled wryly. "You're a great ringer, Colt. My estimation is that he learned of ECHELON through his involvement with Trinity and disclosed it after the split. I think it was a warning shot that Archon used to warn their former Trinity peers and governments about the damage they could do if pursued. The ECHELON disclosure happened at the absolute worst time for the Bush Administration. The Iraq War was going badly at this point. There were rumblings that the WMD justification was incorrect, if not outright falsified, and the public was getting early indications of 'enhanced interrogation.' This started a downward spiral of trust in government we still have yet to recover from."

"So, you think it was a calculated move?" Colt asked.

"I do. To Tony's point, I think Craddock is unstable, which explains this move in part. The other side of this is that there have always been two wings within Archon. One is what I'd call the Wales–Hawkinson side, which is the group who believes AGI is a path to power, to reshape the world order according to their designs. Quentin and Guy were both soldiers who experienced the worst of warfare. Both were deeply patriotic and wanted to ensure 9/11 and—this is important—the subsequent twenty years of war could never happen again. The others, like Craddock, Fleet, and Yoon, they represent the more academic and futurist side. They believed AGI was the pathway to a better world, but that the world wouldn't get there on its own. To that faction, the only way to achieve this utopian outcome is to brute force it. They didn't want violence."

"How does that play into Craddock turning himself in?" Ikeda asked.

"Wales and Hawkinson disagreed on a fundamental point. Guy insisted they elevate him to the board because of the financial and personal sacrifices he'd made. Wales said he wasn't ready. They believed Guy was too visible. Craddock thinks these are all revenge killings for not elevating Hawkinson to the board. Remember, nobody knows where Guy is, so Craddock thinks he went into hiding before striking."

"Archon can't protect him, but Craddock thinks a government can?" Colt asked. His mind immediately went to the DNA-targeted xenobot weapon.

"I can't argue his mind state, Colt. I can only tell you where the profile and the analysis take me."

"That's fair. Who's Craddock turning himself into?"

"Europol."

Now *that* was interesting. Europol was the European Police Force, a kind of multinational FBI, which had statutory authority to make arrests. It was frequently conflated with INTERPOL, which was a coordination and information-sharing body among the world's law enforcement agencies, but INTERPOL couldn't actually arrest suspects, whereas Europol could.

"Craddock doesn't trust the United States government, but he won't turn himself over to an authoritarian either."

"Why not go to the Swiss? Seek asylum?" French asked.

"Hawkinson based his technology group in Geneva," Colt said. "Samantha Klein, who I assume lined up with the Wales faction, had one agent in Swiss intelligence that we know about. The Swiss also have a highly capable multi-domain electronic surveillance platform called

ONYX. We learned the hard way that Archon was all over it." Colt looked over to Ikeda, who nodded grimly.

"My guess is that Craddock is trying to leverage Europol to make it more 'official' from a law enforcement standpoint, as opposed to going to the UN or some similar body. He hopes to win them over and then use that to broker a deal with the U.S.."

"When does this go down?"

"He's still negotiating with them, but I think soon," D'Angelo said. "His tradecraft is pretty bad for someone as paranoid as he is. Solomon got onto Craddock's smartphone by hacking through their chat system. I've been listening in on every conversation he's had with Europol. Ready for the kicker? He's planning to turn himself in here."

"In Vienna?" Tony asked.

"Yeah," D'Angelo said, nodding. "Europol HQ is in The Hague, which he won't touch with a ten-foot pole because of the heavy U.S. presence. NATO's headquarters isn't far from there. Plus, like Colt said, Vienna is just different. It feels more isolated."

"Alison, that was exceptional work. Thank you," Colt said. "First up, we need to get Special Agent Ricci here immediately. I'll handle that. Tony, take Solomon and do some recon of the Vienna International Airport."

"What are you thinking?"

"Remember how we got Liu?" Colt knew that was all he needed to say for Ikeda to know exactly what he meant.

Tony smiled and nodded. "That'll work," he said.

When they'd learned Liu Che was going to attend a diplomatic function in Geneva, Colt and Tony impersonated chauffeurs and, having already hacked his phone with LONGBOW, guided him to their vehicle. If they could get Craddock's flight plan, they could do the same thing here.

Colt smiled. It felt good to be back on offense.

Keith Ricci took the first available flight to Vienna. Colt had Tony pick him up, which gave him a chance to test the routes they planned to use with

Craddock. Tony briefed the FBI agent on the way back, while Colt made an extremely long SDR to get to the embassy.

Colt had to ask the Chief of Station for another favor.

They'd need a vehicle to capture Craddock, and it would have to be something that could pass as executive transport. Colt asked the chief if he had any connections they could use and, of course, he did. Because of its proximity to Eastern Europe and the former Soviet Union, Vienna remained the European Division's nexus for dirty tricks. The chief had ways of getting clean vehicles off the books. They arranged for a three-year-old Audi A8 L that had previously been part of a VIP fleet. Colt had a limited operational budget. When he asked the chief who was paying for this, he just smiled and replied, "somebody."

Colt apologized to the chief for coming, again, hat-in-hand. He wasn't part of the man's staff and was drawing on his resources. The old operator simply told Colt that the DNCS had given him two instructions. One, get Colt and his team whatever help they needed, and two, don't ask any questions. "I've been at this a long time, Colt," he said. "I can connect the dots."

Colt took the opportunity at the embassy to contact Nadia. She'd been at Jeff Kim's for the last week working on their quantum tracing program. Nadia told him the work was going well, and she'd report back as soon as they had a viable prototype.

Colt picked up the vehicle from a support asset outside the city the following day.

That night, the team met again in the living room so they could take advantage of the big-screen TV to project the briefing material.

"Team, here's the ops plan," Colt said, standing next to the TV. "Tony and I will be in the Audi. I'm driving and don't show my face to Craddock because there's a chance Archon can identify me. Tony will handle the interactions. He'll meet the plane and guide Craddock to the car outside the private aviation terminal. Vienna Station has a support asset at the airport who is going to run interference for us with the terminal and make sure we have the requisite permissions. Ricci will stand next to the car, looking like an executive protection detail. You bring sunglasses?"

"I did."

"Good. We've got an earpiece for you as well. We'll all be up on the net, and Tony will communicate movement. Make everything look professional. Tony guides Craddock to the car. Ricci, you greet him, and once you've got a hand on his arm to guide him into the back seat, identify yourself as FBI and place him under arrest." Ricci nodded. "Hood goes on and we bring him to Site Two to question him." Site Two was a small house in a village east of the airport, a secure location the Chief of Station had helped them set up,

"Why not just put Craddock on a plane and extradite him?" Ricci asked.

"Because we need answers now. If we take him back, and he gets put into the system. We lose days, maybe weeks."

"And if he doesn't talk?"

"You're here to negotiate on behalf of the Justice Department."

"I need an attorney for that. The DoJ has prosecutors positioned at certain embassies, but they could send someone here."

"Not yet. We can't risk the leak. Offer Craddock whatever deal they'll let you make, but he needs to tell us how Archon is breaking encryption and where they're doing it from. As soon as that happens, we extradite him. Use his fear of Hawkinson as leverage to get what we need."

"What's our response if he says we can't protect him?" D'Angelo asked.

"He obviously thinks someone can, or he wouldn't be turning himself in. I think the answer is that if he tells us where the quantum array is, we can apprehend Hawkinson."

Ricci pressed the line of inquiry. "What if he doesn't know? And what if it's not Hawkinson?"

"If he genuinely doesn't know," Colt said. "Then you get credit for nabbing an Archon board member and known fugitive. He can help us bag as many Archon elements as we can. And we rely on our Plan B, which is what Nadia's working on with Jeff Kim." Ricci nodded, mollified. "Tony's job is to separate Craddock from any security personnel or aides he might have with him. Mission radio codes are in your inboxes, so please memorize them. If Tony sees Craddock has security with him, he'll say 'turbulence' over the net. If it looks clear, he'll say 'jet lag.'" Colt paused for questions. "Rehearsals start tomorrow."

They practiced the grab for four days while they waited for news of Craddock's next move. There were no new security breaches reported, though the British intelligence scandal was proving to be disastrous enough. Britain's relations with their neighbors on the continent, already strained under Brexit, had become the worst they'd been in modern history thanks to the leaked revelation. There was an unwritten rule in espionage that everyone spies on everyone else. Just don't get caught. The intelligence services all understood this, on a level, but their citizens did not. Nor did their elected officials. The aftershocks were particularly damaging within NATO, who often shifted operational command between American and British forces. Some NATO members refused to serve with UK units or under British commanders. It made an already complicated security situation around supporting Ukraine potentially dangerous.

Each CIA station in Europe now worked around the clock, watching for the Russians to take advantage of the situation.

Meanwhile, Craddock appeared to be losing his mind over the pace of the European law enforcement bureaucracy. In fact, he threatened to contact the Malaysians and ask them if they wanted the scoop (although he didn't explain in his messages or phone calls what "the scoop" was). Craddock's Europol contact was presumably trying to vet this deal with his superiors, who were no doubt also supporting the EU's emergent and sweeping counterintelligence crisis. They set the date for a week out. Craddock argued that he needed to come in *now*, so they agreed on two days hence.

"Here comes the part where we all get fired," Colt said to Tony that night. They were stretching their legs in the woods behind the safe house.

"Maybe having a Fed watch dogging us wasn't the best idea."

"Man, we are so far outside the NTCU's mandate on this," Colt said.

Tony smiled coldly. "Welcome to the CIA, my friend."

Europol expected to meet Reece Craddock at the Vienna Airport VIP terminal in two days to take him into custody. To remedy that, Solomon French, spoofing Craddock, sent a message from the fugitive tech exec's phone to his Europol contact with an updated arrival time of ten p.m., claiming as Reece that he preferred to arrive when it was dark. It was twelve hours later than his original arrival time. When he'd first gotten onto Craddock's phone via the communication tool, French had deployed a version of the LONGBOW program, which gave him full control of the device.

Colt and Tony walked inside, then did a final verbal walkthrough.

Given Craddock's insistence that he come in as soon as possible, they didn't believe they could push it out any further than twelve hours. And this also required someone to be on Craddock's phone to intercept any communication to or from Europol. They'd engaged the NTCU Ops Center at Langley, which was continually staffed, who would monitor the phone while the Austria team slept.

Colt reminded the ops desk of the stakes.

If Europol somehow discovered that the NTCU had infiltrated their communication loop with Craddock, it would create a scandal as big as what their MI6 counterparts had forced on themselves. Europol was an essential partner in the fight against transnational crime and American law enforcement agencies relied heavily on their cooperation.

Failure was not an option.

The morning was gray and cold for late summer.

The heat, at least in Austria, had finally broken.

Colt and Tony both wore off-the-rack black suits. D'Angelo thought it made them look more like professional drivers than properly tailored suits would. He had a point.

Vienna's airport sat in a wide tract of farmland just south of the Danube.

Colt, Tony, and Ricci drove along the perimeter road leading to the VIP terminal. The contrast to any major American airport was stark. All that separated them from the flight line was a ten-foot chain-link fence with barbed wire.

"Do we think Europol has an advance team?" Ricci asked.

It was a fair question and something Colt and Tony had debated several times over the last few days of prep. The logic of the advance team was that given Craddock's status as a flight risk (Europol was not aware of his status within Archon) and his erratic nature, Europol would want to have the airport covered well in advance in case Craddock tried something. The NTCU-engineered delay would raise the level of attention.

Ultimately, Colt and Tony did not agree on the point.

"I would," Tony said.

"I think they will," Colt agreed. "But I also think they won't be here twelve hours in advance."

Their other risk, and there was no way to manage this, was that flight plans were easily discoverable. There were several publicly available flight trackers. While one couldn't glean the passenger manifest from the flight number, it was simple enough to use other data points to figure that out. For example, if Europol knew Craddock's point of origin, all they needed to do was match the tracks. If Europol was watching the inbound flights to Vienna International, they could figure out that a plane landing at ten in the morning probably had Craddock on it.

Colt pulled through the roundabout and took the exit for the VIP terminal, a wide, squat building of alternating gray and green glass. They were in position an hour prior to the scheduled landing. They exited the vehicle and executed their assignments. Ricci's job was to look for indicators that Europol had indeed brought an advance team. Tony was tasked with approaching the terminal employees loitering outside to inform them they were waiting for a pickup. Colt entered the building and connected with the support asset. The man passed the code phrase and said everything was ready. He told Colt that an airport employee would escort "the package" through customs and to this main entry hall to meet them. Colt thanked him and returned to the car.

"I don't see anything that looks like cops," Ricci said.

Solomon was posted a few miles west of the airport in a field, flying the micro drones parallel to each other over the state road and the Autobahn, the two paths that led to the airport. He'd signal any approaching law enforcement vehicles. D'Angelo sat in the car with him, monitoring Craddock's phone for any attempt to contact his Europol handler.

Colt, Tony, and Ricci passed the hour in the Audi.

"Go time," Colt said, once they confirmed Craddock's plane was on its final approach.

Tony and Ricci stepped out. Ricci secured his sunglasses, despite the gloomy clouds, stuck in his earpiece, and took up his position next to the Audi. They did a final comm check.

Tony Ikeda walked into the terminal.

Reece Craddock looked like his reputation.

He was tall and wiry, tanned and sun-spotted with hard lines creased on his face. The stresses of his choices had clearly taken their toll. He appeared gangly and haggard. His chin-length hair, still brown at the roots, was faded gray and stringy from salt spray, and his mottled Van Dyke was peppered with white. His perpetually narrowed eyes immediately scanned the corners of the entryway when he exited the private customs room. Craddock wore a blue suit and white shirt without a tie. It appeared fresh, and Tony suspected he had just put it on. A tactical-style backpack was slung over one shoulder, and a concierge followed with the rest of his luggage. Other than the attendant, he was alone.

Tony closed the distance between them in purposeful steps.

"Good morning, Mr. Craddock," he said. "My name is John Tanaka, with Guardian Protective Services. Europol hired us to bring you into Vienna proper."

"Nobody told me about this," Craddock said, wary.

Tony immediately assessed him for visual clues that he was about to run. He watched Craddock's eyes to see if they instinctively looked for exits, his shoulders for subtle shifts in body weight that would presage movement. Craddock fidgeted, practically vibrating out of his shoes. He looked like a junkie three hours overdue for a fix.

But he didn't run.

"I'm sorry for the inconvenience, sir. They felt it was best to keep a low profile. This is fairly standard procedure with high-value guests."

Craddock didn't relax, but he also didn't bolt.

Tony made a show of raising his wrist to his mouth. "I have the principle. Heading to transport now." He turned to Craddock, the mic still live. "No jet lag, I hope."

"I could use a coffee."

"Very good, sir. Right this way."

Tony led Craddock out of the terminal to the idling Audi. Tony stepped behind him as Craddock approached Ricci, who opened the rear door.

Tony stepped forward, just behind Craddock.

When Craddock was at the car door, Ricci said, "Reece Craddock, I am Special Agent Keith Ricci, and you are under arrest."

17

Vienna, Austria

Tony cuffed Craddock in one expert motion, and they had him in the car before he'd even had time to finish exclaiming "What the—" and slammed the door on his expletive.

Thirty seconds later, the car was moving.

Ricci rode in the back and Mirandized Craddock before they'd left the airport grounds, following a road named for the late, legendary Formula One driver Niki Lauda. Colt sped up to the end of the road and turned east onto the state route that ran along the airport. Site Two was in the village of Fischamend, just east of the airport. They'd question Craddock there and signal the Agency bird, currently parked on the ramp at Ramstein Air Base in Germany, when they were ready for pickup. They'd fly Craddock back to the States once they had the information they needed. Colt and Ricci would fly with Craddock while Ikeda, D'Angelo, and French broke down and packed the gear and sanitized the safe house.

"Colt," French said over the net. His voice was heavy and nervous. "I've got two vehicles moving at a high rate of speed on State Road Nine. They are Mercedes G-Wagons. I've got two more BMWs on the A4."

"Copy that," Colt said. "You see lights and sirens?"

"Negative," French replied.

"Lights and sirens? What the hell is this?" Craddock said. "Who are you people?"

"I already answered that question," Ricci said.

"You're cutting out Europol?" Craddock asked. Clearly, he wasn't so addled as to not understand exactly what was going on here.

"Colt, they are closing fast. Drone has the Mercs doing a hundred and ten."

Colt put the pedal to the floor and the Audi's engine roared as they put on speed. Colt faded lanes and glided around cars. He'd doubled the posted speed limit for this road and nearly every pass or lane change got him an angry honk. They blew past the airport, following the road's curve as it cleared a forest on the left side, showing the A4 Autobahn next to them.

Colt saw the G-Wagons in his rearview.

Mercedes G-Classes were the German equivalent of the Land Rover Defender, a commercial version of a military tactical vehicle. Despite their boxy stature and sharp angles, G-Class SUVs were fast. The Audi A8 sported a twin turbo V8, and while it was certainly slower than its sportier twin, the S8 (which Colt now wished they had instead), Colt reasoned it should be enough to keep distance from the G-Wagons. He was actually more concerned about the two BMWs that were likely to intercept them.

"I've got the G-Wagons in view," he said. "No lights, no sirens."

If these were law enforcement vehicles, they'd have identified themselves as soon as they had the Audi in view.

"Mr. Craddock, I'm getting the impression somebody doesn't like you very much," Colt said.

"Who do you think is following you?" Ricci asked.

"How the hell should I know? I just got off a goddamn airplane," Craddock thundered.

"We can't help you if you don't cooperate," Ricci said.

"Who's going to help *you*?" Craddock spat.

Years before, Audi adopted a button-activated, magnetic parking brake. Right about now, Colt really missed the hand brake. That would've made what he was about to do a hell of a lot easier. You couldn't power slide with a button.

"Hold on," he said calmly.

"I'm not belted in!" Craddock shouted.

Colt hit the brakes and cranked the wheel to the right as he blasted through an intersection. He pushed the gas pedal to the floor, engine roaring in protest. They shot down a long street through an industrial air park. Craddock screamed random nonsense from the back seat, panic words. Colt pulled a hard left at the end of the road, aiming them east again. He saw one of the G-Wagons in the rearview made the turn and the other kept going on their original route. They were looking to close them off.

Colt floored the accelerator again.

"Traffic circle up ahead," Tony said. Colt saw in his peripheral that Ikeda had his phone out, navigating. "This puts us on the road we've been on. Watch out for that other Merc," he warned.

Colt spotted a wedge-shaped parking lot that connected this road with the main street, both ending in a traffic circle. He braked hard and turned left, hoping to throw off one of their pursuers. He cut a hard right, accelerated, and hit the intersection going forty. The trick worked. One of the SUVs hit the circle, veered abruptly, and collided with a station wagon.

Colt blasted through the intersection.

"Okay, four blocks up, you're looking for a left on Donauarmstrasse."

Colt watched in the rearview as the SUV that had crashed into the station wagon reversed and swung around the traffic circle after them.

"Those guys are definitely not cops," he muttered.

"Mr. Craddock, we know you're a member of Archon's board," Ricci said. "Whoever is killing the other board members is coming for you now. Who is it?"

"I don't know what you're talking about!" Craddock screeched.

"Guns out," Colt shouted. "Get down." In the rearview, he saw a machine pistol extend out of the passenger side. Tony dropped his phone, drew his sidearm, and lowered his own window.

Colt drew his pistol and did the same.

The turn would be tricky and he needed to time it exactly, because it required going across an oncoming lane and now there would be bullets. At the combat driving course, they'd trained to shoot on the move. Colt knew he could hit the Mercedes, but the other cars and nearby houses created an unacceptable risk of civilian casualties.

"Here we go," Colt said, and braked.

They heard the staccato rip of automated fire behind them.

Colt cranked the wheel hard to the left. The car fishtailed, tires screaming. They felt a blunt crash, and the car jolted hard in the other direction. Colt had mistimed the turn by a millisecond, and an oncoming car had clipped them into the intersection. They heard metallic clangs in rapid succession as bullets streaked across the Audi's trunk and the rear window became a spiderweb of cracks. Colt fought the steering wheel as the car fishtailed. They slid perpendicular with the street.

Trying to regaining control, Colt punched the gas and pulled the wheel hard to the left.

One G-Wagon cleared the intersection and fired a quick burst from the machine pistol. Colt pulled away at the last instant. Bullets peppered the low building next to them.

"Tony," Colt said, warningly.

"On it," Ikeda replied, unbuckling. He popped out of his window as Colt blasted down the residential street and fired four times, each shot hitting the Mercedes' windshield. Tony dropped back into the seat and buckled. "This is the last time I get into a car with you, McShane. This is Buenos Aires all over again."

"What the hell was Buenos Aires!" Craddock yelled from the back.

"Shut *up*," Colt and Tony both said.

Colt raced down the wide street. Already, he could see the overpass at the far side.

"Looks like the road doglegs to the right, underneath the bridge," Tony said. "So let's not do this at sixty."

"Right," Colt said. The rearview mirror was worthless because he couldn't see out the back window, but clocked one of the SUVs in his side mirror. "I've got one coming up the left side."

"I see the other on the right," Tony said, looking at his mirror.

Colt looked up at the bridge. "This is going to be close."

"I hate close," Craddock whined.

Colt drifted the car left and then right, weaving an *S* pattern on the street, trying to deny the shooters a clear line of sight and not giving the drivers a chance to overtake him.

"Coming up on the left side. Keith, I need you to get ready to shoot."

"I'm on it," the FBI agent said.

They had the length of three house lots to the end of the neighborhood. Then, it was about a block until the overpass. If Colt wasn't the first one through, it was all over.

The SUV on the left sped up to overtake them. "Get ready," Colt said. Ricci dropped his window.

Colt tapped the brakes.

The Mercedes jerked forward alongside them.

Ricci emptied the magazine into the Mercedes. The rear window shattered and bullets scattered across the vehicle's right side. It shook violently and Colt could see the driver furiously struggling for control. Ricci might well have hit him.

The Mercedes crashed into a parked car at nearly seventy.

The SUV's tail vaulted into the air and crashed down with tremendous force. The car it hit crumpled with the impact.

Colt put on more speed, aimed for the bridge, and tried to put the second SUV in the dust.

"Good shooting," Ikeda said.

"Yeah, well, I'd feel better about it if I knew who I was shooting at." Ricci replied.

That makes two of us, Colt thought sourly.

He could confidently rule out his theory that his tail last week was an opportunistic Russian surveillance op. The day after he'd talked to Ava, Carlos Marin had died in a suicide drone attack. Then, two NTCU analysts concluded that the bird impact on Rhett Bolton's air taxi was likely a coordinated drone strike. They'd mocked up a simulator and tested it convincingly enough that Thorpe requested access to the wreckage from the NTSB.

Only a powerful and highly technical actor could carry out assassinations like this. In Colt's mind, it could only be Trinity. Hawkinson was on the run and his assets frozen. Even if he'd squirreled funds away in sheltered accounts, he couldn't possibly afford this. And it seemed unlikely he could coordinate such a campaign while remaining hidden from everyone. Colt just couldn't believe Ava would risk his life to get to Craddock.

Couldn't believe, or chose not to believe it.

Nothing made sense.

Colt let up on the gas, letting gravity do its work. He didn't want to use the brakes, which would signal to the remaining SUV behind him that they were slowing. Roads beneath bridges collected sand and gravel, so he didn't want to have to go heavy on the brakes underneath it. A spinout at these speeds would send them off the road.

They sped through the shadows beneath the bridge and Colt saw the curve was easier than Tony told him, so he accelerated, taking the turn at forty. The road rose slightly, trees whipping by on the left. There was a steep embankment on the other side leading up to the Autobahn.

Colt looked down the road. They flew by a channel that connected with the Danube. Up ahead, he saw what looked like a dirt road perpendicular to this one. It'd be a ninety-degree turn, but he could make it. And the best part was, it was through a forest.

"Keith, have you reloaded?"

"Doing it now," he said.

"I'm going to slow down to make a turn. When I say 'go,' fire everything you've got out the back window. We need to back that other Merc off."

"Got it."

"I don't like this," Craddock said.

"Get ready," Colt said, ignoring Craddock and speeding the car down the street. He flicked his glance to the side mirror, confirming the second SUV was closing in.

"Go!"

Colt hit the brakes, screeching the tires and sending white smoke into the air.

Ricci turned in his seat, fired twice to clear the window, and then emptied the magazine at the G-Wagon. Colt rode the brake through the turn, pressed the accelerator to the floor, and crashed through a chain barrier blocking the road.

"I believe we've just broken a law," Tony said dryly.

The Audi bounced hard on the dirt road and sent a cloud of dust up behind them. Colt could see a little out the rear window now that Ricci had opened a large hole. Because of the dust behind them, he couldn't tell if the Merc had made the turn or not.

The tree cover lasted about a tenth of a mile. Then they crossed a small, green field framed by tracts of forest. The road ended up ahead, at the tree-lined river, with a frontage road running next to it. Colt hit the brakes and turned hard to the right, power sliding around the tight corner before hitting the gas again. The Mercedes cleared the trees just as he did. He cursed. It looked like Ricci had only slowed it down.

The Audi rocketed down the dirt road, bouncing and sliding. A murky channel of brown water appeared on the left.

"They're gaining," Tony said.

Colt put on more speed.

They raced the length of the field, blasting through a copse of trees dangerously close to taking over the road. Branches clawed at the car as they screamed past. Colt hoped the Vienna station chief knew a good body shop. They blasted out the trees just in time to see their dirt road ending abruptly in the field of golden grass. The Audi plowed through the field, shaking and bouncing hard, its suspension mercilessly tortured. The Mercedes was going to eat this up. Colt spotted a two-lane highway on the far side of the field, maybe fifty yards away.

He pushed the accelerator to the floor and prayed the car would hold out long enough to get there. The ground rose slightly here, and the car launched off it. There was a brief sensation of flight and the Audi crashed down in the dirt. Craddock, still not belted, bounced off the car's ceiling and cried out in pain. The impact broke any remaining rear window glass loose, showering the two in the back seat. The Audi's front end bounced, and dirt and grass geysered into the air.

They hit the highway with a screech of tires, sparks, and groaning metal.

Colt spotted a building up ahead. If they could get there before the Mercedes cleared the field, they might set up an ambush and end this thing.

Colt laid on speed.

"Oh, shit," he said.

A pair of black BMW sedans blocked the road.

Colt checked the rearview and, through broken glass, saw the Merc bound over that small hill and slide onto the highway, trailing a cloud of dirt and grass.

The building up ahead on the right looked to be a restaurant, its parking lot fronted by the road. One of the BMWs was in the lot and the other was in the road, angled to block traffic on either side.

Colt calculated his odds. He could speed up to fool them into thinking he was charging, then bank the car right around them. It was risky and dangerous, but risky and dangerous also seemed to be the only two options left.

He saw now that one of the BMW's trunks was open.

They heard the explosion before they saw it and Colt instinctively hit the brakes. Even in the rearview, the flash was so bright he had to squint against it. By the time he looked, the Mercedes was a decelerating, rolling fireball.

Colt skidded the car to a stop.

What in the hell had just happened?

Four men emerged from the BMWs.

Tony and Colt were out of their seats, weapons drawn and using the doors for cover. Ricci pushed Craddock to the floor and covered him.

The reflected light of the still intensely burning SUV lit the car, and now they heard the low rumbles of combustion.

With Ricci covering Craddock, the opposition outnumbered them two to one. Their best bet to get Craddock out of here was to draw fire away from the car and give Ricci a chance to escape.

"What's the plan?" Tony said, as if reading Colt's thoughts.

"I think you and I draw fire. Keith gets in the front seat and takes off. Gets Craddock to the safe house and we call for emergency exfil."

"I'm covered in glass back here," Craddock said from the floor. "And I'm suing the shit out of you."

"Well," Colt replied through gritted teeth, "you're free to do that just as soon as we prosecute you for tax evasion, wire fraud—oh, and terrorism."

That quieted him down.

"You're thinking these guys are Trinity?"

"That's where all the arrows point," Colt said.

But it didn't explain the SUV spontaneously exploding. Unless, maybe, Ricci hit a fuel line when he shot them. He emptied a magazine into the front, so it was possible, but it still seemed too convenient.

"Put your weapons down," one of the men said in accented English. That was an Israeli accent. So it was Trinity, then. Ava would have a deep bench of former Mossad operatives to draw from. "We're not here to hurt you."

Colt looked at his battered, bullet-ridden car with a chagrinned expression. "Could've fooled me," he said. "We're not turning Craddock over to you." Colt declined his head to hide his lips from the four men opposite them. They were about fifty feet away. He spoke in a harsh whisper to Tony. "I don't want to kill these guys if we can help it. On my signal, let's open fire and run to either side of the road, split their return fire. Keith, you get up here and drive."

Tony and Ricci both rogered.

"We aren't here for Craddock," the man said. "At least, not entirely."

Colt shouted back, "Again, could've fooled me. You've been chasing us from the airport."

"No," he said, and motioned to the burning SUV that had finally rolled to a stop on the other side of the road. "We were chasing them."

Colt's body jolted with a surge of fear. If Trinity's operatives were trying to kill Craddock, and they were in what was left of that SUV, then who in the hell was Colt talking to?

Two of the men fanned out of their cars, weapons covering Colt and Tony. The one he'd been speaking to stepped out from behind the door, pistol in one hand and a sat phone in the other.

"Boss wants to talk to you," he said gruffly.

18

Queenstown, Maryland

Thorpe cruised slowly down the long, wooded driveway and pulled into the carport. He sat there for several minutes, unsure of what to do next. He knew what he needed to do, but the act, actually going through with it, was something else. Thorpe's hand brushed past his service pistol on the way to unhook his seatbelt.

This conversation was going to go one of two ways.

Either he was going to get honest answers and valuable intelligence, or he was going to arrest a former deputy director of the Central Intelligence Agency for murder.

It didn't matter that Rhett Bolton was a leading member of a techno-terrorist. He was an American citizen, and he had a constitutionally protected right to trial. It didn't matter who Trinity was, what good they'd done, or how they'd supported the NTCU and the Intelligence Community in the past. If they'd truly become a vigilante group, taking the law into their own hands, there would be consequences.

Thorpe was, first and last, a cop.

He'd embraced the NTCU's mission and was proud to lead it. Blending intelligence and law enforcement capabilities enabled them to prosecute advanced technology threats that didn't stop at national borders. But the more time Thorpe spent in that shadowy world of invisible lines, the less comfortable he was. He feared they were moving into a world where the old rules no longer applied.

Thorpe got out of his car and reluctantly approached Wilcox's front door. He'd said that he needed to come out here to discuss an operational matter, and it was best if they didn't do it at Langley. If Thorpe truly had to arrest the man, he didn't want to do it at CIA Headquarters. They owed Wilcox that much, at least.

Thorpe rang the bell, and Wilcox answered. For once, Jason Wilcox looked retired, in a Tommy Bahama polo and shorts. They shook hands, and Wilcox invited him in.

"Get you a beer?"

"No, thank you. It's a long drive back to Virginia. And I've got more to do tonight."

"I can imagine. Water it is, then."

"Is your wife at home?"

"No, when you said we needed to talk about something mission related, I asked her if she could have dinner with some friends, give us space to talk."

Thorpe nodded and followed Wilcox into the living room. The old spymaster walked over to the bar and fixed himself a manhattan and asked Thorpe again if he was sure he didn't want anything. *Put him at ease*, Thorpe told himself. "Well, if you insist. I'll take a bourbon on the rocks." Wilcox poured two fingers of Bardstown and dropped in a couple of ice cubes. He handed the tumbler to Thorpe, and they sat, Thorpe on the couch and Wilcox in an Eames chair.

"So, shoot. What's got you coming all the way out here after work?"

Thorpe took a sip of the bourbon and set it down on the side table.

He had twenty-five years in the FBI and, by his estimation, had conducted thousands of suspect interviews. *Jesus,* he thought, *is that really what this is?* A suspect interview with Jason Wilcox? It didn't seem possible.

What he did understand was the crushing reality that in the thousands of interviews he'd given, this was the hardest question he'd ever asked.

"Jason, you and I go back pretty far, so I'm going to spare you the bullshit and the preamble. Four members of Archon's leadership team have been murdered in the last month. One of them is an American citizen. I need to know if your organization is responsible, and I need to know right now."

Jason Wilcox calmly sipped his manhattan, said nothing for a moment and simply stared at Thorpe with those intense eyes. He set the drink down.

"I will remind you that Archon murdered a member of the British Parliament," Wilcox replied. "They brought down our air traffic control system and caused a fuel crisis. They've fomented riots among our citizens and nearly pushed us into a war with the Russians."

"Jason, it doesn't matter how bad they are. What matters is how we respond."

"On that, we agree."

"So that justifies murder?"

"I never said we murdered anybody. You and Colt are the ones who keep bringing that up. But, maybe the threat has grown beyond the rules we have to fight them. I created your unit to deal with this threat and got you dialed in with the White House because you couldn't do this without a direct line to the policymakers. I hoped the law would catch up and pace the threats, but it hadn't. Hell, even if Preston Hawkinson wasn't undermining every gain we tried to make, it still wouldn't move fast enough."

"Jason, you haven't answered the question," Thorpe said softly.

"Your people told us we couldn't sit on the sidelines anymore. You told me we had to act."

"I think we can both agree that sometimes Colt's mouth gets in between his brain and his better judgement."

"I'm not talking about that," Wilcox said. Thorpe noticed he never gesticulated, never made wild, angry gestures the way some men did. No, Wilcox was a man of cold and purposeful fury, and Thorpe did not enjoy being on the other side of it. "The NTCU told us that Archon was Trinity's problem, something we created somehow, and we bore the responsibility for solving it."

Thorpe barked a laugh. "That's your euphemism for assassination? Problem solving?"

"Will, I didn't kill anyone, nor did I order it done," Wilcox said coldly.

Thorpe's law school training came back to him then, the precisely honed skill at breaking down the logic of an argument. He instinctively deconstructed Wilcox's every word and assessed it. The man clearly knew how to maneuver from his long years in the Agency and throughout Washington's corridors of power. He'd used many of the same words that the national security advisor, even the president, used in conversations not that different from this one. They spoke of an outcome they wanted achieved, an objective met, an end state . . . never giving the actual order to do it. Plausible deniability was the time-honored Washington term for it.

No, Wilcox would be too smart to give the order. He'd simply say the world would be better off if Archon was gone.

"The problem you need to solve for, Will, is who figured out how to lay all of our secrets bare. Because I'll guarantee you that whoever is doing that is probably the one killing Archon's board members."

"But why?"

"This is the conversation we've been trying to have with you since this shit started. All the intelligence points to Guy Hawkinson attempting a hostile takeover. He's on the run, you've seized all of his assets, and, most critically, branded him a traitor. Guy Hawkinson thinks he's the Keyser Söze of the American Way. Then Archon dismissed him without so much as a 'Thanks for your service.'"

"I sense there's a 'but' coming," Thorpe said, and reached for his drink, which he was now very glad he had accepted. Wilcox had flipped this dialogue like a judo master. He'd accepted Thorpe's aggressive energy and spun it back around to redirect it where he wanted it to go.

"There is indeed," Wilcox said, the old wry light flashing in his eyes. He took a drink and set his glass back down. "Guy Hawkinson isn't that smart. He's an instrument, not a strategist. I've briefed his uncle, and he's no mental giant either. Preston Hawkinson is in the US Senate because his family business brought a lot of jobs to Wyoming, not because of any grand ideas he has. He's as much of a pawn as his nephew. They'll both take the power that comes with whatever bargain they've made, but they aren't driving this. Guy has a better grasp on technology than his uncle does, but he's no scientist."

"You can understand why all signs point to your organization," Thorpe said, trying to steer the conversation back. "Our targeting officer came up with the same analysis on the Hawkinsons." *But you know that already,* Thorpe said to himself. Debating with Wilcox was dangerous, because there was no set of circumstances where Thorpe believed he'd know more than Wilcox did.

"I'll allow that, yes. I also think someone is framing us."

"Framing you," Thorpe repeated skeptically.

"You remember the anti-technologist movement?"

How could he forget it?

It had started two years ago when the world first realized Trinity's existence. They were branded a techno-cult that worshiped AI as a god. Social media and the less reputable news outlets overflowed with stories about how technology was going to take people's jobs and replace humans. Then the rumors began that Trinity was secretly controlling the government. People radicalized. They panicked and rioted. Technology became the enemy. They threw firebombs into electronics stores and attacked tech companies. Mobs harassed tech employees and, tragically, murdered several. Then, a domestic terrorist blew up a Ford plant because it used a robotic assembly line (and had done so since the 1980s, but that seemed to escape the narrative).

The NTCU later discovered that Archon had orchestrated a social engineering scheme. Today, it was mostly gone. But only because the NTCU had aggressively searched for and destroyed the bot farms, the dark web sites, and the fictitious news organizations Archon's AIs had used to execute the campaign.

Wilcox continued. "I think this is a furthering of that effort. Someone is trying to drive a greater wedge between us and the governments who've supported us."

"To what end?"

"Because we're the only ones that can stop them."

"Damn it, Jason, stop who?"

Wilcox turned and reached for his phone, muttering an apology. He spent a few seconds on the screen before dismissing it. "Sorry. I've got motion detectors on the lawn, but the goddamn deer keep tripping them.

The disparity is kind of ridiculous. Sometimes the irony kills me. We've got quantum computers using subatomic particles as storage and at the same time, we have a sensor that can't tell the difference between a deer and a—"

The bullet came as a whispered *thud* and Wilcox's eyes pooled like saucers. Thorpe saw a wave of shock wash over Wilcox's face, followed quickly by pain. His eyes narrowed and a widening stain flooded his chest. Wilcox staggered out of his chair.

Thorpe's gun was out. "Jason, get down."

Between the brightly lit living room and the exterior lighting that ended at the tree line, Thorpe couldn't see their attackers. They'd used suppressors to mute the sound and mask the muzzle flash. Thorpe fired three times through the massive picture window. The glass didn't shatter, rather cracks lanced out like lightning bolts frozen in time. He didn't expect to hit anyone, but hoped that the sound might get a neighbor to call the police. Thorpe dove for cover and crawled over to Wilcox. He'd taken a round in the chest and it was bad.

"You're going to be okay, old friend, just hang on for me," Thorpe said, forcing calm he didn't feel into his voice.

Wilcox's jaw moved, but words wouldn't come out.

Using the large Eames recliner as cover, Thorpe leaned out to the right and saw two men in black tactical gear with long guns emerge from the woods. Thorpe sighted one of them and fired. He lost count, four or five rounds, maybe more, but he knew at least one of them hit. The assailant pitched backward and fell to the grass.

The other attacker swept a stream of semiautomatic fire in a tight arc, obliterating the chair.

Thorpe felt lances of fire burst in his chest, knocking him back against the coffee table. He landed on his right side next to the table, with his pistol lying a few inches from his hand.

Thorpe heard three quick shots and the discordant twang of metal bending, followed by glass shattering. The assailant must have shot the lock off the patio door and kicked it in. Thorpe fought the encroaching darkness, following the man's position by the sound of the glass crunching under his feet. His eyelids were so heavy, he just wanted to close them, just for a moment. To give in.

Thorpe clenched his teeth and fought to stay conscious. He concentrated on the pain in his chest, used that to keep him aware.

If he could just move, he could get the attacker. Then, reach his phone to call 911. Then he could sleep. Sleep for as long as he needed to.

Two dull taps punctured the air, and he knew his friend was gone.

Thorpe's eyes went hot as tears flushed his face. A primal fury the likes of which he'd never felt before filled his body. It was all he could do to hold in his screams of raw, pure rage.

In that moment, he knew what his last act would be.

Revenge.

And he would take this son of a bitch with him.

A shadow fell over him. Thorpe still lay on his side, his back next to the coffee table. The attacker said nothing.

With a move like lighting, Thorpe grabbed his pistol and corked his torso. The motion sent an explosion of pain through his chest. He emptied the magazine into the attacker. Thorpe couldn't even tell where he was shooting, he just aimed for the shadow. The man fell backwards, out of view.

Thorpe heard him crash, heard the rifle bang against something hard.

He heard something else, something far off, a sound he recognized but couldn't place.

Darkness took him.

19

Vienna, Austria

So far, this was the strangest day Colt McShane had ever seen, and it was only the afternoon.

Ava was waiting for him on the satellite phone.

"Get in the car," she said. "Don't argue. My men will sanitize your vehicle. They'll get you somewhere safe so we can talk. We're holding off the authorities, but we cannot do it for long." Ava disconnected before Colt could say a word. He doubted the Audi would last and they wouldn't want to drive a damaged car through their Austrian village.

Colt didn't argue.

Ava's team wiped the Audi down, removed the license plates and registration, and pulled the VIN stickers from the window and doorframe. There would be one more on the engine block, but they couldn't get to it in the field. This was a delaying tactic, not a vanishing act. Colt and Ikeda rode in one car, Ricci and Craddock in the other. Colt didn't like being separated from the other two. Neither side trusted the other, so they'd agreed on a mutual détente.

As they drove, Colt asked the driver, the man he'd spoken with on the road, what happened to the SUV. "Suicide drone," he'd answered brusquely. "Once we figured out where you were probably going, we parked and set it up to loiter. As long as you stopped within a few miles of where we were, we could get them."

"How'd you know we'd go along the river?"

"Computer," he said. "The system will work out your escape route based on your transport, the aggression of our pursuit, and civilian casualties allowed. Plus, some other things. We designed it to find terrorists in urban environments. They repurposed it."

Colt didn't ask who "they" were. Nor did he ask the men if they were actually Trinity operatives or just contractors Ava had hired.

They drove to a farmhouse, surrounded on three sides by thick forest, an hour south of Vienna, where they waited. The men had water, food and coffee, which they shared. Colt phoned D'Angelo—Ava's men hadn't disarmed them or removed their devices.

"We've got Craddock, but there's been a complication."

"What kind of a compli—" D'Angelo began, but Colt cut her off.

"I can't get into it now. You and French clean the safe house, pack up our gear, and get home."

"Roger that," said D'Angelo, and the line clicked. She knew better than to ask any more questions.

They handcuffed Craddock to a chair in a barn behind the farmhouse, abutting the trees.

Colt walked across the lawn between the farmhouse and the barn, a styrofoam cup of coffee in one hand, an unopened bottle of water in the other. Ricci was standing outside the barn on his phone as Colt approached. Ricci screwed his face into a concentrated frown. The two men traded glances and Colt stepped into the barn. Ikeda stood a few feet from Craddock, arms folded, his cheap suit jacket dumped on a nearby table.

"Would you care for some water?" Colt asked Craddock.

"Lawyer," he growled.

Colt half-smiled and took a sip of coffee. "Mr. Craddock, that only works with cops. Any questions you have about your rights, you need to save for Special Agent Ricci back there."

"What, is he your boss, or something? Then why am I not talking to him?"

"One, he's not the boss. Two, he's a cop, and we are not." Colt watched the grim realization of his predicament blossom in Craddock's eyes. "Three, we have questions for you, which you will answer. If you choose not to answer them, then Special Agent Ricci locks you in one of those national security prisons we don't have names for."

"And that's only once we're back on U.S. soil," Ikeda added. "Lot can happen between now and then."

"So, shall we start over?" Colt asked.

"No," Craddock said with equal parts malice and arrogance. "We *shall* not. I don't care who you are and I don't care who he is," Craddock jutted his chin toward the barn door and Ricci on the other side. "You're looking at an international incident, pal. I have an arrangement with Europol, which your FBI pal over there can explain to you is a big problem. For you. I shouldn't even be telling you this, but I've been collaborating with them for some time. You're getting in the way of that and it's going to go poorly for you. You're going to embarrass the U.S. government with this. And, I suspect, cause a lot of problems between several governments and your own. I can't wait until they arrest you for conducting an illegal operation on Austrian soil."

Colt didn't take Craddock as the "nervous bluster" type. He'd assumed someone in Archon's leadership team would be more circumspect.

Ricci stepped in. "Can I get a word?"

Colt followed the FBI agent back outside. Clouds the color of cement covered the sky, and it hadn't warmed. There was a slight, chilly breeze that shook the trees around the house. "That was the legal attaché in Vienna. He just got off a call with a liaison officer at Europol HQ in the Hague. They've never spoken to Reece Craddock."

"What?"

"Yeah. Someone played him."

Colt exhaled sharply. "Okay. Let's break it to him. That should shake him loose."

They returned to the barn. Craddock still looked smug and angry.

"Mr. Craddock, I've just spoken with the FBI's legal attaché at the U.S. Embassy in Vienna. The LEGAT is the senior American law enforcement—"

"I'm familiar," Craddock interjected in a deadpan.

"Right. Well, there's no deal with Europol."

Craddock barked out a laugh. "You think you can just kill that with a phone call? Good luck."

"I'm afraid you don't understand. There never was a deal. You've never spoken with them. Someone is using the same tricks your organization has to impersonate legitimate authorities."

"You think you're the only ones with classified units," Craddock countered. "There's plenty Europol doesn't share with the FBI. Believe me."

"I don't doubt it," Ricci said. "Just not this time. So, I believe my colleague here was asking you some questions about how your group developed the technology to break encryption."

Craddock dead-eyed Special Agent Ricci and said, "I don't know what you're talking about."

Colt said, "Quentin Wales, Rhett Bolton, Mariano Emmanuelle, and Carlos Marin are all dead. Someone has declared war on your organization. You stay alive as long as you're useful."

"My attorney is going to have a field day with that statement," Craddock said.

"Let's talk about your lawyer for a second. The only hope you have of staying alive is by cooperating. I've no doubt you've got the money to make whatever bail the government would set, assuming they do. But let's play this out. Your lawyer gets you back on the street. How long do you think you last? Quentin Wales was killed in his Range Rover surrounded by a protection detail. Emmanuelle was shot with a fifty-caliber sniper rifle in his home. Of course, you could try running, though they seem to have that angle covered too, because Rhett Bolton was in an air taxi and our best guess is they dropped a drone swarm on him. So, Reece, how long do you last?"

"Longer than you," Craddock sneered.

Colt had one last card left to play.

"Possibly. I wonder, though, what if Wales's contingency plan—you know, that thing that kicks in if he dies—what if that includes taking out people like you so they can't expose the broader operation? Now you've got three groups coming after you."

"There's no backup plan. You're making that up."

That pattern dragged on throughout the rest of the afternoon. Colt and Ricci traded leads in questioning, trying to get Craddock off balance. Their profile said Craddock believed the U.S. government had been after him for decades and they played to that. They never said who Colt and Tony worked for, other than that they weren't law enforcement. Then they tried using Ricci's status as an FBI agent to provide a kind of lifeline. None of it worked, at least not yet. Though Colt hadn't expected it to. He didn't believe Craddock would crack until he was back on American soil and truly understood Europol was not coming to save him. Until then, he would hold out.

Craddock contended he didn't trust the lot of them, was not interested in helping them, and had no clue about anything related to encryption. Craddock cradled the argument that his liaison with Europol was a classified unit that Colt, Tony, and Ricci wouldn't know existed.

They could not convince him it was all a ruse. At least, Craddock wouldn't admit it to them if they did.

Colt's phone buzzed later that afternoon. It was a notification from the Trinity-designed app he and Ava used to communicate (and one which Thorpe had to authorize to be loaded on Colt's Agency-issued phone). The message said: I'm here.

Colt suggested they take a break, and he went inside.

Ava was in the kitchen, alone.

Colt stepped in and walked over to the coffeepot, grabbing a fresh cup.

"Colt, we need to talk," she said. Her voice was thick, and Colt knew immediately that something was wrong.

"What is it?"

"You need to sit down," she said. Colt joined her at the table, cradling his coffee cup between his hands and leeching the warmth from it. Even once he sat, Ava didn't immediately speak. He was about to repeat his question when she finally said, "Colt, Jason is dead."

Words escaped him, and the blood drained from his face.

He felt nothing.

It was as though someone had popped the top on his soul, upended him, and dumped it into a bin, leaving him a vacant shell.

"What happened?" Colt eventually said. His voice was distant to his own ears, hollow.

"He was murdered in his home. Two gunmen. They were professionals."

Colt was about to ask how she knew, but then stopped himself. Trinity probably had monitoring devices on the home, and they could easily tap into the local public safety systems. Did the Agency know? Surely there were protocols in place for them to be notified if something happened to Wilcox.

"There's more," Ava said. "Will Thorpe was with him. He was shot as well."

"Is he . . ."

Ava shook her head. Her voice quavered. "We don't know. Paramedics removed him, and he was alive then, but they reported a gunshot wound to the chest. He . . . he killed both of the attackers. The FBI is trying to identify them now, but their names don't appear in any law enforcement or U.S. government database. We don't know what hospital they took Thorpe to. We've tried to find out, but presumably he's listed as a John Doe."

Colt did some fast mental math. He guessed this happened around the same time as Craddock's arrest, or earlier. Why in the hell hadn't the unit contacted him? They would've known by now.

Another realization sobered him. Colt, as number two, was now the acting head of the NTCU.

He needed to get home. The team would fear for their boss, and possibly for themselves. Wilcox had recruited many of them personally when he set the unit up, and Thorpe had led them well ever since. This was a serious blow. Colt needed to be with the NTCU.

But there were a few things he needed to do here first.

A sudden surge of raw fury that he could barely contain welled up inside him.

Wilcox had been a friend, a mentor, damned near a second father. Colt worked for him for eight intense, incredible, and challenging years. He hadn't known what to make of Wilcox's admission that he'd been a member of Trinity since the nineties, when he'd found out. It hadn't felt like a betrayal, necessarily, but something definitely less than honest.

Colt returned to the same question he'd tried and failed to answer. Did Wilcox authorize this assassination campaign against Archon, or was Ava acting on her own, fulfilling her role as an avenging angel?

"I guess it was only a matter of time before someone pushed back," Colt said icily. It was all he could do to hold himself in check.

"This wasn't on us."

"Isn't it? Archon's leaders are being systematically eliminated. Seems natural they'd counterattack."

"Despite what you think, we're not fielding a private army. I wouldn't even know where to start."

"That so? I assumed those four that picked us up this morning were ex-Mossad."

"They are currently Mossad. One of them is a friend. He owed me a favor." Ava reached across the table to touch Colt's hands. He left them flat on the table and didn't move closer to her. "I know what Jason meant to you, so I want you to know that I'm here for you. Whatever you need, okay?"

Colt mumbled, "Yeah." His mind was elsewhere. The fury had subsided, a tide that washed out, and now the emptiness returned. He knew this was how he processed grief. There was a kind of numbness for some indeterminate amount of time, and then he'd feel a rush of conflicted emotions all at once. It was a terribly unhelpful way to grieve.

"What are you going to do?" For one of the only times in their relationship, Ava looked apprehensive, if not outright nervous. She had the look of someone who'd just discovered they were no longer in control of the car they were driving.

"Thanks for telling me about Jason, Ava," Colt said, ignoring her question entirely.

"Don't shut me out, Colt. I'm here to help."

"You told me that our work and our relationship were air-gapped," Colt said flatly, if not a little harsh. "I'm just doing what you asked."

"Don't be an ass. I just asked if you're okay."

"No, you didn't. You asked what I was going to do about Jason's death."

"I don't make much of a distinction there," she said.

"Ava, you can't change the rules. You told me, quite clearly, there were no free rides. I couldn't use our relationship for intel. Well, now I'm telling you the same thing." Colt felt his self-control slipping away. It was all too much.

"I think the situation has changed a bit since we had that conversation."

"Has it?"

"What are you going to do with Craddock?"

"That's up to the FBI," he said dismissively.

"I want to talk to him."

"Absolutely out of the question," Colt said.

"He won't talk to you. And you wouldn't have him if it wasn't for me."

Colt pushed himself up from the chair. "Heather Fleet is an American citizen and on U.S. soil. I'd advise you to steer clear of her. Braithwaite is a member of Parliament. Given the status of things between MI6 and the continent, someone might take assassinating an MP the wrong way," he said. "Friendly advice."

Colt left the farmhouse, ignoring Ava calling after him, and returned to the barn. He placed a quick phone call and then entered the barn, where he motioned for Tony and Keith to join him outside. When they did, he explained what had happened to Wilcox and Thorpe.

"That's all I know right now," he said. "I still haven't heard from the unit."

"Any chance they don't know?" Keith said.

"If a former deputy CIA director wasn't also murdered, I'd say maybe. This has to have triggered alarms all the way to Washington. I can't imagine they're in the dark. I just called the plane at Ramstein. They're on their way now. Should be on the ground in Vienna in two hours. You two escort Craddock back home. Keith, book him and put him in a hole. Do you have anything you can arrest Heather Fleet on?"

The FBI agent shook his head and scowled. "I don't know, man. Except for what Hawkinson has done, it's almost impossible to draw a direct line from the Archon board to any action they've taken. Hell, even the cyberattacks they launched last year were all from servers in Russia."

"Try to think of something. Even if it's protective custody. I just want her off the street before someone tries to take a shot at her. Maybe we can play her and Craddock off each other."

Tony looked over at the farmhouse. "You think Trinity might try something?" Colt hadn't told him Ava was here, but Ikeda was a smart man and Colt assumed he'd figured it out.

"I put them very high on the revenge index right now," Colt said.

Colt called the NTCU Ops Center from Vienna Station on a secure phone. They told him Thorpe was alive, but in a medically induced coma. His location was being withheld for security and he had a protective detail at all times. When Colt asked why no one had contacted him, they said the Technology Mission Center director had instructed them not to say anything until he spoke to Colt himself. Colt checked his watch. It would be four in the morning at Langley.

"He said that if you called in, you're directed to fold up your operation and come home immediately," the watch officer said.

The mission center director wouldn't know about the covert action.

Colt would head home quickly, but not immediately. He had to run the NTCU, but there was something he had to do first before this entire thing spun so far out of control they'd never get it back.

20

San Francisco, California

The *New York Times*'s San Francisco bureau was two blocks off the Embarcadero, in the heart of the Financial District. Lacy used to love working downtown. She'd started with the *Chronicle* and then did a short stint with TechCrunch before getting picked up by *Wired* as their cybersecurity writer. She'd worked for the magazine two years when the *Times* hired her. San Francisco had changed a lot since then. Colleagues didn't meet for drinks after work very often, or if they did, it was outside the city. The New York office fought them constantly about the exorbitant parking costs until the bureau chief explained no one felt comfortable riding the Bay Area's rail system. They eventually relented.

Though with the attention Lacy was bringing the paper, she thought they should spring for a black car and a driver every day.

Her story on the Chinese diplomatic cable hacking had been one of the *Times*'s most read articles of the year, and the follow-ups were just as popular.

Lacy was now looking over an email from "Bashe" and wondering how long she was going to be here tonight. He'd become one of her best sources in years, if not her entire career. Bashe had given her the scoop on the social media leaks and the hacked cables between the top echelons of the Chinese military and intelligence departments.

Though he'd stayed clear of any details that could identify him personally (something about Bashe's communication style told her he was a man), Bashe described himself as a hacktivist, a data-libertarian. He broke into systems as a kind of public service. He reasoned that if he could get into a system, it wasn't being protected well enough and he should expose those responsible. Bashe told her a week ago that he had a source within the CIA who wanted to provide some damning info. Said the guy knew about something that was gnawing at his conscience, an illegal operation. Maybe she could look at it.

Lacy ran it by her bureau chief, Bradley Finch, and they agreed to review the material, if the source's bona fides checked out. The leaker, through Bashe, provided time-stamped photos from the CIA parking lot, blacked out paystubs, and email traffic.

The email she'd just received, on the dummy email account she used to communicate with Bashe, directed her to an onion router and a document repo on the dark web. Lacy closed the door to her office and drew the blinds. She was one of the few beat reporters with an actual office, a condition of her taking the job, because of the sensitivity of sources and leads she worked with. It didn't make her popular with the people stuck in the bullpen, but she didn't care.

Lacy entered the password Bashe had provided and spent the rest of the day reading everything he'd given her.

When she was done, Lacy picked up the phone and dialed Finch's extension. "Can you come in here, please? And don't tell anyone."

A few minutes later, the bespectacled bureau chief appeared in her doorway, decked out in a blue gingham shirt and Patagonia vest.

"What's up?"

"Close the door, please," she said. When he did, she turned her laptop around—the cheap one she used to communicate with confidential sources.

"What am I looking at?"

"Bashe just connected me with a leaker at CIA. He's provided evidence of an unacknowledged joint FBI–CIA unit that is conducting a massive domestic surveillance operation. They have an AI system called CERBERUS that is allegedly hooked into nearly every government computer system." Finch whistled.

"That's not all," Lacy continued. "According to this source, they've also connected it to numerous commercial systems, from travel to banking, social media, you name it. This is one of the biggest data collection efforts I've ever seen."

"Why is he coming to us? We're not going to expose an intelligence operation just because we learned about it. The government will sue us into the ground."

"The source claims they're spying on American citizens. He said he's coming forward because his conscience can no longer tolerate it. He says they're deploying spyware on government and commercial systems."

Finch paused to read. "Sounds like ECHELON, but without the telecom's blessing." He turned the laptop back around to her. "It's groundbreaking, but it could put us in serious danger to expose it."

"I mean, with everything else going on with digital security, the very idea of privacy is at stake. And now we've got evidence of a massive domestic surveillance campaign." Lacy waved at her laptop.

"What's this group called?"

"The National Technical Counterintelligence Unit," Lacy said. "NTCU, for short."

"Here's what we do," Finch said. "First, we need to secure all of this. That laptop needs to stay locked in the safe at night. Don't take it home. You haven't accessed this on any other device, have you?"

"You know me better than that, Brad."

"Right. Sorry. We need another piece of info, something to tie all this together. Have Bashe contact the leaker and see if they can provide something more concrete. We need evidence of actual domestic surveillance."

"Okay. I'll see what I can do."

"And not a word of this, to anyone. I'm going to call New York and see how they want to handle it. If this is true, though, this is the Pentagon Papers all over again. Or worse."

21

Cambridge, United Kingdom

If nothing else, Colt had to appreciate the British sense of humor.

He was meeting his contact in the wooded courtyard outside Cambridge's Trinity College.

Ann had been Colt's first real connection to Trinity. Before he'd known anything about them, before he'd known they were an unlikely ally in the fight against Archon, Ann had attempted to recruit him. Colt rebuffed the effort, but the two struck a partnership and, once he'd gained her trust, he learned that she was the one who'd recruited Jason Wilcox into the group during the nineties. Ann appeared every bit a proper English grandmother, but that appearance belied her past as a Cold War veteran and career code-breaker with GCHQ. She also had a PhD in theoretical mathematics from the very institution on whose grounds they now walked.

Europe, and seemingly the rest of the world, was still locked in the worst heatwave in a generation, and Colt found the shaded lawn welcome. To his left, the ancient stone walls of Trinity College rose like castle battlements.

Ann entered the courtyard from the north and walked over to him. Colt stood.

"Colt," she said, holding out her arms. "I just learned about Jason. I'm sorry."

"Me too," Colt said. They embraced.

Ann wiped her eyes and reached into her purse. She drew a water bottle out and handed it to Colt. "Thought you might need one of these," she said. Colt thanked her and they sat on the bench beneath the thick, leafy canopy. Between the high walls and thick trees, it would be nearly impossible to surveil them from above. The shade was just an added benefit.

"To what do I owe the dubious honor of a visit from Colt McShane, on this of all days?" Ann asked.

Colt couldn't help but smile at her lilting, almost whimsical tone.

"I need your help and I don't have a lot of time."

"I imagine not," she replied lightly.

"When I last spoke with Jason, maybe a month ago, we talked about whether Archon was behind these security breaches. I asked him what Trinity was going to do about it and he told me not to wait on others to act. Now, four of their board members are dead."

"You'll forgive me if I don't shed a tear. Especially Wales. Bloody psychopath, that one," Ann said.

"Ann, I have to know, are you behind this?"

"What? Me, personally? That's a laugh. Can you imagine me as a hit man, at my age?"

"This is serious, Ann. I have a source inside their organization. He's said they have a kind of doomsday plan. If one of them dies, they've all got a contingency plan that kicks in and now we've got any number of mini-Archons spinning up. Groups we know nothing about. We have to get these people in custody so we can question them, not only so we can figure out how they're beating everyone's encryption, but to stop these dead man's switches from tripping."

"What does Ava say about all this?" Ann asked in a way that suggested she already knew the answer.

Colt had taken a tremendous personal risk in coming here. If Ava learned he was going around her, that would be the death knell of their relationship. But Colt's duty went beyond his feelings for her. He had a responsibility to unravel this, to stop whoever was behind the murders and the cyberattacks, and that was more important than any future he might have with Ava. He hated it. Colt felt like he was operating in a world entirely without rules. He hoped the operator in Ava would understand this decision, even if the rest of her did not.

Colt couldn't be sure what Ava might or might not have told Ann, so he decided on the truth. "I asked Ava the same question. She told me that if I wanted to know what Trinity was doing. I had to join."

"Fair point."

"That was before they murdered Jason. And Ava didn't know about their contingency plans."

"I've never heard of it either, to be honest." Ann folded her hands in her lap and looked out across the courtyard. "We did not kill Wales, Emmanuelle, or Bolton."

A cold feeling washed over him.

"What about Marin?"

"Something you need to understand about Carlos, is that he's the one who authorized the murder of Ava's parents."

"I thought that was Samantha Klein," Colt said.

"Oh, it was her idea, to be sure. But she wasn't on the board yet. Carlos needed to give her the okay. Once someone started taking out board members, Ava saw that as her opportunity to kill the man who killed her parents."

"You don't think the Spanish government or Europol might have wanted a say in that?"

"Had long enough to speak their bit, don't you think?" Colt didn't immediately respond out of sheer frustration at the logic. When Ann spoke again, she'd softened her tone considerably. "I'm not saying it's right, I'm just saying to try to look at it from the perspective of an only daughter who became an orphan that day. Consider how it shaped her."

"Does it stop with Marin?"

"Jason did not want us killing people. We're scientists. We want to build a better world."

"That is *literally* Archon's main talking point," Colt deadpanned.

"Well, they got it from us, the bastards. Listen to me, Colt, we're not doing this. It's someone else. If Wales hadn't died first, I'd think it was him. If we were in Vegas, I'd be pushing all of my chips on Guy Hawkinson."

Colt nodded slowly.

"I agree that he seems like the most likely candidate, but the part that I can't square is, well, why? I mean, Archon wants to put his uncle in the White House. They're actively working toward that. And not just in the U.S.."

"Oh, Braithwaite is going to make a run at PM," Ann said. "And I give him a damn good chance of it, especially the way things are now."

"Right, so why does Guy risk that by killing them? When Uncle Preston becomes president, the first thing he'll do is pardon Guy."

"Both things can be true. One thing I've wondered about for some time is how much of Archon's leadership actually needs to be a human. You've met Kim's Saturn system. You know how advanced it is. We know Guy probably had an early version of that, and has had nearly two years to work on it. Certainly he's nowhere near Jeff Kim's level, but after a point, the machine just takes over. Maybe Guy decided he doesn't need Archon anymore."

Colt made for London.

Ann shared Wilcox's belief, which the national security advisor and head of Colt's service also now held, that Archon possessed a quantum computer capable of defeating any existing encryption. Ann believed they were behind this global campaign and agreed with Colt that it was all a preparatory action to solidify Preston Hawkinson's candidacy.

She promised not to tell Ava that Colt had gone to see her and told him to be careful. Ann also said she would urge caution and try to convince Ava to stop at one.

Colt was glad he'd gone to see her. The revelation was important, and it only underscored the importance of his next step.

It took another ninety minutes to get back to London and from there, he spent two more hours on a varied route to get him to a sidewalk along the Thames.

"You can't demand we meet like this, just on a whim. It's dangerous, especially now," Hazlett spat when Colt approached him.

Colt hated agreeing with Hazlett because the man was such an insufferable prick, but that didn't make him wrong. Weeks, if not months, of planning would usually go into a meeting like this. This was criminally poor tradecraft, and he was knowingly putting an asset at risk. In a pre-Brexit world and without the extant crisis between the Brits and the EU, Colt would've at least had them meet across the channel in Calais. Now, though, he reasoned that forcing Hazlett to cross through passport control would raise too many unnecessary flags.

Colt gave Hazlett a few hours' notice and told him the meeting wasn't negotiable.

Hazlett met him in the early evening on a walkway along the Thames, outside of Imperial Park. Hazlett wore a five-thousand-euro suit and did it impatiently.

Colt ignored the man's verbal barrage and just started walking north. Hazlett eventually took the hint and Colt heard his brown oxfords gently scraping the sidewalk next to him. "Where is Hawkinson?" Colt asked.

"How should I know?" Hazlett stammered. "No one knows where he is." Hazlett lowered his voice to a harsh whisper. "No one's seen him in nine months."

"Find him," Colt said.

"How am I supposed to do that? If my superiors couldn't find him, what makes you think I can?"

"Your superiors are an endangered species, Howard," Colt said. "Rhett Bolton is dead, which makes you isolated. You convinced me that some of the other board members know who you are because of the financial work you did, but the more of them who disappear, the fewer options you have. And the less value you are to me." He was not going to tell Hazlett they had Craddock in custody. "Listen to me, Howard, and listen good. Things are escalating quickly and dangerously. This is going to spin out of anyone's control if we don't put a stop to it. Someone is taking advantage of the current security crisis to take out your organization's leaders, and they have been powerless to stop it." Colt paused. He'd always known it was possible that Hazlett was, in fact, working for Hawkinson all this time. The more empty chairs, the greater the likelihood that was true. He wouldn't put it past the snake, either. Time to stress test that theory. "Where is Guy?"

"I told you, I don't know."

The alternative, Howard, is that I tell Ava Klein about you."

"W-why would you do that?"

"Now, I don't know if you know this about Ava, but your superiors murdered her parents. They felt her father was going to cause trouble for them. She took that about as well as you'd expect. She joined Mossad and started hunting them down." Colt stopped walking and turned to face the murky river, staring across at the south bank. "If I don't get what I need, I'm going to tell her where to find you."

Colt knew he was crossing a line now.

This was not how the Agency treated its assets, however morally repugnant they might be.

It wasn't being at the brink of war with China or even the leaking of diplomatic cables or the exposure of military operations that had pushed Colt this far. It was the death of one good man . His entire adult life, Colt had been a small part of "big things." So, it was perhaps understandable that it was a personal loss that had the greatest impact on him.

It would be wrong to say that he knew what he was doing now and didn't care. In fact, Colt was sure that if Wilcox could see him right now, he'd be in for a stern reprimand. Wilcox would tell him this was not how they did things. He could practically hear the man's voice: *We have to work in a dirty world, but we cannot let ourselves become stained by it.*

Sorry, boss, Colt said to himself. To Hazlett, he demanded, "What's it going to be?"

"Guy killed Quentin Wales," Hazlett said, finally. "We can't conclusively prove it, but he blamed Wales for his being left in the cold. Guy thought he deserved a seat at the table and he learned that Wales always intended for him to be a smokescreen, something for people like you to chase. I don't know who killed the other three."

"What is the rest of the board doing?"

"Yoon feels fairly safe because he's in South Korea. Fleet is scared. Braithwaite . . . he's an arrogant ass and assumes he's untouchable. No one has heard from Craddock in weeks, but that's not abnormal. He's a nut."

No argument there, Colt thought.

"They think if they can wait this out until Preston is in the White House, they'll be safe."

"It's four months to the election and another two after that before he'd take office. At the rate they're being assassinated, that math doesn't work out in the board's favor."

Hazlett shrugged.

"You don't strike me as a true believer, Howard," Colt continued. "I think you're in this for the proximity to power. You weren't a member of Trinity and, I suspect, only accepted the invitation into Archon because you saw it as a path to influence. To be a part of the court. You don't want to lead, because you know people like me eventually learn who those leaders are and take them out. You've made a career out of being useful enough that you're not expendable, but not so much that you're a threat. It's a fine line to walk." Colt released his casual grip on the railing and stepped back, a sign that he was about to depart. "Your group has put certain things in motion over the last several years that are coming to a head now. You've almost started one war, and we're now looking at another, possibly several. Obliterating the very ideas of privacy and security will have consequences. Immediate and violent ones, most likely."

"This was never the plan, you understand."

"If you think this is where you get to explain your worldview and hope for sympathy, you're going to be very disappointed," Colt said, but Hazlett continued anyway.

"Your governments are cumbersome and inefficient. They're broken. The whole reason we could shut down your air traffic control network is because your officials couldn't bother to upgrade it. A system that is foundational to public safety, and they just kick the problem down the road because it's too expensive, too hard, or some contractor who lost the bid files a protest. We're here to show that there's is a better way. Remove unnecessary bureaucracy from the decision loop—"

"Right, and entrust everything to you," Colt retorted.

Hazlett chuckled bitterly. "No, and that's where you and your kind continually miss the message. Our organization only sought to replace the inefficiencies of human systems with artificial intelligence to make society function as intended. Critical systems that didn't require patching or upgrade, because they were always top of the line. A justice system that was blind and fair. An education system that met the individualized needs of its students. A—"

"Howard—I don't care. I also don't think you truly believe any of that techno-utopia bullshit, and neither do your bosses. If they did, they wouldn't have turned the gas off for millions right as winter started." Colt turned to face Hazlett. When he spoke, there was no anger in his voice. Colt's tone was calm, even a little tired. "Archon is being dismantled. Guy is taking out the leadership and after what you've done, my country, the British, and probably now, the Chinese are going to obliterate what's left. If you want to be on the 'unhelpful' side of that equation when it's all over, good luck. So I'll ask you for the last time. Where is Guy Hawkinson?"

Hazlett looked away, his jawline tight.

"I don't know where Guy is, truly. Believe me or don't. What I can tell you is the organization spent over a billion dollars investing in Hawkinson's quantum computing design. Which is to say, Jeff Kim's design," Hazlett said, chagrinned. "They built five facilities. Geneva, Singapore, California, and two in Buenos Aires. Your FBI and the Swiss police confiscated the lab in Geneva. An ironically timed generator overload at HawkTech's Buenos Aires office destroyed one of Argentine labs. The other, which was owned by a shell company, was destroyed in a suspicious explosion. The lab in Santa Monica belongs to an organization under the name New Futures Foundation. Heather Fleet is the senior technical advisor."

"Why didn't we know about this?" Subtext: *Why are you only telling me now?*

Hazlett shrugged. "She hid her involvement there for obvious reasons. Officially, she believes in anonymous altruism. The NFF raised significant funds on their own. In addition to the Los Angeles facility, they also have a lab in Seoul. Our organization didn't directly fund that project, but Fleet and Yoon did use Jeff Kim's work to influence the design. The organization invested in eleven of the UK's forty-eight quantum tech startups. As an MP, Braithwaite also allocated government investment for the National Quantum Computing Centre, which we assisted with. If I were you, I would concentrate on my search on the places I've named. Of the ones I've mentioned, I'd start in Singapore."

"Why?"

"It's the kind of place where someone like Guy can hide in plain sight. The Singaporeans have some of the strictest laws in the world regarding foreign intelligence, and no one in the West is going to chance upsetting them at the risk of pushing them closer to the Chinese. It's a modern, high-tech city where an American businessman wouldn't look out of place. Most importantly, it's one of the few places on earth Archon doesn't have any assets."

"Thank you, Howard." Colt said. "You've been helpful. I know this is dangerous for you. Keep your head down. If you need it, I can arrange a protection detail with MI5."

"I'd just as soon not have them know my name."

"Then you should've picked a different line of work," Colt said, and left.

Colt took a red-eye from Heathrow to Dulles. Nadia picked him up at the airport and briefed him on the drive home.

"Latest leak happened while you were in the air. Two actually. First, Europe's two biggest pharmaceutical companies just had their next five years of R&D leaked. This one didn't go public, though. It showed up on servers belonging to one of their major competitors here. They're screaming industrial espionage and saying an American company was trying to take advantage of the security situation. Stock market is freaking out."

This was a distinctively troubling turn. Before now, the leaks had simply been dumped on dark web servers, chat rooms, and other publicly available locations. This was the first instance where the leaker sent information directly to another party.

"Christ. You said there were two?"

"Yeah. The Chinese know we helped stop their invasion of Taiwan. They've gotten ahold of internal comms, Colt."

"It shouldn't be that much of a surprise that we'd help Taiwan."

"Beijing is calling it an act of war. The China Mission Center thinks this might be the tipping point for an all-out war. Since the covert approach didn't work, they might just try to level everything."

Colt made a mental note to contact Liu as soon as he could.

"I think I know where Guy is."

"EMBER?"

"Yeah. Get the team together. I'll be in as soon as I can."

"Okay, but Blankenship wants to see you right away."

Blankenship was the director of the Technology Mission Center and Colt's effective boss until Thorpe was out of the hospital.

"When did you get in?" Colt asked, changing the subject.

"Last night."

"How was California? But, before you answer, remember that I haven't slept in two days and just flew here from London."

"I think this thing is going to work. It's fascinating stuff. Jeff showed me—"

"Nadia," he said calmly.

"Right," She laughed. "It went well. We worked on computer stuff. I have a plan."

Nadia dropped him at his home in Falls Church. Colt showered, got a quick breakfast, and headed to Langley. The TMC director couldn't fit Colt in until late morning. After the perfunctory statements of remorse for Thorpe, he moved into business and expectation setting. He spent twenty minutes talking about "meeting cadences" and "battle rhythms" before asking Colt about his operation. Which was fine for Colt, since the director wasn't cleared to know about it, anyway.

Nadia, D'Angelo, French, Ricci, and Ikeda were waiting for him in the conference room when Colt returned to the unit. They had a pot of fresh coffee for him. Colt poured himself a mug before beginning.

"I want to start off by saying that the last forty-eight hours have been difficult for all of us. Jason Wilcox recruited me, and I worked directly for him for eight years before joining the unit. I've run the gamut of emotions from wanting to personally shoot Guy Hawkinson in the face—"

"I get that," Nadia agreed.

"—but I know Wilcox would want me to do the job. Focus on leads, run them down, work the intelligence and follow it where it goes. We owe it to him to do this right."

"Any word on the boss?"

"All I have on Will's condition is that he's still in the ICU, listed as 'critical.'" Colt took a deep breath. "Let's get these bastards and hit them hard."

Colt briefed them on his meeting with Hazlett, admitting to them he had committed a breach in tradecraft and possibly put the source in danger.

"Don't be too hard on yourself, Colt," Tony told him. "It's not like Hazlett's hands are clean. He just didn't want to be the guy without a chair when the music stopped."

"EMBER is convinced Guy is most likely in Singapore, so let's concentrate our search there." Colt shared Hazlett's reasoning and the team agreed it was sound. "Nadia, where are we on the trace algorithm?"

"I've been working with Jeff Kim for the last week to develop a program that will isolate quantum signatures, allowing us to triangulate their point of origin. With the intel Colt just shared, we can target our efforts much more precisely. Now that we know where to look, we should be able to home in on the source fairly easily. This should help us confirm if Guy really is in Singapore."

"Great work, Nadia." Colt took a sip of coffee. It burned like hell in his throat, but snapped him awake. "My working hypothesis is that Hawkinson is the culprit. I've gone back and forth on this a lot, but I always come back to the same conclusion. Archon used Guy as a lightning rod. Expose him so they could keep themselves hidden. He realized they were intentionally hanging him out to dry, so he took them out. This code-breaking effort was already underway. Guy will co-opt, if he hasn't already. There won't be a list of demands. It starts with getting Preston Hawkinson elected, then he makes it possible for Archon-designed AIs to subvert and take over governmental functions."

"But as soon as he does that, he knows someone is going to take him out," Ikeda said. "Bin Laden made it ten years, and that was because he was willing to live most of those years in a cave."

"Yeah, Guy is way too bougie for that," D'Angelo said.

"Here's what doesn't make sense to me," Nadia said. "In addition to helping me with the algorithm, Jeff gave me a PhD survey course in all things quantum."

"Of course he did," Colt said.

"What Hawkinson is doing right now is, like, table stakes. Quantum computing has nearly infinite processing power and infinite speed. It's theoretically capable of computational problems that classic computers couldn't do in a thousand years."

"Like breaking every code on the planet," French said dryly.

"That, and modeling cancer. And mapping the neurological connections of the human brain. And creating accurate models of atoms, which right now we can only do for hydrogen, and it practically melts the hard drive to do it. The scientific breakthroughs give you more credibility and agency than terrorism can. Like, by orders of magnitude. He could be a savior to the world, but he's doing this? It doesn't make sense. Or, to put a more negative spin on it, he could conceivably take over the global economy with this technology. Just revealing people's secrets and getting them to fight more than they already are? That's bush league stuff. I don't understand that as a strategy."

D'Angelo tapped her pen against a notebook as her mind worked. "I agree. There's something about this that doesn't ring true to me. Remember, when Hawkinson first founded HawkTech, he deployed his AIs to foster secure voting and clean water distribution in Africa. They partnered with rural and inner-city school districts to deploy an AI-based educational initiative. Most of these, especially the voting technology, had underlying objectives that were pretty scary, but the idea was to cover their evil in good works. This whole code-breaking scheme seems to be evil for the sake of evil. It doesn't fit Archon's profile."

Colt considered D'Angelo's statement. "Does this mean we're back to not knowing who's behind it?"

"Kim was pretty adamant on that point. He believes he's the only one whose tech is far enough along to do this," Nadia said. "And they stole from him."

"Well, Jeff has a fairly high opinion of himself."

"He's probably the smartest guy on the planet," Nadia said, and Colt noted a touch of defensiveness in her voice.

"Could Archon have given their tech to someone else? DPRK, Iran? We ruled out Russia and China earlier. Should we revisit those?"

"I don't think so," D'Angelo said. "Of them, only the Chinese have the infrastructure or the expertise to do anything with it. None of the other threat states or terrorist groups could use this stuff for years. And Colt showed the Chinese that Hawkinson wanted them to adopt his technology so he could subvert it, hide behind them. They won't forget that."

"Let's remember that we have multiple things playing out simultaneously here," Colt said. We have to be careful that we don't conflate them. Archon is revealing all of the world's secrets as a precursor to putting their people in key leadership positions around the world. At the same time, Guy Hawkinson is killing Archon's leadership and, most likely, will take over the organization when he's done. I met with a Trinity contact." Colt flushed red and looked at Nadia. "A *different* Trinity contact. Who told me they think Guy's plan is to replace the board with an AI based on Jeff Kim's Saturn. If that's the case, it looks like we're still fighting a war on two fronts."

"Does Thorpe's situation change anything?" Ricci asked. He scribbled something on a scrap of paper, folded it, and slid it into his binder.

"In the short term, no. Longer term, that's a more complicated answer. Until we hear otherwise, we press forward. Alright, I think we've got our assignments. Nadia, I want you focused on finding those labs."

"Got it, but just because the machine is in one of those places, it doesn't mean Guy is."

"Something tells me he won't be far from it."

As he was filing out the door, Ricci gave Colt the slip of paper he'd written on. It read: GWUH, Pat Milton.

George Washington University Hospital. That was where they were keeping Thorpe, and he must be under the name "Patrick Milton."

Colt didn't leave Langley until seven that night. He was tired beyond words, but there was more he had to do. He drove to Foggy Bottom. The George Washington University Hospital had the distinction of being where President Reagan was taken after John Hinckley's assassination attempt.

Colt entered and went to the critical care wing. He asked the ICU nurse to see Mr. Milton and, after giving him a quizzical look, she directed him to the room.

Two officers from the FBI's uniformed service stood outside. Colt gave them his name and they let him in. They wrote nothing down.

Colt walked to Thorpe's room, knocked, and entered.

Will Thorpe had oxygen tubes running into his nose to help him breathe. He was awake and quietly conversing with a visitor.

Fred Ford.

22

Washington, DC

Colt took a seat next to Thorpe. The sounds of the various devices keeping him alive provided a constant, grating background noise.

"I'm sorry," Thorpe said. His voice was just above a whisper. "I couldn't save Jason."

Colt took his boss's hand and closed his eyes against the tears that welled up within them.

"Will, don't do this to yourself," Colt said. He could see from the creases in Thorpe's eyes, the lines of pain on his face, that he'd been torturing himself over it.

No one spoke for some time. Colt held Thorpe's hand, which felt cool and weak in his. The only sound was the respirator's flush and the steady, electronic beat of the machines around them.

"We got Craddock," Colt said. "He's in custody now."

"He talk?"

Colt shook a negative. "Not yet. Now that he's back in the States, I think his tone will change. Ricci is working on getting Heather Fleet into custody. They don't know what they can hold her on yet, but they're working on it.

Just having her will give us leverage over Craddock, though. Play them off each other."

"They were waiting for us," Thorpe wheezed. "They wanted to get me and Wilcox together. Target of opportunity. Take out the two heads . . ." his voice trailed off and Thorpe closed his eyes, obviously in pain. "I know they were watching me. You need to be careful."

"TMC is shutting us down," Colt said. "I spoke with Blankenship today. He's folding everything up, rolling it into his group."

"That's . . . stupid," Thorpe managed.

"Listen, I'm not giving up. There's going to be plenty of fight left for you when you get out, okay? Just focus on getting better."

"Jason told me . . ." Thorpe paused to take a breath. "Jason told me it wasn't them. Trinity didn't kill anyone."

That means Ava's acting on her own.

"I'm going to get these guys, Will. You have my word." Colt said.

Across the bed, Fred Ford stood and laid a gentle hand on Thorpe's shoulder. "I'm going to walk out with Sparky," he said. "Make sure he doesn't screw anything up on the way to the elevator. I'll see you soon, pal."

The two former partners walked out of the room and gently closed the door.

"Pal?" Colt said.

"We forgave each other," was all Fred said. He hit the elevator button. "There's a Starbucks on the first floor. Let's get a coffee." On the way down, Ford explained that Thorpe's wife had just been here, but was going home to be with their kids. The FBI had twenty-four-hour surveillance on them and had uniforms at the kids' schools. They arrived on the first floor, ordered coffees, and found a dark corner to talk in. The coffee shop was empty, cold, and dimly lit. Colt brought Ford up to speed on the investigation, the highlights that he'd missed since retiring. The Agency's security division would lose their mind over Colt talking operational details with a retiree in a hospital coffee shop, but Colt could also count on one hand the number of people he could actually speak to about this.

"I knew moving under TMC was a bad idea," Ford said from behind his cup. "I said this shit was going to happen." He shook his head. "God, I hate it when I'm right."

"So do I," Colt said, smirking despite himself. "How's work?"

After retiring, Ford had signed on with a private intelligence firm run by a former senior CIA officer. They contracted with the Agency and most of the IC.

"The FBI is going to announce tomorrow that they rounded up a cell of Russian illegals in Silicon Valley. Want to know what tipped them off?"

An ugly feeling of premonition came over him.

"Don't tell me it was an anonymous tip."

"With transcripts and backtracking to their COVCOM."

"Jesus."

"Plans for the Air Force's sixth-generation fighter leaked five days ago. The language models for Google and Microsoft's next generative AI appeared on the dark web this morning. We expect the tech index is going to tank tomorrow. Colt, you have to stop these guys. You can't let the suits shut this operation down."

"What leverage do I have? My boss is upstairs fighting for his life. I'm expected to be at HQS, running things in his place. The only other man who'd really intervene on our behalf is dead. We're looking, Fred, but it's like trying to find a needle in a stack of needles. And something about this just feels . . . out of place."

"What do you mean?"

"Archon's leaders are being assassinated. I know Ava was behind one of them, and I know Guy Hawkinson was behind another. Trinity's theory is that Guy wants to take over Archon, replace the leadership functions with the AI he stole from Jeff Kim."

"Well, if that isn't a stiff swig of irony," Ford said.

"My source inside Archon also said their leadership has backup plans that kick in if a board member dies. Basically spins up mini-Archons that no one knows about. We could spend the next ten years chasing those down and only find half."

"Meanwhile, Preston Hawkinson slides into the White House."

"The last conversation that Jason and I had, we talked about these leaks and what Archon had to gain from them."

Ford's face darkened. "When we first went up against them, we thought it was chaos for the sake of chaos, right? They were trying to show the existing system didn't work. Then, when we stopped them, we realized we just defused the bomb before it went off."

"Right. They never offered an alternative. They said, your government doesn't work, but never followed up with, 'Well here's a totalitarian one that does.' Ultimately, because they never surfaced before, all of that still serves what I think they're doing now. It's setting the stage for Preston Hawkinson. It gives him a crisis to come in and solve with some sweeping new authority that he never relinquishes."

"Sort of like Caesar. Makes sense to me."

"Jason laid out a pretty convincing plan of how a President Hawkinson and his backers would gradually erode constitutional protections. It would be a gradual thing, and they'd have the ability to put forward candidates from both parties, all while making it look like we were still electing them."

"Preston becomes the necessary villain and then gets voted out of office, but his successor is from the opposition so no one sees it coming."

"Exactly. Ok, so back to these assassinations. Four of Archon's leaders are dead. My source tells me Guy Hawkinson took one of them out. Mostly, old beef over them not putting him on the board. Ava killed Carlos Marin."

"I can't believe Jason would authorize that."

"He didn't. Probably didn't know about it and maybe couldn't stop it if he did. Apparently, this was the guy who ordered her parents killed. That leaves two more that I can't account for. Both could be either of them. The idea of Ava going off on her own, with Trinity's resources—that scares me. And there's really no one to stop her."

Ford said, "Listen, tiger, I never trusted your girlfriend, and you know that I think your judgement is really clouded on this." He smiled softly. "But I don't know. I wouldn't be so hasty to lay all of those killings at Ava's feet. I'll spot you the revenge hit, but I just don't see Ava going Dirty Harry on this. That feels off to me. Now, can I see Guy being a bitch and murdering the board because they didn't invite him to join their club? Yes. Yes, I can."

A grim laugh issued from Colt's mouth and he realized how much he HAD missed Ford's uniquely sardonic flavor of gallows humor.

"Nobody with this kind of tech," Ford continued, "believes that anarchy is a viable end state."

"Exactly. So, my question is, why now? If Guy is responsible for all of the murders but the one, why not wait until January? We've got no evidence that Archon was after him. We've been assuming they helped hide him."

"I see what you're getting at," Ford said. "Why bite the hand? Guy needs his uncle elected so he can get a pardon. What are you getting at, Colt? Do you think there's a third party here?"

"The only people who know enough about Archon to mount this kind of campaign are Trinity, the NTCU, and Guy Hawkinson. I'm just afraid that we're missing some detail, some angle we haven't considered."

"Yeah. Look, fighting these guys always felt like freeclimbing with a blindfold on. I think your instinct is right about some additional detail, but don't let that distract you from what you know needs to happen. Don't let them get away with this."

Colt's phone vibrated. He looked down and when he saw "UNKNOWN CALLER," Colt swiped to dismiss the call. His phone vibrated again, this time with a text message that said: pick up.

"I need to take this," he told Ford.

"I'll see you around, kid. I'm going to head home. Keep your head up."

The unknown caller rang him again, and Colt answered.

"2121 Mass Ave. Give the name 'Mark McAllister' to the doorman." The line clicked.

Colt looked at his phone on the way out the door. 2121 Massachusetts Avenue was the address of the Cosmos Club. Not being much of a socialite, Colt had to look it up, finding it was a social club created for "men of science."

"That fits," he said aloud.

Colt drove the few blocks to club and then spent another ten minutes looking for a place to park. Looking at his watch, Colt saw it was nearly nine. He'd passed "tired" a long time ago and was moving to levels of exhaustion he hadn't known existed. He shouldn't even be driving, let alone going to clandestine meetings at DC social clubs.

The main building of the Cosmos Club was a nineteenth-century stone mansion on the southern end of DC's Embassy Row. It was early September and still quite warm. DC didn't give up its summers easily. Colt ascended the massive stone steps, where a doorman greeted him. "Mark McAllister," Colt said. "I believe I'm expected."

"Right this way, sir." The doorman led him inside, asked him what size coat he wore, and handed him a navy blazer from a closet. He then escorted Colt through a series of brightly lit corridors, ornately decorated with crimson carpet, ivory walls, and gold accents. They went upstairs to a small library.

Inside were the president's national security advisor and the head of the National Clandestine Service.

23

Washington, DC

"Thank you for joining us on such short notice," Jamie Richter said. Richter was dressed conservatively in a black suit, white shirt and blue tie. The suit was rumpled, as though he'd donned and doffed the jacket repeatedly throughout the day, and his hair was just short of disheveled.

Hoskins, by contrast, appeared every bit the Ivy League stereotype of CIA leadership. He wore a double-breasted navy blazer, gray twill pants, and a white shirt with a red and gold striped tie. A white silk square bubbled out of his chest pocket like a cumulous cloud. He looked like he belonged in a private club.

"How is Will?" Hoskins asked. The deputy director was tall and lean, an intense and brooding scarecrow. Not for the first time, Colt wondered how this man would recruit an asset in the field. Not that Hoskins didn't have the aptitude for clandestine work, he clearly did (or at least, for political survivability). It was more that he just didn't look like a spook.

He was a white shoe lawyer who traded in the nation's deepest, darkest secrets.

Maybe that was the point.

"How did you know that's where I was?" Colt asked.

Hoskins gave Colt a bemused stare and poured him a glass of whatever was in the decanter on the table between them.

"I'm very sorry about Jason," Hoskins said. "He was a great man, and he was one of us. I learned a lot from him over the years. He was . . . Jason was the best of us." His voice wavered slightly, and it was obvious Hoskins was uncomfortable talking about it.

"Thank you, sir," Colt said.

"How did Europe go?" Hoskins asked, changing the subject.

"We got Reece Craddock. He's now in custody here, and not coopera-tive. My FBI liaison is working on getting Heather Fleet now. We'd like to get her before someone else does."

"That's good. Even if Craddock doesn't talk, he's been a thorn in a lot of sides for twenty years. You capturing him at least gives us a favor to cash in with Justice. What do you think we'll get from him?"

"Hard to say, sir. Like I said, he's uncooperative, but I suspect he knows where the code-breaking effort is being run from. Or we can use intel we've gotten from other sources to corroborate what he says."

Hoskins nodded and swirled his drink, but didn't sip it. "I've met with most of my counterparts, friend and foe alike. The Chinese still think this is an elaborate plot to hide some new technology we have. The others mostly agree that some unknown actor is responsible. These leaks are so random, targeting public and private institutions that people assumed were secure. Nothing feels safe. No one knows what to protect or how to respond." Colt picked up on something in Hoskins' demeanor. *Everyone* looked scared and exhausted, but this was something else. If Colt had to put a word to it, he'd choose "acceptance." It was strange to see that in a man who'd carved an Agency career by outmaneuvering rivals with such skill and precision it put him at the top of the clandestine service.

"Colt," Jamie Richter said behind his glass tumbler of what looked like scotch. "The president is unlikely to win reelection in November. There's a lot of lingering sentiment over the crises from last year, that we should've done more. People aren't wrong, but the president is bearing the brunt of the last two decades of poor decisions and delayed actions. It's not fair, but that's democracy. Naturally, the Hawkinson campaign has pounced on these leaks as conclusive proof of our incompetence. I've tried to explain on the talk show circuit that Hawkinson has blocked every attempt by the Congress to upgrade our cybersecurity or establish national standards. Given that this is happening worldwide, they're able to deflect pretty well. This thing with the Turks probably seals it."

Turkey, Colt mused. That was so many problems ago, he barely remembered it. Turkish intelligence had caught the Agency trying to bug a private meeting between the Russian and Chinese presidents. The CIA knew now that it was one of these myriad leaks plaguing the world that led the Turks to sniff it out.

"Anything new on Erica Cano?" Colt asked. He didn't know her personally, but everyone in the Clandestine Service knew her name now.

"The Turkish Government has her in custody and will not let us speak to her until we accede to their demands," Hoskins said.

Richter continued. "Which we will not do. POTUS will not let the Turks blackmail us. We're not inviting them back in the F-35 program, and we're not agreeing to any of their other concessions. So they'll tell the Russians and the Chinese about our eavesdropping op. With every other secret laid bare, how much more damage can it do? We're not exactly worried about relations with either of them at this point. The Turks overplayed their hand. They'll threaten to leave NATO, but they won't actually do it. Once that blows over, we can negotiate for Ms. Cano's release."

The geopolitics lesson is fascinating, but what am I doing here? Colt asked himself. He still hadn't touched his drink.

"While you were in Europe, Preston Hawkinson secured the nomination. With POTUS almost sure to lose now, that means we're looking at having an Archon agent in the White House come January," Richter said. "And, Dwight has some other . . . news to share."

"Forty-eight hours ago, I authorized a unit from the Special Activities Center to capture and extradite Jin Yoon from his home in Seoul. Archon knew we were coming. Through some intermediary, they tipped the South Korean National Intelligence Service. They were waiting for us and arrested our team for conducting an unsanctioned intelligence operation on their soil. I've tried to convince my opposite number that their celebrated scientist is a member of a techno-terrorist organization, and he laughed before he hung up on me. The CIA director and the secretary of state are in Seoul now to try and repair the damage. The director, at least, knows about Archon." Hoskins lifted his glass but still didn't move to drink it. "He's asked for my resignation once this is all over."

"I'm sorry, sir," Colt said.

"It was a risky move. It was also the only one I could make under the circumstances."

Colt considered Hoskins, seeing the head of the clandestine service in a new light. He'd put his entire career on the line for this fight, and lost. That was contrary to everything he'd come to believe about the man.

It was an act of selfless bravery.

"What do you make of these assassinations, Colt?" Richter asked.

"My team believes Guy Hawkinson is responsible. It's a power play to seize control of the organization. But there's something that Guy doesn't know, which is that the board members have contingency plans that activate if they die. A board member's death will activate these spin-off groups with their own agendas. Because no one board member knows what the others' subordinate organizations are or who is in them, we have no way of knowing who is leading these efforts. EMBER says he doesn't know. As of right now, we have at least four Archon spin-off groups activating."

"Why? I mean, what does it give them?"

"Because it's something else for us to chase. These guys understand asymmetric warfare very well. Each time we make ground, they give us a new fire to fight. It also makes sure that their objectives live on after they die. We're assuming some of this is codified in the systems they've developed as well. Those likely live on."

"And your source, EMBER, knew this about Archon," Hoskins said, "but Guy does not?"

"Does it change things materially if Guy does?" Richter asked. "What if creating these spin-offs is Guy's intention in killing off Archon's leadership? Or at least an intentional by-product?"

"Archon has all but eliminated secrecy and privacy to give Preston Hawkinson an existential crisis to solve when he takes office. More smoke and mirrors. Guy decides to take advantage of that and starts killing off leadership once the plan is in motion. He reaps the benefits of their plan and eliminates his rivals. And once his uncle is in the oval, his pardon is secured."

"The longer we wait, the more board members are killed, the more of these spin-offs, as you call them, can launch. Is that right?"

"Yes, sir," Colt said. He opened his mouth to say more, but closed it.

"Was there anything else?" Richter asked.

"No, sir." He didn't want to bring up anything about his earlier speculation with Ford about the illogic of Hawkinson moving against the board before the election.

Richter held his gaze a moment and Colt felt like his soul was unravelling. He immediately regretted answering in the negative, because he could see in Richter's eyes that the man knew he'd held something back, something possibly vital. At least, vital to Colt.

To his surprise, Richter didn't press the point.

Perhaps he had renewed faith in the value of secrecy in a world where it seemed to be nearing extinction.

Richter turned to look out the window next to him. He studied something on the Cosmos Club's back lawn for some time, exhaled, and turned back to the other two. "I'm afraid we waited too long to act. You can save the 'I told you so,' but know that you're correct and that I agree with you. We only have one course of action left, I fear." Richter paused in silent contemplation. When he spoke, Colt could see the grim resolution etching its way into his face. "Colt, the world would be better off without Guy Hawkinson in it. It's the only sure way to neutralize the threat if his uncle wins the White House. I understand what I'm asking of you. I also cannot protect you if it goes wrong."

24

Langley, Virginia

They wanted him to kill Guy Hawkinson.

Well, at least now Colt understood why they wanted to meet in a private room inside a members-only club.

Giving him that instruction in front of Dwight Hoskins meant the move was, at least implicitly, authorized by the CIA. Though with Hoskins' days numbered, that didn't count for much. The Agency was politically shielded since it was coming from the White House, but Colt was not. Jamie Richter had been quite clear on that point. *If it goes wrong, you're on your own.*

Colt couldn't blame the man.

The Agency had a complicated relationship with assassination. And this was among the murkiest orders ever given, Colt reasoned. Over-the-horizon drone shots on terrorist leaders were one thing. The Bin Laden raid had been the culmination of a decade-long, global manhunt with the president watching live to give the final kill order. This was . . . different. Hawkinson was an American citizen and, therefore, constitutionally protected.

Asking Colt to kill him blatantly violated the law. Several laws.

If Colt failed, or worse, if he succeeded and was discovered, the government would try Colt for murder. Senator Preston Hawkinson would see this the most egregious violation of presidential authority in U.S. history. It would bring down the entire administration and would undoubtedly stain the presidency—any presidency—for decades to come.

The CIA worked every day to thwart those who killed to stay in power.

This is third-world dictator shit, Fred's voice said in his mind.

"You're not wrong," Colt replied aloud.

Richter was also correct.

There could be no due process for Guy Hawkinson.

If they arrested him, now, his uncle would claim it was a political stunt, the only desperate card that a failing president had left to play. Even if the president somehow won the reelection, the senator would still claim retribution. Rumors suggested Senator Hawkinson would work to impeach if he lost. Assassinating his nephew would unquestionably add fuel that fire.

If Colt didn't do it, Guy Hawkinson would almost certainly succeed.

It was the worst of all options, yet it was still unequivocally the right thing to do.

It just happened to be the most profound violation of the Constitution Colt could fathom.

Third-world dictator shit.

"They sure didn't teach this course at the Farm, Jason," Colt said. He wished Wilcox was there to talk it through with him.

Colt returned home to a restless stretch of hours and a world full of nightmares, whether he was asleep or awake.

The next day started off strange.

Strange for Colt, which was saying something.

Blankenship called and said that he'd spoken with Deputy Director Hoskins and they'd agreed it was best for the NTCU and the Technology Mission Center to remain separate for now.

Reading between those lines, Colt guessed Hoskins was giving what little support he could. That alone was staggering, given the revelation that

Hoskins was being forced to retire. Instead of shuttering all Archon-related ops, he was doubling down.

Nadia was waiting for him at his office with a welcome breakthrough. Jeff Kim and the Agency's Sci-Tech Division engineers had finalized their prototype post-quantum encryption algorithm. Hypothetically, at least. If it worked, they would have protected communications in the field that, by Jeff's estimation, would stand up to any attempts to break it.

Probably.

"We don't totally know that it works," Nadia said, hedging.

"We're not playing a 'second chances' kind of game here," Colt said.

"Look, I get it, but no one has attempted this sort of thing before. Because the encryption key is based on the quantum states of subatomic particles, theoretically, it cannot be broken. The key is unknowable to an adversary. But, like I said, no one has ever tried this, so we won't know until we get into the field. No one has ever tried using a quantum computer to hack a quantum encryption algorithm. It isn't supposed to be possible . . ." Nadia trailed off with a shrug. She didn't know what else to say, or how else to explain it. They were trying to apply an uncharted area of science to a real-world espionage challenge that was unfolding by the minute.

"This takes us back to the problem of the quantum network you brought up in Austria, right?" Colt asked.

"Exactly. Regardless of the type, computing is ultimately about how much power you can throw against a math problem. Jeff has a quantum computer. The Agency has a prototype and, for obvious reasons, we're not linking the two of them. We could only use the assets we had available. Archon might have as many as fourteen quantum computers, based on your brief."

They now had a way to isolate quantum computing traffic on the internet, which meant they could trace it back to the source and the ability to communicate securely in the field.

Nadia said, "So, what's the plan?"

Colt asked her to get the team together while he considered how much he could tell them.

Once the group assembled in the unit's conference room, Colt closed the door.

"We're going after Guy Hawkinson. I'm trusting EMBER's intel that he's in Singapore. Alison also worked late into the night on some additional analysis backing that up. This is a risky play, though, because we don't know exactly where he'll be. Nadia, that's where you come in with the work you did with Jeff. I want you and Solomon deploying the trace program. Alison, I'd like you to work with CERBERUS and try to connect any Hawkinson or Archon datapoints with Singapore. Guy got there somehow. He's certainly traveling under a forged passport, but he's got lodging, he's got transportation, and all those things get paid for somehow. Let's see if we can find the front company. He's also going to have a security detail, and I bet most of them are ex–Hawk Security Group. Forging passports is difficult, expensive, and illegal."

"So, Guy probably did it for himself. Not for his team," Angela said.

"Exactly. We know that Guy kept the executive protection business running after he sold off the rest of HSG. We have those names."

"If it's just as simple as looking up his entourage, why didn't we start with that months ago?" Keith Ricci asked.

"This is only a theory, and it might be wrong. Guy would have disappeared alone. Once he thought he was safe, though, he'd have contacted his most trusted men and had them meet him. Most people wouldn't assume he'd go back to his old team once he was in the wind, but Alison's profile of him suggests that's exactly what he'd do."

"Wouldn't he just hire new mercenaries for this?" Ricci asked.

"I don't think so," Angela said. "He puts a high value on trust and personal relationships. He's also on the run and knows that intelligence services in half a dozen countries are trying to get him. He won't work with people he doesn't know well." As a targeter, D'Angelo's job was to immerse herself in her subject, become an expert on them. It was as much human psychology as it was intelligence analysis.

"Keith, next up, I'd like you to head up Heather Fleet's arrest."

"I've already got tickets booked for LA. I leave tomorrow. I'll be working out of the LA Field Office."

Colt nodded. He didn't like having to deceive to one of his team, but he knew how the FBI agent would respond to the real plan, and there simply wasn't time for any more debate. Colt had his orders, whether he liked them or not. For a moment, he wondered if he was making a mistake in not giving Ricci, who'd served as the team's conscience, a chance to object.

Of course, Colt hadn't shared the full scope of their orders with the rest of the team either. He'd said only that they were going after Guy Hawkinson. He didn't say how far that extended.

Colt remembered a lesson Wilcox had once given him on the streets of Vancouver. His mentor explained the need for conscience, how it was the most important tool an intelligence officer had. "The country may ask things of you that aren't right and justify it in the interest of national security. That's how we get caught up in things like mining harbors in Nicaragua and Iran-Contra," Wilcox had said. "To paraphrase General Patton, your job is to get some poor bastard to break the laws of his country, so you defend the existence of yours. Never conflate the two. If it doesn't feel right, it probably isn't."

"That just leaves Braithwaite, who we can't touch," D'Angelo said. "And Jin Yoon."

"Let's assume he's off the table for right now as well," Colt said. Tony shot him a hard glance, but said nothing. Of course he would know.

Colt ended the meeting and sent his team off to their respective tasks. Tony stayed behind.

"One second," Colt said. He opened up the app on his computer that accessed the covert communication app on Liu Che's phone. Colt sent the Chinese spymaster a message that they needed to talk ASAP.

Once they were alone, Tony said, "We deployed a team to Seoul to get Yoon and they didn't come back." The Agency's Special Activities Center, once known as the Special Operations Group, was home to the blackest of the CIA's black operations. Referred to as "the third option" in Agency parlance, the SAC was used when there were no choices left and failure wasn't an option. It was a small, tight group and they tended to know what one another was doing. Though, Colt guessed, Tony was the only one who knew why they were trying to capture a South Korean scientist and doing so without talking to their counterparts in Seoul.

"I know. I'll share this with you, but I couldn't tell the others. Hoskins ordered the grab. Archon knew they were coming and warned the South Korean government. Used a cutout or an agent or something. The director and secretary of state are there now trying to patch things up. The move cost Hoskins his job."

"Shit," Tony said. "And they still want us to get Guy?"

Colt nodded. "The part I didn't tell the rest of the team, and this comes from the White House, is that we're not arresting him."

Tony immediately understood.

"I don't know how to do this stuff," Colt said heavily. "My background is in economic intel and tech. I'm good on the street, I know that much, but I've never planned something like this before and I don't even know where to start."

"Normally, I'd jump in with both feet, you know that, Colt. This is . . ." Ikeda shook his head. "I have to think about this."

"I understand, and if you say 'no,' I'll understand that too."

"And there are no other options?"

"There are not."

"I'll get back to you when I've considered it. The White House not giving us top cover scares the shit out of me."

"You and me both, brother. Can you help me with an ops plan, though? Even if you don't go, I need your help putting this together."

"Of course."

Colt and Tony worked late into the night. Not knowing where Guy would be made planning this nearly impossible, so their first task was to familiarize themselves with the city and how to create the conditions for success.

They had a break late that night. D'Angelo had also stayed late, working with the unit's highly sophisticated AI, CERBERUS. CERBERUS had originally been designed to conduct pattern matching and link analysis at scale and at machine speed, meaning it could finish actions that would tie up teams of human analysts for months. Angela focused on the members of Hawk Security Group, Guy's former private security company, that the Agency believed stayed with him after he sold the company off. She got a hit on a man named Jordan Kirk. Kirk was a former

U.S. Army ranger who had served with Guy in Iraq and then joined him at HSG.

CERBERUS was networked throughout the unit, so they could pull feeds up on any screen. D'Angelo joined Colt and Tony in the conference room. It was nearing ten.

"I've got him," she said, and gave a quick summary of Kirk's background. "Kirk has made three trips to Singapore in the last six weeks. He varies his route each time. Once he flew through Kuala Lumpur, once into Singapore direct, and once into Batam."

"How do you know all that?" Tony asked.

"CERBERUS is hooked into the State Department, so with the new chipped passports we can see any time it's scanned into a country, if they have that technology. The Singaporeans do. Each time he stayed at the Travelodge Harbourfront."

"Can we figure out what credit card he used? That might help us find how Hawkinson is paying for things. It'll be owned by a shell company, but probably the same one."

"I can," Tony said.

The CIA had originally recruited Tony out of UCLA's computer science program because he'd gotten a reputation as an exceptional software developer and spoke Japanese fluently. Instead of entering the clandestine service after the graduating from the Farm, he was sent to then SOG, where the Agency trained him as a hacker. Tony accompanied black ops teams in the field and supported them with cyber capabilities, deactivating municipal power grids, sensors, and alarms, that sort of thing. When the CIA learned about his extensive martial arts experience, they offered him an opportunity to join the ranks as an operative, combining both his technical and physical skills.

It wouldn't take him long to hack into the hotel's reservation system, especially not considering the resources available to them at the NTCU. Tony said he'd need about an hour.

While Tony was doing that, Colt checked his COVCOM app and found he had a message from Liu, asking to speak.

Colt went to his office and closed the door. He opened a VPN tunnel, plugged a headset into his computer, and dialed.

Liu answered and gave the current code phrase to prove he wasn't under duress.

"We can confirm Archon is responsible for the security breaches," Colt said. Confirmation might be a bit of a stretch, Colt thought, but he wasn't going to tell Liu that. He wouldn't disclose how the CIA knew this, or the technology Archon used to do it. Though, of the latter, Colt assumed Liu would eventually reach the same conclusion he had.

Despite their being on opposite sides, Liu was one of the few people outside the NTCU that truly understood Archon for the threat it was.

"I assumed as much," Liu said softly. "Though my leaders still believe this is a grand American scheme. The party is dismissing this as American propaganda, but internally they are terrified. The president is furious. After all, one cannot bluff when the opponent can see one's cards."

"When we met last, you mentioned having a network in Singapore. What can you find out about Guy Hawkinson?"

"In Singapore?"

"Yes. And as soon as you can get it."

"Let me see what I can do."

Tony easily accessed the hotel's reservation system and got the credit card Jordan Kirk had used to pay for his room. They put a global alert on it. The next time he used it, they'd know. In the meantime, Tony was working on the transaction history. It was a corporate card, registered to a company called "Apex Systems," which, in turn, was registered to a succession of holding companies.

The hotel Kirk stayed at was within line of sight of two marinas and not far from the city's industrial center.

Kirk was at the hotel now, so they agreed Tony would deploy immediately for Singapore and set up surveillance on him. Tony hadn't fully come around to their ultimate objective, but he could create a mental wall between that and surveilling a target.

Three days later, Colt heard from Liu.

"One of my sources reported a meeting between the Singaporean government and an American entrepreneur, Cooper Barnes."

"Okay?"

"Cooper Barnes is an alias Guy Hawkinson used to do business in Singapore."

"How do you know this?"

"Because he told me," Liu deadpanned.

Before Colt trapped him and flipped him as an asset, Liu had tried recruiting Hawkinson. Guy believed it was the other way around. *A useful reminder when dealing with Liu Che*, Colt told himself. "When I met with Guy in Geneva, he mentioned having investment in a project in Singapore. He tried to convince me to embark on a joint venture. I informed him this would be problematic, since they are an American ally and he was under investigation at the time. Guy told me he worked under an alias, bragged about it, in fact. He was trying to impress me and told me the name. I had it checked out later and then gave it to one of my agents as a standing information requirement."

"When does the meeting take place?"

"Next week."

25

Singapore

Colt left for Singapore on the first flight he could get after speaking with Liu. He met up with Tony, who'd already acquired a safe house and had been tailing Jordan Kirk for several days. Other than his hotel's rooftop bar, Kirk had only made three stops. The first was to pick up one of two black Range Rovers Apex Systems had recently purchased. The second stop was to a mixed-use office park on Singapore's west side. The third was to the Keppel Bay Marina, which was less than a mile from his hotel.

Tony agreed to stay in Singapore on one condition.

If Tony called the operation off, Colt couldn't question him, couldn't override him. Colt was free to go about it on his own, but if Tony said it was too risky, that was it. Colt agreed. They also agreed that if they found evidence they thought the FBI could use for prosecution, regardless of what the White House or Langley's Seventh Floor said, they would get Ricci out there immediately.

Their careers would be over, they both knew, if they bucked a White House directive—even an unofficial one. They could both live with it.

Before departing, Hoskins set them up with a black bank account, an off-the-books pot of funds for them to use in the operation. It was close to a quarter of a million dollars. Colt didn't ask where it came from and didn't want to know. Tony knew how to secure weapons abroad, even in a place as tightly regulated as Singapore.

They rented a two-bedroom apartment near the city center using an Agency front company that wasn't traceable back to Langley. Same with the car. They had ways to buy the other things they'd need, but first they needed to determine where Hawkinson was so they could decide how best to get at him.

Colt's first morning in Singapore, Colt and Tony were planning over coffee when they heard three sharp knocks on the apartment's door. Tony gave Colt a concerned look and Colt got up and walked to the door.

He opened it and Ava walked in.

"Good. Now tell me what in the hell I'm doing here."

Colt was relieved to see her, and after their meeting in Amsterdam, he wasn't sure she'd show.

"I'm going to go do some recon," Tony said, and left the room without missing a beat.

Colt assumed Hawkinson had Ava under surveillance. Contacting her post-Austria was challenging and problematic. Knowing they didn't have time to work out a more complicated, virtual solution, Colt had loaded Kim's new encryption model onto an NTCU-modified smartphone, put it in a diplomatic pouch to London Station, and had one of their officers deliver it to a dead drop in the city. To let Ava know where it was, Colt applied some real-world tradecraft to the digital world, stashing the message within a virtual server he'd spun up for a short time. Ava navigated to it using Trinity's version of a TOR browser, obfuscating her trail through cyberspace, and found the file where Colt identified the phone's location.

Colt included a handwritten note explaining that the phone was safe and for her to call him immediately using the encryption app.

"We think we know where Hawkinson is," Colt said when he answered her call. "He's here, or will be soon."

"Why are you telling me?" Ava's words frosted over him like an icy winter morning.

"Because I'd like you to meet me. I can't explain on the phone, but we can end this thing and I need your help."

"The last time we spoke, you blamed me for Jason's murder."

"That was wrong, and I'm sorry. I spoke with Thorpe. One of the last things Jason said to him was that Trinity didn't do it."

That didn't let Ava off the hook entirely. After all, she *had* murdered Carlos Marin. As Trinity's leader, Wilcox was a target no matter what, but Colt still believed they might not have come for him had someone not been targeting their leaders. It was impossible to know.

Then why contact her? Why bring her in on this if he wasn't positive he could trust her?

Because Colt had nowhere else to turn. He couldn't use official assets for this, beyond the black money Hoskins had dumped into an offshore bank for him. He was completely on his own and that meant he had to go to the only person who knew Archon for the threat that it was.

Maybe it was the fact that Ava was one of the few people on Earth who could relate to Colt in this, have some understanding of what he was going through. And what he was up against.

Ava told him he couldn't trade on their relationship for intel, but she'd gone back on that herself after Archon murdered Jason, and Colt had Craddock in custody. Maybe it wasn't an absolute. Maybe they should work together and let any personal consequences work themselves out later.

Also, if she was here with him, she couldn't also execute Guy.

"I'm waiting," Ava said. "I flew here for whatever this is. You said you know Hawkinson will be here. Great. Why am *I* here?"

Apparently, flying all the way here from London had not put her in a good mood.

But she'd come anyway.

Colt showed her into the living room.

"Let me start with what we know, and that'll explain what's going on."

Ava's eyes narrowed and Colt knew from long experience that her temper was held together by rapidly fraying threads. "I think you'd better start with the latter."

"I have authorization to kill Guy," he said.

The color drained out of Ava's face. "I wasn't expecting that," she said.

"Can we sit?" Colt said. He brought her a cup of coffee and a bottle of water and they went to the couch. "You know what will happen if it ever gets out that I told you this, but you're also the only one who'd understand. The White House authorized me to take Guy out. They're convinced his uncle is going to be elected in November. Even if the rest of Archon's leadership is taken out, as long as Guy is free a President Hawkinson can do irreversible damage to our country. If not, the world."

"This is what Jason was most concerned with," Ava said. "But he wouldn't want you to kill Guy."

Colt was about the press the issue and then withdrew it. This was not the time. Just having her sit down with him was a kind of victory.

"We think there's a split in Archon's leadership."

Ava barked out a bitter laugh. "Again?"

"After investing, what, fifty million into his tech retreat in the Virgin Islands that the Russians wiped out? Then being forced to release that bioweapon before it was ready, which we, Mossad, and MI6 all picked up. Finally, using HawkTech's assets to launch cyberattacks against the West, which we wouldn't have detected but for Jeff Kim's help. At least, not in time. Guy believes he made all the sacrifices and was still denied a seat at the table. He snapped. He killed some of the board members. Personally, I think he only wanted to eliminate a few—the aggressive ones, like Quentin Wales. Guy likely thought he could reshape things as he desired after that."

Colt had only realized this in the last few days, as he continued to pour over D'Angelo's analysis and worked with CERBERUS to further explore Guy's patterns.

"So, you don't think that I did this?"

"I don't think you did *all* of them," Colt said. He wouldn't tell her he knew about Marin, or how he knew. That would create a crater too wide to cross in his relationship with her, or with Ann, not to mention what it would do between Ann and Ava.

To his great surprise, Ava did not explode.

"I don't know if you knew that he'd killed Wales or not. We know Bolton died with a drone swarm downing his aircraft. There aren't many people with the technology to do that. I'd put even money on you and Hawkinson for it. Emmanuelle died from a gunshot, but it was a remotely operated fifty-caliber rifle, not unlike the mechanism that they shot you with in Greece last year. Given what we know about Emmanuelle, I'd put that one on Hawkinson. Marin died by a small scale suicide drone, and—"

"That one was me," Ava admitted. "And Jason didn't know. He never thought we should kill them. We argued that point a lot. I told them, why would you bring someone like me into this if we're just going to play computer games? Jason wanted us to subvert Archon, use our technology to defeat theirs, buy time for Western security services to catch up and make arrests. But Marin ordered my parent's death. I couldn't let that stand. I was prepared to act on the others, but what you told me in Amsterdam made me reconsider."

Ava's expression softened, and Colt could see in her eyes that she knew she had gone too far. "I'm sorry," Ava reached across the space between them, put her hand on his, and squeezed. "These last few months have been . . . a lot."

"I know," he said. "I got called into a meeting at this private club in DC a little over a week ago. The national security advisor and the head of the Clandestine Service were there. The NSA told me, in so many words, to kill Guy, but that they couldn't protect me if things went badly. I shouldn't admit this to you, but . . ." Colt finished his sentence with a tired shrug.

Ava's face flushed, and she jerked her hand back. "So, what, you call me in so *I* can do it? You figure I do your dirty work, we have a roll in the sack, and everyone goes home. What the f—"

"Ava! Damn it, listen to me."

"Believe me, I am. Every word."

"I called you here to help me, not to do the job for me. I've got nothing left. It's me and Tony. I'm not even sure I can go through with it."

"Your service has killed plenty of your country's enemies."

"Just because there are no better options doesn't make this right. And CIA doesn't kill citizens. I don't know if I can do it, and more than that, I don't know if I *should*. If we can justify murdering our own citizens, regardless of what they've done, how are we better than the people we're supposedly fighting? Yes, Guy has dodged justice at every step. And Jamie Richter isn't wrong. If the FBI arrested Guy tomorrow, his uncle would just pardon him the day he's inaugurated. Then he's free to use the full power of the United States government to go after everyone he considers a threat."

"Explain to me again how this is a debate?"

"Because Guy Hawkinson is an American citizen, and he has rights, whether or not I like them."

Ava stood and walked over to the window, looking out at the daytime bustle below. "Colt, everything you say is true. Guy Hawkinson is a monster. I know you're familiar with Operation Wrath of God."

Of course he was. Every intelligence officer in the world knew about Mossad's yearslong mission to get revenge for the Munich Massacre.

"The public perception is that we ruthlessly pursued the architects of the Holocaust. The truth of it is, we were far less successful hunting Nazis as we were at killing Palestinians. Yes, we got Eichmann and some others, but so many escaped and died of old age." She walked back across the room, arms folded. Her delivery was professorial, almost clinical. Though Israeli by birth, she'd spent half her childhood and her university years in the U.S. When she spoke of Israel as a nation, it tended to be dispassionately. "Israel had too many existential problems to worry about—invasion from our neighbors, terrorism, assassinations of our leaders. We had more crises than we could manage, so hunting down Nazis fell by the wayside. So, yes, we killed the architects, but so many of the construction workers survived. *That* is why I joined Trinity." And the fire in her that he'd always known, that fearless fury, was back in an instant. She'd gone from lecturer to revolutionary in the span of a breath.

"Archon's criticisms of our governments aren't wrong: they're slow, they're mostly ineffective. The British were tricked into leaving the EU and they even screwed that up. Then they spied on them to understand how much damage it really did, rather than just having a conversation about it. My country reelected a prime minister convicted of corruption. Your country is about to put an Archon agent in the White House. That should be impossible. I'm telling you these things because classifying 'right and wrong' as 'black or white' isn't always easy. The lesson with the Nazi hunting is twofold. One, that honest leaders have to make hard decisions about what problems they can solve with the time they have in power. Two, that sometimes there are problems leaders can't solve with the tools their people give them. We should have punished them all. We didn't, and most escaped."

"And that makes killing Hawkinson okay?" Colt spoke in measured, analytical tones. He didn't want to Ava to feel accused.

"I can't answer that for you. I know what's okay for me, but as you already said, I have a different perspective." Ava's words took on a razor's edge with that last phrase. "I'll support whatever you decide, and I won't do anything unless you ask me to. For your sake, as much as for ours."

Colt stood.

Before he knew what he was doing, he took Ava into his arms and held her. She just stood there for a moment, as if considering how to respond. He felt the muscles in her arms and back move subtly, but didn't know how to interpret it until she returned the embrace. She rested her head on his shoulder. Colt drank her in. Sometimes, he missed her so much it hurt, but he forced himself to think about anything else just so he could get through the day. In that moment, it was almost overwhelming.

"We only seem to see each other when the world is about to end," she said softly. The line had become a running, dark joke between them.

"I know," Colt said. A million thoughts ran through his mind at once. "When this is over, we need to figure us out. I love you, I want to be with you, I just want the world to give us a damn chance."

"Me too," she said. Ava stepped back and that dry, sardonic grin slid up one side of her mouth and her eyes lit. "Now, we just have to kill Hawkinson so we can have proper dates again."

"You're trouble," Colt said.

Colt went to check current intel and any updates from the unit back home.

"How are you going to locate him once he gets here? This is a relatively small city, but it's still heavily populated," Ava asked as they were digging into their takeout lunch.

"We learned he was going to be here because of one of my assets," Colt said. "They passed the information along that Guy would be here, and we already knew Archon had invested in a quantum computing facility here."

Ava snapped her fingers. "I have an idea. One thing Jason had me doing was using our AIs to uncover Archon shell corporations and roll them up. We were looking for all the places they were hiding money or ways they used fake companies to hide their moves. We dropped a lot of anonymous tips with law enforcement agencies and revenue services across the world. But, more than once, I called some banks pretending to be a cop and had them shut these down."

Colt laughed.

"With our systems working continually on these, we found and rolled up a lot of these shell corporations. We've been working with groups like the Internet Freedom Foundation and Bellingcat and gave them a huge document dump for them to go after. The point is, Hawkinson has far fewer places to park his money than he did a year ago. What if I give you all of my intel? Could your analysts do anything with it?"

Hell yes, they could. This kind of pattern matching was exactly what CERBERUS was designed to do. "My source is supposed to tell me where Hawkinson's meeting will be. Knowing where that facility is located is just as important." Cold grinned slyly. "I don't have the same reservation with property damage."

Ava transferred the files to Colt from her laptop. He put them on a hidden container online and had the NTCU ops center download them for Nadia to work on when she got in the next morning.

Tony returned by early afternoon. He could tell that whatever tension had existed when Ava arrived had dissipated, and he asked no follow-up questions.

They made plans for the following day. Colt wanted to familiarize himself with the city and needed to check in with Liu. Hawkinson's meeting with the Singaporeans would take place within the next few days, but they still didn't have any details.

———

Shortly after nine p.m., all of their phones erupted in sync .

They'd stopped working about an hour before and were having a beer at a bar down the street from the apartment when Colt's phone started vibrating. Ava's went next, Tony's last.

Colt's phone had multiple notifications on it, but the one he paid attention to was the encrypted chat tool Nadia had roughed out with Jeff. Colt opened it, scanned through the message, and by the time he got to the end, his body was practically vibrating with nervous energy.

"What is it?" Ava asked.

"Hold on," Colt said, voice edged with tension, and clicked on the link Nadia sent. It was to the front-page story of the *New York Times*, identifying the National Technical Counterintelligence Unit by name. It described them as "a kind of high-tech black ops group" that operated both within and without the United States. There was no mention of the FBI's role, or their authorization under the Foreign Intelligence Surveillance Act. The article alleged they had a sophisticated artificial intelligence program they used to conduct "a sweeping domestic espionage program."

The most damning allegation was that the NTCU worked alongside the cyber-terrorist organization known as "Trinity."

26

By midnight Singapore time, Langley had a solid four hours to get themselves into a full frothing panic.

Colt spoke with Nadia, who he learned was calling from somewhere on the Agency campus. Apparently, Blankenship had ordered a full stand-down for all NTCU personnel and demanded to know why Colt wasn't at Headquarters Station.

"I don't know what to do," Nadia said. "People are really freaking out here."

"Don't stick your neck out. Whatever Blankenship asks you to do, you do, understand?"

"Okay, I got it, but I have to update you on what we've been doing first."

"Is this going to get you in trouble?" Colt asked, warningly. He knew that Nadia's relationship with the rules was more of a "casual understanding" than an acknowledgement of absolutes.

"I don't know," she said dismissively. "Maybe, probably. Whatever. Listen. D'Angelo said Guy is only going to travel by private jet or boat, like a Class A oceangoing yacht. Part of it is because he's a pretentious asshole, but it's mostly for the security. We took the data you gave us last night and ran it through CERBERUS, like you said. We linked the private aircraft entering Singapore's airports to their registration and who paid for it if the flight was a charter. Normally, this would take the system a lot of time, but it wasn't a large dataset—a few hundred flights over seven days. Anyway, we ruled out air travel because we could verify the origin and provenance of every flight."

"Did you check Malaysia?" The city-state of Singapore was an island just off the top of Malaysia, connected by a pair of bridges and innumerable ferries.

"We didn't, but don't get distracted. We found a ship that's got a berth at the Keppel Bay Marina. It's registered to a charter company owned by a firm called International Transportation Services."

"Jordan Kirk, one of Guy's security detail, is staying at a hotel within earshot of Keppel Bay Marina. He's made several trips there. I think Kirk is acting as an advance team, getting vehicles, things like that."

"That has to be it. One of those Archon shell companies owns ITS. I'm assuming that you got this from Trinity. They did some serious legwork here. I can see from the logs how many nested layers of corporations they unraveled. Anyway, the boat is registered in Bari, which is on—"

"Italy's Adriatic coast. I'm familiar with it."

"Records show it docked yesterday."

"Nadia, thank you. This is incredible work. Now, *please* keep your head down, okay?"

"Yeah, I probably won't, but I appreciate the sentiment. Not sure how much more help I can be. Blankenship ordered us to shut down CERBERUS."

Colt reiterated his instructions, hoping that if she heard them again, maybe it'd take.

He shared what he'd just learned with Ava and Tony.

"As soon as the sun is up, I'll go recon the marina," Tony said. "I'm sure they'll have private security, but I can't imagine they'll be much good."

"Assume Hawkinson is armed."

"I've gotten us clean weapons. I'll pick them up tomorrow," Tony said.

"Do I want to ask?" Colt asked.

"You do not," Tony said. He opened his laptop and started thundering on the keys. "I'm going to hack into the marina's admin system and see if Hawkinson has a vehicle registered with them."

"Good idea."

"There's an avenue we haven't considered yet," Ava said.

"What's that?"

"What if I go talk to him?" She held up her hands. "Think about it before you say no. I come in waving the white flag. He'll take a meeting with me—he did just murder my boss. It'd be a reasonable next step to say I want this war to end. Guy knows you, but he doesn't know Tony. He can come as my security guard."

"To what end?" Colt asked. "Hawkinson is going to have his own security on the boat, and they'll check both of you for weapons."

"We're not doing it there. At least, not on the first try. This would give us a chance to interrogate him first. Tony gets firsthand intel."

"I'm looking at satellite photos of the marina now. I can easily set up a sniper position."

"Can you get a rifle in time?"

Tony shrugged. "Probably not. Just throwing ideas out. Another option, though I like it less, is that I swim aboard in the middle of the night and take care of it. I can pretty much guarantee his people aren't doing twenty-four hour patrols. He's not going to travel with that big of an entourage, it'll attract too much attention. Especially if the ship captain doesn't really know who he's working for."

"Any chance of getting him out of the marina?"

"We could get him on the way to or from his meeting with the locals," Ava mused. "That introduces some complications, though. Namely, it increases our risk by orders of magnitude. I'd rule that out, and you already know my predilection toward taking risks," Ava said, a slight smile breaking across her lips.

"I know. I mean, the safest thing to do would be to put a charge on the ship and detonate it when they're at sea. That's the only way I know of to limit our exposure. But that creates the possibility for civilian casualties that I'm not comfortable with. That crew is just driving a boat. They probably don't even know who he is."

"I think we've got our answer," Tony said.

The Keppel Bay Marina complex sat on Singapore's southern shore facing the South China Sea and a tight cluster of islands belonging to Indonesia. Colt crossed the Keppel Bay Bridge. It had a single span in the center, angled slightly with guy wires extending out from it, giving the aesthetic of being a ship's mast and sail. Beneath them, waters of a perfect teal rippled softly.

The marina itself was located on a small island within the bay, situated amid a rippling mass of lush green plant life. The marina's stark white construction contrasted sharply with the verdant surroundings, which only served to make the main building's large, domed structure stand out that much more against the jungle backdrop. Palms lined the walkways abutting the water. Tony parked in a spot reserved for prospective members.

They drove separately. Tony would eventually identify himself to Hawkinson, and they didn't want to appear together on the marina's security footage.

The sky was mercifully overcast, but the tropical heat permeated everything.

Colt had rented a vehicle for the day using the alias and credit card they'd spun up for this operation. He parked in the visitor's lot and made his way to the member's lot. He wore a yellow polo, lightweight tan golf pants, designer sneakers he'd purchased that morning, and squared-off aviator sunglasses.

Security here was better than Colt expected. Member parking was in an enclosed garage secured by a key card. He simply entered the building and was immediately stopped by an aggressively helpful concierge in a uniform of a white polo, matching shorts, and too-high socks that reminded Colt of the Royal Navy's tropical kit. "I'm a guest of the Tans," Colt told him. "I left something in the car. I'll just be a minute." Before the concierge could argue, Colt vectored left for the parking garage. Tan was the most common surname in Singapore, so it was a decent bet at least one of the marina's members would share it. Colt stepped into the garage and walked around as though he were looking for a car (which, of course, he was). He was the only person in there, but wanted to make a show for the cameras. He spotted a black Range Rover, one of several, actually, and it took him a minute to line up the license plates.

Colt approached the vehicle. He palmed something from his pocket as he approached the vehicle, bent down to tie his shoelaces and, as he brought his hand up, slid the quarter-sized magnetic tracker up to the rear bumper's underside.

Colt walked to the end of the row and dipped between two cars, out of the line of sight of the cameras, and hung out for a few seconds. He checked his phone to make sure the tracker's signal was good, and then left the garage.

Tony spent an hour with the staff, letting them pitch him on becoming a member and why he should berth his vessel at Keppel Bay. He knew from researching the marina's security that access to the gangways and berths was controlled by a security terminal that required an access code. Tony had to convince them he was a whale in order to get the time, and now they weren't going to let him out of their sight. He impressed upon the sales rep how valuable his time was and that he was quite pressed that day, having an important engagement later that day.

"Shall we look at some berths?" the rep asked. Tony gave his best nonchalant nod.

The rep opened a small refrigerator in his office, handed Tony a branded bottle of water, and led him outside through a blue-tinted glass door flush with the wall. The full weight of the humid tropical air fell on them as they stepped outside.

The rep guided him down a ramp to the small security station, a glass-enclosed booth with a numbered cypher lock. As he walked, he discussed the security features in great detail, explaining how Keppel Bay would dutifully protect Tony's investment. Vamping interest in the security, Tony edged in and looked over the man's shoulder as he typed in the security code on the keypad. Tony committed it to memory.

Once they were through the security gate, Tony stepped forward and guided them in the direction of Hawkinson's ship.

"Let's go this way," he said with a rakish grin. "I'd like to check out the competition."

"Of course," the rep said indulgently, doubtless smelling a fat commission. The two headed down the dock.

"You know what?" Tony paused, surveying the yachts around them. "I think I've seen enough."

"You have?"

"Yes, I'm ready to sign, my good man. Can you give me a moment to speak with my broker? I also want to know how quickly I can have my ship moved down from Hong Kong."

"Absolutely, sir. Take all the time you need. I'll be in my office."

"Wonderful. I'll be up in just a few."

Tony pretended to make some calls until the sales rep had dashed up the ramp, and then walked toward Hawkinson's ship. As he approached the enormous graphite-and-tan vessel, Tony muttered, "Tell me you're a megalomanic without telling me you're a megalomaniac."

He approached the ship and caught the eye of a crew-cut blond man in khakis, a navy polo, wraparound sunglasses, and an earpiece standing just off the gangplank. These idiots couldn't be more obvious.

"I'd like to talk to Guy," Tony said from the dock.

"Don't know who you're talking about," the man growled back. His tradecraft was terrible. Typical grunt, a hammer in a world of nails.

"Okay," Tony said smugly. "Tell you what," he reached into his suit jacket pocket and smiled as the guard flinched. He withdrew a card with a phone number written on it. Tony held it up so he could see, then he walked up the gangplank to the guard and handed him the card. "Give your boss this and when he's ready to talk, we'll talk."

"Who?" the man asked.

"Trinity."

Colt and Tony individually returned to the apartment once they were certain no one had followed them.

Colt returned to an urgent message from Nadia to call her back, which he did.

"It's official. We're totally shut down. The NTCU is offline. Everyone on the team is on administrative leave until they can figure out what to do with them. Since I was never here officially, I'm kind of sidling back to the language school."

"That's smart."

"They confiscated everyone's devices and laptops. If you call back, it'll get rerouted to the Technology Mission Center's watch desk. And they've got orders to patch you into Blankenship. He's demanding to know how to get ahold of you so that he can order you home."

"You and D'Angelo are the only ones who knew where I was. She's got the same order, hide nothing from Blankenship. If he asks a question, tell him everything you know."

"Well, luckily for me, we don't actually know what you're doing."

"If they confiscated phones, how are we talking?"

"The NTCU didn't issue my phone. Logistics did, and I just loaded the encryption program on it. They know nothing about me. Blankenship knows nothing about me either."

"Good luck, Nadia. Thank you."

"Take care, Colt. Good hunting."

Colt disconnected the call. He was glad Nadia was covered. Colt had planned this op assuming they were on their own, but having absolutely no reach-back support would complicate things. Especially if they needed cyber support above what Tony could handle.

He hoped Hoskins would tell Blankenship to hold off on shutting current ops down, though that might also arouse suspicion. If things went poorly, it would create a line of culpability within the Agency. It was a terrible feeling being on the tail end of that, but Colt understood it.

Tony walked into the room, holding his phone.

"That was Hawkinson's people," Tony said. "He wants to meet."

27

Singapore

Tony and Ava rode to the marina in a black car, both dressed for the evening. Tony wore an off-white linen suit and navy shirt that he'd purchased that day and paid an exorbitant amount to have it tailored while he waited. He wasn't worried about the expense reports on this one. A ceramic stiletto was concealed in a sling beneath his left forearm, which had stood up to several frisks in the past. He did not carry a firearm. Singapore had some of the toughest gun laws in the world and the harshest penalties to go along with them. They could hold a suspect indefinitely without trial if they were deemed to be a national security risk. Foreigners with illegal weapons automatically fell into that category. Tonight's objective was not to kill Hawkinson, but to determine whether he should be.

And to plant additional surveillance equipment on his boat.

The stiletto was a precaution, and Tony knew his hand-to-hand combat proficiency would be more useful than a handgun on the boat's close quarters.

Ava wore cream-colored pants, a light blue blouse, and a navy jacket. There was a pistol in her handbag, which Tony didn't know where she had gotten or how she had smuggled into the country. Colt had advised her not to bring it along, but she told him she wasn't stepping foot onto an Archon boat without it. Ava concealed the weapon within her small bag inside a quick-release panel. Tony asked her to show how that worked out of sheer curiosity and she'd shown him. It still seemed like a bad idea to him.

The black car dropped them at the marina. They'd paid him for the evening, so he'd remain until they were ready to leave. Colt was, ironically, less than two hundred feet away, positioned on a public walkway on the mainland side of Keppel Bay. Hawkinson's boat was in the second slip from the end. He'd be using one of their micro drones—about the only gear from Headquarters Station they could smuggle in—for overwatch.

Tony stepped out into the brightly lit violet sky and took up a position in front and to the side of Ava, acting as a security guard. He guided Ava into the marina's main building, making a show of dead-eyeing passersby and valets alike as potential threats to his principle. After being informed that they were guests of "Mr. Barnes," a concierge escorted the two through the building and out to the marina, where he guided them through the security pavilion. They followed the man down the dock to Hawkinson's boat. None of the staff working now had been there when Tony delivered the message yesterday. It didn't matter. If someone recognized him, he'd just have told them he was acting on behalf of Ms. Klein. The concierge led them to the boat and Tony saw Colt in the distance, separated by the water. The marina employee waited until the ship's company acknowledged Ava, and then bid them both a good evening.

Tony guessed the ship was about 108 feet long. It had a dark gray hull with a long line of darkly tinted windows that gave way to a white upper hull. The deck was teak with a blond stain.

A security guard brusquely waved them aboard and waved a metal detector over them. It did not pick up Tony's stiletto or Ava's gun. Tony had used a lead weave pouch before to conceal small firearms and assumed that's what Ava had stashed her gun in. The guard instructed them to place their watches, phones, jewelry and, unfortunately, Ava's handbag in a small box. Ava protested about the bag, but the guard told her the rules weren't flexible and he didn't care. She relented. Next, another guard asked them to remove their shoes, jackets, and belts. He patted each one down individually, testing for secret pockets, transmitters, or other devices. Once that was done, he handed them back, and they were "welcomed" on board.

A guard, the one Tony had interacted with the day before, led them up to the second deck. If he recognized Tony, he made no mention of it.

Four curved couches were arranged in a wide ring next to a long table that the stewards were currently preparing for dinner. Guy Hawkinson stood in the center of the couch ring. He wore off-white pants, a shade close to what Tony had, though his sported a dark gray pencil stripe. Guy wore a black polo with a white accent line around the arms and collar.

He even *dressed* like an asshole.

"Welcome aboard, Ava. It's been a long time," Guy extended a hand, which she accepted, an unreadable expression on her face. She withdrew her hand before he could do anything worse, like make a show of kissing it. Guy turned his thousand-watt smile to Tony, and he found himself surprised it was the man's uncle running for office. Hawkinson had a charisma, a kind of dark charm that was undeniable. Not that it was working, just that Tony detected how this man could pull people into his orbit. "And you are?"

"This is Tony," Ava said. "He's one of my associates."

"Ahh. Bringing in some fresh talent. Just the one?"

"I have fewer holes to fill, so I can afford to be a little more selective."

"Touché. Joseph. The lady will have a glass of the Sancerre, a martini for me. And for you, Tony, was it?"

"Gin and tonic," Tony said flatly. Guy made a show of repeating the order and invited them to sit as their drinks were prepared. A steward brought the drinks and set each down, then disappeared.

Guy lifted his glass and toasted magnanimously "to old and new friends."

Ava, mouth drawn tight, said, "We're not quite at the toasting stage."

"Okay, what stage are we at? Why are we here? I won't ask how you found me, though I'll admit that was some impressive detective work."

"I want to know what your end game is, Guy. You've proven the damage you can do, but I want to know what the point is."

"You're assuming I'm behind it."

"This is going to take a very long time if we have to bandy about on each point."

"I have all night," Guy quipped. "But, fine. Let's just say, for the sake of discussion, that yes, the organization has showed this capability."

"You know there will be consequences. Even if your uncle ends up in the White House and pardons you, there are a multitude of other governments, not to mention my organization, that will take action. There's nowhere on this earth you can hide."

"Is that a threat?" he asked, amused.

"You know me far better than that, I think."

"Why are we here, Ava?" Guy asked again.

"This is a chance to reframe the conversation. You've already done irreparable damage to global security. I cannot imagine that, even if you offered a solution, anyone but your uncle would let you off. Assuming he succeeds, of course."

"You're still assuming I'm the mastermind behind all this," Guy said, dramatically waving his free hand. "My country's government is pursuing me for alleged crimes. That's between me and them. And you're correct, if the American people elect my uncle this fall, that gives me an opportunity to tell my side of the story without fear of an unjust reprisal. You shouldn't count on his charity. However, he and I are not nearly as close as you're making us out to be."

Tony considered this as he studied Guy. He knew this to be a convincingly delivered lie. Guy might even believe it himself.

Guy continued. "What reason would I possibly have to do what you're alleging? I'm not an anarchist. I don't see anyone offering a list of demands or an alternative. What's the point of all this, you're asking me? I put that question back on you, Ava."

Ava's response was ice cold, clinical. She leaned forward in her chair, affecting a pose like a journalist on a talk show. "Four members of your group's leadership are dead. The Americans have Reece Craddock in custody. If they don't have Heather Fleet now, they will soon. Neither of us were part of these organizations when they were formed." Ava sat back in the chair. "Why don't we reframe the discussion?" she said, matter-of-factly. "Your group split from ours because they said we weren't practical. They wanted to use AGI to build a different model of society, a new Athens. Trinity wanted to achieve AGI for the sake of the achieving it and allowing society to determine how best to apply it. You've shown that governments are poorly equipped to deal with the challenges of technology that advances beyond their ability to control it. But you never followed up with the 'so what.' You never used that to broker a seat at the table and force a discussion on what we do next." Ava leveled her gaze at Hawkinson and locked eyes with him, holding him in there by sheer force of will. "That was, after all, Archon's whole point."

"That's an interesting theory," Guy said slowly. "But if I'm already damned in the eyes of the world, what do I care? You've already said even if I came forward today with a solution, to paraphrase, Mossad, MI6 . . . or perhaps Tony here, would exact vengeance. So, what's the point?"

"But you're not coming forward. And Archon, what remains of them, isn't offering an alternative. I'm suggesting there is a way out."

Tony leaned forward. They'd agreed that Ava would lead the discussion and do most of the talking, try to set a logic trap for him and see how he'd respond. Tony said, "The intelligence services who acknowledge Archon's existence assume you were the face. What Ava is proposing is that since no one really knows what's happening inside Archon, you control the narrative now. If you architected the security breaches, you can stop it and come forward to frame a post-quantum solution. If you didn't, you can still come forward and help frame a post-quantum solution. And then springboard that into reframing the drive to reach Artificial General Intelligence. But, as Ava said, four members of Archon's board are dead and one is in custody. Two, perhaps three, remain at large, but they likely won't for long. Your value decreases with every board member that gets arrested. Reece Craddock is a cartoon, but Heather Fleet and Jin Yoon are not."

"I didn't kill them," Hawkinson said.

"You didn't kill who?" Ava said.

"The board. That wasn't me. I have no desire to seek control of that organization."

Tony's mind came screeching to a halt.

"If it wasn't you, who was it?"

Hawkinson shrugged. "Beats me. In Ava's recounting of the litany of people who might want to kill me, she listed off several that are capable of it. Every major intelligence service has some facility with deniable wet work. And I think we can agree that if groups like Trinity and mine exist, it's not a stretch of the imagination to suggest there may be others. We can't be the only ones who believe that seventeenth-century democracy has outlived its usefulness." Guy's mouth upturned in an eerie and especially grim Cheshire smile. "I'd say you'd need to round up more than the usual suspects." Guy sipped his drink and studied Ava and Tony for a moment. "I want nothing to do with them. I believed in the initial interpretation, as you say, the desire to create a new Athens. People are free to think and create, and machines can do much of the work. It's a lofty goal and one I don't think human nature actually allows for. I'm more of the opinion that if we take the quest for power out of the equation, perhaps we have fewer wars. I spent my twenties as an infantry officer in Iraq. It was a wake-up call to the absurdity of executive decision making and the people we put our faith in. I'd hoped that what you call 'Archon' was a pathway around that."

Tony's mind immediately latched onto what Hawkinson had just said. *What you call 'Archon.'* As though he or they didn't use that term themselves.

"However, when I became part of them, I realized they were just as disillusioned and dysfunctional as the governments I'd hoped we could evolve." Hawkinson shrugged and drank from his martini. "I've since given up."

"Running in style, then?"

"Beats living in a cave and dying in Pakistan."

"What's your end goal?" Ava asked.

"Ms. Klein, I simply want to survive. I suspect the battle between Trinity and," he extended a hand to her, "Archon will be over shortly. But that won't be an end to the conflict. They will play it out in different spaces."

"But—"

Guy stood. "I'm afraid I'm going to have to interrupt you. We have another guest joining us this evening, and I'd be rude if I didn't introduce him." The door to the communicating salon slid open, and Tony looked over to see Liu Che emerge from inside the ship.

Tony stood, immediately looking for the fastest way off the ship.

He knew Liu Che and, more critically, Liu knew him. They'd been together in Argentina when Colt ran him on an operation against Hawkinson. What in the actual hell was going on here? Hawkinson's lieutenant, Matthew Kirby, had tried to kill all three of them. Tony fatally shot Kirby, allowing them to escape, which was the only reason Guy didn't know who he was.

Liu wore a crisply tailored black suit, white shirt, and dark tie. "Now this is interesting," Liu said as he walked casually toward the circle of couches. "Ms. Klein, I presume. I've heard so much about you. And this, Guy," he said, gesturing to Tony, "is Anthony Ikeda of the Central Intelligence Agency."

Tony caught the look of pure shock on Guy's face.

Well, at least he could still be surprised.

The night suddenly erupted into an electric blue cyclone of spinning lights. Tony looked over at the water to see several dark boats entering the bay. In the distance, the sounds of sirens pierced the night as police vehicles raced across the Keppel Bay Bridge.

Tony put his hands on his hips, held them there for a few seconds, and then ran his left hand up to scratch the back of his neck.

"And those will be my close friends in Singapore's Internal Security Department," Liu said. "They will no doubt have questions about what the Central Intelligence Agency is doing here unannounced and in the company of a noted terrorist."

Hawkinson's guards appeared from inside the boat.

"Hope you've got an explanation for all those guns, Guy. I understand they frown on that here," Tony said.

Hawkinson shrugged, fake sheepish.

Liu Che just smiled, and it was an ugly thing to behold.

28

Singapore

Colt watched in horror as the police boats stormed into the marina and then hit their lights. Another set of lights drew his eyes to the Keppel Bay Bridge, and he saw a long line of vehicles racing across it with lights and sirens. The Police Coast Guard boats quickly swarmed Hawkinson's vessel.

Colt checked his phone and saw no messages from either Tony or Ava.

He should have a robust electronic and video surveillance capability and listening devices on Tony and Ava. Instead, he had a micro drone hovering over the boat's aft-castle with eyes on Hawkinson, Tony, and Ava. Colt could see them speaking to someone off camera, but whoever that was, they were underneath a covered portion of the deck.

God, he'd give anything for audio right now.

Colt could interpret a little from body language, but even that was hard to tell, because he was directly overhead.

So, he didn't actually know who the police were racing in to get.

Hawkinson was an international fugitive with a well-crafted alias and the boat was registered to a (seemingly) legitimate holding company.

Tony was under a non-official cover and Ava was part of an organization that much of the world wrongly believed were cyber-terrorists.

Colt watched on the feed Tony put his hands on his hips. That was the prep-signal. He paused a beat and used his left hand to scratch his neck.

Colt swore. That was the signal he desperately hoped he would not get. It meant they'd been burned.

Colt turned and walked away.

He didn't bother recalling the drone. If it didn't receive instructions after a set amount of time, it would crash itself into the bay. It'd be better not to get caught with it.

Colt hopped the metal fence and entered the grounds of the condominium complex that overlooked the bay. The buildings were tall, mirrored structures, shaped like sails. Each looked to be thirty to forty stories. A dense green hedge, precisely manicured, and at least thirty feet high, surrounded them in a wavelike contour. Excellent cover. Colt disappeared into the shadows. He didn't know how, but Hawkinson had sold them out to the Singaporeans. There was no way to complete their assignment now.

But maybe there was still a way to get that son of a bitch.

He pulled out his phone and considered the consequences for a flash of time. If he did this, his CIA career would probably be over. He would expose the operation, but, if things worked out badly in the fall, it was possible this could end up in court.

It was also the only minor chance they had of getting Hawkinson.

They were exactly twelve hours ahead of DC.

Colt opened up his encryption app and dialed.

"Colt?" Special Agent Ricci answered. "I'm just on my way in. Traffic is a bitch today, so I got stuck on the Beltway. I'm going to miss the morning brief but—"

"Keith—I don't have a lot of time. Guy Hawkinson is in Singapore. He's using an alias, 'Cooper Barnes.' The Singaporeans think he's a tech investor. I need you to call the LEGAT in Singapore immediately and have them connect with their liaisons here."

"Wait, you're in Singapore? What are you—"

"No time, Keith. Call the LEGAT. Tell them everything I just told you. Hawkinson has a boat in Keppel Bay Marina. Here's here under the name Cooper Barnes. The ship is registered with a company called International Transportation Solutions. Have it seized so he can't leave."

Colt moved quickly through the condo complex, taking advantage of the darkness.

"I got it," Ricci said. "LEGAT can arrest him and we can have the embassy Marines detain him until we can get Marshals out there. Or, the Singaporeans can do it."

"Next, I need you to update the Red Notice with his last known location, just in case he slips out. Hold on." Colt reached the complex perimeter, which was a six-foot-tall wire fence. He scaled the fence, which was challenging because the gaps between the wires were rectangular rather than oval, and then dropped onto the other side. There was a minor road in front of him, the perimeter drive around the condo complex, and a line of trees with a golf course beyond it.

"Anything else?" Ricci said.

"No. Just make that call right now."

"Hold on—I've got questions."

"Keith, I gotta go," Colt said. "I think I'm about to be arrested."

Four times as many police vehicles as Colt would assume necessary flew around the corner and closed off any escape he might make on foot. Doors opened, guns were out, and angry cops shouted for him to get on the ground.

Colt sat in an interview room in what he assumed was a police station.

The door opened, and a man entered carrying a manilla envelope. He was shorter than Colt, perhaps five foot seven, and in his mid-forties. He wore tan dress pants and a dark blue shirt, no jacket or tie. He was clean-shaven and his hair was cut short.

"Good evening, Mr. Egan," the man said, using Colt's alias, Jesse Egan. "I am with the Internal Security Department." Colt noted the man did not identify himself. They'd confiscated all of Colt's possessions, so he didn't know exactly what time it was, but he'd spied a wall clock before being brought into the interview room and that had read eleven-thirty.

The ISD officer pulled out a chair and sat opposite Colt.

"May I ask what you're doing in my country, Mr. Egan?"

"I'm here on business," Colt said.

"Yes, that's what you told the arresting officers."

"I'd like to speak with the U.S. Embassy, now," Colt said. He had no expectation the ISD would allow this, but it's exactly what an American civilian would do when braced by a foreign security officer.

"All in time, Mr. Egan. What sort of business are you in?"

"I am a technology consultant. I'm here on a business development trip."

"'Technology consultant' is a broad term. What exactly do you do?"

"We help businesses find and use advanced technology."

"So, you're in IT, then?"

"It's a little more complicated than that." Colt recognized the technique. The ISD officer was probing into his legend to see where the holes might be. Colt used one of his existing Agency covers for this op because there hadn't been time to fabricate a new one. That in itself was risky, because Langley would have a record of that legend and thus, could link Colt to whatever was happening here. Assuming this got back to them.

"Tell me, do you know a Ms. Ava Klein?"

"No," Colt said.

"How about an Anthony Ikeda?"

"I'm afraid I don't."

The ISD officer opened the envelope and removed a photo. It was an overhead shot of Colt standing at the water's edge watching Hawkinson's boat. Actually, what he was doing was looking at the drone feed.

"Is this you?"

"Looks like it? Do you spy on all visitors to your country?"

"Only the ones we receive tips on," he replied.

That explained how they caught him. They'd had persistent surveillance over the site.

"It is interesting that you left at that moment, and quickly."

"Well, with the police presence in the harbor, I just assumed they would have a bunch of cops on the sidewalk there where I was. At least in the States, cops tend to ask people to clear out. Figured I'd save them the trouble."

"I see." The ISD officer removed another photo. Colt looked at it and felt a cold, heavy pooling in his stomach. It was a shot of him in the passenger seat of their rental. "And this is also you?"

"That's correct."

"And who is this?" He removed another photo and set it next to the one on the table. This was a shot of Tony driving. It was slightly grainy, probably from a traffic camera.

"That's my colleague, Shinjo."

"Shinjo," the ISD officer repeated. "Not Anthony Ikeda?"

"No, again. I don't know that name. I'd really like to know what this is about and I'd like to contact my embassy."

"That's very interesting, because we arrested this man earlier tonight on suspicion of espionage. Tell me, Mr. Egan, do you know the name Colt McShane?"

Colt's blood turned to ice in his veins.

"No, I don't," he said.

"Neither does your embassy."

29

Singapore

Liu Che reclined on a large couch on the Marina Bay Sands hotel's fifty-seventh floor rooftop lounge. It was late morning, the day after Singapore's ISD had arrested McShane and his cohorts. It had been a late night for Liu. He'd spent about two hours with Kwong, the man from ISD, and then another two writing up reports for his own service. Still, duty called, and here he was.

Liu considered the previous evening as he sipped his coffee, his eyes on the skyline opposite the harbor in the hazy morning. The Marina Bay Sands was Singapore's most iconic and notable structure. A crescent-shaped platform connected three towers with a sky-bar, lounge, park, and infinity pool.

"Che, good morning," Guy Hawkinson said. He dressed in white pants and a white polo wearing sunglasses that probably cost as much as Liu's car. "Thank you for meeting me here. We had to leave the marina, unfortunately."

"I hope there was no undue inconvenience at the marina," Liu said in low tones. "I could not inform them of the operation beforehand because of security concerns, as I'm sure you understand."

"Yeah, they kind of asked me to move my boat," Guy said, dragging it out.

"In that case, I apologize for the discomfort."

Guy shrugged it off. "Well, I appreciate the warning. Though I admit to being highly surprised to hear from you."

Now that the world was aware of the NTCU, and its officers facing prison sentences or at least termination, Liu had found himself in a position to reconsider that relationship.

"So, what can I do for you?" Liu asked.

"I wanted to see where you and I stood."

"In what regard?"

"We've had some . . . call it, misunderstandings . . . in the past," he said smoothly. "I don't see why that prevents us from aiding each other in the future."

"I see," Liu said. *Guy is looking for allies*, Liu mused. The balance of power had shifted abruptly in the last week and Liu would be the first to take advantage of it. If events unfolded the way he expected, Guy would have an asset close to the President of the United States. This would be an even bigger coup than having a three-star admiral on the national security staff.

"I think it highly likely that my uncle becomes president," Guy said, without prompting. "When that happens, we'll be looking for a strategic reset with the People's Republic."

"Is that so?"

"Yes," Guy said, nodding emphatically. "Frankly, we don't care about Taiwan. It's yours. We will not waste half the U.S. Navy and millions of lives defending a seventy-year-old pact that was signed out of spite. If anything, this will be a way to rejuvenate chip manufacturing in my country."

"I think cold wars have proven much better at stimulating economies than hot ones," Liu quipped.

"Great. We'll be in touch." Guy stood, flashed a smile, and extended a hand.

Liu stood and shook Guy's hand. "I look forward to it."

Guy returned to his suite just a few floors below the rooftop bar where he'd met Liu. He was anxious to be back on the ship.

The craft, a 108-foot oceangoing yacht, had been a gift from his benefactor, a man he knew only as "the Doge." Guy estimated the ship was worth about twenty million dollars, though when you can silently manipulate entire economies, generating wealth becomes little more than a mental exercise. More importantly, the ship had been his home these last several months. The Doge had helped Guy escape from Switzerland before American and Swiss law enforcement agents arrested him the previous winter. He'd provided Guy with expertly forged passports, money, and a clean car. Guy drove through Austria and Slovenia to Croatia, where he'd taken possession of the ship.

Guy had one of his people send up dinner and a bottle of wine. As he was waiting, Guy opened a bottle of scotch from the suite's bar and poured one. Then, he opened his laptop and connected to the TOR browser and the email client he used to send emails under the "Bashe" alias.

His contact at *The New York Times*, Lacy James, needed one more disclosure to really push this over the edge.

30

Singapore

Colt saw the nameless ISD officer just once more in the two days after they arrested him. He asked Colt a version of the same questions he had that first night, and then asked if there was any part of the story that Colt wanted to change. Colt told him he did not. The man gave a bemused smile and said, "We shall see, with time," and then he left. Colt hadn't seen him since. A day had passed. He was alone in a holding cell, wearing an issued jumpsuit. They did not give him access to an attorney or the consular staff at the embassy.

Colt had been to Singapore before. The country was a technology center, a crossroads in southeast Asia and a longstanding U.S. ally. The Chinese had strong ties here. Seventy percent of Singaporeans were ethnically Chinese. The two nations described themselves as having a "special relationship," not unlike that of the United States and the United Kingdom. Espionage operations here had to be handled carefully because of that dynamic. When Colt had worked here before, under his cover as a venture capitalist, he'd visited companies or attended conferences to gain economic intelligence.

Ford had a lot of stories from this place.

Before that fateful posting at Beijing Station with Thorpe, Fred Ford was assigned to Singapore. While the Agency worked closely with Singapore's foreign intelligence service, the Internal Security Department and the Security and Intelligence Division, Ford also cautioned that the Singaporeans took their internal security and sovereignty seriously. They didn't give foreigners a lot of leeway, regardless of how tight the partnership might be. Their national security laws were strict and did not have the same evidentiary standards as those of the U.S.

Colt could be here for quite a long time.

He took no consolation in the knowledge of how close they'd come.

This was not a game where second place counted for anything.

Wilcox was dead, Archon severely degraded, but not destroyed. And worse, they still didn't know with any certainty who was behind the assassinations. All evidence pointed to Hawkinson, but they were no closer to knowing if that was the truth. The intent behind Ava and Tony's meeting with him was to trick him into admitting it. Colt realized that was a mistake now. He'd never been comfortable with the idea of killing the man, regardless of what his crimes were, and had felt they needed some kind of proof before they carried it out. He still believed that had been the moral decision, but in retrospect, had it been the right one?

Colt had failed.

He tried to console himself with the fact that Wilcox would have approved of his decision to vet Hawkinson first, to find proof before resorting to lethal violence. However, as the hours wore on and doubt seeped through the cracks, he thought of Ava's admission that she'd killed Marin. Had Wilcox known? Did he approve? Had he turned the corner to Machiavellian statecraft, or had Ava worked outside the lines to become both judge and executioner?

If the former was true, Colt's memory of his mentor would be forever stained. If it was the latter, it was his estimation of the woman he loved and any future they might have.

These were the thoughts careening through his head when his cell door opened.

Colt had been awake for some time and they'd already served him breakfast, so he guessed it to be midmorning yet. He didn't know for certain because there was no clock in here.

The ISD officer stood with two armed guards in dark uniforms.

"Let's go," the officer said.

Colt stood. "Where are we going?"

"Out," he said gruffly.

They led him to another room where a police officer gave Colt a bag and told him to change. "Knock when you're dressed." They closed the door behind him. Colt opened the bag and saw that it contained the clothes they arrested him in. It did not have any of his electronics. Colt dressed and hammer-fisted the door. A police officer opened it and ushered him out.

"What's going on?" he asked the ISD officer.

"You're being released," he said.

They led Colt down a long, bright and cold hallway without windows to another room. Inside sat an Afro-Asian man. He had salt-and-pepper hair, a tightly groomed beard and dark, and piercing eyes with a slight almond shape. He wore a loose white polo and navy pants.

"Good morning, Mr. Egan. My name is Rittenauer. I'm with the U.S. Embassy. We can go now." He handed Colt a clear plastic bag that contained his cellphone. "Here's your phone." He leaned in as he handed Colt the bag, putting his mouth a few inches from Colt's ear. "Say nothing else until we're outside."

The American led him out of the building via a subterranean garage, escorted by the armed police and the nameless ISD officer. Rittenauer and the ISD officer exchanged a few words Colt didn't catch before withdrawing back into the building. The American started walking, and a very confused Colt matched his stride until the man said only, "Wait."

He led Colt to a silver Toyota Land Cruiser, dinged up from being driven in such a congested city. He unlocked the car with the fob and they got in. As Colt climbed inside, he saw a bottle of water, sweating with condensation, and a stainless steel travel mug. "I brought coffee and water, wasn't sure which one you'd need more," Rittenauer said, his tone a little more amiable now. Once he'd backed out of the space and was navigating his way out, he said, "My name is Hendrix. I'm the Chief of Station here."

They left the garage and Colt saw the imposing, dual tower police complex behind them as they drove through the security cordon and onto the street. Colt picked up the travel mug and drank. It was still warm. There was something reassuring about a hot cup of coffee, even in the tropics.

"I suppose you'd like to know what's going on, Colt," Hendrix said. Well, that answered one question.

"Yes, I would," Colt said, looking out the window numbly, watching the city pass by.

"First thing's first. I am not here in an official capacity and you and I have never met. If anyone from HQS calls, I will deny ever having met you. Fair?"

Colt smiled. "Seems like the least I could do."

Hendrix gave a throaty chuckle and then said, "Fred Ford is an old friend of mine."

A lot of things immediately fell into place.

"I got a very strange phone call from him yesterday telling me that his young protégé, who is capable of getting himself into—and I'm quoting him here—'cosmic levels of shit,' was in my AOR and needed help."

"How did he know?"

"He said you'd ask that and told me to tell you he's got a finely tuned 'Colt's fucked up again' alarm."

Colt laughed for a good, long time. All the tension of the last two days seemed to flush out of his system with that act.

"Ford told me that one of yours called him and said they'd lost contact with you."

Nadia, Colt thought. She'd risked her career reaching out to Ford with this.

Hendrix continued. "Ford called me. He didn't tell me exactly what you're up to and—for the record—I don't want to know. But, he said he figured you were after the people who killed Jason Wilcox."

"How did you get the Singaporeans to let me out?"

"They can do easy math. INTERPOL blew up the wires yesterday with a refreshed Red Notice and my FBI counterpart is shitting his pants trying to figure out how to make an arrest. However, to answer your question, once they figured out who Hawkinson really was, they made the connection that you were part of that." Hendrix was quiet for a minute.

"ISD arrested two others the same night as me. Any word on them?"

"Tony Ikeda will be out within the hour. I don't know about the woman. I take it she's not one of ours."

All Colt said was, "Ex-Mossad. Jason knew her too."

"Where can I drop you?"

"I've got an apartment in the city center."

They drove in silence. Hendrix guided them toward the huge metro station in the Sekang District. He pulled onto an adjacent street in the shadow of a cluster of residential towers. Once the car was stopped, Hendrix twisted in his seat and pulled a small, nondescript backpack from the back seat. He handed it to Colt and looked at him expectantly. Colt opened it. Inside was a ball cap and glasses. Colt recognized each immediately, as he'd used them before. The cap had a liner in the bill that would baffle electromagnetic transmissions, such as those coming from surveillance cameras. The glasses had a coating over the lenses that would prevent cameras from imaging his eyes and foil video identification and facial recognition. Together, they'd make him look like a fuzzy blur on a video feed. There was also a small voice recorder. "That will record, and there's some useless chatter on there. I think it's a shopping list. Once you activate it, it'll scramble EM signals around you. Between those three, you should be free of electrooptical surveillance, which is how they picked you up."

"Thank you," Colt said, and meant it. He was truly grateful.

"I can do simple math too, Colt," Hendrix said. "The pack has a false bottom. There's the newest version of our compact disguise kit in it. Should be enough for two people. Fred said you know your way around it. There's also a nine-millimeter pistol in there. It's a Czech model favored by our host police. A support asset got it. It's clean, but I don't need to tell you not to get caught with it. Whether or not you use it, it's better off at the bottom of the river when you're done."

Colt put his hand on the door.

Hendrix said, "I worked for Jason. I wouldn't have this job without him.

He was my friend, and he was a good man. You get this son of a bitch. I bought you twenty-four hours. If you're still here this time tomorrow, you'll be arrested for espionage."

Colt put on the hat and glasses, activated the "recorder," and made his way back to the apartment. He used a route that included the metro, a cab, and a circuitous route that included random interval double-backs to see if anyone had followed him. He also camped out near the entrance to their four-story apartment building, just to see if they were being watched.

When he was sure it was safe, Colt entered the apartment.

Ava was waiting for him.

Seeing Colt at the door, she rushed over and embraced him. Colt just stood there, numb. Eventually, his arms came up and wrapped around her. He was exhausted. Not only from the adrenaline rush and subsequent action crash of their arrest, the tension and release of interrogation and eventual freedom, or even of the demands of their largely off-the-books assassination mission. Colt was worn down, burned out by the unrelenting tempo of the last eighteen months. He had Ava right there, for whatever that was worth. A stretch of calm within a turbulent and stormy sea.

"How did you get out?" Colt asked.

"We've got a few friends," she said dismissively.

Tony showed up about an hour later, having taken similar surveillance detection steps as Colt had. Colt filled him in on his car ride with Hendrix. Tony then shared what had actually happened on Hawkinson's boat, including the double-cross by Liu Che. Colt made a dark joke about pulling the same move as they did in Geneva, where they'd captured him for the first time.

"What's our next move?" Tony asked.

It was midafternoon.

"Well, everybody seems to know Guy is here," Ava said, looking at her laptop. Colt stood next to her. "INTERPOL reissued their Red Notice and plastered his last known all over it, along with his alias. The police have blocked off Keppel Bay Marina and, just to be safe, the Singapore Navy has a patrol vessel on station outside Keppel Island. Hawkinson's boat isn't going anywhere."

Colt returned to his seat and turned the laptop to show Tony what was on the screen. "Hawkinson's car is at the Marina Bay Sands hotel. I called Keppel Bay once I got back to the room, pretending to be an embassy consular officer with a question for Hawkinson, using the alias he checked in with. They told me he'd left the night we got arrested, but wouldn't say anything else. If he's still at the Marina Bay, he's got to be under a different name and is probably trying to figure out his next move. His clock is ticking."

"So is ours," Ava said.

Colt said, "Right. We have twenty-four hours to wrap this up and get the hell out of here, or the ISD is going to arrest us. I'm not joking when I say we'll probably spend the next twenty years in a dark hole if that happens."

"Remind me why I keep hanging out with you," Tony quipped.

"Ava, see if you can make any connections between the shell corporations your team identified and Singapore. We know Archon has a quantum computing lab here, but they probably used Hawkinson to purchase it. There might be a correlation between the company that leased his boat and that."

"On it."

"Tony—how does he get out? We have to assume the airport is closed off."

"This is where Guy's strategy backfires on him. Singapore has some of the tightest border control in the world. They don't screw around with national security and have pretty broad definitions for what that might be, as we have experienced. The Red Notice has Guy's photo and known aliases, so figure any customs-controlled exit is out. There's a bridge connecting Singapore with Malaysia. Assume that's locked down and they are probably checking vehicles. This country is an island, but it's a littoral one. Malaysia and Indonesia are just miles away. Small watercraft is probably the most likely. Figure he holds off until dark and slips out off of a beach and into one of these other countries. Guy has ranger and special forces training, so I'm pretty comfortable with his ability to even swim out to meet a boat."

"That will all take time to set up," Colt said, picking up on Tony's line of thinking. "Which might explain why he's still at the hotel."

"I think I've got something," Ava said.

"That was fast," Tony said.

"My people have been working on this for months. When they didn't hear from me the other night, they assumed he got me and they had to continue the work. We've been gradually peeling back Archon's shell companies for nearly a year. Check this out: There's an R&D entity called the Quantum Research Institute. Private, not affiliated with the government or the Ministry of Education. A company called Lion National Labs is their primary backer. Again, no connection to the government." The lion was one of the key heraldic elements in Singapore's coat of arms, and the country was also known as the Lion Republic. "LNL is owned by a holding company." She showed Colt the screen.

"Tony, check this out," Colt waved him over. "It's like shell companies, all the way down. Do any of those connect to what you've already found?"

"Not yet," Ava said. "But, I think it's interesting that this lab would be owned by a bunch of front companies. Here's something else. I may or may not have had my people hack into their network." Ava gave a tight-lipped smile. "They're expanding the lab and are under construction. They've just taken delivery of a large shipment of industrial equipment and building material. I have the manifest, but it's not relevant. What is relevant is who owns the ship."

"It's an Archon holding company," Colt said, flatly.

"Yes, but that's not what's interesting," Ava said. "The ship is a proto-type. It's an electric container ship, battery powered." Ava typed feverishly and then sent a link to Colt and Tony's machines. "It's got to stay close to ports, so to go from the U.S. to Asia, it goes up to Seattle, then to Alaska, over to Japan, and finally down here so it can recharge. It's considerably smaller than one of the big container ships, though it's got about a third of the crew of a comparably sized ship. Looks like they made some big PR showing when they made the trip, and we just missed it."

"Well, I don't think any of us added 'electric boats' to our search para-meters," Colt said.

"Is the ship still in port?" Tony asked.

"Yes," Ava said. "It's at the main cargo port in Pasir Panjang. The Faraday. Looks like it's registered to an Aethon Ventures. This ship delivered hardware to the quantum startup that Hawkinson used to build the array he's using for the crypto attacks. That's enough of a line for me, but I'll keep digging."

"Tony, could he get out as a member of the crew?" Colt asked.

"He'd still need to clear customs, but if it works like our airports do, the flight crew just holds up a badge and TSA barely gives them a second glance. I suspect Singaporean customs officials won't be scrutinizing the cargo lanes either. Let's also remember, yes, a Red Notice went out and their ISD is engaged, but he's still one guy."

"If you were him, which way would you go?"

"Me? I'd still try to slip away at night."

Colt looked back at the screen. "Shit, he's moving."

31

Singapore

"We've only got enough time to guess once," Tony said.

"We're in downtown core, which means he's got to pass us to get to the port. We can pick him up on the Keppel Viaduct. I'll drive. Tony, the tracker I put on the car has the two-way transmitter on it, so it's got send/receive and bridging."

"Already on it," Tony said. The Agency had devised these devices specifically to hack into modern automobiles. Newer model cars had numerous digital access points—Bluetooth, satellite, or cellular. One just needed to know which. The GPS tracker acted as a bridge, which would enable an Agency hacker to connect with the vehicle remotely. From there, it was a relatively simple matter of taking over certain vehicle functions. A few years earlier, demonstrating the cyber threat landscape for civilians, the Defense Advanced Research Projects Agency (DARPA) hacked into a Jeep Grand Cherokee via the vehicle's Bluetooth. They took complete control, remotely speeding up, decelerating, and even stopping. The intent of the demonstration was to show the dangers of the interconnected world and urge the government and manufacturers to adopt tighter security standards.

The three of them raced for the car. Once inside, Colt angled south toward Keppel Road, the route that followed Singapore's southern coastline. Ava rode in the passenger seat working on her own laptop. Tony rode in the back. This was so hastily cobbled together, one couldn't even call it a "plan." They hadn't even had time to discuss how they'd handle Hawkinson when they caught him. If they caught him.

Colt knew what he should do, which was to call the FBI's LEGAT at the embassy and advise them of Hawkinson's current position and expected escape route. Colt had engaged the law enforcement apparatus when he'd gotten Ricci involved two days prior. Ricci knew where he was, which meant the broader FBI knew where he was. Which, in turn, meant any cover they'd previously had was effectively disintegrated. If Colt carried out Richter's instructions now, there would be a line connecting him and Hawkinson. He and Tony would have no legal protection.

He'd tried to do what he believed was the right thing. When it looked like they were about to be arrested, Colt used the only backup he'd had, which was to engage the FBI and try to take Hawkinson down legally. What he hadn't counted on was the organizational inertia of the Agency's clandestine arm, or their desire to get revenge for the killing of a beloved former leader.

Now Colt was trapped.

People knew he was here.

Law enforcement could not react in time. Hawkinson had too many resources at his fingertips. Christ, he had a container ship.

"He's not taking the Keppel Viaduct," Tony announced from the back seat. "Keep heading south on Neil." Colt was still getting used to Singapore's unique concept of urban planning. The high-rise structures were not confined to any one area. Rather, they blended into collections of industrial, office, and mixed-use facilities. Shopping centers, townhomes, apartments, recreation, and commercial facilities were scattered between the high-rise clusters. Singaporeans showed a great dedication to green space, with parks and gardens growing in any available location. When there wasn't enough room for a park, they designed ivy trellises and other vertical plantings up the sides of buildings and bridge abutments. They passed a small neighborhood of white townhouses with red-orange tile roofs on one side and a high-rise apartment complex on the other.

"Okay—get ready. They're about to pass us coming in the opposite direction," Tony said.

Singaporeans followed the British standard, which meant the driver was on the right side of the vehicle and on the left side of the road.

"Now," Tony said, and the black Range Rover rolled past them. Colt made a left turn into the neighborhood, looped around the block, and reentered Neil Road about a quarter mile behind Hawkinson.

"Looks like they've got a chaser," Colt said, seeing a second Range Rover behind it. That would contain more of Hawkinson's security team. He liked this less and less. Colt followed the Range Rover convoy through the congested city streets. He knew they were roughly parallel to Keppel Harbor and the city's primary cargo port, where the Faraday docked. He expected them to make a left turn toward the coast at any point.

Except they didn't.

Instead, the two Range Rovers took a bridge over the Keppel Viaduct, still cutting across the city. Colt saw the port and warehouses to their left as they drove across the bridge. Still, Hawkinson's vehicle continued its parallel path with the coast and the port.

"What are they doing?" Colt asked.

"I've hacked into the vehicle. They aren't using the nav system," Tony said. Then he added, "Not that I expected them to."

Colt followed at a distance onto Kampong Bahru Road, which curved south to travel alongside the outer fence of an overland freight terminal attached to the port.

"There's another entrance to the port up ahead," Tony said.

"We need to stop them before they get inside the port," Ava said. "They'll have credentials, we don't."

It was midafternoon on a weekday, and the roads swelled with cars. Tony could shut the Range Rover down remotely, even lock the brakes, but to what end? Was Colt going to walk up to the window and shoot Hawkinson through the glass? He began to see the flaws in not turning this over to the FBI or, hell, even to the ISD.

"What do you want me to do?" Tony asked.

They were stuck in a line of cars approaching an overpass that marked the boundary with the port. Though they were about twelve cars back from the traffic light, Colt could see the port beyond the bridge. Once Hawkinson hit that, he'd be gone.

The Singaporean Navy could certainly stop that ship, but it would mean contacting Hendrix and hoping he could call in enough favors to pull it off. The only other option was to contact Langley and get the military liaison officer to contact the U.S. Coast Guard and interdict the ship, as the U.S. Navy didn't have the legal authority to make arrests at sea.

There was no way those dominoes all fell into place. And both options would put Colt and Tony in a shit storm with CIA bureaucracy when they got home.

So it was back to the port. Colt racked his brain. How could they convince the port authority that the three of them had a justification to be there with no semblance of credentials?

"Colt," Tony said in a warning tone. Hawkinson had answered the question for them. The convoy turned right under the bridge.

"Where are they going, Tony?"

Colt still had several cars ahead of him before he could make the turn. Not that he would try to cut around the cars by jumping into the oncoming lane, but even if he'd wanted to, there was a concrete median with a metal fence in between them, anyway. "Come on, come on, damn it," Colt growled impatiently at the line of cars ahead of him. The light turned red with two cars to go. In another country, where traffic laws were more akin to "oral tradition," he might have jumped around them and made the turn, but not here.

"Hawkinson has merged onto the Sentosa Gateway," Tony announced.

"What's that," Colt barked.

"Causeway between Singapore and Sentosa Island. Looks like a bunch of high-end resorts, a Universal Studios, golf courses and . . . one really big marina. I'll lay odds that's how he's getting out of here, but you won't want to take the bet."

"What kind of marina?" Colt asked.

"Hold on," Ava said, jumping in. She'd largely been silent, working on her laptop, and Colt hadn't been paying attention to what she was doing.

"It's all small craft, personal boats." The light turned green, and Colt sped into the turn and pulled under the bridge. He followed that to the exit, approximately a block later, for the Sentosa Gateway. "I doubt he's got another multimillion dollar yacht up his sleeve. Probably this is a smaller ship that he can take across the Singapore Strait to Batam. I think it's only like, ten, twelve miles across," Ava said.

"If he gets into Indonesia, he's gone," Tony said.

Colt navigated onto the causeway. Traffic was lighter here, giving him some room to catch up. The Sentosa Gateway was a short stretch connecting the two islands, with three lanes of traffic in either direction and an overhead rail. There was a dense line of hedges and trees on the left, separating the port complex from the road and proving a pleasant visual aesthetic.

"He's about a quarter mile ahead. They look to be doing about forty-five and they are speeding," Tony said.

"On my signal, engage the parking brake."

"You want me to do what now?"

"Parking brake is electric, right?"

"Yeah," Tony replied.

"Good. Stop the car."

"What are you doing, Colt?" Ava asked.

"Rear-end collision at forty-five miles an hour." Colt looked over to the right. There was only a low, grassy median separating the two sections of road. Once they stopped the car, he'd get out to inspect the damage and finish the job if need be. He could leverage Hendrix to get them out of Singapore, or perhaps Ava's Trinity contacts.

Colt was pulling around several cars. He closed the gap, now able to see the two SUVs in front of them.

"Go!"

All he heard in response were several hard keystrokes.

Going from forty-five to a dead stop was a violent enough reaction to launch anyone not wearing a seatbelt like they were being shot out of a cannon.

Colt heard the scream of tires and saw a cloud of smoke before the second SUV hit Hawkinson's from behind with as much savage force as the sudden stop. The back end lifted off the ground, the residual energy being directed backward. It crashed back to the pavement, bouncing on the suspension.

The cars around them all mashed on the brakes, skidding to a stop to avoid the collision.

For a blunt moment, nothing moved but smoke.

Colt, along with everyone else, had stopped and people were already getting out of their cars to help. "Tony, I need you to get up here and get ready to drive."

Colt stepped out of the car.

"Colt, what are you doing?" Ava demanded. "Get back here."

He slid out of the car and sidled along the hedge next to a stopped car. From this position, Colt had a better view of the damage. The first SUV's rear end looked like an angry giant had kicked it like a soccer ball. Similarly, the front end of the second vehicle had buckled almost back to the shattered windshield. No one moved in the first Rover. Colt was maybe thirty feet from it.

Quick steps to the SUV, open the rear door and finish the job, keeping the weapon out of view.

Time to end it, Colt told himself.

An early conversation with Wilcox crept into his memory. *The job will compromise you if you let it*, Jason told him.

And Guy Hawkinson will murder millions if I don't, Colt responded to Wilcox's memory.

The rear door opened and Guy Hawkinson stumbled out, blood pouring down his face from several lacerations. He braced himself against the door. He was dazed and staggering, but had the presence of mind to look around to check his surroundings, and when he did, he saw Colt.

The two locked eyes and Colt saw the recognition in them.

Colt reached for the pistol in the concealed holster beneath his shirt.

Hawkinson reached inside his suit jacket.

Colt's fingers snaked around his pistol's grip. An image of Jason Wilcox flashed in his mind and then he thought of the countless innocent others needlessly murdered because of Guy Hawkinson's actions. Colt pulled the pistol and held it level. Maybe this wasn't entirely legal, but it was *right*.

He could live with that. Or at least, he could find a way to.

Guy was uneasy on his feet, dazed. He braced himself with his left hand against the vehicle. Colt saw movement inside it. Guy's security detail would be out here in the span of a few breaths.

Colt sighted Hawkinson.

Then, something clawed his attention away, pulling it like someone had pointed out a car crash and demanded he look. Colt saw a blur in his peripheral vision. A bird. Gaze still locked on Hawkinson, he saw the other man's eyes go wide.

Colt turned his head just as the "bird" flew into the rear passenger side window of Hawkinson's SUV. Some primal part of Colt's mind registered that this was impossible. The object was traveling too fast for it to be an animal, and as it crashed through the window, he knew it should've splattered against the side—even if Hawkinson didn't have armored windows.

Colt took a step forward.

He saw a flash, like lightning.

Hawkinson's Range Rover exploded in a thunderous ball of orange.

32

Singapore

Raw, concussive force threw Hawkinson's body forward like a rag doll, followed by a burst of fire that rolled out from the Range Rover and consumed him. The same force knocked Colt to the ground, and he bounced his head off the pavement as a wave of heat washed over him.

For a few blurry seconds, all Colt could hear was a ringing sound, like someone had hit a bell with a hammer and was just letting it ring. The ringing subsided, and gave way to the wet, rolling crackle of fire. Colt rolled over onto his side and pushed himself into a seated position. He saw the Range Rover, flames gushing out of the windows and black smoke roiling into the sky.

He saw a body face down in the street, and everything snapped back into place.

Guy Hawkinson was dead.

"Colt!" He felt powerful hands pulling him backward. Tony helped him to his feet.

"Hold on," Colt said, recovering his breath. He took a few hesitant steps toward the vehicle. The explosion hadn't been as large as he initially thought. There had certainly been a massive concussion—even from some distance away, the shockwave had knocked Colt to the ground. If this had been something on the order of an antitank weapon or even the kind of suicide drone they believed killed Carlos Marin, Colt should be dead too.

He clearly wasn't.

"What are you doing? We have to go," Tony said.

Colt ignored him and jogged over to Hawkinson. His jacket was scorched black and smoldering, but the fire only glanced him. Colt rolled him over and checked for a pulse. There was none. His expression was shocked, face frozen in a horrible rictus, his eyes glassy.

Guy Hawkinson was dead.

Colt reached into Guy's pocket and removed his phone. He returned the body to its original position on the street.

Sirens mounted in the distance.

Tony shouted his name.

Colt peered into the Range Rover's back seat. The interior was scorched from a flash-fire, and there were traces of smoke, but it wasn't still burning. Everyone inside was dead. The guard in the back seat had been decapitated and the two in front weren't much better off. Colt tore his eyes away from the terrible sight.

Colt spotted a ballistic nylon laptop bag on the floor. He grabbed it and was gone.

A door in the chase vehicle opened. Colt looked at the vehicle for the first time and saw that the blast knocked out the front windshield and shredded the inflated airbags behind it. Both the driver and front passenger appeared to be unconscious. One of the rear doors opened and Colt broke into a run for his vehicle. He slammed the SUV's door shut as he ran past it, smashing it into the emerging mercenary's face.

Colt dropped into the passenger seat of their car and Tony was moving before he'd even closed the door.

"What the hell were you doing?"

"Intel," Colt panted, catching his breath. "Evidence. There's going to be something useful on this." He slid Hawkinson's phone into one of the laptop case's side pockets.

"What *was* that?" Colt asked. His words sounded a little thick and gauzy to his ears.

"I don't know, man," Tony said. "I saw you walking up, and it just blew."

"Colt, look at me," Ava said, and he turned to face her. She leaned forward and shone her phone's flashlight in his eyes.

"Ow! What the hell are you doing?"

"Trying to see if you have a concussion, dummy," she snapped and put her phone away. "You're fine," she pronounced, and turned back around.

Tony was across the causeway just as the police rolled up to establish a cordon.

They raced back to the apartment and quickly sanitized the place. They'd packed their personal gear already, so it was a fast sweep to wipe everything down and double check they didn't leave any personal effects behind. Colt was, admittedly, still numb from seeing the explosion and how close he'd come to being killed. His clothes carried traces of ash and dirt. Another few feet closer and he might have been caught in the blast.

He also couldn't get the image of Hawkinson's smoking body lying in the street out of his mind.

It was no less than Guy deserved, but it was an image Colt knew would haunt him for a long time.

That sense of incompleteness fit well with Colt's growing realization that in death, however violent it was, Hawkinson got away with it. The world would never hold him accountable for his actions. There would be no justice for the millions he terrorized, for the governments he undermined. Nor for the businesses, the lives, or the whole industries Archon had upended in their fabricated "anti-technologist" campaign. The people duped into believing that was a genuine movement would learn the truth that they'd been deceived or see justice.

Colt could only take consolation in knowing Hawkinson could never do it again.

It was a shallow victory. Perhaps it wasn't even one.

Despite all this, Archon still existed. Two of their members were in the wind and untouchable. The NTCU knew so little of the organization beneath them. What about when these contingency plans activated, if they hadn't already. Or would they fracture into smaller, more focused groups like so much shattered ideological glass?

A shard was smaller, but it could still cut deep.

"I'm ready," Ikeda said. He dropped his two bags next to the door.

"Same," Ava said. She'd said little after their hasty exit from the causeway. Colt hadn't pressed it. At first, he'd been stunned by the blast and in shock from what he'd seen. Once he felt like he was in control again, his mind tried and failed to draw connections between the explosion and the crash.

There was a hard knock on the door, and all life seemed to stop.

Colt lifted his shirt to show Tony the pistol in the concealed holster. There wasn't another way out of here—another failure in their shoddily cobbled plan. Of course, a dedicated adversary would have the alternate egress points covered, but that didn't mean they shouldn't try. No one knew they were here and, according to the property owner, this was a long-term corporate rental.

Ikeda nodded and opened the door.

The Internal Security Department officer who'd arrested them earlier stepped into the apartment.

He took a quick look around, locking eyes on each of them.

"I see you're taking my advice to leave the country seriously," he said, a faint smile pressing at the corner of his lips. He stepped close to Colt. "My name is David Kwong." It was the first time he'd identified himself. That was not normal. Colt understood the Singaporeans guarded their security service identities the same way the CIA did. "It's been an interesting day. An American businessman who also happens to be an international fugitive, named Guy Hawkinson, was just killed in a tragic, if . . . curious . . . traffic accident."

Colt and Tony's eyes met. Tony also picked up on Kwong using Hawkinson's real name, not his alias.

"Apparently, their vehicle stopped abruptly and rear-ended by the car behind them, which triggered the gas tank to explode. Very tragic. Strangely, the men in the second car appeared to be personal security for Mr. Hawkinson and were all carrying illegal firearms. They'll be arrested once they're out of the hospital." Kwong walked past Colt and deeper into the apartment, pushing apart the blinds and peering out the window at the street below. He turned back to Colt. "Mr. Hawkinson funded a startup here focused on advanced technologies. We understand that Mr. Hawkinson may have been using this company as a basis for a concerted cyberterrorism campaign. I can't get into the specifics, of course. However, my country takes these allegations quite seriously." Kwong clasped his hands at the small of his back. He considered Colt with a bemused expression. "We take our sovereignty equally seriously. We don't take kindly to operations being carried out on our soil without our knowledge. Though we appreciate acts of terrorism even less. I don't suppose that you would have any information on Mr. Hawkinson's untimely demise, would you?"

"I would not," Colt said gruffly.

Colt flicked his eyes first to Tony and then to Ava. Where was he going with this? Colt would've given anything to have a camera in the hallway to see if there were a squad of ISD officers ready to pour through that doorway and arrest them.

"Well, in that case, I bid you good luck and safe travel, Mr. McShane."

A shock went through Colt's nervous system. So Kwong did know his name. He'd said it during their interrogation, but Colt hadn't acknowledged it. That was an old interrogation trick. Spool out a piece of information to see if a nervous subject confirms it. This was different. Kwong had said his name with knowledge and conviction.

"I suspect we won't conclude our forensic investigation for a few days yet. As one professional to another, I'd suggest you be gone before we do." Kwong regarded the three of them, then flashed a half-smile and said, "Good day."

He left, closing the apartment door behind him.

"Anybody else feel like they just finished a book, but half the pages were missing?" Tony said, this time sincerely, and with no hint of his usual deadpan humor.

Colt held up a hand to stay anyone else from speaking. He tapped his earlobe and then pointed to the ceiling. Ava and Tony picked up on the signal immediately. Kwong knew they were here, so it was possible the ISD had bugged the apartment to see if they'd reveal anything worthwhile, anything that might condemn them.

The trio silently grabbed their things and left.

They left the apartment in the city center and drove to Kallang Riverside Park, several miles away. Tony drove and though he checked for tails, did not make a full surveillance detection route. They parked and exited the car. No one spoke until they were safely enveloped by the palms and dense tropical foliage, sight lines broken. The air around them felt like a warm, sodden towel.

"That was unexpected," Colt said. He was bone weary, hungry, and his brain wanted nothing more than to just shut down.

"The only explanation I have is that arresting us complicates an already convoluted situation. Plus, this lets ISD avoid any embarrassment over not figuring out Hawkinson was here to begin with," Ava said.

It was a good thought and one that aligned with the facts as they knew them. Like Hawkinson's death, however, it still felt incomplete.

"Tony?" Colt said. The other man only shook his head.

"I got nothing. What Ava said makes sense. That's probably good enough."

"Yeah," Colt agreed. "The part I'm most uncomfortable with is how Hawkinson died." Colt knew from his combat driving course that cars rarely exploded. A gas tank rupture would certainly catch on fire, but what he'd seen was a detonation. He also knew what he saw. Something flew into that vehicle, and it exploded.

But it was a small, contained explosion.

Tumblers fell into place in his mind. The years of Agency-honed pattern analysis, the mental matching he could never turn off.

Someone had killed Hawkinson, it just wasn't Colt. Whoever did it wanted to limit the collateral damage to just the vehicle's occupants.

Who would know to do that? Or care about limiting casualties?

Colt locked eyes with Ava and held her gaze for several moments.

She said nothing.

A question hovered over him like a dark specter. It haunted his mind, begged him to learn its truth so that it could rest.

Ask. Seek what you shall find.

The CIA's motto, *The truth shall set you free*, echoed in his mind.

Colt's business was secrets and lies told for the greater good. The world was built on secrets. They'd learned over the last few months how jealously guarded those secrets must be, and how easily they were to unravel. There would always be some novel way to protect those things, until there was a novel way to unravel them. Security would forever be an elaborate dance between the technological attempts to protect and steal.

Ultimately, no hidden thing was truly safe from discovery.

Unless it was a question that went unasked.

Perhaps the only safe knowledge in the world was that which we wish not to learn.

It was clear to him that Ava was the only one who could've done it. Trinity wouldn't act without her authorization.

Colt had believed that by bringing her here—one of the only people on the planet who truly understood the threat for what it was—Ava would join him, help him. Instead, she'd used that to collect the last bit of intel on Hawkinson and kill him with it.

It shouldn't matter to him. After all, the intent *was* to kill him. Though Colt told himself he'd have brought Guy in if he could. Ava doing it, though, robbing him of the responsibility the White House placed on him —whether he wanted it or not—was wrong. It felt *wrong*. And they were forever changed because of it.

"Travel safely," Colt said to Ava. There was an unreadable expression in her eyes. She looked at Tony and then back to Colt.

He wasn't sure what he wanted at that moment. An admission, an expression of something?

"I guess it's over," she said and Colt agreed, though later he would wonder exactly what she meant.

Had she done it for him? For *them*?

Colt didn't know and Ava didn't say one way or the other.

Somehow, that made it worse.

Colt didn't ask. He didn't want to hear her say it.

Ava left.

After she was gone, Colt looked at his phone to double-check his flight information. He was leaving in a few hours on a flight to Doha, where he'd be on the ground for several hours before connecting to Dulles. Tony would fly to San Francisco and then on to Washington the next day. Colt saw a notification on the COVCOM he used to communicate with Liu. He opened the messenger and saw that Liu wanted to meet.

He was still here. In Singapore.

Interesting.

A move as bold as it was curious, after double-crossing them with Hawkinson.

Colt had questions.

"What's up?" Tony asked as they reached the car, seeing Colt preoccupied.

"I've got to take care of something before I leave. I need you to drop me somewhere."

33

Singapore

Liu suggested the Marina Bay Sands Hotel.

This was a level of extravagance that Colt didn't expect to experience in his lifetime, and certainly not when he was in the CIA. Hollywood always portrayed intelligence work in places like this, buildings with impossible geometries set against dramatic backdrops. The real world of intelligence was dirty alleys in the third world, the back seats of cars with profusely sweating assets surfing a wave of panic, and lots of public transportation.

Yet here Colt was, in one of the world's most exclusive hotels to meet another spy.

Naturally, Liu wanted to meet at the sky lounge.

Colt took a high-speed elevator up to the fifty-eighth floor. It was like nothing he'd ever seen. The skyway was eleven hundred feet long, vaguely serpentine and spread across the Sands' three wedge-shaped towers. Colt could see the entire city. His eyes were drawn to the Gardens by the Bay park where he and Liu met several months before when this crisis first began. It seemed like a lifetime ago.

It was early evening, around five, and the sky was still the sun-washed, faded blue of day, but from this height, he could see the first ribbons of night on the eastern horizon. Colt navigated to the rooftop bar, gave them the name Liu had made the reservation with, and was shown to a red sectional sofa next to the edge of the skyway. The only thing separating them from the open sky was a pane of glass that came up to Colt's chest.

Liu was perched on a couch with a glass of wine. Colt remembered from the FBI report of their raid on Liu's home in DC that the spy had a sizable collection of French wine. Colt approached the table and sat, immediately feeling the pressure of the concealed holster at the small of his back. A server appeared, and he asked for a gin and tonic to get rid of them.

Colt sat in silence until the server returned with his drink.

He had exactly an hour to be at the airport to make his flight. He didn't have time to dick around with Liu.

"Why am I here?"

Liu smiled.

What Colt hated most about their interactions was that Liu continually played games with him, the sly jabs and reminders that Liu was himself, a master of spies. It was the subtle things, like seizing the initiative in their meetings and peppering Colt with questions when it was he who was there to report. Or times like this, where he told Colt they needed to meet.

Seeing Liu about to speak, Colt cut him off. He was sick of being pushed around by Liu's mind games. "Actually, let me ask a different question. What in the hell were you thinking?"

His face impassive, Liu set his glass down in front of him and ran a hand across his pants to smooth them over.

"Once I read the reports that of your unit's exposure for spying on your countrymen, I naturally assumed that you would be arrested. Or, at least tied up for some time."

"That's rich, coming from you."

Liu shrugged, deflecting the jab.

"I was a little surprised to see you here, I admit. I think it was only natural that I tried to slip out of my obligations, yes? You'd have done the same in my place."

That was true, but it didn't excuse the betrayal, in Colt's eyes. He also knew that couldn't be the only reason.

"Why did you really do it?"

"I wanted to finish the work we started in Argentina," Liu said. "I knew Hawkinson would never stop. With your organization effectively shut down and with what was sure to come in your next election, I knew there would be no check against his ambitions. Even when I'd learned you and Tony were here, I knew you could only go so far. "

Colt said nothing to refute it, just a dry half-smile.

Liu picked up his wine glass and leaned back into the thick cushions.

"It appears I underestimated you."

Colt, again, said nothing.

"Hawkinson attacked my country. I wanted to lure him back to Beijing so he could face consequences."

Thoughts of Hawkinson suffering the rest of his life in a prison on China's western frontier flashed through his mind. For a moment, Colt wondered if Hawkinson had gotten off too easily. Though, it was just as likely that even if Liu was telling the truth (which Colt hadn't yet determined), that the Chinese government might just grant Hawkinson clemency for his technology and his access.

Guy was, Colt mused, safer to the world dead.

"Justice denied, I suppose," Liu said and took a drink.

Beads of condensation flowed down Colt's untouched glass.

"I don't know," Colt said. "I probably have the same concerns you do about anyone's ability to prosecute him. Being able to attribute actions to someone in an intelligence context is a far different test than it is in a court of law. At least in my country."

"So, it is true, then. That was him on the Sentosa causeway," Liu said.

"It was," Colt replied.

"How much of Archon remains?" Liu asked.

"Alive? Four," he said, and the admission surprised him. Though, even in this game, there was value in truth. "Two of them are in FBI custody. Two remain at large. I think we can agree that nobody runs forever."

Liu considered that for a time. "And what about our work together?"

"What do you mean?" Colt asked, even though he already knew. He wanted Liu to say it. Colt could play that game, too.

"Have I satisfied my obligation to you?"

Colt was impressed. It was the most direct Liu had ever been.

"Do you remember what I said when I got you out of Argentina?"

"I will never forget it. You told me it was the right thing to do, even though we agreed I would not have done the same were the situation reversed."

"If you hadn't sold me out to Hawkinson and the Singaporeans, I'd have said considering his death the end of your obligation to us. Then I spent two days in a jail cell and Hawkinson almost got away because of it," Colt narrowed his eyes. "That makes me a hell of a lot less charitable."

Liu didn't speak, didn't move. Colt couldn't even detect a ripple on the surface of the wine glass in his hand.

"Before I answer your question, I'd like you to answer one of mine," Colt said. It felt good to be back in control of the conversation. "Why did Hawkinson agree to meet with you? The last time you met him, he knew you worked for me."

"I merely explained that with the recent exposure of your unit, it released my obligations. He was so eager to do business with me, he didn't care. I gathered Mr. Hawkinson believed he could outmaneuver me."

"What did he want?"

"He wanted to deliver his uncle an early foreign policy win. He believed he could negotiate a cessation of hostilities between our two countries. I gathered that would be all the reputation laundering he'd require. I said that in exchange for such a consideration, he would need to stop the cyber-attacks against my country. He agreed. When I pressed him for assurances that he could deliver on this promise, Guy assured me it was his sole province to do so. I share this with you in hopes that it helps your superiors reconsider our arrangement."

So, there it was. Guy had admitted to Liu that the quantum decryption was him and not Archon at-large.

Colt didn't know how to answer Liu's broader question. He didn't know what his own future held once he got back to Langley.

"The reality, Liu, is that I honestly don't know. You're a valuable source and to the extent that you can help us calm the waters between our countries, I don't see my service letting you off the hook. This sort of thing isn't up to me."

"This places me at considerable risk," Liu said.

Colt shrugged. "Did you give that kind of consideration to Admiral Denney?"

Liu flushed red. His lips pursed and his jaw tightened around the words he so wanted to speak, but did not.

Liu was a curious asset. One of a kind. Most of the assets Western intelligence agencies recruited in repressive governments did so out of conscience. They could no long countenance the evils they saw their leaders commit and wanted to do whatever possible undermine it. In a rare few cases, those had even prevented wars. In modern America, very few recruited spies did so out of an ideological motivation. Most did it for the money.

Liu was neither.

He was not a true believer.

He was a communist in name only, maintaining party affiliation because it was required, not because he believed in it. Liu's belief was in the job. The Ministry of State Security was a means to an end. He would be identical, Colt believed, if he were somehow transplanted into CIA, MI6, Mossad, or the French DGSE. Liu's faith was espionage. Dead drops were his church, covert communications were his liturgy.

The nation it supported didn't matter.

In another life, they could easily have been peers.

Who am I kidding, Colt thought, *I'd be working for him.*

"We move around a lot. What usually happens is that agents change hands when the handler moves on or retires."

"I see," Liu said softly.

"There's another option."

"Defection," Liu answered flatly.

Colt nodded. "That might be a difficult proposition, given your . . . complicated . . . history with my country. But, I think in exchange for intel on your service, we'd be willing to make a deal."

"They would find me. Our sister service, the Ministry of Public Security, is actively hunting dissidents throughout the world. My disappearance would not go unnoticed. The KGB had many defectors. My service? No."

"Think it over. Discuss it with your wife. If the Agency approves, we can resettle you, give you a new identity. If you're worried about being in the U.S., we have agreements with other countries."

Liu looked out over the lights of Singapore and the burgeoning night. "There is much to consider," he said.

Colt knew that besides weighing the security concerns, Liu would also think about what his identity would be if he weren't a spymaster. Yes, everyone left the service eventually, though Liu had at least another decade, or more. And this would be a different sort of retirement. The party would label him a criminal and a traitor to his homeland. His extended family, his friends, would think he betrayed the motherland. Worse, the families of relocated spies didn't always take to the new country, the new life.

Colt and Liu had once been bitter enemies. Then, momentarily aligned in the fight against Archon. Two days ago, Liu had betrayed Colt to use Hawkinson for himself. Did he deserve defection? Was there any guarantee that Liu wouldn't become a double agent? Report on the Agency's relocation program back to his superiors, or feed the CIA false information on his service, the party, or the PLA? There were methods to uncover these things, of course. Any defector from an intelligence service had to pass a rigorous counterintelligence vetting to prove they weren't a double agent. Most were never approved.

Colt leaned forward. "Think about it and let me know. You know how to reach me."

Colt adjusted his collar, the all-clear signal.

Somewhere in the bar, Tony Ikeda disappeared into the hotel.

Colt stood and left to begin the long journey back home.

34

Venice, Italy

Giovanni Soranzo watched the drone's progress through its onboard camera in a small panel on his laptop. A second window showed the small aircraft's position superimposed over a map. It flew up over a large hedge and dropped to the ground in a maneuver that pilots called nap-of-the-earth. The tiny drone, not much larger than a tablet, streaked toward a black SUV that was stopped on a road. It flew into the vehicle's rear passenger door and the image on the screen immediately dissolved into static. A second drone, this one much smaller, hovered above the kill zone. Giovanni switched his attention to that feed, which showed the smoking SUV and a body lying on the ground.

Another man ran up to Hawkinson's body, hovered a moment, and then went to the vehicle. He appeared to remove something from it and ran back to his own vehicle.

Soranzo couldn't see the man's face, but there were other ways to figure out who he was. That would come in time.

The important thing was that the Americans would be blamed for Guy Hawkinson's murder. That he possessed surveillance footage showing them removing items from the scene would only amplify this theory. If, in reality, it turned out they weren't Americans, who would care? The narrative would hold, and that was all that mattered.

This worked out better than he imagined.

He closed the laptop.

"*Arrivederci*, Signor Hawkinson."

Guy had served his purpose and, frankly, Soranzo was grateful to be rid of him. He'd only met Guy in person once. The interaction lasted less than five minutes, and he found Hawkinson to be a self-absorbed fool with an opinion of himself orders of magnitude beyond his potential.

Smuggling him out of Europe cost a small fortune, even before the boat. Though Soranzo was less concerned about the money. His family wealth predated most nations. The money he had spent on Guy was a sound investment and already paying dividends.

He stood and walked over to one of the floor-to-ceiling windows in his study. He'd decorated the villa in a style consistent with its sixteenth-century origins. In fact, his family had commissioned the famed Renaissance architect Andrea Palladio to design the home in 1562. This "study," which Soranzo used as his office, might have qualified as an aircraft hangar in some parts of the world. One could sprint from the desk to the door and get a workout. A long red carpet, with gold filigree at the edges that looked like gilded flame, ran the length of the room, a decorative tongue extending from the door. A crystal chandelier hung in the center of the room.

Family lore held that during the Second World War, an SS colonel tried to appropriate that chandelier and several artworks from the villa. Giovanni's grandfather informed Il Duce, then residing in nearby Lombardy, that the Soranzos' ancestral property was off limits to the Nazis. The SS colonel was undeterred, and even had the audacity to park a troop transport on the grounds with the intent of loading artifacts. Giovanni's grandfather suggested to the colonel it would be in his best interests to move along. He did not. So, the colonel was invited in for a drink. He was never seen alive again, nor were his men. As the tides of war began to shift, Soranzo's grandfather became a key ally in the region for the American Office of Strategic Services (OSS) commandos and aided in the final overthrow of the fascist government.

Giovanni Donatello Soranzo was a rarity. He'd studied computer science and physics with a minor in theoretical mathematics at Cambridge before going on to postgraduate work at Princeton. There, he studied under a prominent physicist before earning an MBA at the London School of Economics. This was all standard, in preparation to take the helm of the family's shipping and construction empire. What made him a "rarity," though, was the fact that his family dated back to the thirteenth-century Venetian Republic and was part of an unbroken line of its ruling class. Though his title was only now used on formal occasions and the rare state function, Soranzo was still a duke.

Which was why when Guy Hawkinson demanded to know who he was, he'd simply called himself "the Doge."

The intercom on his desk beeped softly and Soranzo walked to his desk to answer it. "Yes?"

"Sir, your guest has arrived."

"Thank you. Please send him up."

"Is the Alzero ready?"

"Yes, sir."

"Excellent. Please send it as well."

"At once."

Soranzo returned to the window and stood, hands clasped behind his back, to once again consider the grounds. He liked greeting guests in this way. Their first view of him was a dramatic turn from the window, backlit by sunlight. It also saved him the long walk from his desk to the door to meet them.

There was a knock at the massive doors to his office.

"*Entra*," Soranzo said.

The doors opened and Howard Hazlett stepped into the office.

"Good afternoon, Howard," Soranzo said, and then turned to face his guest.

"Good afternoon, sir." Hazlett wore a gray, three-piece wool suit with a windowpane pattern, a white shirt, and a green tie. Soranzo grimaced inwardly. Hazlett's unconscious tic was that he dressed like a 1960s Connery every time they met.

"I trust we were successful," Soranzo said, already knowing the answer.

He invariably did this, letting his functionaries report known information to him. It made them feel important, valued.

"Yes, sir. Very much so. Guy Hawkinson is dead."

"Excellent," he said. At that moment, one of his staff appeared and served the '97 Giuseppe Quintarelli Alzero, from right here in Veneto. Soranzo had them decant it an hour ago. He wouldn't normally share a wine such as that with the likes of Hazlett, but, as the French were fond of saying, *c'est la guerre.*

Soranzo motioned to a pair of large chairs facing one window, and the two men sat.

"I fed my CIA handler the intelligence on Hawkinson, just as we discussed. He swallowed it whole." Hazlett favored him with a dark smile. "He believed I was quite terrified." Their conversation stopped as a butler approached with the decanter and two glasses. He poured the wine, waited politely to be dismissed, and then disappeared when instructed, closing the enormous doors behind him.

"I'm disappointed in Guy," Soranzo said, lying.

"It was an unfortunate necessity," Hazlett said. "You did all you could."

"Indeed."

Once Western law enforcement had enough of Mr. Hawkinson and threatened to arrest him, Soranzo had secured a forged passport and a clean car for Guy to escape to Switzerland with. Once he was in Croatia, Soranzo got him onto a chartered ship with a different passport and put him at sea. Soranzo, anonymously through Hazlett, divided and sold Hawkinson's businesses to entities controlled by Archon.

He preferred his formal title, Doge, though "architect" would be just as appropriate.

To a certain line of thinking, one could make the argument that Soranzo was responsible for Archon.

Soranzo had learned of Trinity at Princeton.

The physicist he'd studied under was Dr. Benjamin Kurtz, a protégé of John von Neumann, who had taken over leadership of Trinity when von Neumann died in 1957. Kurtz asked Soranzo to join in 1989, just before his own death, but Soranzo declined. His reasons for this were varied and capricious. He supported Trinity's objectives and debated machine intelligence with his mentor for many hours, debates that sometimes even included Trinity co-founder and Manhattan project alum Edward Teller. Soranzo maintained that Artificial General Intelligence was likely not achievable, but a worthy goal of striving toward. If for nothing else, the technologies realized in the effort would benefit all.

Soranzo remained on the fringes of Trinity, however, and that group invested heavily in the computing company he started as well as a research institute he founded in Rome, the Società per L'informatica Avanzata. In time, Soranzo realized that Trinity would never succeed because their desire was the technology itself. They'd forgotten the lesson that the founders had learned so profoundly in developing and then witnessing the destructive potential of the atomic bomb: that one day, thinking machines might help man end the destructive race for technology that they had just begun.

The latter-day Trinity leaders were a faded reproduction of those men, a copy of a copy.

By the nineties, there was no one left in the organization who'd known any of the founders, let alone studied with them, debated with them, learned from them. In time, Soranzo understood he was the keeper of the flame, so to speak. None of those he'd termed "the final generation" were worthy. He'd named them thus because that was the last group before the schism that shattered the organization, the schism that gave rise to Archon and a more militant, yet less focused, Trinity.

Soranzo was the true architect of the schism.

By this point, Trinity believed Soranzo was a kind benefactor, but an anachronism. He was one of the many "elder statesmen" of technology that quietly supported their organization. Working in the shadows, he convinced Quentin Wales, Rhett Bolton, and Cameron Braithwaite that Trinity was doomed. The seeds of what would become the schism were planted and there they would grow. Each of those men had noble aims to begin with, but as Trinity's wealth grew almost immeasurably, their goals became corrupted. This wealth grew exponentially in the tech-dominated 1990s and 2000s.

It actually amazed Soranzo they would invite such men as these to join Trinity.

What would Teller or Kurtz think if they learned Trinity argued over whether they should weaponize their technologies in order to confront modern threats?

Soranzo gently pushed for those men, and a few others, to break off and form their own group—one with the wherewithal to accomplish what the founders set out to do. Create a better society. They did, but not in the way that men like Braithwaite and Wales defined it. Soranzo kept his influence hidden, and nobody suspected his involvement.

The Trinity–Archon war was foolish and wasteful and lasted far longer than he'd intended. But it was also the only way to purge the zealots and the megalomaniacs from the organization. Wales wanted to run the world, to subvert governments because he believed he could do a better job. Marin and Yoon believed a sufficiently intelligent machine would do a better job at managing the day-to-day affairs of a government than humans ever could.

When it was simply taking too long, Soranzo emerged from the shadows and assumed a role of "board advisor" to Archon's leadership. He recommended they recruit the Hawkinsons, and it was he who suggested Guy be their sword. All the while, the Doge quietly whispered in Guy's ear that Archon had gone too far and that together, they could reframe the organization, rebuild it.

That Trinity had actually killed Carlos Marin for him was a fortunate coincidence. It also provided serendipitous inspiration for how to handle Hawkinson.

"Unfortunately, four board members remain. Craddock and Fleet are both in custody." Hazlett said. He leaned forward, awkwardly sloshing his wine to affect a dignified swirl, then took a gulp. Soranzo's eyes bore into the man's Adam's apple as it bobbed.

"I wouldn't worry about them," Soranzo said. "You were aware of the xenobot project, yes?"

"Of course. I secured the funding," Hazlett said archly.

"A bit before its time, but useful, I think." Hazlett tried to interject another superlative, but Soranzo just spoke over him. "I had Hawkinson do something for me when he first created the weapon. Or, rather, I had some-thing done. Working through a trusted asset, I secured the board members'

DNA samples. Then, I had a version of the xenobot created from the original model. Now that we're ready, we'll just release that into the area near Braithwaite and Yoon." He paused and smiled archly. "In fact, that's already been done. I suspect we'll soon learn on the news that these gentlemen have expired from unfortunate heart failures."

Hazlett was aghast. "But everyone knows Archon is responsible for the xenobots."

"Everyone knew Hawkinson created and used that weapon. Hawkinson is dead. And so is Archon. There will be no further speculation as to the provenance of this weapon. Craddock, as you pointed out, is in custody, so he'll be a little harder to get to, but he *will* have to appear in court at some point."

"What of Dr. Fleet?"

"Ah, yes, dear Heather. I rather liked her. She was a pure scientist." Soranzo set his wine down and stood. As he walked back to his desk, he said, "Tell me, Howard, are you familiar with the term *slaughterbot*?"

Even Soranzo had to admit the term sounded comical in his Italian-accented English.

A nervous titter issued from Hazlett's mouth. "I'm afraid not."

"Some activist coined the term in 2017 after learning that America's Defense Department was creating micro drones equipped with shaped charges to be used as battlefield weapons. The explosion would kill the subject just as easily as a gunshot and would likely resemble being hit by a large caliber round." Soranzo opened a drawer in his massive desk and removed a device. He walked back over to Hazlett, showing him the palm-sized quadcopter with a small protrusion on the front. "This identifies the target, and then there's a shaped charge that completes the task. Rather ingenious."

"Quite so," Hazlett agreed.

"We'll be deploying one of these to California to retire the good doctor. It is a true pity. Of them all, she had the most potential to realize our vision. Sadly, the campaign to expose Archon worked a little too well." Soranzo made a show of setting the drone down on his desktop. He reached down to another drawer and pocketed something. "Let's take a walk," he suggested.

"Of course. I was admiring the grounds on the way here." Hazlett hastily changed the subject from killer drones, but he did not calm.

As they descended to the ground floor and navigated the wide, Renaissance corridors, Soranzo explained the home's history and his family's place in the pantheon of Venetian nobility. If one were to ask Soranzo of his nationality, he'd say "Venetian" first, and only if pressed, "Italian."

In time, they made their way outside the villa and descended the steps from the rear portico to an expansive patio. Soranzo led Hazlett to the grounds, plush grass barely registering the footsteps that passed over it. Hazlett preened about his accomplishments. He talked at length about finalizing the transfer of the rest of the Archon-owned businesses, the ones they hadn't allowed Trinity to discover. Working through agents like Hazlett and using systems of his own design, Soranzo had enabled Trinity to unravel enough of Archon's operations that they concluded they'd struck the decisive blow against their nemesis. That they were pushing toward the endgame.

"We have always isolated the organization from the leadership, operating most activities as franchises. All of that to say, most of the lower tier never knew who they served. Certainly, they couldn't put a name to it. I'm the only one who has any real linkage."

"Excellent. And when did you last meet with your CIA handler?"

"In London, perhaps ten days before Hawkinson's death."

"Excellent," Soranzo repeated. The early autumn air was still warm. The sun lit the grounds with a golden light, though the trees cast long shadows in their wake. "Where Archon failed was that they forgot what Trinity was created to do. Create 'thinking machines' that would make warfare obsolete. Further, that machines could one day do all the mundane tasks that humans belabor their lives with. Thus, freeing humanity up for philosophy, art, debate, and the pursual of pure science. The intent was to create a new Athens, not a benevolent dictatorship run by AI with a ruling class above it."

"Yes," Hazlett said, hedging, because Soranzo knew he didn't believe that. Hazlett desired what the rest of them did, power for its own sake.

"I knew the last surviving founders of Trinity. This was their vision, not what Archon is or even what Trinity, today, has become."

"Well, some leaders would be required, certainly. Society often needs a bit of a nudge," Hazlett said.

"It certainly does," Soranzo agreed.

He drew the object he'd slid into his pocket out, a Beretta 8000, barely larger than the drone he'd shown Hazlett in his office. Without a word, Soranzo shot Hazlett in the head.

Hazlett's body dropped to the ground.

Soranzo had dedicated his life to unlocking the highest technologies. But sometimes, a simple solution was the most elegant.

One of his men would be along shortly to collect Hazlett. After sanitizing him, they'd dump the body in any of the salt marshes near the coast where no one would be likely to find it. And if they did, no one would care, because he was English.

Giovanni Soranzo now controlled all. The last vestiges of Archon were his. Good had already come from this. Global investment in artificial intelligence had increased fivefold in the last three years. The gains achieved far surpassed what the scientific community expected. Now that he'd shown the world what quantum computing could do, he predicted a similar sea change. Far too soon to suggest they were on the cusp of a new golden age, but it was at least within reach.

Hazlett had been correct about one thing. Society often needed a nudge.

Soranzo returned to his office, passing two of his men on their way to dispose of Hazlett's body. He informed one of his butlers that he would work until dinner and closed the doors. He retrieved his wine and sat back at his desk. Soranzo opened his laptop.

"Good afternoon, Paolo," he said.

"Good afternoon, Doge," the machine, named for Paolo Scarpi, the Venetian historian, scientist, and statesman, replied.

"We have much to do today." said the Doge.

35

Washington, DC

Senator John Treadwell loved Washington in the fall. The air became crisp after the unrelenting summer heat and the trees turned to gold. The senior senator from New Hampshire had maintained a residence in Georgetown ever since he was a freshman congressman in 1990. He served in the House of Representatives for four terms before securing a senate seat in 1998, which he held to this day. Unlike many of his colleagues, Treadwell remained in Washington as long as they were in session and relied on his home office to manage constituent services. Particularly now. There was simply too much to do to return home for fundraising and glad-handing and, he noted with some derision, campaigning. Treadwell was part of the old guard. A shrinking generation of politicians who believed that divisiveness and rancor were things to be rooted out and purged, not cultivated for short-term popularity. As he'd told his colleagues on more than one occasion, "this is the United States Senate, not the Roman Colosseum."

The party expected him to be home campaigning for Preston Hawkinson's presidency. He was not going to, however. Treadwell's heart wasn't in it any longer. He was exhausted. Treadwell was in the middle of his fifth term in the senate and he'd known for a long time there would not be a sixth.

Now in his seventies, he was even contemplating an early retirement. Preston Hawkinson was sure to win next month. The president's approval rating was lower than Bush's nadir during the first years of the Iraq War, and lower than Carter's generally.

Treadwell couldn't blame the American people for the sentiment. They'd stumbled from one global calamity to the next and the country had never been more divided. The rioting and civil unrest had largely subsided as people aligned to one camp or another, but many still believed "computers were going to take their jobs." Deep divisions remained, but it seemed that furious candle of civic violence had guttered out. While there was much about the current pace of technological advancement that concerned, if not outright frightened him, Treadwell believed it was ultimately progress. He was one of the few in his party that hadn't latched onto the anti-technologist narrative and the populism that followed it. One of the many areas where he'd grown beyond his party. Or, perhaps the party had transformed into something he no longer recognized.

Frankly, he could say the same about either side of the aisle, if not the entire system.

Treadwell tried to push these dark thoughts from his mind, recognizing that he felt them with increasing frequency of late. Instead, he just tried to enjoy his weekly walk through Georgetown's Montrose Park. Warm sunlight broke through the tree cover and it felt good. He might go a little farther today, taking the trail down into Rock Creek.

As he was walking, a young woman jogged past him, looking over briefly. He heard her rapid footfalls stop as she passed, and then she turned and paused. "Excuse me, I hate to bother you, but are you Senator Treadwell?"

He smiled. "Yes, I am."

"I thought so," she said, beaming. "I saw you on *Meet the Press* last week."

Treadwell chuckled slightly. It happened less and less these days, particularly as he sought the limelight less and less, but it was nice to be recognized. He'd put the young lady at, perhaps, thirty. She had a slight frame, blonde hair cut short. Her face angled slightly too narrow at her chin, giving it a rounded V shape. She had bright, expressive eyes.

The girl looked up and down the trail and then leaned in. As she did, her smile dropped to a serious expression. "Senator, I think you should go to the Senate SCIF today and look at a file marked 'SCARAB.' I think you'll find some interesting reading. Have a good day, sir," and she was off.

What in the hell was this?

The Senate intelligence committee had a Sensitive Compartmented Information Facility in the Capitol so that they and their staffers could review the classified materials essential for them to perform their oversight responsibilities. But how had this young lady known about a that, or a specific code-worded file?

Treadwell turned around and returned home as quickly as he could. He had to know.

Legislators often requested access to classified materials at unusual hours, so his being there on a Sunday didn't raise eyebrows among the Capitol Police. Treadwell walked through the silent Capitol. The only sound was his heels on the polished marble floors. When he'd arrived at the nondescript, oxblood colored doors, Treadwell removed his phone and set it in a locker outside the door. The senator entered the room, closing the door behind him. He was alone.

The senator opened the document safe and searched for the file the jogger mentioned. Sure enough, there was a file labeled "SCARAB." Treadwell removed it from the safe and walked over to a table. He opened the folder and scanned the contents. The senator read it three more times before dropping it on the table in a mixture of disgust, horror, and complete confusion. He didn't know what to do, but he felt sick.

Treadwell read the file one last time to ensure there was no mistaking its contents. There was not.

The senator put the file back where he'd found it and left the SCIF. He went up to his office, opened up a bottle of fourteen-year Oban that he kept there, and poured a couple fingers into a tumbler. Treadwell drank the scotch and contemplated what to do.

Finally, he picked up his cell phone and dialed his chief of staff.

"Tim, I need you to set up a meeting for me."

Off the Record was, perhaps, the most archetypal Washington bar. Located in the Hay-Adams hotel, it was dark, with red walls and dark brown wood paneling. The chairs and tables continued the red-on-brown motif, interspersed with lights ensconced in bright brass. Long held as a place to be "seen and not heard," Off the Record was a place where the District's political and business leaders met to grease the wheels of government.

It was the physical embodiment of the axiom, "If these walls could talk . . ."

It had been four days since Treadwell had read the SCARAB file. He shared the contents with an old friend and ally on the Permanent Subcommittee on Investigations, the congressional body charged with probing criminal acts such as fraud and conspiracy, anything the Congress deemed damaging to the health and welfare of the nation. Treadwell was not ready to begin an inquiry yet, but he wanted his friend's read on the matter. His old colleague reached the same conclusion—that it was irrefutable.

Treadwell spotted the other party sitting in a far dark corner, looking at his phone with a glass of bourbon in front of him.

Treadwell approached the table and sat.

"Good evening, Preston," he said curtly.

"What's this about, John? I've got to be on a plane in two hours. You know how much I hate flying at night."

The job's aged him, Treadwell thought. Preston Hawkinson resembled a bitter scarecrow, stooped and ragged. He dressed like he had family money, though given his otherwise haggard appearance, Treadwell thought Hawkinson looked like someone had draped expensive fabric over old bones.

Treadwell hadn't wanted to be bothered during their conversation so he'd left instructions with the maître d' that he was to be served two fingers of Oban upon being seated and not to be disturbed thereafter. Per his instructions, a waiter deposited the scotch in front of him and vanished.

"My condolences on your nephew's untimely death. Tragic accident."

"Yes, well, you know in some of these countries there are barely any laws. Driving is like a," Hawkinson waved his hand theatrically, "game to them."

True, Treadwell allowed. *But not Singapore.*

"I've had some interesting reading lately," he said and took a sip of his scotch. He set the glass down but didn't release the grip.

"I don't have time for this, John. You know I'm due on the stump. Now, you got the last twenty minutes I had. What are we talking about?"

"Synergy Automated Systems. Do you know that company?"

"No," Hawkinson said brusquely.

"They are the company that designed this 'secure voting technology' you've been pushing. I noticed that many of the pilots are in swing states."

"It's a test project. Limited rollout. I don't have much to do with it."

"Do you know who designed these systems?"

"Of course I don't."

"Your nephew, Preston."

"That's ludicrous. And anyway, all of his business was wrapped up in this goddamn FBI witch hunt. He was a patriot and a veteran. He doesn't deserve this kind of treatment. POTUS can't win the reelection on his own so he's going after—"

"Preston, stop it. Your nephew's company, HawkTech, built these systems. They're the same ones they sold abroad under these UN contracts they had. When his company folded, someone quietly sold off his product lines. They were rebranded and in April of this year, you made an impassioned speech on the Senate floor about how we needed to invest in technologies to ensure safer elections. Then, ironically, the very technology your nephew built is the one you're championing? Curious, isn't it?"

"That's preposterous."

"On that, we agree."

Hawkinson drank his bourbon. "What's your point, John? This isn't exactly novel technology, is it? Anyone could develop this. Especially after Guy's company did good work restoring democracy to some parts of Africa. Nothing stays secret for long in this world. This is probably the work of some imitator. And, it's not as if I gave them the contract, is it? All I said was that the American people deserved free and fair elections, free from the kind of nonsense we've seen the goddamned Russians try. I did this because I don't need them muddling with another election. I can beat President Harrison myself. The Russians are right to be scared of me. You know why they want him to stay in office? Because he's weak. They know what they can get away with."

"The FBI has records. They can show how the technology was moved between, I believe, twelve different shell companies before landing at Synergy Automated Systems. Which, if you'd cared to look, only exists on paper," Treadwell said.

"If you called me in here today to tell me that the Federal Election Commission didn't properly vet a contractor, all I can tell you is that it's just one more example of how this administration is failing the American people and why I can do better. Frankly, this is a message you should be pushing for me on the stump, John."

"You don't think the public would believe it's just a little bit suspicious that your nephew built the voting technology being used this election? What will people say if you win?"

"They'll say, 'Thank God, now we can get back to business.'"

Treadwell considered his drink for a moment. Hawkinson's strategy here was exactly how he'd manage this accusation were it made in public. Delay, delay, delay, until the election was over. Then, make it disappear.

"Don't know what you hoped to accomplish with this, John. I do think that you haven't gotten with the times. I've spoken with some others," Hawkinson paused and pursed his lips, as though weighing some heavy decision. In truth, both men knew it was for show and whatever he'd decided had been set long before. "We won't be supporting your reelection in two years. Be good of you to retire, get some fresh perspective in your seat. Someone . . . a little more visionary."

Treadwell took another drink, pretending to hide behind his whiskey and make Hawkinson think he'd scored a point. If he'd been on the fence about leaving the Senate, Hawkinson had certainly convinced him. If he weren't so tired, he'd run again just to spite the bastard.

"Tell me, Preston," Treadwell said, and set his drink down on the table. "Do you know Reece Craddock?"

"The crackpot? Just what I read in the papers. Fugitive, isn't he?"

"He knows you."

"I'm a United States Senator running for president. Of course he knows me."

"According to the FBI, the relationship is a little more intimate than that. They arrested him in August, along with a woman named Dr. Heather Fleet. The Justice Department is having a very interesting conversation with him right now. Craddock admitted to a sweeping money laundering scheme, which made its way into your campaign through multiple political action committees. He also cooperated their speculation about this voting technology and confirmed the intent is to ensure you get elected."

"You're lying, John. If that were even *half* true, I'd have heard from the Justice Department, not from a wheezing old draft horse long overdue for the pasture. And *anyone* can contribute to a PAC. I don't know who they are. You know that just as damned well as I do."

"That's good. Craddock has a lot to say about your associations and the people who stand to gain if you're elected."

"I've had enough of this. I came here in good faith, at the request of an old colleague. Someone I once considered a friend and ally. I won't listen to these baseless accusations. Furthermore, I won't hear this deep state nonsense. The FBI will have a reckoning when I take over." Hawkinson waved a long, skeletal finger accusingly at Treadwell. He looked every bit a fire and brimstone preacher.

"You seem awfully sure of yourself," Treadwell said calmly. "That's not really what I wanted to talk ago you about, though. Not entirely." The SCARAB file. "Did you know your nephew met with a Chinese intelligence officer before he died?"

"I'll not let you scandalize the memory of a war hero for this . . . nonsense." Hawkinson's righteous indignation took him to his feet.

"Sit down, Preston. I'm not finished with you yet."

"I'll do no such thing."

"You'll talk to me or you'll talk to the FBI. What's your choice?"

Hawkinson begrudgingly lowered himself to his chair with equal measures of effort and spite. "I'll listen, but just so I have something to scratch onto your tombstone."

"Your nephew had an association with this intelligence officer. Met with him on multiple occasions. On the last one, Guy attempted to broker a deal in which the United States would relinquish any claims to the defense of Taiwan in exchange for a cessation of hostilities with China. He said this came from you."

"Preposterous."

"It was recorded," Treadwell said.

"Then how do *you* know about it?"

"Because what your nephew did *not* know, was his contact was a CIA asset. He reported it to his handler immediately. Who, in turn, handed that recording over the FBI."

Hawkinson, white faced, said nothing.

"The part that troubles me the most, though, is that Guy's contact asked him for something in return. A sign of good faith. He wanted the cyberattacks to stop. End the security crisis, at least, for the People's Republic of China."

"Why did he think Guy could deliver this for him?" Hawkinson's tone was flat and cold.

"Because Guy was behind it. I think we can spare ourselves the technical discussion. I don't believe two wheezing old horses like us would understand it. Especially you, who, until a few months ago championed the push against technology. But suffice it to say, Guy possessed the capability to break open everyone's security systems like they were eggshells."

Treadwell leaned back and took up his whiskey again.

"Here's what happens now, you son of a bitch. You're going to withdraw from the race and resign from the Senate. Immediately. Cite health concerns. I've spoken with the House Committee on Investigations and the Attorney General. If you go quietly and *immediately*, you'll avoid prosecution. If you tarry for one day, Preston, by God they will handcuff you on the Senate floor." Treadwell pushed himself back from the table and stood. "Given our long history together, I'll give you the courtesy of a day. Which is more than you deserve."

"I don't think you'll be so smug when the organs of government are turned against you in four months," Hawkinson said.

He had to give the old bastard credit, he didn't go down easily.

Treadwell leaned in across the table. "The CIA said these people, the ones who back Reece Craddock, killed your nephew because he crossed them. What do you think they'll do to you if you step out of line?"

Treadwell left the bar and returned to his townhouse in Georgetown.

The next day, he watched with grim satisfaction as Preston Hawkinson announced he was withdrawing from the presidential race and retiring from the Senate, on the advice of his doctor. He referenced an undisclosed health condition and asked for privacy during this very difficult time.

36

Her phone rang in the dark and Lacy James snatched it off the nightstand before it woke the house.

Lacy slept little anymore. Her job had her awake at odd hours to respond to sources, many of whom were hackers that kept odd hours. But since that first message six months before from Bashe, she hadn't slept more than four hours at a stretch.

Because once she ran with it, Lacy was worried someone was going to break the door down.

Despite what they tell the electorate or the press in those heady, early days of an administration, no government truly enjoys accountability. They each justify secrecy in the name of fulfilling an agenda for the American people. The Nixon Administration started a dark trend of pursuing journalists who did their jobs, and it continued to greater or lesser extents with every subsequent presidency. No president liked their secrets exposed. Instead of refraining from doing the things that scandalized administrations, they tended to shoot the messengers.

Fortunately or unfortunately, Lacy James was the messenger of the moment.

Lacy muted the ringer but didn't pick up until she was out of the bedroom. She heard her husband stirring and hoped he'd get back to sleep. It was just creeping up on four-thirty. She'd have declined the call, but it was her editor, Brad.

Lacy pulled the door to her office shut behind her and picked up the call. "I'll assume they announced the Pulitzers early, and that's why you're getting me out of bed," she said.

"It's all gone, Lacy. All of it."

"What's all gone?" Her pulse spiked, and Lacy was fully awake now.

"The Trinity files and the CIA stuff. Everything you got from your Bashe, guy, it's all gone."

"How is that possible? It's locked in a safe."

"I'm at the office now. New York called, freaking out. They had some source material on their hard drives and it's gone. So, they called me—"

"They had *what*? Damn it, Brad! We talked about this. You gave me your word. New York gave me their word that we were not putting any original source on any electronic media. Jesus Christ, do you people even read what I write?"

"I had nothing to do with it. This was a decision New York made, and they didn't tell me."

"They were supposed to follow the same protocols they did with Snowden. What the hell, Brad?"

"I think it was a mistake. Someone must have—"

But Lacy wasn't listening. She powered up the clean laptop that she used for communicating with sources. The laptop booted to the login screen, Lacy entered the fake username and password and nothing happened. Then, she saw the computer cycle through the new user dialogue.

Someone had wiped the machine completely.

Lacy closed the machine's lid and stared into space. Distantly, she heard Brad on the other end of the line, asking if she was still there.

Later that morning, Lacy drove to her local bank branch and asked to access her safe deposit box. She opened it and pulled out the sealed and taped envelope, first checking to ensure that the seals were still in place. Lacy closed the box and drove home. She went out to the backyard and used a letter opener to break the packing tape seal she'd used to secure it. Inside were the physical copies of everything she'd gotten from Bashe, the files she'd printed out before deleting them from the virtual server. These were the source documents that served as the foundation for her stories, as well as things she hadn't yet reported on. Some were items Lacy was saving for future reports, others were things she believed too damaging to put into the public. What New York had were copies of some of this, which she'd flown there herself. They'd wanted to see them in person before running the story.

Lacy put the contents in their backyard fire pit. Next, added her notebooks. She covered the pile in lighter fluid and struck a match.

Numbly, Lacy James watched it all burn to ashes.

Whoever sent that message, she received it.

37

Langley, Virginia

Colt missed Wilcox's funeral because he'd been in Singapore.

One more reason he was glad Guy Hawkinson was on a slow boat to hell.

He did make it to the Agency's memorial for Jason at headquarters. Colt listened to Deputy Director Hoskins's speech about a career that embodied duty, honor, and integrity even in the murkiest circumstances. About how Wilcox held true to his belief that what he was doing was right, just, and necessary to protect the republic.

Hoskins hadn't announced his retirement yet. That would come in a few months, when the world was quieter.

Colt was alone now. An orphan within the CIA bureaucracy.

Hoskins hadn't spoken to Colt since he'd returned. In fact, their eyes met only once during the speech. Hoskins looked at him and gave a barely perceptible nod. The expression could mean anything from a simple acknowledgement to "I'll deal with you later." Colt was too mentally fatigued to read any more into it.

He and the entire NTCU team were on administrative leave pending a formal investigation. The CERBERUS AI was legal and covered by multiple statutes governing electronic surveillance, but that didn't make it any less of a scandal. The media coverage painted it as "legal" the same way torture had once been.

Colt acknowledged that during their two-year campaign against Archon, they might have bent some of those rules, but they never broke them. The NTCU's prosecution of that conflict showed, to Colt at least, that the laws governing where intelligence ended and law enforcement began were woefully outdated. It was entirely possible that their next adversary might, in fact, be an AI. And you can't prosecute a computer.

The *Times*'s breaking of the existence of NTCU and CERBERUS had created a political firestorm that gained momentum daily. There hadn't been a new security breach in weeks. While the administration claimed victory over that, the public outcry over the so-called "sweeping domestic surveillance program" filled the void left in the news cycle by the resolution of the security crisis. The NTCU knew, now, that Hawkinson was the leak. He'd covered his tracks well, but Nadia figured it out. It wasn't hard, not with the tools that the NTCU had available to them. Once they had the journalist's byline, they could work it back. She'd hidden her moves well. Someone that knew InfoSec had taught her well, but not well enough for the unit.

Congress would investigate. Some in the Agency feared this would be like the Church Committee, the post-Watergate bloodletting that many in the Agency believed had been more to extract a pound of flesh than to drive necessary reform. If that happened, Colt knew he'd be done. They'd be looking for a head to put on a spike, and he was the only choice. It wouldn't be Hoskins and Blankenship, and the Technology Mission Center had only overseen the NTCU for a few short months. Thorpe had taken a bullet in trying to protect Wilcox and was, rightly, called a hero. That would leave Colt, the number two and the senior CIA officer in the unit.

Whatever happened, Colt knew he did what was right. Without the NTCU's intervention, Archon would still be alive, and it was entirely possible that America, after a few years, would be unrecognizable.

Hoskins mentioned Thorpe in his speech, giving rare praise for the FBI man who'd been present when Wilcox was assassinated. Thorpe had risked his life trying to save him, and the CIA owed him a debt they could never repay, Hoskins said.

Colt agreed with that.

Thorpe was a good man, a good friend, and Colt would miss working with him.

Thorpe was at home recovering and would be medically retired from the FBI. They had also awarded him the FBI Medal of Valor.

Hoskins concluded his remarks, and the somber gathering dispersed. The memorial had taken place on a cloudy October day, in front of the Agency's original entrance, where Hoskins announced there would be a statue erected.

"Wilcox would hate the shit out of that," a gruff voice said, and a meaty hand dropped onto Colt's shoulder. "Get you a beer, Sparky?"

Colt smiled, despite his bitter mood.

"Man, they'll let anybody in here," he said to Fred Ford.

"I had to bribe the gate guard," Ford said. It was strange seeing him with a visitor badge.

They started the long trek around the massive complex to their cars.

"So," Fred said in a heavy voice. "Is it over?"

"I think so. We got Guy's laptop in Singapore. We can put all of the cyberattacks on him. That was the part we got wrong. We thought it was Archon, but by the time he started it, Guy had already split from them. The tech was based on stuff he stole from Jeff Kim, but with two years of AI and human research on top of it. It was originally Archon's plan; Guy just took it over and then went to war with them. We know Guy killed at least one of Archon's board members. Ava was good for one. I don't think Guy did the other two, that's the only part of this I can't square."

"You think she did it?"

"Somebody killed him," he said dismissively. "I mean, I was right *there*. It was a small, concentrated blast, our analysts think intended to minimize collateral damage."

"Like someone knew you'd be there?"

Colt shrugged. "He was the leaker, by the way. To the *New York Times*."

"No shit," Ford said. "What an asshole."

"Yeah. Craddock didn't break until he learned Hawkinson was dead. We still don't know if it was the fear that Guy could get him or the realization that Archon couldn't get him out. Cameron Braithwaite and Jin Yoon both died of heart attacks that were curiously similar to Sir Archibald Chalcroft's." Chalcroft was a British MP and former MI6 officer. He was also a member of Trinity, and was the man Archon had directed to be assassinated using their biological weapon. "We'll probably keep that connection quiet. Heather Fleet is in custody."

"What about those contingency plans you mentioned? The doomsday scenario?"

"Far as we know, that was bullshit. I haven't heard from my source in weeks and he's not responding to COVCOMs. The FBI asked Fleet and Craddock about those plans independently and they both denied their existence. As near as I can figure, my source was trying to protect Archon's board. My best guess? He thought we were behind the assassination campaign and wanted us to back off."

"Hedge bets that they could beat it in court?"

"Yeah. God, but they did a lot of damage. Some of this is going to take years to untangle. None of the financial markets have recovered."

"Global recession, I'm hearing. Maybe worse," Ford said.

"China is a total shit show right now. The party fired half of their general staff once they saw them question whether they could take Taiwan. NATO's secretary general resigned, and the French and the Turks are demanding that they kick the British out of the alliance." Erica Cano was still in Turkish prison. The current thinking in the State Department was the Turks wouldn't release her until after the election. If the president lost, they'd use it to gain favor with his successor. If the president won, it would be a way to recalibrate the relationship in Turkey's favor.

"What's going on with our friend in Silicon Valley?"

"Who, Jeff Kim? He got what he wanted. Hawkinson is gone. He hired Nadia, by the way."

"He did what?"

"Yeah. She's leaving at the end of the calendar year. Two hundred and seventy-five thousand dollars a year to be a senior researcher. She's going to be at the forefront of AI. Can't say I blame her. That's pretty far from the blast radius here."

"Think you're going to be okay?" Ford asked.

"I don't know, man. My faith in this place is shaken. I'm not sure. And what's next? Leaving the NTCU to be a case officer at some station somewhere is a bit of a letdown. I don't have enough seniority for a deputy Chief of Station gig and anyway, nobody knows me."

"Well, I have a spot for you if you decide to leave."

"Thanks," Colt said.

They walked in silence for a while. Ford didn't ask about Trinity, because that would bring up questions about them, and about Ava, that neither of them wanted to discuss.

Colt loved her, as he always would. But he couldn't see past her having killed Hawkinson. Colt recognized the hypocrisy. After all, that was the job they had sent there him to do. But Colt was, at least, acting on behalf of some duly constituted authority. It was different in his mind. He also wasn't sure that he'd have gone through with it. He might have captured Hawkinson and held him until the FBI's legal attaché could come over from the embassy and arrest him.

Colt didn't know, but what he did know was that Ava had taken that option away from him. That would always hang over their relationship.

As would her killing of Carlos Marin.

They hadn't spoken since Singapore.

Colt didn't know what was next for Trinity. They'd militarized, for lack of a better term, over the past decade as they rose to meet the challenge Archon mounted. Would they return to the race to achieve AGI, or had they concluded that it was too dangerous for anyone to achieve? Colt knew there were some in Trinity who believed humanity wasn't ready for AGI and that the group should work to stall, even subvert those efforts until society was ready. That thinking scared Colt more than anything else because the desire to be a gatekeeper for humanity's future was exactly what had given rise to Archon.

Perhaps they'd return to pure science.

Whatever they did, Colt hoped they'd abandon their "operational" side.

Colt knew from hard experience that one could only chase ghosts for so long before it wore down their soul.

Colt and Ford reached their cars.

Colt told him he'd pass on the drink. He knew he would not be good company today and wanted to send Wilcox off on his own. They agreed to meet up soon and Ford told him his wife, who was fond of Colt, insisted he resume their monthly dinner engagement at the Ford home. Colt promised he would. On his way home, Colt stopped at the Vienna Inn. It was a popular Agency hangout about ten miles from Langley and close to Colt's house. He parked and walked inside.

The Inn was a dive bar, converted in 1960 from single-story house, sporting a black and white checkered floor, blond wood tables, and a simple, long bar at the back. It was a favorite hangout of current and former spooks, as much for the proximity to Langley as for its status as the antitheses of the archetypal pretentious DC watering hole.

Colt ordered a Vienna lager and raised a silent toast to his friend and mentor. He took a sip and said, "Good hunting," in a quiet voice. He was on the edge of breaking. Wilcox's assessment of Archon's end goal had been largely correct. Craddock admitted once they maneuvered Preston Hawkinson into the White House, they planned to gradually but quietly undermine America's constitutional protections, while at the same time replacing government functions with AI under the guise of "modernization." They would wrap the scheme in good works and most citizens would never see it coming. Quantum AI, with its nearly limitless processing power, could unlock advances in medicine and technology the world had never seen. Sustainable clean energy would be within reach. Archon would subtly shift the American economy and infrastructure away from petrochemicals. The savings realized from eliminating millions of civil service and contractor positions would be an incredible boost to the economy. Machine-made pharmaceuticals in quantum labs could lessen healthcare costs, increasing accessibility for all. Eventually, Archon expected this would allow them to eliminate the need for health insurance. Within ten years, they expected to implement a universal basic income. Robots would cultivate and harvest crops genetically engineered to be drought resistant. They would reduce food scarcity. Archon calculated that if most citizens received a free education, had basic healthcare, and received a basic income, they would have no incentive to revolt.

And all that Americans would have to do to live in this utopia would be to give up their personal freedoms. Craddock estimated it would take them a decade to implement. By then, they would have unraveled the fabric of American democracy enough that there would be no stopping them. Archon would start with the United States, with "pilot projects" in other nations. The rest of the world would follow or be left behind. It was a terrifying scenario, and Colt was relieved it would never happen.

Colt noticed someone pull up to the bar next to him and order a beer.

"I think 'cheers' would be inappropriate, so I'll simply say, 'I'm sorry.' Jason was a good man. He'd be proud of you."

Colt looked over at the voice. It was Jamie Richter.

"Were you there?"

"I was. I stayed toward the back." The bartender handed Richter his beer and disappeared to the other end of the counter. "I know I said I couldn't protect you, but I don't want you to worry about what the Congress may or may not do about this latest thing. It's impossible to handicap the election with Hawkinson dropping out, but even if his party wins, they won't come after the Agency. Everyone wants him to go away as quickly as possible. I've already spoken to Hoskins. All NTCU personnel will be reassigned without consequence. I know we put you in an impossible position, Colt. And I also want you to know I didn't forget it."

"There's any number of ways I could take that," Colt said.

"Well, take it like this. You are in the rare position that the number two man at CIA and the national security advisor both owe you a solid. At a minimum, you get your pick of jobs. Personally, I'd like to see you get back in the field."

"Why is that?"

"Something Jason said to me once. We got to be friends after he left the Agency and we spent a few late nights drinking bourbon and solving the world's problems. He's the one who helped me understand what we were up against. He said the Agency got so focused on killing terrorists over the last twenty years they forgot how to recruit spies. Forgot how to work on the street. But that's just not the game anymore. We need people who are good on the street and who understand the technological threat well enough to articulate it to people like me. Hoskins has his faults, but he does get it. He knows the clandestine service has to evolve. I'm trying to talk the director into changing his mind about the resignation."

"This sounds like a pitch," Colt said.

Richter laughed. "Sometimes I forget who I'm talking to. Hoskins is going to propose an idea to you, and I'd like you to hear what he has to say."

"Kind of curious that I'm getting this from you, isn't it?"

"Not so much. Like I said, I owed you one. The NTCU filled a vital hole in the Intelligence Community. That need doesn't go away."

"So, what, they're going to remake the NTCU and just change the packaging?"

"Not exactly. Just that there's a recognition that we need to blend old school tradecraft with current tech, stay ahead of the opposition."

"Isn't that what the new mission center is for?"

"That's the brain. What don't have right now are hands." Richter took a long drink. "It's interesting, Preston Hawkinson dropping out of the race like that."

"Health concerns, I heard," Colt said.

"Yeah. Scuttlebutt is an intel committee peer had a quiet word with him. Guess he came across some interesting information. Whatever it was, must have scared old Preston half to death. Timing was curious too, because if it would've come out after the election, particularly if he'd won, they'd have been able to bury it."

"Well, Jamie," Colt said, staring ahead. "You know this town. It leaks like a sieve."

Jamie Richter set his glass down, half finished, clapped Colt once on the shoulder, and left the bar.

Colt drank alone with his secrets and his ghosts.

Colt finished his beer and ordered another. He didn't even see Nadia come in. She grabbed a stool next to him and asked the bartender for whatever Colt was having.

"Hey," she said, and Colt finally looked over. "Fred thought I'd find you here. You doing okay?"

Colt shrugged. There wasn't a way to answer that question.

Was he doing okay? He'd just come from the memorial service for his boss and mentor, the man who taught him everything he knew about being a spook. *Maybe not everything, Sparky.* He could hear Ford's voice in his head, and he smiled.

"I'm fine," he said, and it was somewhat true. "What's up?"

"I, ah, wanted to thank you," Nadia said. She cradled her hands around her beer glass.

"For what?"

Nadia turned to face him. "For Hawkinson, Colt. Archon. All of it."

"I don't follow," Colt said, confused.

"You said we'd get them and you kept your word. They tried to kill me. I was resigned to living the rest of my life looking over my shoulder. If he was still around, I'd always be worried that he was going to finish the job. I don't know what it took, but I want you to know how much I appreciate it. I can have a life now."

Not sure I'm the one you should thank, Colt said to himself.

"I don't suppose you'd reconsider quitting," he said, before he'd even thought about it.

"Why?"

"Oh, nothing. Rumors are that they're standing up a new unit."

Nadia barked out a laugh. "Is this where you put on a *Top Gun* hat and tell me you're coming back as an instructor?"

"Something like that," Colt said, chuckling. "They just offered me the job."

"What'd you say?"

"That I'll think about it. Would you come work for me if I did?"

"I'll think about it," Nadia said, the corner of her mouth twisting in a smirk. She left her beer mostly untouched on the bar. "Well, I'll leave you to it." Colt stood and they embraced. "Thank you," she said and left.

Colt's first commanding officer in the Navy told him once that the only thing that truly mattered was his shipmates, his fellow sailors. Lofty national security objectives didn't make a damned bit of difference for a ship taking on water, or when a crewman went overboard. What mattered was the team.

The global economy was in shambles, but it would recover in time. Governments and corporations might even start taking information security seriously, now that they'd seen exactly what could happen if they didn't. The world order depended on secrecy, or at least on privacy and confidentiality. Colt couldn't control those decisions, he could only hope that those in power finally learned the lesson. He could find solace, though, in knowing that the sacrifice he'd made gave Nadia closure, if not security. That was more valuable than anything.

Especially considering it was he who put her in that position to begin with.

Colt thought of Ava and wondered where she was, what she was doing. Would she try to reconstitute Trinity, try to return it to its original mission or would she move on? He hoped for the latter. Not out of some naive belief that it would mean a future for them, but because he didn't think that kind of power should exist without accountability and controls. Trinity's foundational problem was they answered to no one. They were on the right side until they weren't. Ava didn't always acknowledge that distinction. That, more than anything, was the reason he knew he'd stay away. And if she agreed to leave Trinity in the past? Well, there were still the things she'd done.

Richter's words lingered as well. Colt had come in here thinking he would resign the next day. He might still, but the opportunity to stay in the fight, the one that mattered, was a powerful incentive. He thought about that quote from Director Woolsey that he'd shared with Ava about the threat landscape after the Cold War. They'd used it in context of pursuing Hawkinson and ignoring Archon, but perhaps that wasn't exactly accurate. They lived in a dangerous new world, one that would evolve every day.

They'd just killed a dragon.

What snakes remained?

No Prayers for the Dying
Book 1 in The Gage Files by Dale M. Nelson

In the high-stakes game of international spycraft, the most dangerous weapon is the truth. And Matt Gage is about to unleash it.

Ex-CIA operative Matt Gage believed the covert world was firmly in his rear view. But the untimely demise of a Silicon Valley powerhouse drags him back to the subterranean chessboard of spycraft. At the behest of the tenacious Elizabeth Zhou, the magnate's daughter, he starts an inquiry that promises more shadows than truths.

From the vibrant alleys of Chinatown to the imposing skyscrapers of the tech giants, a sinister web unfolds, where the line between friend and foe isn't just blurred—it's non-existent. Each revelation is a grenade with its pin pulled. Every move is made on a knife's edge. And with every step, Gage walks closer into the subtle battle being waged far from the public eye.

Get your copy today at
severnriverbooks.com

ABOUT ANDREW WATTS

Andrew Watts graduated from the US Naval Academy in 2003 and served as a naval officer and helicopter pilot until 2013. During that time, he flew counter-narcotic missions in the Eastern Pacific and counter-piracy missions off the Horn of Africa. He was a flight instructor in Pensacola, FL, and helped to run ship and flight operations while embarked on a nuclear aircraft carrier deployed in the Middle East. Today, he lives with his family in Virginia.

Sign up for the reader list at
severnriverbooks.com

ABOUT DALE M. NELSON

Dale M. Nelson grew up outside of Tampa, Florida. He graduated from the University of Florida's College of Journalism and Communications and went on to serve as an officer in the United States Air Force. Following his military service, Dale worked in the defense, technology and telecommunications sectors before starting his writing career. He currently lives in Washington D.C. with his wife and daughters.

Sign up for the reader list at
severnriverbooks.com

Printed in the United States
by Baker & Taylor Publisher Services